THE
SAMSON
HEURISTIC

THE
SAMSON
HEURISTIC

THE SAMSON HEURISTIC

Danny Rittman
&
Brian Downing

iUniverse LLC
Bloomington

THE SAMSON HEURISTIC

iUniverse books may be ordered through booksellers or by contacting:

iUniverse LLC
1663 Liberty Drive
Bloomington, IN 47403
www.iuniverse.com
1-800-Authors (1-800-288-4677)

ISBN: 978-1-4917-2142-1 (sc)
ISBN: 978-1-4917-2143-8 (hc)
ISBN: 978-1-4917-2144-5 (e)

Library of Congress Control Number: 2014901193

Printed in the United States of America.

iUniverse rev. date: 01/23/2014

Computers are not intelligent. They only think they are.

—Epigrams in Programming, ACM SIGPLAN Sep 1993

Barry's first taste of battle was only a skirmish against a small rearguard of Frenchmen who occupied an orchard beside a road down which, a few hours later, the English main force would wish to pass. Though this encounter is not recorded in any history books, it was memorable enough for those who took part.

—Stanley Kubrick, Barry Lyndon

"This meadow," said Bertin, as he slipped his arm through hers; "could be held by one machine-gun against two companies; they could never cross that stream down there. And the edge of the forest would be a first-rate emplacement for anti-aircraft guns." The meadow was a blue sheen of cuckoo flower and stork's bill. "Yes . . . the woods by Verdun looked like that, only much thicker, when we got there."

"I wish you could forget those woods," said Lenore tenderly. Secretly she, feared it would be long before this man of hers found his way back out of those magic woods into the present—into real life. Within him the conflcit had not died; still it surged and thundered . . .

Like any pair of sweethearts they passed into the shadowed green splendor of the forest, and the gleam of her yellow frock could still be seen after his blue suit had disappeared from view.

—Arnold Zweig, Education before Verdun

New Mexico

"Everything looks overexposed out here," Barrett grumbled to himself as he drove into the studio parking lot. The direct sun, treeless yards, and cloudless skies make for a brightness which caused people to comment that his photos were too harsh and that software could take something off. "But that's what New Mexico looks like," he'd tell them. "Overexposed . . . *way* overexposed." He found a place to park in the visitors section and walked toward the television studio that did contract work for international news stations. "At least it's easy to park here, even in downtown Albuquerque."

Barrett stiffened and looked warily as a man exited the building and came toward him. The man walked past him, got into his car, and drove off. Barrett continued to watch him a few moments more before entering the building.

"Barrett Parker," he announced to the receptionist, "I'm scheduled for an interview on Al Jazeera at two." She made a quick look on her screen and replied, "Studio 4, just down the hall to the left." He nodded and walked down the hallway, stopping to check his longish hair and short beard for the proper amount of dishevelment which he thought conveyed aloofness from convention. No security badge or sign-in book. New Mexico isn't like that. Los Alamos and Sandia Labs are like that. The rest of the state is low-key. It was like that in Billy the Kid's day and before.

New Mexico received a fresh infusion of offbeat people when hippies flocked there in the sixties. Some of them lived in buses converted into houses of sorts or in dwellings built to resemble flying saucers. Most of the offbeat New Mexicans weren't his crowd though he shared their eccentric spirit. Most of them mistrusted him because of his expertise in military matters. It just didn't fit with their world; no decent person should know what a Raptor or a Misagh-2 was. Barrett thought that was part of the problem with the country. Most people who oppose involvement around the world know nothing about world affairs and simply repeat old rallying cries from the sixties. In the absence of thoughtful criticism, national security institutions roll on and foreign policy gets messier and messier, deadlier and deadlier.

He sat in the black leather chair in a ten-by-ten chamber and looked into the camera three feet in front of him. Behind him a large LCD television showed a Jpeg of the stately Sandia Mountains to the city's east, providing an attractive backdrop to his head and shoulders atop a six-two frame whose athleticism was still immediately recognizable despite being fortyish. A technician adjusted the camera and handed him an earpiece and lapel mike.

"Hi Barrett," came the mellifluous voice of Khadija, the producer in Qatar, the small principality in the Persian Gulf that funds Al Jazeera and seeks to become a force in world affairs. "Another tweed jacket, I see. I presume you're wearing jeans and Tony Lamas beneath it."

"These are Luccheses, my mysterious Qatari friend," Barrett said as he raised a boot up for the camera. "I don't have Tony Lamas."

"I was right about the jeans though. I thought everyone wears Tony Lamas in New Mexico and Texas."

"That's like saying everyone where you live wears—"

"Sound check, please!"

Barrett began counting to ten as Khadija got the volume and compression right. "We'll go live in two minutes," she said. The anchor gave an intro on the increasing tensions with Iran then launched into the interview.

Anchor: We're pleased to have Barrett Parker with us to look more deeply into the situation. Barrett, is war with Iran imminent?

Barrett: I don't think so. We're still quite a ways off from anything serious. Right now, we have a geopolitical game of good cop, bad cop. Israel is threatening to attack while the European Union is trying to negotiate a settlement.

Anchor: But the talk out of Israel is very ominous.

Barrett: The prime minister doesn't have sufficient support for war. Only 32% of Israelis support unilateral attacks, and major figures in Mossad—that's the Israeli equivalent of the CIA—and the military are expressing skepticism about the judiciousness of an attack. A former Mossad chief called it the stupidest thing he'd ever heard of. His words, not mine.

Anchor: Of course. What about an American strike?

Barrett: At present, that's highly unlikely. The US has a different "red line" for attacking Iran than Israel has. Israel wants to attack before Iran moves its uranium enrichment facilities into mountain sites that are very difficult to destroy. The US is not as concerned about uranium enrichment. Iran can do that as long as it's for peaceful purposes.

Anchor: Are Iran's purposes peaceful?

Barrett: We have no firm evidence that Iran is making a weapon. It can have enriched uranium, even highly-enriched uranium. Without a triggering mechanism and warhead though, the uranium is not an immediate threat or even militarily useful.

Anchor: Isn't the United States under pressure, from both congress and the general public, to go along with the Israeli prime minister on this?

Barrett: Yes, there's a good deal of such pressure. However, the president knows that war with Iran would unleash a wave of bombings and assassinations around the region and oil prices would skyrocket. Rising oil prices will weaken world economies amid a sluggish recovery. Furthermore, the president has a very high opinion of himself and he does not want to go down in history as a president who continued the military ambitions of predecessors he opposed. Remember, he criticized the muscular foreign policy of his predecessors—and rather harshly too.

Anchor: His predecessors being the Neo-conservatives.

Barrett: That's right—the Neo-cons. The president and most of his advisers oppose reliance on military force.

Anchor: So you see nothing imminent.

Barrett: Correct. Watch the number of aircraft carriers the US has in the waters around Iran. Also, watch oil prices on the London and New York exchanges. They've been flat during all the recent sound and fury. Just a small bump here and there. In other words, people with billions of dollars at stake aren't greatly concerned.

Anchor: Anything going on behind the scenes you can tell us about?

Barrett: Well, I imagine the US and Israel are very eager to find out if Iran is currently going beyond uranium enrichment and building a weapon system.

Anchor: How would they find out?

Barrett: Satellite imagery and eavesdropping can provide some information, but my guess is that they're trying to get people inside a couple of research facilities to see for themselves. That will be difficult—and very dangerous too.

Anchor: Any idea where those research facilities are?

Barrett: Sure. Fordo, which is near the holy city of Qom, and Parchin, which is near Tehran. Fordo is a uranium-enrichment site and Parchin is where weapons production *might* be occurring. No one knows for sure, at least outside of the IRGC. Those are the places to watch.

Anchor: Fordo and Parchin. And the IRGC is the Iranian Revolutionary Guard Corps?

Barrett: Yes, the IRGC is Iran's military elite. It's also involved in many business enterprises and intelligence operations. Many people think the IRGC has political ambitions. They'd like to wrest control of the country from the religious figures.

Anchor: Do you think the IRGC has political ambitions?

Barrett: Yes, I do. Generals have been getting into politics since Julius Caesar marched his legions across the Rubicon. It's gone on quite a bit ever since.

Anchor: Indeed. How might the IRGC realize their ambitions of wresting political power from the mullahs?

Barrett: Historically, wars have shifted power and prestige to militaries, and the present crisis will give the IRGC the opportunity to expand its influence. Wars are run by military experts, not religious ones.

Anchor: Thanks for your insights, Barrett.

Barrett: Thanks for having me.

Khadija added her thanks as Barrett relaxed for a moment to enjoy the exhilaration of finishing a crisp interview.

"Khadija, how is it that I've never had the chance to see you, not even on a monitor."

"I'm a woman of mystery, Barrett. Seriously though, you should live here in the Gulf and become a regular. You'd know the region even better than you do already. You might look less intense and perhaps smile a bit more, even if it's just for the camera."

Barrett rolled his eyes playfully, knowing she could see him.

"Not much to smile about in the Middle East these days, Khadija. Besides, I spent some time in the region, as you will recall from my CV."

"Yes, but Qatar is quite different from Iraq, especially when you were there."

"I still prefer the tranquility of New Mexico. But you will say hello to Farrah Esmail in your sports department for me," Barrett said as he loosened his tie and leaned back.

"I'll tell her you were thinking of her. Hey, I saw a slight smile come across your face. Maybe now you'll come here."

"I'm afraid I must remain here with my wolf. Remember him?"

"Yes, you sent me the photo of him with a hat on his enormous head. What did the hat say on it?"

"It said, 'Dysfunctional Veteran—Leave Me Alone'. He lets me wear it sometimes. Speaking of Jesse, the old boy needs to be fed soon. Otherwise, he'll start looking at the neighbor's cattle as jumbo burgers—rare, no fries."

"Give him a hug from me—if you dare! But why do you wear that hat, Barrett?"

"Khadija, I'm a man of mystery."

Barrett removed his earpiece and mike and headed for lunch at Kelly's on Rt 66.

The sports bar section wasn't crowded and the gaggle of regulars sat about watching a rerun of a college football game from the eighties. Barrett settled in a booth that allowed him to see anyone walking in.

"Still solving the problems of the world?" the lithe blonde waitress jibed as she brought a Guinness and menu. Barrett was an enigma to her, though a somewhat appealing one. Handsome but standoffish. Witty but reserved.

"I'm sure trying, Dee Dee. Yet things get worse everyday."

"Not wearing your veteran cap today, I see." she said holding back a laugh. "It makes a lot of people here wonder!"

"It makes me wonder too, Dee Dee." Barrett smiled slightly as he watched her walk back toward the bar.

Kurdistan, Iraq

The Kirkuk airport in northern Iraq grew impressively after Saddam's ouster in 2003. Once chiefly a base for suppressing the Kurds and ensuring Baghdad's control of Kurdistan's oil, Kirkuk now served the hundreds of engineers, construction crews, politicians, and diplomats who came and went.

More than a few intelligence people also came and went from Kirkuk. Kurdistan was now practically independent from Iraq and it held a critical strategic position in the region. Anthony Sabatini had been in northern Iraq before and felt a measure of pride in its independence and growth. His ranger team had trained local militias in explosives and sniper tactics and tried to get them to coordinate operations. The latter mission wasn't entirely successful with the fractious Kurdish tribes. Nonetheless, when the US invaded Iraq in 2003, Saddam was pushed out in surprisingly short order and Kurdish troops, including Anthony's people, played an important role in tying down an Iraqi mechanized infantry division.

Along the way, Anthony learned some Kurdish to mix into the Farsi he studied in army schools. Skills like that proved useful over the years as the special forces and the CIA worked hand in hand. The two organizations composed the backbone of American foreign policy in the Middle East—and increasingly elsewhere too. No longer in the military, though still involved in related activities that used former rangers with exotic language skills, Anthony was back in Kurdistan.

Walking through the airport, he felt sure he could spot others in the intelligence field. They had a certain look, especially the American ones. "Too big, too athletic," he'd complain to others. They looked like Big Ten running backs. The faces of the diplomats they claimed to be were less determined and conveyed acceptance of doubt—an unwelcome characteristic in the army and CIA. He recalled the CIA employee nabbed in Pakistan in 2011. The instant Anthony saw his photo he knew that he wasn't with the State Department and that Pakistani intelligence likely knew that for a long time. It was as plain as his broad shoulders and stout neck. Anthony was no running back. He was six feet and just over 190 pounds. A Big Sky Conference safety at best. Undersized, but a hard hitter.

Many countries had intelligence people in Kurdistan. India and Britain each had them there seeking ways to increase their influence in the area. The US and Israel used Kurdistan to conduct operations inside Iran. So did the Saudis, though they were there chiefly to write checks and listen to briefings. That's what they did best.

Iran undoubtedly had Revolutionary Guard officers there. They were all over the rest of Iraq, primarily in the Shia south. The IRGC officers were welcome down there, though not in the Kurdish north. The Kurds saw the IRGC as oppressors of their kin across the border in Iran, and Tehran saw Iraqi Kurds as intent on acquiring the Kurdish areas of Iran. The Kurds were now getting plenty of foreign help—from intelligence officers.

Anthony was escorted to the military section of the airport where he met with the CIA station chief and a local colonel. A Black Hawk with Kurdish army markings awaited him. The Kurds of northern Iraq had their own army, constitution, and flag and were for all practical purposes a separate country. Fear of Turkish and Iranian reprisals prevented a formal declaration of independence, but every Kurd in Iraq, Turkey, Syria, and Iran prayed for the day.

As the Black Hawk lifted up noisily and executed a stomach-churning pitch to the east, Anthony saw construction cranes rising up from the ground throughout Kirkuk. Off to the north, shiny metal tubes of a new pipeline system glistened in the late afternoon sun as they stretched north into Turkey where they fed into the pipelines that took oil out of Kazakhstan. The pipelines brought energy to Europe and hope to the Kurds—hope that empires and statesmen and secret agreements had long crushed.

Anthony carried no elaborate communication gear or transponder. They would be giveaways if found at the border and get him into worse trouble than what the Big Ten running back in Pakistan had faced. No pistol either. For now, he had an iPod Touch. There was nothing out of the ordinary on it except encryption programs for the camera and the Skype app. There was some Kurdish music loaded from an iTunes account under the name of Agrin Saleh. It was the same name on his passport and other papers.

The iPod would automatically erase the encryption programs and recent data if he didn't enter a code every twelve hours. A security measure, in case of capture. A transponder and pistol awaited him at a safe house in Tehran.

Santa Clara, California

Silicon Valley was waking up. Unlike San Francisco, which stayed overcast until late morning, Santa Clara was accustomed to clear morning sun that suggested bold new things ahead. It had a palpable eagerness only rarely found elsewhere. People wanted to get to their workplaces and discover things, create things—things that changed how people lived and communicated.

The forecast said it would hit the low nineties and the prospect of an unpleasant afternoon made people head for work early, before their energy and creativity wilted. The Valley had this defining energy since the late 1970s when a handful of young people built empires with their enthusiasm for computers. The best of them weren't motivated by money, though there was a great deal of that as housing costs ably indicated. The best of them were driven by imagination and will. A few were motivated by ideas that were vanishing fast—an appreciation of beauty and a need to do good.

Ethan Alon began his mornings by letting the sun creep up through the open curtains and by idly listening to the cuckoo clock rap out its rhythms.

Switzerland's peaceful gift to the world—the cuckoo clock. Breakfast shall be . . . oh, cantaloupe and pomegranate juice. I'll stop for coffee on the way in.

After a bracing shower, he donned beige corduroy slacks and an Aztec-design shirt then headed into the still uncrowded streets.

It was just before seven and other early risers were driving or biking down the roads to the glass office buildings along El Camino Real. A few trucks were on their way to the supermarkets or heading back to warehouses in Oakland to the north. Ethan pulled his Prius into the Boudin Bakery—part of a small chain that made coffee, breads, and pastries. It originated in San Francisco and expanded throughout the Bay Area and even as far south as San Diego.

"Good morning, Paul. How goes it this beckoning morning?" Ethan spoke in a distinct accent with only occasional mastery of American idioms.

"All is hunky dory, my brilliant Israeli friend. From your chipper voice I trust all is well with you," replied the cherubic manager, his apron dusted with a flour from the morning's work.

"I take it 'hunky dory' means good. Just two coffees, large, decaf. Maybe an Ethiopian?"

"Ethiopian Harar it shall be—decaf. A croissant with that? On me, of course." It was a familiar enough routine. Paul offered a croissant and Ethan politely declined.

"If I ate them, I'd start to look like a Boudin baker and I wouldn't be able to run up the stairs to my office."

"Then you'd be a little plump and very happy!" Paul laughed and handed him the coffee in a cardboard tray.

"I'll remain trim and at least somewhat happy—at least until my company goes public and I become as rich as Monsieur Boudin."

A baking tin clanged on the floor behind Paul, momentarily distracting Ethan. A faint memory flashed almost harmlessly through his mind, one that once held devastating power over him. The harmlessness of the memory allowed him a comforting smile.

"Ethan, you *will* let me know when your company goes public, won't you?" Paul sheepishly asked as he picked up the tin. "And maybe get me a slice of the IPO? You know, for your plump baker friend. That would *sooo* make him even happier."

There was jest in his request but perhaps a hidden need as well, especially in the hard days the recession brought. "I'll see what I can do, Paul. When you go public though, you lose control of your business to Wall Street. You lose your soul as well. You become part of a machine, with no will of your own."

"No house in Napa Valley then. And no Maserati either."

"For now, I shall have to get by with just my soul and my Prius. They've both served me well, though each needs a little maintenance now and then." Ethan turned around in the doorway. "Oh, I also need your coffee. Have a great day!"

Paul bowed operatically as Ethan disappeared into the street.

Another reason not to go public occurred to Ethan. Even fleeting conversations like those with Paul would have to be guarded, lest he give away information on the company's health to a passerby or someone worse. The restaurants and bars had more than a few stringers who traded information to Wall Street analysts and hedge fund managers. And woe betide the employee who left a smartphone prototype in a coffee shop.

Freelancing for big microchip corporations—ones that had gone public long ago—had taken him places. Those companies earned niches for their products in the first generation of PCs and network devices and were now in most computers, servers, and cell phones around the world. He even helped design the chip that ran the US air force's missile system and the software architecture that secured the Israeli military systems, though he couldn't put those details on his resumé.

After fifteen years with the big shots, he looked for his own way—in large part owing to the dry corporate cultures which lacked appreciation for the higher things in life. He developed a software system that analyzed microchip designs and identified faults well before production began at the fabrication plant, or "fab." It saved time and money. He patented it and formed Micrologic Design Automation, Inc.

The morning air was brisk, the skies promising, and the Harar strong. "What new worlds await me today?" he thought as he pulled into the office parking lot. "A morning in the eBeam room looking at old chips and getting the product ready to ship. Not bad."

Ethan parked behind the beige, five-story building that housed Micrologic Design and briskly ascended the stairs to the top floor. Panting considerably, he unlocked the door, switched on the overhead lighting, and walked down the hall lined with enlargements of masterful chips he'd studied and in some cases worked on. It was to him a gallery of magnificent artwork. He sometimes stopped and looked into the detail of one such masterpiece and felt appreciation for the designer's hand. Certain units on a chip were like the distinctive brushstrokes of a Goya or Matisse or Brueghel, knowable to the initiates in the chip design world. He saw the works of the masters and occasionally an area where a master had allowed a promising student to add a few strokes. He'd look at some units and faces would come to him—a speaker at a convention, or a colleague at Yale, or a venerable guru at the Palo Alto Research Center.

His girlfriend, Rina Hardin, had a different opinion on the wall decor. Though she appreciated the craftsmanship in the chips, she wanted to replace Ethan's silicon hall of fame with images of Yosemite and the Mojave where they camped on increasingly infrequent weekend getaways. Rina said that he looked to be in a different world when in the hills and ravines. "Indeed, I am," he thought while musing over a private irony.

They agreed, however, that chips were living creations at work in the world—mostly for the good, they liked to think. The decor was in debate, though not yet in transition.

Donning his NASA lab coat, Ethan entered the eBeam machine room. He picked up the lab coat at a flea market in San Mateo. The NASA logo resonated with boyhood dreams of becoming the first Israeli on the moon, and after a little haggling it was his for twenty bucks. He'd hope to get him down to fifteen but Ethan's interest was too obvious and the dealer dug in. Since then, the coat was part of his eBeam ritual. He thought it made him look masterful. Rina had a different view on that too.

The eBeam room was the most intricate chamber in the company. Silicon, the key material of chips, is sensitive to the finest dust and dirt, so the air in the room is purified by elaborate filters and the floor is surfaced with honed ceramic tiles. It's crucial to exercise great caution to prevent any contaminant coming to rest on the open silicon. The eBeam machine resembles a large microscope with a sealed chamber in which the opened chip is carefully placed where it can be examined in astonishing detail. The device fires a concentrated beam of electrons onto a chip, creating an image of the surface on a computer screen. The instrument gives a wondrous tour of intricacies, including silicon layers and metal-oxide wires whose dimensions are measured in microns, which make a strand of hair appear like a sequoia.

Ethan switched on the eBeam. A low, droning hum built up, announcing that the electron-beam cannon was revving up. Green lines on the monitor read out the preparation sequence. "Time for another cup?" he thought but decided against it. "Enough coffee for the day." A microchip, the renowned and ubiquitous PAMD microprocessor, lay in the sampling tray, stripped of its plastic housing. The tiny piece of silicon was ready for scrutiny.

"I'm about to perform open surgery on a microchip. No anesthesia for you, my silicon patient. Don't worry, you won't feel a thing. Say 'aaah'. No, I won't ask you to turn your head and cough."

The PAMD microprocessor under the eBeam that morning was from the early nineties. It was a breakthrough in its day owing to innovative subsystems, including one for communicating with other systems. It became the standard microprocessor for almost all personal computers and workstations and servers around the world. Parts of its architecture remained in generational descendants, like the DNA of parents and grandparents and great-grandparents. The internal structures of a chip, even a venerable one, held possibilities for exploration that Micrologic Design could learn and benefit from. Ethan was about to run a "reliability analysis" on the chip to search for problem areas that might have developed since it was manufactured in one of the PAMD fabs.

The communication circuitry was his main interest, especially its error detection protocol circuitry. That circuitry enabled more reliable delivery of data over communication channels, both within a computer's system and throughout networks it was plugged into. Communication channels are subject to channel noise or intentional communication disruption such as sabotage, hacking, and the like. Error detection finds such errors; error correction repairs the original data. The circuitry contained highly advanced encryption and decryption units. All this on a tiny part of the PAMD chip visible only under an eBeam.

Ethan navigated the eBeam inside the chip's structure, down various segments until he neared the communication circuitry.

"Down a little more . . . a little more . . . yes . . . Hmmmmm . . . I must have made a wrong turn back at the intersection of Flash and ALU. Let's put her in reverse and go back a block or two. Sorry, officer, it won't happen again."

He retraced his steps and soon determined he had not taken a wrong turn at Flash and ALU. He was nonetheless in an unfamiliar neighborhood. He increased the zoom.

"Weird . . . I don't see any identification on these blocks."

He looked for the blocks in the microchip's "documentation"—the PAMD guide that describes circuits and their functions in great detail for purposes of patenting and for the benefit of engineers on the next generation of microprocessors. The most important documentation is the electronic schematics which are a full representation of the chip's circuitry.

"This neighborhood isn't on the map even though it was built years ago."

He navigated through the undocumented section more intently and found a maze of circuits—most of them of astonishing sophistication. He ran through the basics of chip design: density, package terminations, heat dissipation, logic units, control sections, bit size, caches, and the like.

"I don't know who did this . . . but my heavens, they did it very well."

On the chip's lower side, he expected a blank area and indeed it was, but there were a few specks on the silicon. Usually such things turn out to be anomalous silicon fragments, but these had discernibly sharp corners and slivers. He amped up the zoom and the specks turned out to be minute circuit structures—not in the same nanometer scale of the rest of the chip. Only one fabrication process is normally used to make a microchip, yet this chip's undocumented parts were much smaller than the rest of it.

"Very weird."

He navigated further, activated the Ultra Zoom, and an entirely new circuit appeared!

"This just can't be right."

"What can't be right? Did you ask the chip to turn its head and cough again? And it complied?"

Rina Hardin—grad student, intern, girlfriend—entered the room, Stanford sweatshirt draped around her shoulders. She gently placed her hands on his shoulders as he sat before his screen. "Have I ever told you that you look ridiculous in that NASA coat?"

"Many times. Just not this week."

"I'm sorry I let you buy it. You shelled out forty bucks for something that makes you look like a twerpy kid playing Asteroids in his parents' basement."

"It was only twenty bucks—and people tell me I look like a strapping Neil Armstrong."

Rina rolled her eyes. "More like a napping Neil Cavuto."

Ethan's eyes never left the screen. "I don't know Neil Cavuto. Is he in a band you like? Anyway, there's something more interesting here than any rock band."

Rina imagined a head-slap emoticon. She was in a doctoral program at Stanford, preparing a thesis on automation algorithms. She was slender with long, straight brown hair and wore brown horn-rimmed glasses with round lenses. Her green eyes often enough had a mischievous sparkle that made her irresistible to many men though off-putting to some. Her boldness and wit attracted Ethan the day she arrived from grad school. Even the most analytic of tekkies have human impulses running through their circuitry and in time, no more than a couple of months, the two became close.

"Rina, I've found extra layout on a PAMD microprocessor—something not in the schematics, something with a smaller design process than the rest of the chip. I've never seen anything like this. It makes the manufacture of the chip more difficult and more expensive, and I assure you the PAMD suits watch costs."

"Maybe it's just proprietary information. Something the company doesn't want the world to know about yet," Rina offered before exhaling audibly. "This must be important if he doesn't even look at me," she thought in disappointment. She delighted in his attention, originally only for professional reasons.

Still no words from the NASA escapee.

"So what's the big deal?" she asked as she looked at the screen. "It's something for PAMD's internal usage. Maybe some kind of signature, manufacturing data, or the like. We saw that in a Korean flash memory chip last year. It turned out to be an interface for a new smartphone."

"He'll acknowledge my presence now—he has to," she thought. She stood above him, activating all her feminine vibes, lowering her head to just above his, but he remained in eBeam Land.

"Ground Control to Ethan Alon!"

"It's an old chip. Look at these specks," he said pointing them out on the screen with a cursor. "Now let's go to Ultra Zoom. *Pow!* See all the circuitry? Bizarre."

She looked over the anomalous circuitry with interest but not astonishment.

"Note the layout, Rina. It has flash memory, logic arithmetic sections, mathematical parts, and more. Someone went to a great deal of effort to design and manufacture this. Furthermore, someone made sure there was no schematic correlation, no documentation—at least not published and available to the industry."

"Very nice . . . I hope you're not thinking of making a blowup for the hallway gallery."

Ethan remained fixed on the eBeam image. "It's so tiny. Why would someone hide the circuitry? Why would they hide an entire *chip inside a chip?*"

He could smell her perfume and for a second he was distracted, as he was her first day. She smiled as she realized she had finally made contact with the lost astronaut. She gently shook her head, letting her hair roll along her shoulders. But in an instant, he was drawn back into eBeam Land.

"I can clearly make out complex circuits . . . they hold and process data. I know it." He gave her a quizzical look which Rina saw as a small sign of progress. "They can hold a large amount of information. They can calculate and make logical decisions. Who knows, maybe even execute them in some way."

"So what do we do with this discovery, captain? Plant the flag and send in missionaries? It's an old chip, Ethan. Who cares about what's on old chips?"

"I do. I'm intrigued and want to learn more. We've invested a princely sum in this eBeam device. I can look into it and determine the section's function." He continued staring at the screen until his excitement burst forth again. "Rina . . . just *look* at this stuff!"

"I might have thought we had more pressing matters," Rina said as she turned to leave the room. "Like running Micrologic Design—you know, the company here? No, no, you have all day. Really. I'll handle the release of our software. We have customers waiting, but exploring an antique chip is more important right now."

He lifted his head to her and smiled to her. "The business can wait a few hours. I want to reverse engineer this thing. Can you join me . . . maybe?"

She turned back to him.

"Why, Colonel Alon, suh! How very kind of you to think of me," she said in a sultry southern voice, eyelashes batting rapidly.

"Can you call over to Boudin's for sandwiches?" The batting of eyelashes stopped instantly, alarming Ethan and making him grasp for an escape. "And then we can work on this chip inside a chip—you know . . . together. Like a team . . . like a *couple*."

"Much better, Ethan. Much, much better. Things may work out here yet."

"Rodger dodger. By the way, Rina, I was only a lieutenant."

"Yes, Lieutenant Alon of the Israeli Defense Forces. I *love* guys in uniforms," she teased. "Actually, you're the only person I've ever known who's been in the military. *Any* military."

They saluted each other then pressed their lips together in a manner undefined in any army manual, Israeli or American. Some civilian manuals depict it as a timeless preliminary.

Northwest Iran

Penjwin was an intel hub long before Anthony Sabatini was born. It lay just to the south of a protrusion into Iranian territory that Agency people called the Parrot's Beak in honor of a storied stretch of the Cambodian border where North Vietnamese troops infiltrated into the South.

In the sixties and seventies, American and Israeli intelligence routinely passed through the small town on the Iraqi side of the border. Iraq was a Soviet ally—someone to harass and distract. Iran and Israel saw Iraq as a common enemy and part of a coalition of Sunni states hostile to Shias and Jews alike. It was best to stir up Kurdish trouble for Iraq and tie down a few divisions that might otherwise be used against Iran and Israel.

The CIA station chief introduced Anthony to a colonel in Kurdistan's army intelligence and a few men in civilian garb gathered in an untidy stone house on the edge of Penjwin. Not the colorful local dress as might have been imagined; Dockers and sport coats.

Anthony was what his father called "FBI"—full blooded Italian. His dark, angular Mediterranean features were not dissimilar to those of the Kurds, who in turn didn't look Persian or Arab or Turkmen, though they were an indeterminate blend of all three and not the mysteriously distinct people they claimed. He had posed with Afghan fighters in local garb and thought he blended in, especially if he wore the woolen Pakol cap of the mujahideen warriors. No Pashtun would have agreed.

Tehran was a cosmopolitan city with international firms and embassies. He wouldn't stand out too much. Tehran also had many spies. A number of assassins too, but that wasn't Anthony's mission this day.

Idris and Barham, Anthony was informed, were rug dealers—real ones. They smiled engagingly and shook his hand gently, which contrasted with the show of strength and determination when meeting new people in the rangers or the Agency. They would escort him across the border and into Tehran where he'd meet members of an intelligence cell.

"Whose cell is it?" Anthony asked.

"The cell is well placed and highly reliable. This comes from reliable people," replied the station chief after a slight pause, which instantly alerted Anthony. It meant that the cell wasn't an American asset and that it was impolitic to inquire further.

If they're so reliable, why are you sending me?

Idris, Barham, and Anthony walked out of the house and over to a black Safari Storme, an Indian SUV popular on both sides of the border. His associates warmly embraced the colonel in a manner that suggested to Anthony that they were relatives. He suppressed any sign of surprise or annoyance and climbed into the backseat.

The old-timers in the Agency told Anthony they used to sneak across the frontier on smuggler trails. There'd be a skirmish arranged a few miles away. A few mortar rounds would thump and a few thousand tracer rounds would lash from a machine gun. The excitement would cause a distraction and a few men would scurry across the line. The Pakistani army still does it for Taliban fighters and Kashmiri guerrillas.

That afternoon, the three men would drive down Rt 46 to the border crossing east of Pe;njwin and cross into Iran. The border was tense, even unfriendly, but trade was trade and with international sanctions coming down on Iran over the last year, Iran needed as much trade as possible.

The wait at the crossing was only an hour and when they reached the guards, Idris greeted them as he had in previous times with fulsome praise for Persian artisanry and a surreptitious gratuity in the form of silver coins much appreciated by underpaid border guards.

"Last month we found many splendid carpets in the Sewan villages along the Caspian. On this day we are bound for Tehran's wonderful bazaars."

Anthony kept quiet of course. He could likely pass a border guard's queries but why take the chance. It was the Revolutionary Guard that concerned him. They were mostly ethnic Persians and wary of non-Persians, even if they were one of the dozens of other peoples who made up Iran.

"Why not Qom?" the guard asked, more as conversation than as a challenge to their authenticity. The question was undoubtedly leading somewhere.

"Qom rugs are indeed magnificent, as all in our trade know. Alas, the wealthy people in Kirkuk and Mosul want tribal pieces for their homes this year and I must buy what they buy. Do you come from the holy city?"

"No. My wife is from there . . . and she wants a Qom rug."

"With dome medallion?" Barham asked.

"Yes, with dome medallion—and *signed*!"

"We shall search all Tehran, my friend," replied Barham. He sensed an implication in the guard's words that future crossings might be adversely affected and that a silver coin or two didn't get all it once did. "And we shall bring back only the finest for you to give to your fortunate and virtuous wife."

The guard knocked abruptly on the car door and motioned for the three to be on their way. "Signed!" he shouted gruffly as they drove off.

In a few minutes they were up to highway speed and headed down Rt 46 on the way to the Iranian capital.

"If you, ever plan to motor east . . . " Anthony sang in a low voice. Idris and Barham stared ahead and talked about the business ahead in Tehran. Anthony thought about his business in Parchin.

Santa Clara, California

The quick run to Boudin's came in handy for Ethan and Rina. It was well into the night before the tedious "reverse-engineering" paid off. The process entailed translating intricate material on the eBeam screen into an equally intricate schematic drawn up, piece by piece, on a software program. Normally, it's the other way around, with layout designers given software schematics with which they then manufacture a physical chip.

As they toiled and moiled, Ethan told Rina of Russian tekkies reverse-engineering entire American microchips. When US corporations learned this, they were amused. Developing an entire chip from scratch would take less time. That was commentary on the state of chipmaking inside the Soviet Union and later Russia. Their best fighter jets were still using vacuum tubes. The tubes were expertly made though, and found loyal fans with western audiophiles who loved the warm sounds tubes delivered.

As dawn neared, Ethan remained focused while Rina was crashed out on the couch in the next room. He eagerly fed the reverse-engineered schematics into a program that would simulate the data and reveal the circuit's purpose. Scores of graphs and symbols popped up on the screen. Numbers came up, then whole block diagrams. Ethan looked at the screen intently, trying to put it all together. His mind raced and looked for an answer to the puzzle, yet after a full hour he was no closer to one. He thought of Rina next door in slumberland and pondered joining her for the rest of the night on the couch's foldout bed.

He looked back at the screen, yearning for the solution but willing to settle for a clue. Through the haze of a flagging caffeine buzz, ideas flashed through his head, albeit too fleetingly for him to fix on and analyze. It had PAMD hallmarks, mid-to-late eighties, but other parts of this odd chip section were out of time and place. It was like looking at an old Chevrolet, apparently stock and unmodified, that had 21st-century innovations under the hood. Who were the lead engineers at PAMD in the eighties? A few names and faces flitted through his mind.

"Whitt . . . Verma."

His eyes ran across the screen over and over and he began to grasp the meaning of the chip-inside-the-chip. Though he didn't fully understand it, he recognized the level of sophistication and that was key to unraveling the mystery. He was in the presence of masters and had to think like one to understand them and their chip section.

"Rina, you've got to see this!" he called out into the hallway. No answer came, which in a way was an answer. He heard Rina rouse briefly then roll over and with a snort and a sigh return to sleep.

Ethan turned the machine off and listened to the ticking sounds of the electron-beam cannon cycling down before coming to a stop and then to the hum of the coolant as it ceased coursing through the machine's insides. His brain wasn't far behind the machinery as he walked over to the chair next to the couch and plopped down.

He closed his eyes but the colorful patterns of the layout had become all but embedded into his neurons and synapses. He felt as though he made a great discovery, something the world needed to know about. But he only discovered someone else's great work. He had to know who and why, and learning when the chip-inside-the-chip had been first placed on the PAMD microprocessor would be a start. That investigation had to wait till tomorrow.

The names "Whitt" and "Verma" flitted repeatedly through his mind, mixing randomly with recollections of military chips he'd worked on in Israel and the US and how he hoped his work would help the cause of peace.

The Southern Coast of Lebanon

The Israeli frigate *Moledet* made soughing sounds as it languidly plied the eastern Mediterranean while on picket duty near Sidon. It was almost dawn and a light mist hovered just above the water. According to the navy's meteorologists, the fog would lift within the next hour and yield to a clear day.

Lt Yossi Sagy sat near the helm, tired, occasionally training his binoculars through the haze to look for small craft that might be headed down the coast to attack Israel. There had been more than a few such raids over the years and dozens of civilians had been killed—some of them children. None had happened under his watch and he was determined that it would remain that way. He knew, however, that there were people and organizations as determined to get through as he was to stop them.

The ship was outfitted with a slew of electronic devices that could detect even small craft as far away as a hundred kilometers. It had missiles that could devastate a light cruiser and knock a streaking MiG out of the sky. There was a complement of multi-barreled machine guns that could fire a hundred rounds a second. Rather than giving off the staccato of regular machine-gun fire, they emitted an eerie whirring noise and their tracers resembled angry, short-lived sparks from a piece of metal pressed hard against a giant grindstone. The crew was proud that their little ship packed so much firepower.

Yossi waited for his relief after which he'd head for his bunk in the bow. Not so much *his* bunk as *a* bunk. There weren't enough beds for all the crew. They used the "warm-bed" system—one sailor slept while another stood watch. Such were the privations on a small patrol ship and all knew it was necessary. It was part of everyone's military service, part of everyone's duty.

Yossi's eyes looked up from the water to the orange sphere rising above the hills of southern Lebanon. The sun was starting its ascent and the sea and land welcomed it by fusing into a single, almost living entity. It was a glorious view that ended his watch by filling him with a sense of wonder and beauty.

Military life could drain such appreciation from a young man and war could do it faster and more completely, perhaps even irreversibly. Yossi thought of the great poets of the First World War who clung to their humanity through appreciation of life's beauty even amid the misery and death on the western front. They looked for a cloud passing silently across the moon or a small bird perching unexpectedly on the sandbags above a dank trench. Yossi looked again at the sunrise over the Levant.

A blue window suddenly opened on the combat intelligence center's main computer screen. "What's this?" he thought aloud. "It shouldn't be doing this." An urgent message from the command center in Haifa looked similar to the odd window now in front of him, but this window was blank and Haifa's messages had the navy logo and jargon-laced text. The cursor blinked a few seconds in the upper left corner then letters and numbers appeared. The pace of the letters and numbers increased to a dizzying speed. Yossi saw a few words here and there but the rest was an incomprehensible barrage of arcane code.

"Wow! . . . What the hell? . . . Stop it!"

Yossi hit a few keys to try to regain control but the maniacal alphanumeric scrolling would not relent. As best he could guess, the system was performing routine checks, internal ones and systemwide ones with other ships and with Haifa and with who knows what. However, no such maintenance was scheduled nor would it be done while on combat patrol. The operation was distracting.

The lines disappeared as quickly and inexplicably as they appeared. Only an empty window and a blinking cursor could be seen. Then a single line appeared.

Records check complete—S. is logging off.

The window disappeared and the computer became responsive again. Yossi immediately ran a program that checked the system's operational level then he turned to the clearing seas to the east. Still nothing along the coast except some fishing boats. The program ran its tests and in time determined that nothing was amiss. But it did not sit well with him. He checked for messages from Haifa or from another ship or from the Iron Dome and Arrow antimissile sites in Galilee. Nothing. He checked for records of external access to the ship's computer. Nothing.

"Morning, Yossi. Went the night well?" Lt Ronen Tal, his relief, arrived at the bridge with a cup in hand and his Zeiss binoculars around his neck. "Here's some herbal tea for the outgoing watch. Just don't spill it on the bunk—again." Ronen saw Yossi was busily looking at the screen and knew something was up. He shifted into duty mode.

"Someone heading south?"

"No, nothing at all. The fishing fleets are gathering in port. They should sail west toward the shoals off Cyprus. We'll track them. An odd thing happened with the computer. A window popped up a few minutes ago and ran a procedure."

"What procedure?"

"I don't know—a *procedural* procedure! There's no record of it though. Something was done on our system—or *to* our system. There's no indication of a firewall breach or a message from Haifa. There's no evidence that any data was stolen or altered or damaged. *Something* certainly happened. I know what I saw."

"Let me have a look for this *procedural* procedure."

Ronen knew the system and indeed knew most other systems too. He knew how to get into just about any system and had helped get into the Syrian air defense net in 2007. Syria was temporarily blinded and Israeli fighters devastated the nuclear site near Deir ez-Zor. Such knowledge required great discretion and character as it had potential for tremendous mischief, crime, and cyberwarfare.

Ronen took over the keyboard and deftly entered access codes while his eyes stayed fixed on the screen. Yossi had only recently gone from two-finger typing to five or six. Ronen pursed his lips as he skimmed through the records. A fellow officer's concern could not be taken lightly. Ronen ruled out Haifa and other Israeli military sources and thought of hackers. Hisbollah, Russia, China, the US—it didn't matter. It could even be some kids in their parents basement in Tel Aviv or Des Moines.

"Nothing," he mumbled as he continued typing away and searching other locations. Yossi was tired but determined to stay inside combat control until his colleague found an answer. *Or maybe just for another twenty minutes,* he soon said to himself.

"There you are," Ronen exclaimed. "I am a true computer savant and you are fortunate to have me aboard the *Moledet!*" he said with irksome self-satisfaction. "That was a tough one though."

Yossi was pleased the problem was solved and prepared to absorb a cyber-lesson, exhausted and ill-disposed to Ronen's lectures though he was.

"It was the work of a subprogram written in machine language—a program embedded within a microprocessor or a micro-controller. It's permanently burned into the microchip and performs routines like checking the system's motherboard and other key components."

"*Burned* into a chip, Ronen?"

"That's right. Permanently embedded there, like the fondness in your brain for poetry. It's done in the simplest computer language so it's only for local checks—battery life, chip temperature, and so on. It woke up this morning, ran some checks, and verified functionality and correctness. Nothing to worry about. Think of it as something like an antivirus program that wakes up and runs a system scan."

"I see," Yossi said, though he only barely did. "I was worried. You know, with all these things like Stuxnet and Fire going about."

"It's Stuxnet and *Flame*, Yossi. Stuxnet and *Flame*. They only hit Iranian systems. Everybody thinks that the US did it or that we did it, but from what my colleagues from grad school in Mossad say," Ronen turned a perplexed face to his friend, "no one really knows."

"I thought you did it, Ronen—when you were on leave last year."

"Not me. I was with Stella on a beach near Eilat. I tell you, no one really knows where those viruses came from. I'm glad they struck though. A nuclear Iran would be a disaster for us."

"We have nuclear weapons. You've seen the cruise missiles with the distinctive warheads loaded into our subs at night. You know about those fighters in the air 24/7. A nuclear Iran wouldn't dare attack us," Yossi replied wearily. "We'd respond instantly and devastatingly. They know it."

"Maybe. I can't really say. I *can* say that all is well on the *Moledet* this morning." Ronen patted himself on the back. "But there is one problem."

"What?"

"Your tea's cold—and so is your bunk."

Yossi smiled. "Well, someday you'll write a 'rewarm' program for the world. I'm going straight to the sack, cold or not."

As he was halfway to his bunk he remembered the message that flashed on that blue window—"S. Logging Off." He wondered who or what "S." was.

The *Moledet* continued its patrol along the coast of Lebanon and the ship swayed gently with the morning waves. Yossi relished the motion as would a young child in his mother's arms. He rolled over and was asleep in minutes.

California

"Today we're going to have some old-fashioned fun," Ethan said after they both freshened up in the office washroom. "We're going shopping!"

"Shopping? My hair's a disaster!" Rina protested as she looked at her disheveled appearance in a mirror.

"Not to worry, Rina. We're not going to Neiman's."

"I'm so not surprised. Where then?"

"You'll see."

Rina accepted the mystery, tucked her disastrous tresses inside her sweatshirt's hood and hopped into the Prius. Her hopes of a good time vanished as they pulled into a 1970s strip mall with a payday loan store, a tattoo parlor, and more than one closed-up shop. Ethan parked in front of a thrift shop.

"You really know how to charm a girl. I was hoping for a "Born To Write Code" tattoo next door. Harumph!"

"Harumph yourself! This place is a treasure trove of old computer gear." Ethan gallantly opened her door and gestured her toward the thrift shop.

"Okay, what's the deal here, Ethan? You know the hard drives and memory are gone the first day. There's nothing here but vaporware."

"Today, we like vaporware." Ethan led her to the electronics section, past some old TVs, clock radios, clunky wireless phones, and CRT monitors the size of small microwaves. "Dear, could you please find me a few old computers—machines from the eighties and nineties? Kaypros and Leading Edges will do. Actually, we just want the microprocessors . . . and it doesn't matter if they work or not."

"What's a Kaypro?"

"An old PC. Mid-to-late eighties. Much admired, at least for a while. Same with Leading Edge. Quite popular in their day, especially for students on tight budgets."

She looked at him with greater puzzlement. "Why do we want medieval CPUs?"

"Because history tells us something about the past and present—and maybe a bit about the future. That's what an eccentric friend in New Mexico tells me."

"Those words would make a good tattoo."

"Where do you want it?" Ethan's eyes looked down Rina's frame until coming to a likely place.

"Oh! But that's where my 'Micrologic Design' tattoo is!"

"Ahh. You'll make employee of the month for that someday."

* * *

Keith Douglas's weekend with his kids hadn't gone well. All the bickering and complaining took a toll and the following Monday he was not "on task" as the managers and consultants like to say. He worked at the PAMD design center in Sacramento along with a thousand electrical and software engineers where the family of microprocessors that ran the world were created. Caffeine and office chatter couldn't put a disappointing weekend behind him but he had work to do and he was determined to get through it that day. More importantly, PAMD was determined that he got through it that day. Working on an upgrade for the famed microprocessor was initially daunting and exciting but the later stages were tedious and annoying.

He'd arrived to work at eight-thirty. It was now almost ten.

"On task . . . get on task, boy."

He sat at his desk and stared at the screen for a while, hoping something would inspire him. He felt he was starring in a Dilbert cartoon. This upgrade would be an appreciable improvement in the line—greater speeds, larger caches, and less power consumption. Keith was in charge of an Arithmetic Logic Unit, or ALU. Its main task was to perform calculations and logical operations—the building blocks of microprocessors. Even the simplest ones contain ALUs for numerous purposes such as maintaining timers. Newer microprocessors have several incredibly powerful and highly complex ALUs.

The ALU design was almost finished. Almost. There was a glitch somewhere. It was a small one, almost insignificant. Almost. In time it would cause quirks and errors and complaints. Ken discovered it during simulation runs. External circuitry was influencing his unit— "crosstalk" in chip-design jargon. Crosstalk takes place when a signal transmitted on one circuit or channel creates an undesired effect in another circuit or channel. It's usually caused by unwelcome capacitive, inductive, or conductive coupling between circuits—more jargon. The exasperating thing for Keith was that there was no other circuitry near his ALU.

Ten-thirty.

He decided to start digging into the design again but then looked through the news. He saw a few items about upcoming elections and demonstrations in the Middle East and how world markets were responding. A desk utility told him that PAMD opened up a full dollar per share on NASDAQ based on Wall Street's expectations of higher revenue from the new chip—the one Keith was working on, or thinking about working on.

"They're counting on you, boy."

Keith sighed and typed his user name and password into the PAMD site. Nothing had changed since Friday. He looked over a piece of design that he'd taken whole cloth from the previous generation. It had the same functionality, so why try to reinvent the silicon wheel? It was common practice in chip design and his manager had approved it, just as previous managers had for earlier versions of the microprocessor. It would save time and money.

"Isn't that what management wants? Isn't that what shareholders want? I know it's what Wall Street wants."

Another two hours of scrutiny failed to uncover the flaw. He could not delay things any longer. There were schedules to meet, announcements to be made, and orders to fill. A fab was waiting in Scotland— Silicon Glen, as it was called. Wall Street analysts were calling the chief information officer everyday and being told everything was on schedule. No worries!

"I'm worried."

Three o'clock.

"The flaw appears only once in a great while . . . a truly great while. Billions of operations go by without a problem. I can declare this unit complete. Worst case, every once in a great while the computer will hang and have to reboot or run some checks. It happens with the present chip . . . It'll continue to happen with the new one."

He looked at his screen and debated running one more simulation. He went back and forth on it and then clicked "Run." It dived into the heart of the circuit, assigning zeros and ones as necessary to perform millions of Boolean functions. The circuit became alive. Logical components quietly received input and produced output in picoseconds. Critical paths operated faster, reminding Keith of Porsches with the tires and lubricants warmed up. The paths calculated, analyzed, and executed until a set of operations driven by a series of decisions approached, unbeknownst even to Keith, a critical intersection. One path led into a basic routine, the other into a risky one. This routine mimicked human behavior and hence had the potential for error. It was an heuristic—a hi-tech rule of thumb. The outcome was not entirely predictable, even to gifted engineers.

The signal raced to the intersection. Millions of instructions pushed it forward, overcoming practical transistor propagation delays. More jargon. But it was all calculated, it was all known. Everything went well with over a million instructions. Then another instruction arrived and was routed away from the heuristic. It skipped the rule of thumb and executed its function perfectly. A green light illuminated on Keith's screen.

"Yes!" Keith exclaimed, as though he'd just gotten the checkered flag and could coast into the winner's circle.

He entered the ALU into the database and signed off—Complete. The ALU, minute heuristic glitch and all, would be passed on to the next generation of PAMD microprocessors, like a recessive trait in the human gene pool. The flawed heuristic was there awaiting a signal to take the risky path. The heuristic had been on all PAMD microprocessors since it was placed there, in updated versions, by a team of secretive engineers in 1986. Keith was carrying on an old tradition at PAMD. He just didn't know it.

Keith relaxed and looked at the news.

"Man . . . the world is filled with trouble these days. Sure glad it has nothing to do with us here in Sacramento."

* * *

Ethan focused the eBeam on the layout of an older microprocessor from a Compaq that he and Rina had cannibalized from the thrift store. The image was blurry. "This will take some doing," Ethan mumbled "The section we're looking for isn't in the same place on every generation of chip." For the next several hours he went through the CPUs of a half dozen old PCs—Dell, Acer, IBM, Gateway, Leading Edge, Hewlett-Packard, Packard Bell, Kaypro, Wang, and Everex. They even found some Wellfleet, Banyan, Ascend, and Cascade servers in the storage areas of friends' businesses and garages, all sporting PAMD chips.

Word spread of Ethan and Rina's obsession with old chips. Colleagues were amused that anyone would find something of interest in such things. More than one, though, suspected that they must be onto something and spent hours trying to figure out what secrets the stuff held. They talked about it at the water cooler and at lunch, sent email inquiries, and asked on industry bulletin boards and chat rooms. Word of Ethan Alon's investigation even spread outside of Santa Clara into hi-tech centers in Korea, Taiwan, China, and Israel. No one had a clue, so they all went back to work. Yep, Ethan was an eccentric—a guy who wore a NASA lab coat at work. Downtime around the world.

A day and a half of eBeaming along memory lane brought a conclusion.

"The mystery chip-inside-a-chip isn't on microprocessors prior to 1986 . . . but it's on every one of them made from late 1986 to the present—with upgrades every few years of increasing sophistication."

"And twenty-five years later, there's still nothing in any industry journal or schematics or anything. I've searched them all." Rina shook her head. "Most peculiar, Mr Alon. As peculiar as can be, as the song goes."

"Indeed it is, Ms Hardin . . . though I don't know the song. I thought it might be some sort of industrial espionage . . . circuits to collect information from devices made by competitors that are on the same motherboard. But there's no valuable data to be collected from microchips that are working with this microprocessor. PAMD itself makes most the chipsets and the rest are dull-witted clones."

"Maybe there's a political angle?" Rina suggested. "International espionage? Or maybe our own government looking in on us?"

"Back then? I don't think so. We don't know what it does, only how it does it—very cleverly." He sampled some Sumatran coffee he'd made in a french press and grimaced when he found it only lukewarm. "These circuits do not function as part of the normal microchip operation."

Rina poured some fresh Sumatran for them. "Somebody's using that section for something."

Ethan turned back to the eBeam machine.

Sirjan, Iran

Gamal Esmaili fidgeted as he prepared a presentation for the military and religious figures who'd flown in from Tehran. War was no longer an abstraction, something to think about for the future. Talk of war was flowing everyday from think tanks and media around the world, and Iran had to be ready. Esmaili and his missiles had to be ready.

Iraq was once his country's principal danger. That is, until the US defeated him soundly in 1991 then ousted him altogether in 2003. Iraq was now a friend of Iran, thanks to the US. Esmaili pondered another irony: the Iranian missile program began with the help of Israel in the shah's days—Project Flower, it was dubbed. And now the missiles were trained on Israel.

"With enemies like these, who needs allies?" Esmaili and his colleagues liked to note. IRGC officers were known to enjoy the line.

As tensions built between Iran and Israel, especially with the recent assassinations of Iranian nuclear scientists, Tehran allocated funds for better computers, servers, and communication gear at the Sirjan base. The simulation programs though, were from the days of Project Flower. They were supposed to have been destroyed but there are always loose ends when partners have a falling out. The programs only needed updating to run on the new architecture. Esmaili worked on a simulated strike on Israel. That afternoon he would demonstrate it to a gathering of generals and mullahs.

Esmaili stood next to the base commander and greeted General Qasim Suleimani of the Revolutionary Guard Corps, his coterie, and a senior mullah who accompanied them with a few younger clerics. Postures, speech, and body language suggested that the general was the most

41

important figure in the delegation. They sat in the control center and Esmaili began the briefing.

"Esteemed guests, through your wisdom and foresight, we have created a potent missile system that is second to none and capable of striking targets within 2000 kilometers of Sirjan."

"Would that include Haifa and Tel Aviv?" the mullah interrupted.

The military figures were annoyed by the question but knew it would be impolitic to show it. Everyone knew the Shabab-3s could hit all of Israel. That's the main reason they were built and that's why they were positioned in the western part of Iran. General Suleimani was practiced in dealing with clerics he deemed dilettantes on matters of war. He manifested no reaction at all.

"I'm pleased you asked of that matter, esteemed guardian," Esmaili replied obligingly, even solicitously. "Yes, our missiles are capable of reaching Haifa and Tel Aviv, as shall be seen in tonight's simulation, to which we now turn. We shall begin with two feints. First, five MiG-29 squadrons will fly west over Iraq—with Baghdad's approval, of course. Second, there will be ground and rocket attacks on Israel from Gaza and Lebanon. This will focus Israel's defense systems on incoming planes and short-range missiles. Soon thereafter, we will fire a series of volleys of Shabab-3 missiles, only a portion of which will have warheads. Thus, the Israeli defenses will be expending their missiles on our unarmed missiles, making themselves vulnerable to ensuing volleys of armed ones. I humbly call your attention to the big board."

Eyes turned to the large screen, thirty feet by ten, showing a map of the region from Tunisia to Afghanistan. There were small arrows over central Iraq, representing the Iranian MiGs streaking toward Israel and IDF fighters scrambled to intercept them. Simulated missile volleys began and the first wave was entirely destroyed by Israeli defenses. Other volleys, each more numerous than the previous one, followed in random intervals and all could see that with each ensuing volley, first one then more Shabab-3s got through, striking Haifa, Tel Aviv, and military bases where missiles and fighters were positioned. Two hit the Dimona nuclear site in the Negev desert. In less than an hour, the simulated attack was over and several Israeli population centers and military sites were devastated. Some of the men in the room were happy, even effusive.

Not so General Suleimani, not so his retinue. Their countenances remained sober.

"So the war will all be over in forty-five minutes and we shall come out of it unscathed?" the general asked, with obvious irony.

"Would we not be starting a long war much like the one we had with Iraq?" a colonel asked.

"Can we defend against their Jericho missiles which will surely launch in response?" another colonel posed.

The senior mullah simply nodded.

These were not questions for a missile scientist and the officers knew that. The simulation was not intended to consider Israeli retaliation, only the destructiveness of a complex first strike. Nonetheless, Esmaili was put off by a perceived slight. The retinues of the general and the mullah were surprised that their superiors expressed their concerns about war so openly. None of them would have dared to.

"That is for our superiors in Tehran to judge," Esmaili replied. "And of course their judgment will be wise and beneficial," he quickly added.

A reception followed the presentation. Despite the critical questions, the feeling was positive, upbeat, even celebratory. After some desultory chatting with midlevel officers, Esmaili went to his office for Turkish coffee. As much as he needed a lift after the stressful presentation, it would not be polite or wise to imbibe caffeine in front of a senior mullah. Besides, General Suleimani was uncomfortably intense and reportedly mercurial as well. Esmaili sat at his desk to check his mail and took noisy sips of the strong concoction, taking in as much air as coffee.

As he clicked on the mail program, a blue window opened instead. An empty white window filled his screen. He hit a few keys, shoved the mouse back and forth, and hit ESC. No luck. The cursor remained frozen in the upper left corner. Lines of alphanumeric data raced down the screen, far too fast for him to identify more than a handful of numbers and words. He hit more keys. Still no luck. After a few minutes, the lines disappeared and ended with one line in the middle of the screen.

Records check complete—S. is logging off.

Back in control, he started to search the system for a security breach or malfunction. Nothing. He alerted the security expert who went through the system all the way to its roots. "Another virus from the US and Israel?" Esmaili wondered.

After almost two hours, the security figure concluded there was nothing to worry about. The computer's microprocessor was running a self-check routine which all computers did periodically, though usually in background. Esmaili breathed easier and was again grateful that the simulation went well.

Thank the stars that this didn't happen during the simulation or I'd be sent off to Zahedan or some such place in the east. Dreary work on the frontier with Afghanistan or Pakistan.

Esmaili asked an assistant if Suleimani was still in the building. He obligingly went downstairs then returned with the unsettling affirmative response. Esmaili shuddered and returned to his screen.

Washington, DC

Just to the side of the White House stands an old structure in the French Empire style called the Executive Office Building. Opinions vary on its beauty but no one disputes that the power inside is second only to that of the White House. Joseph Burkett entered his office and clicked on his machine to read the morning intel briefings.

Since becoming head of the Middle Eastern desk of the National Security Council, or NSC, he wondered if the news weren't more reliable than the intel coming in from Langley. The whole region was aflame with revolution, political strife, war and rumors thereof. The Iranians were boasting of their missiles systems and practicing small-boat strikes on shipping in the Strait of Hormuz.

The insurrection in Syria was still going on and there were concerns that Assad's chemical weapons might fall into the wrong hands. The Turks were maintaining their pressure with artillery and the occasional angry denunciation. Assad would not last much longer, Joe was sure. Some Syrian Kurds opposed Assad; others were supported him because he'd defend them against the Turks. Sectarian fighting was spreading into Lebanon.

Joe wondered why he didn't study a calmer part of the world in grad school but didn't know where that might be.

Antarctica? No, they'll find oil there someday. Or rare earths. Then the rush will be on. National Intelligence Estimates on the strategic value of glaciers. There'll be an ice gap with the Chinese.

He was becoming disenchanted with the national security world and he had to hide it at meetings. A white window appeared on his screen and the cursor jumped to the upper left corner.

"Hmmm, where did you pop up from, little buddy?" Joe tried to get rid of the window but without success. It seems to be stuck there and had a mind of its own.

The stubborn cyber-imp remained there even though Joseph hit various keys and muttered numerous rude words. Neither had any effect.

"Cursing usually helps. At least it does in NSC meetings. I've seen it work countless times—goddammit!"

"Did you need something, Mr Burkett?" his PA asked from the doorway.

"Sorry, Susan. I'm just briefing my computer."

Hundreds of lines of code started to scroll down and Joe could only watch them go by like the cars of a long freight train as he sat in his SUV at an intersection.

"Time to get the IT people up here."

"There's no need to worry, Dr Burkett," Mark, the IT chief for the NSC, later assured him. "It's simply an internal system check. No security breach whatsoever."

"Are you sure? It's never happened to me before and with all these viruses running about . . . " Joe shot a look of skepticism.

"I'm quite sure. Such checks usually go on in the background, usually during updates of the operating system. Sometimes they try to grab screen time."

"So they're like goddam congressmen? Wait, Mark, let's keep that one confidential."

"Hah! Yes, that's an excellent analogy—one I'll keep to myself. Anyway, the chip manufacturer knows about it and assures all of us in the IT world not to worry about it."

"This is the first time my entire system has hanged like that."

"Well, we'll soon have the new microprocessors and new operating systems as well. I think our publicity-seeking cyber-congressmen will refrain from future screen appearances."

"Welcome news. Who makes these chips, by the way?"

"PAMD. They're based in California and have fabs around the world."

"Oh yeah. They're one of the hotshots of NASDAQ. A basketball friend suggested I invest in them back in the early nineties."

"Sound advice. I hope you got a slice or two of PAMD. The stock's done—"

Joseph's annoyed glance ably conveyed that he ignored his friend's advice and that further discussion of the issue was unwelcome.

"Oh, Mark, one more thing. Do you guys in IT know anything about that Stuxnet virus that hit the Iranian nuclear site?"

"I've seen some of the logarithms that were posted on the net. Wow! Whoever did it was absolutely brilliant."

"Any idea who could have written it, Mark?"

"Dr Burkett . . . I was looking for a chance to ask you the same thing. We kinda thought you would know."

Kaliningrad, Russia

The old Soviet cities named after Lenin and Stalin were renamed Saint Petersburg and Volgograd, but Kaliningrad has retained its old name honoring a Bolshevik stalwart. This is because the former name, Königsberg, is German. So was the population until the Red Army vanquished it in 1945 and Stalin redrew the boundaries of Eastern Europe. Reverting to its German name might raise the question of why Russia was holding on to a city that had been German for almost eight centuries.

Kaliningrad was now a home of the Russian army and navy. Cut off from the rest of Russia by Poland, Lithuania, and Belarus, the Kaliningrad garrisons felt besieged. That was a sentiment that pervaded Russian culture, which was shaped by devastating invasions from Mongol khans, Charles XII of Sweden, Napoleon, and Hitler. The twenty-seven million dead in the last invasion was in the living memory of older Russians and the younger ones know well of their parents' and grandparents' ordeal.

In one of the dozens of Kaliningrad's military bases was a secretive cyberwarfare department housed in a cheerless concrete building of 1960s vintage. It was like the ones in East Berlin that westerners pointed to from across the checkpoints as signs of communism's failure—or at least its lack of imagination.

The section was tasked with defending against computer attacks from foreign governments, but the department, staffed mainly by young people, delved into other matters. It hacked into banks from London to Dubai to Singapore to New York. The hackers didn't do any harm. They just went in and out, quickly and stealthily, taking notes on the security systems. It became a competition among the best young people who were doing their military service and hoping to parlay work in Kaliningrad into a job in the security section of one of the banks they'd hacked into.

One young man, a Lt Dimitri Rublev, hacked into the Pentagon, the CIA, and even Brad Pitt's laptop. He joked that Jennifer Aniston helped on all three. A dour colonel found out about the entry into sensitive American sites and ordered a halt. Intriguing and potentially useful as the information was, he was concerned that American hackers were far better than Russian ones and that the Pentagon and CIA might retaliate and bring his section crashing down along with much of the Russian military system, along with his career. "Civilian institutions only," he barked. "Initiative be damned." He was curious about Brad Pitt's bookmarks, though, and had the artful lieutenant send them to him.

Dimitri was annoyed at the scolding, but he reasoned that there was a better future in hacking into America's banks than into its military.

What does a Russian colonel make compared to an American hedge-fund manager? Not much.

He and a colleague in the Ukraine were attempting to get into the "mergers and acquisition" section of Goldman Sachs—M&A, as it was called in the industry. Knowledge of imminent business moves and an options account in Zurich could make them incredibly wealthy in a few years. They could triple their money every two months, depending on how long the merger talks dragged on and how many deals were shot down by the Securities and Exchange Commission. On further reflection, Dmitri and his Ukrainian colleague determined to hack into the SEC, examine its disposition on pending M&A cases, and act accordingly on the options markets.

A few decryption keys were at work when his computer froze and a bewildering array of code scrolled down for several minutes. At length, a window read:

Records check complete—S. is logging off.

He looked into the audit trail system to see all recent activities but there was no record of an outsider accessing the system. He went through an exhaustive check of the security and firewalls but there was no indication of penetration. The PORTS accessibility and blockages offered no reason for worry.

Dmitri remained worried. What if this was American retaliation for his recent forays into their systems? What if Goldman Sachs had better security than he thought and this anomaly was precursor to a punishing retaliatory strike? Either way, Dmitri was determined to find out more. He'd either get promoted captain or exiled to a Russian airbase in Kyrgyzstan. That's where the military sent troublemakers, at least since the end of the Chechen war. Troublemakers and people with initiative.

"*In-ish-i-ativ*," he kept muttering. "We had to import that English word into our language. We have so little use for it in Mother Russia."

Dimitri thought admiringly about the Russian wheeler-dealer who recently bought an American basketball team and moved it to Brooklyn. Dimitri preferred baseball and wondered if Brooklyn might like a baseball team too.

California

In between daily business routine and well into the nights, Ethan and Rina scrutinized every nanometer of the anomalous chip-inside-a chip—the "CiC" as they were calling it. The work was baffling, mind-numbing, hard on the eyes, and led to many dead ends. It came to take more time each day.

Rina was intermittently intrigued. Ethan was obsessed. It wasn't just a mystery story to him; the CiC had tremendous import for the chip industry and for Micrologic Design—both of which were dear to him. The CiC was in many respects well ahead of anything out there and understanding it would bring advantages, as would getting to know the ingenious designers.

"Now we've got some information to work with," Ethan concluded with satisfaction as he at last extracted a set of instructions from the CiC's memory circuits.

Rina pored over them as they appeared on her screen and made partial sense of them. "These are opcodes—assembly language. I recognize some code . . . but the rest is a corrupted program as best as I can tell."

"There must be some order to this silicon chaos," Ethan said as he looked through the opcodes. If you count the number of occurrences of a specific word, there is some consistency." He counted some of selected words. "I counted every fourth word and there's the same key, but it's not universal. In some cases, a different key accompanies different words." He raised his eyes to hers. "So, we have an algorithm within the data stored in the memory."

"Encryption?" She rocked her head back and forth in amused thought, surprised by a new layer of intrigue.

"Exactly—and not a simple one either. Can you work on cracking it while I tend to business?"

Rina rolled her eyes. "I left my decoder ring at home, Daddy Warbucks . . . but I'll give it a try."

"You know, Rina, I love listening to your voice, even when I have no idea what you're talking about."

"I'm on the case, big guy. I'm on the case."

* * *

Even senior chip designers like Vaughn White come across surprises in their work. This was the second time he verified the microprocessor and gotten anomalous results. The end of the project was at hand and final chip verification due. He was the "tape-out owner," meaning he was the person tasked with sending the microchip's completely verified data to the fabrication plant. The term "tape-out" remained from the old days when chip manufacturing information was stored in large reels of magnetic tape and physically delivered to a fab. Today, of course, only one large file was delivered, electronically, to a fab, but the old term stuck and acquired an endearingly archaic quality, even to younger people on the team who laughed at the sight of tape reels in old movies.

Vaughn was to run the chip through sign-off software to make sure it met the electrical and geometrical rules. The software would run through the entire chip, a process that even with today's equipment takes a few days. Upon completion, the software would hopefully declare the chip "clean." Upon approval, the chip was ready for manufacture and it would be sent to the fab where nanotechnology would print it onto silicon wafers.

A few days ago, he'd submitted another run on the verification software just out of curiosity and it returned with discrepancies. "That ain't right," Vaughn said to himself staring in annoyance at the screen. The program reported circuits that weren't there before. "I couldn't miss *that* many circuits. Something's amiss in Sacramento." He visually inspected the design for anomalous circuits, but he couldn't find any.

"I must have done something wrong. We'll just do another run."

Everything came out clean this time. That was it. The software system upon which PAMD relied, upon which its reputation had been built, passed the chip. Vaughn breathed easily and signed off on the update.

He walked down to the tape-out party later that day and was met by scores of elated team members. The affair was lavishly catered and featured a live band that played music from the nineties, including a number by Hootie and the Blowfish whom he loved since his college days. Vaughn gave a short speech thanking everyone on the team for their hard work and professionalism. The applause was effusive. He was proud of what they'd done and the thought of the anomalies never crossed his mind. PAMD rewarded them all with hefty bonuses in the form of stock options.

There was also a senior engineer present. Peter Whitt had been with PAMD since the mid-eighties and he had unspecified oversight on the chip now headed for the fab. Most engineers thought he was just a senior guy with time on his hands. Whitt made a point of congratulating Vaughn personally and shook his hand vigorously.

Vaughn tried to think of something pleasant to say to the old hanger-on. "There's so much you could teach us about the company's early chip designs."

Whitt sensed the empty sentiment and simply nodded. "It's important to pass things on to the next generation," he said.

Whitt's departure from the celebration a while later went unnoticed.

* * *

Ethan was awakened by Rina's nudge. "Hey, hotshot, I think I got something . . . and I trust you've finished up the work for Micrologic Design. That's the name of your company, sleepyhead." She began to poke his rib cage and collarbone. "C'mon, c'mon! You're supposed to wake up when I press any key bone structure. You *have* finished up the customer inquiries, haven't you?"

Ethan mumbled incomprehensibly, hoping to duck the question.

"Well, Ethan, it's made in the most primitive programming language— Assembly. It's definitely encrypted and very well too—256—or even 512-bit type. It's embedded in the silicon like flash memory. It can store and restore instructions and data." She mimicked wiping her brow. "That took only six hours to discover! No nap either," she added saltily.

He looked at her and smiled silently. She read his mind.

"No, no," she said shaking her head. "I'm not decrypting this thing. It's the weekend and I want to relax."

"Yes . . . but . . . "

"You want me to go for that right now?"

"That's why I hired you—your inspiring perseverance, our shared appreciation of wall art and lab coats." Seeing no positive response, he added, "And because you're a genius . . . a beautiful genius . . . and a wonderful hiking partner . . . and of course, certain other things."

"Maybe we can discuss those other things more often. Maybe even *pursue* them. Now back to the CiC. If someone took the efforts to manufacture such a complex unit, we can assume that the encryption will be . . . ." She looked at the ceiling, pretending to be calculating.

"Okay, like, *impossible* to crack. Maybe like something out of the National Security Agency."

"There is no such thing as impossible, Rina. It was made by humans, it can be unmade by humans. It's a law of nature or physics. One or the other. Maybe both. Anyway, it's just a matter of perseverance and talent. However, I like your idea of the National Security Agency. That might come in handy."

Rina arched an eyebrow. "Wait, Ethan, you are *not* going to—"

"Just a thought . . . or a last resort. Let's get back to your perseverance and talent. We know that you have lots of both. Terabytes of both."

"This I'll do tomorrow. It's three am. I'm tired and we still don't know what we're looking for."

"Well, we pretty much know what we're looking for. We just don't know what we're getting into."

Several days later, Ethan and Rina were still struggling with the CiC encryption. They made a program to run sequences of combinations, but without any success. They even checked with friends and colleagues who specialized in security methods. He had a colleague at the National Security Agency but knew he couldn't ask about cracking codes. That would put him on a list somewhere and being on such lists was bad. It can sneak up on you later in life—say, when you wanted a security clearance. "Mr Alon, I see you tried to get a friend to give you sensitive decryption information. What can you tell us about that?"

No thanks. Besides, he had another way of getting NSA information.

The chip encryption proved not to have a straightforward structure. It had an irregular pattern derived from keywords and defining the keyword combos proved elusive. Ethan had already seen the most "unbreakable" encryptions cracked in his days with the Israeli military and he knew it was only a matter of hard work. Hard dull work. They had the knowledge to work the mechanism but they needed creative thinking to find the encryption algorithm. As much as Rina liked challenges, she had exhausted her skill set.

Ethan continued thinking—even at home.

He sat on the balcony of his apartment and sliced a quarter from a soft, fragrant honey dew. The sun was already heating up Santa Clara with all its considerable might. He listened indifferently to the news from his television in the living room. The anchor was talking about tensions in the Middle East, a bombing in Damascus, another bombing in Baghdad.

"I'm afraid that's not news," he lamented, with not a bit of sarcasm.

He thought of the sun and the weekend, but there was no getting away from the dogging matter of the encryption. Beyond that, there would be the task of figuring out what the system was designed to do. He had a hunch and thought of getting thoughts from someone outside the hi-tech field, someone far removed from clean rooms and algorithms and eBeams of Silicon Valley. Someone who could be trusted, for he suspected this CiC business would lead to something complicated, probably something political and dangerous.

Ethan thought of a friend who lived by himself out in the desert of New Mexico and read loads of history.

New Mexico

"Keep saving the world, Barrett!" Dee Dee cheered Barrett as he left Kelly's on Rt 66, the landmark watering hole in the Nob Hill section of Albuquerque built out of a Texaco station from the forties.

"All for you, my dear." Barrett added a wink to which Dee Dee responded in kind.

He drove east on I-40, the long interstate that runs from Los Angeles all the way to North Carolina then entered Tijeras Canyon which separated the Sandia Mountains from the Manzanos to the south.

"No radio or cell service for a while," he thought as he looked up at the reddish-brown sedimentary walls of the canyon. It always reminded him of the radio blackout that astronauts go through on reentry. "A moment of splendid isolation for me."

Barrett thought of his convoluted path to rural New Mexico. Four years in the army, including a small part in the 1991 Gulf War. College and grad school at the University of Chicago studying counterinsurgency, a little teaching, then off to Iraq and Afghanistan to consult for people that thought they knew it all and wanted consultants to tell them they were doing just fine. It diversified any blame that might come down one day.

He moved out to New Mexico to be with an old girlfriend but it didn't work out. Things were especially difficult after he returned from his second time in Iraq. Writing and consulting on his own out in the desert suited him best. A little investing here and there worked out well most of the time but the glory days of the nineties were long gone. It wasn't for everyone, however it meshed with his independent views of the world and mordant wit.

As he came out of the canyon and neared the town of Tijeras, his cell phone signaled that a call had come in while he was reentering the world. A quick look told him that it was from Washington, DC. Senator Gregory's national security aide was calling. "What does he want from me? Those guys take their cues from party hacks and K Street lobbyists, not from anyone like me." He decided not to get back to the senator's aide.

He pulled into the driveway, opened the iron gate, and drove up to the adobe house. Jesse, an immense aging Timberwolf, trotted up stiffly to greet him.

"Hey, buddy! You're the biggest and baddest wolf in the Southwest." Jesse gave him a doggy smile, the openmouthed, soft panting that some people mistake for shortness of breath. "Jesse, do you know there are people in this world who can't recognize a doggy smile?" The great wolf dropped his cheerful demeanor, as would any sentient creature on hearing Barrett's grim assessment.

Barrett had entered middle age gracefully. Pushups and walks with Jesse up the deer trails of North Mountain kept him in good shape. Sunday was time for *The New York Times* crossword, in ink, and often enough an answer came while looking off into plains that led out to Moriarty and eventually to Tucumcari. The cholla cactuses were in late bloom, giving the cheerless, foreboding landscape improbable bursts of fuchsia and yellow. The empty expanse resonated with his disdain for cities and offices and most people in them. He wasn't in the running for a humanitarian award.

"We should move out there," he found himself saying to Jesse from time to time.

Back at work inside, he was pleased that an article on Iranian influence in Iraq and Afghanistan was coming into place. Shia militias in Iraq had been tied to Iran since the Iran-Iraq War of the eighties. It didn't lead to a whole lot during the war but afterwards, with the ouster of Saddam in 2003, Iranian influence became considerable. Off to the east, Iran supported the Northern Alliance against the Taliban and the Northerners were grateful. More grateful to Iran than to the US.

"Why didn't Washington know this? It wasn't classified. Sometimes I think ten people who read the news regularly could give better foreign policy advice than the 'intelligence community'. Man, what a term."

The draft was going well. He hit "save" every now and then and dragged the document to a thumb drive. "I'll take the old boy out for a walk and polish it up later before sending it out. Can't trust their copyeditors anymore."

Jesse was sitting by the door expectantly. A Skype window announced an incoming call.

"Who do I know in the 408 area code? Okay, *whom* do I know out there?"

Ethan was so excited that he neglected to apologize for intruding on Barrett's weekend. They'd known each other since the late nineties when they both taught at the University of Chicago. Fresh out of Yale, Ethan taught chip design in the new computer science program. Barrett taught international affairs in the government department. Afternoons, they played basketball at Henry Crown Fieldhouse where an assortment of teachers, students, local kids, and a high-handed community organizer played together. The games were "spirited" and status was based on what you could do with the ball, not on your degrees. Neither Ethan nor Barrett was blessed with exceptional physical talent, but they set picks, hit the boards, and if left open, they'd drain a jumper.

Nor was either at home in an academic setting. Ethan was a doer, Barrett a loner. Each escaped academia after a few years. Ethan headed off to Silicon Valley, Barrett to his old girlfriend. At least the desert environs turned out well for him.

"Barrett, I have something interesting for you."

"Can it wait for Monday. I was just on my way out to—"

"To play basketball?"

"Not at 7500 feet, Ethan. I'd drop dead in ten minutes, even if I were still in my twenties."

"To walk your wolf friend then."

"You got it."

"Can I ask you to hold off with big Jesse a minute? I've come across something strange in a chip."

"You're asking *me* about a chip? I can install RAM and hard drives. That's about it."

"This will intrigue you, old man. I think there might be a political angle . . . maybe an *international* political angle."

"Okay, let me get my clipboard and pen. But I'll expect free tech support for a year."

"You should have a PC, Barrett. Aren't Macs still using RISC chips?"

"Okay, fill me in on your find—and by the way, Apple went to PAMD chips years ago."

"It's good to hear that Apple is catching up. Now, speaking of microprocessors . . . "

Ethan told him about the CiC. Barrett didn't see where he fit in but he listened patiently and took in as much as he could.

"We need to crack the encryption code. We can't figure out what this program does until we get inside," Ethan paused to gauge Barrett's reaction.

"Maybe the CiC simply prevents you from bootlegging Metallica albums or it sends out emails saying you've won a lottery somewhere. Okay, I'm kidding . . . and out of date. No one listens to Metallica anymore."

"This is serious, Barrett. Well, it might be. I think there's something going on here and I think it has politics in it. I don't know . . . espionage, surveillance, intelligence outfits."

"There've been concerns that China has been putting stuff on circuit boards to collect data. The Manchurian Chip, as it's called."

"I know, Barrett. I was called in to study that concern."

"Called in by whom?"

"By a friend in a certain organization in Israel. There was nothing to that Manchurian Chip stuff. Anyway, this is on the microprocessor, not the circuit board. China doesn't know how to make microprocessors. They're all made in the US or Israel or Britain."

"Well, Ethan, isn't the NSA doing all sorts of obnoxious things to us? Maybe this is part of their guardianship over us—or should I say, *über* us."

"That's PRISM and ECHELON. They do it with software, not with hardware," Ethan replied instantly.

"Ethan, how the hell do you know that? Your friend in a certain Israeli organization?"

"No, a friend in the Ukraine told me about all the NSA snooping. He watches the watchers, guards the guardians. That's another matter entirely. The odd thing is that the CiC, as best as we can tell until we break its encryption, was designed by someone long ago. We're not dealing with a kid straight out of Stanford or an internship at Palo Alto."

"I'm intrigued, I'll say that. You do read more sci-fi than most people do, and you might get drawn in far more than most people."

"Yes, that's true. But someone very clever—no, someone *incredibly* clever—has gone to great pains to put this program on the chips and hide it in an ingenious way. The program's covert and brilliant nature makes me think it's related to the Stuxnet virus that struck that nuclear facility in Iran."

"Natanz . . . the Iranian nuclear facility is Natanz."

"That's the place. Stuxnet sent Natanz's centrifuges into such high speeds that it burned out whole banks of them. That was one amazing program, Barrett. Do people in your world know who wrote it?"

"My world? The New Mexico desert? I thought *you* wrote it, Ethan. Weren't you in the Israeli military and didn't you work for a certain organization over there?"

"Yes, I did, but it wasn't me. My friend in a certain organization over there says no one there knows who wrote Stuxnet. And trust me, they've tried to find out so they can hire them for similar projects."

"That's what my friend in a similar organization over here says too. Well, whoever it was, they did a damn good job. Iran's uranium-enrichment program was set back a year or more and it kept Israel from launching air strikes."

"You're getting on track now, Barrett. The chip's tied in to big things. I know it!"

"Such emotional speculation from a chip designer. I thought you guys were all logic and numbers."

"There are exceptions, Barrett. You should meet my assistant Rina. We'll be out your way soon. Oh, one more thing. The CiC suddenly appeared on PAMD chips in 1986. No CPU before 1986 had the CiC, every CPU after 1986 has it."

"1986 . . . " Barrett talked as he was thinking. "Who would hide a microchip inside a microchip. The most obvious answer is that the company itself created it for business purposes, but you don't believe it and you know that world. Second, a US military or intelligence function, but they use software. Third, some electrical engineers went off on their own venture . . . Oh, I don't know. Ethan, you must have more thoughts."

"I really don't at this point beyond placing it in the political world— *your* world."

"That's a cheap shot if ever I heard one!"

"Well, it's a world you know and detest. Barrett, the circuits are incredibly well designed. They have a definite and important purpose. If—no, *when*—we break the encryption code, we'll know more. For now, what was going on in the world back in 1986?"

"Oh, many things were going on. Wars . . . more wars." Barrett could sense Ethan's impatience. "I'll need some time on this stuff. Ethan, there's probably nothing terribly interesting going on. I'll think about it though and I'll be in touch."

"What? Can't you give me something now?"

"I have to think through a decade of geopolitics. You can't rush sound analysis. Look what happened in Afghanistan."

"You mean back during the Russian war or now?"

"Either one. I'm off to run with the wolves—or at least one of them."

Cedar bushes and trees thrived along the slopes, nourished by the moisture the Sandia peaks bestowed by pushing the clouds higher until they burst and gave the East Mountains the rain that Albuquerque was only taunted with. The altitude and incline caused Jesse to walk more stiffly and Barrett to breathe more deeply. The wolf's glance suggested they take a break, so Barrett sat on the rust-colored rock where he liked to sit and think.

"Nothing will bother me with such a big critter at my side. Talk about credible deterrence." At night the coyotes could be heard on the hunt and in celebration, but they dared not come within a quarter mile of Jesse. Never. It was in their DNA to avoid wolves. It was in human DNA too as the occasional startled hiker demonstrated. Jesse and Barrett got along fine though. Each looked upon the other as someone uncomfortable with his surroundings and as someone who made those around them uncomfortable. It was a match made in New Mexico.

Barrett brooded up there on North Mountain, often for hours, replaying things he'd seen in Iraq and was still trying to make sense of or at least stash somewhere in the back of his mind for a while. He did that elsewhere too—sometimes while drinking at Kelly's, ostensibly watching a game. A loud noise or two people simply shaking hands would take him back to the desert of southern Iraq.

"So what do we have here, Jesse? This chip is used all over the world, starting in 1986. It's every computer's brain. But whose brains are embedded in it? Assuming Ethan's right about a political dimension—a dubious assumption, Jesse—what was going on back in the mid-eighties? Reagan's in and building up the military. Star Wars was just getting underway."

Barrett looked out to the east where the sky was getting dark.

"The first Lebanon war was in 1982. Israel went in to chase out the PLO which led to the rise of Hisbollah—and a long war. The Russkis go into Afghanistan even though the old generals thought it a bad idea. Another long war."

Jesse stared at him.

"What am I forgetting, buddy? Oh yeah . . . the Iran-Iraq War 1980 to 1988. Stalemate and poison gas, just like in World War One. Over a million dead. Missiles fly. Russian ones, western ones. Everyone has an interest because of all the oil going through the Strait of Hormuz. Oil tankers get attacked, even an offshore platform or two. Hi-tech missiles and radar, low-tech gas and rifles. Very nasty, even by the demanding standards of the twentieth century. Over a million dead. Yeah, I already mentioned that . . . Mostly under twenty-five, I'll bet. Kids . . . poor kids . . . So, is there a connection to what Ethan found?"

The wolf stared down to the flat land where they made their home.

"You're right. It's probably nothing. Just something PAMD thought up, printed out at a fab, then dropped. Let's go home, big guy. Dinner awaits us."

"Dinner" being a keyword in the wolf lexicon, Jesse took note.

As they wended their way down the deer trails, Barrett's mind continued to churn. Looking down at the sandy soil, he thought about all the blood that the Middle East had absorbed and about the copious amounts he'd seen and been responsible for.

Farther down the trail, he passed an Iraqi tank he'd put a Sabot round through and the remains of a Republic Guard crewman nearby, a gnarled arm reaching up despairingly from a charred torso. GIs took turns shaking his hand. Barrett displayed no such etiquette that day.

"After the war, Saddam is broke so he invades Kuwait. We send troops and wallop him. Bin Laden is outraged that the US has troops on Saudi soil and we know what that led to—9/11 and Afghanistan and Gulf War Two. Then al Qaeda metastasizes from A-stan to Iraq and Yemen and Somalia and Indonesia and Syria. And now Mali. Jesse, al Qaeda's in Mali now . . . That's near Niger. But you knew that."

They arrived back at the iron gate and wire fence.

"There's no getting away from the wars, Jesse. They keep coming back."

An old, obnoxious visitor would be with Barrett for some time, until they wearied of one another and the visitor went away, though promising never to be far away.

Barrett fell asleep around two and dreamed he was back in the Middle East—a common enough occurrence in the years after his two trips to Iraq, rare now though. He woke up more than once as he saw an Iraqi man walking toward him, several bleeding GIs behind him. One of the wounded, though faceless in the dream, he knew was from a small town in Texas.

The University of Tehran

"Professor? May I ask a question, please? I hope I'm not impertinent." The meek and undersized young student stood outside of the office of Dr Abbas Karroubi, an elderly professor at Tehran University.

"Yes, of course. Come in," came a brisk but not uninviting reply.

The student peered tentatively into the cluttered office and saw the renowned professor focused on his computer screen. Hearing no motion, Karroubi turned to the doorway and saw the young man still standing there. "Come in, young man. I have not bitten anyone in many months and I've just finished a good lunch," he jested as he motioned him in. "So then, what can I do for you?"

The young man was a new graduate student who was enthralled by Dr Karroubi's reputation as an able computer scientist and a helpful teacher who placed his students in prized positions upon graduation. Though older by academic standards, Karroubi retained an analytic edge and abundant generosity.

"Thank you," the student replied nervously.

Dr Karroubi turned away from his screen once again and scrutinized the youth, assessing his intellect, disposition, and potential. Someone had to speak. The young man found courage.

"I am interested in worms—computer worms. I am especially interested in complex ones that invade whole systems, not just the laptop of someone surfing the web or downloading music illegally."

Karroubi again observed the man and tried to discern his motives. He passed his hand through his thin gray hair. "Computer worms. There's certainly been interest in them recently. I suspect we shall remain busy with them for a few more years at the very least."

"I completely understand if you don't have the time, Dr Karroubi. I could come back at a time more convenient if—"

"No, no. Please have a seat. As chance would have it, I am right now looking into an especially pernicious worm that found its way into our country's systems. What is your name, young man?"

"Hussam, sir."

"Good." Karroubi thought of Plato with a young student such as Thrasymachus and opted for a dialog. "Hassam, can you define a computer worm?"

"Yes, of course. A computer worm is a program that duplicates itself like a bifurcating worm and spreads by means of networks into other computers. Often many computers."

"Often *very* many computers—and very *important* ones too. And how does a worm differ from a virus?"

The young man reached into the research he'd done in previous weeks. "A worm is a separate program. It doesn't need to sneak into another program already in a system . . . and it doesn't corrupt files as viruses do. Worms jam operations though—especially networks."

Karroubi was pleased by the young man's preparation and delivery. The professor's respect showed and Hussam grew more comfortable and confident. Karroubi directed Hussam's attention to the screen.

"This is a computer worm called Stuxnet. I'm sure you've heard of it."

"Yes, of course," the youth replied eagerly as he leaned forward to look at the screen.

"Parts of it—only parts of it—have been made available on the web. It was detected in one of our nuclear facilities."

"At Natanz."

"Yes. At Natanz. That's no secret anymore. It has done great harm to the uranium-enrichment centrifuges there. Even our leaders admit that. And Hussam," Karroubi added, lowering his voice to convey humor rather than concern, "if they admit that, the damage must be *quite* severe."

Hussam smiled cautiously then moved closer to see the screen where dozens of lines of intricate code were displayed—most of it far above his understanding. He made out a few basic commands and had occasional glimmers of insight as to Stuxnet's power. He was fascinated, as though a young apprentice in the presence of a master-artisan's work from which he would learn to be a master himself.

"May I ask, professor, what harm the Stuxnet worm did—and how did it do it?"

"Those are questions that can be answered through hard work. A more important question just now, young man, is who wrote it. Our experts in government are convinced that Stuxnet could not have been done by an individual and I've supported that view in meetings with the IRGC. The complexity points in the direction of a large team of highly-skilled people, perhaps in the employ of a state. Which state or states would you suspect, Hussam?"

"There are only a few countries with both the resources and interest to attack our nuclear program. And I have read that it was done by the United States with Israeli help."

"You have *read* this?" Karroubi wondered how a young man could know of this information which was a matter of debate in the highest councils of the Iranian government. "But where?"

"In a review of an American book, from a reputable author and publisher. Many people in the US government were upset by the revelation."

"Well, such revelations can be harmful, though perhaps by directing our attention in misleading directions. Such things need not concern us scientists. Let us entrust that to the politicians and generals." Karroubi saw no recognition of his irony in the youth and he grumbled imperceptibly.

"Professor, what exactly has Stuxnet done to our Natanz facility?"

"It invaded the software engineered by Siemens to operate the thousands of centrifuges which spin rapidly and expel uranium particles thereby enriching the uranium from U-238 to U-235. Stuxnet sped up the centrifuges then slowed them down. The vibrations damaged many centrifuges, indeed whole cascades of them. Worry not, young man, we have located the worm and eradicated it."

"How was it located? Such things are expertly disguised."

"I was called in, as I often am for such matters, and I saw something amiss with the control servers. Commands were sent to the machinery that ignored the guidance of the hundreds of sensors in the centrifuges. I went into the operating subsystems and noticed unusually high network traffic—a reliable sign of a worm, as you know. I calculated the traffic and bandwidth that should be on our network given the amount of data flow and the traffic indicator immediately showed abnormally high values."

"The worm was overloading the network traffic."

"Indeed, it was. From there, finding the worm was fairly easy. I wrote a network trap to sample data, the content, and quantity. This was still tricky since Stuxnet did not operate consistently. In order to camouflage its operation, it operated at random times. It was painfully hard to find."

"Amazing . . . frightening," Hussam was concerned and fascinated as his education and his country's security were intertwined.

"Stuxnet had other ruses. It periodically sent meaningless data into the network to cause more confusion. That made my detective work more difficult, I can tell you." Karroubi took in some herbal tea then continued. "One of the most devious aspects of Stuxnet was its method of spreading itself. It picked a random host through the network, duplicated itself, and pretended to be one of the system's files. After completing its mischief, it erased itself."

"It came, it conquered, it left."

"So you've read Caesar's Gallic Wars. A promising sign! Now back to our worm infestation. It was as if Stuxnet had never been there, except for the damage it left. Except for the *considerable* damage it left." Another historical analogy came to the professor's mind. "In this respect, it was like many great men in history. They leave behind horrid ruins and immense cemeteries, as the poet said of Generalissimo Wallenstein."

Hussam reached again for information from his readings of history and literature. "Wallenstein . . . Albrecht von Wallenstein—the seventeenth-century mercenary commander who tried to take too much power. The Habsburgs had him killed."

"That is he. Impressive, Hussam. Breadth of education is rare these days. I wonder if General Suleimani of our Revolutionary Guards knows the name Wallenstein. He should. Indeed, he should."

"Military history is a hobby—and so much revolves around military matters today. My mother says that too much revolves around military matters."

Dr Karroubi nodded. "Only a foolish lad ignores his mother's counsel, Hussam."

Hussam was beginning to recognize the professor's wit, making him feel more comfortable. "What about the Stuxnet program itself? Did it have unique algorithms and methods?"

"You may be sure it did. Perhaps the most sophisticated part of Stuxnet targeted the Programmable Logic Controllers which operated the motors and pumps. Remarkable programming techniques accessed the motors and sent them off into ruinous spin rates. Someone had their hands on highly confidential Application Programming Interfaces."

"They must have had help from the manufacturer of the centrifuges."

"That could be the case."

"Eventually we detected it and stopped it. I mean, *you* stopped it." Hussam looked with great admiration at Dr Karroubi and enjoyed the prestige of having a great man impart his knowledge to him, if only in small, easily digested amounts at this point. For the moment, the nagging senses of worthlessness and futility that haunt graduate students eased inside him. He'd demonstrated worth and perhaps found a mentor.

"Stuxnet destroyed perhaps a thousand centrifuges and caused considerable delay in our enrichment program. Ah, but the centrifuges are back up and the control program is more secure now." Dr Karroubi sank into his thoughts, pondering what promise there was in this young student. "Are you aware of any other centrifuges in our country, Hussam?"

"Yes, there are centrifuges at Fordo. They are much deeper underground than the ones at Natanz. So they are invulnerable to enemy air attacks."

"We build deeper facilities and they build bigger bombs, Hussam. The Americans are building an enormous one."

"Yes. The Massive Ordnance Penetrator." He enunciated the foreign words slowly. "It is being built in White Sands, New Mexico." More slow enunciation. "That is the same place the Americans detonated the first atomic bomb."

"Remarkable, young man. You are promising."

Hussam positively beamed. "Like you, I hope to see our country take its place in the forefront of world affairs."

Karroubi smiled faintly. Anyone who knew him would have discerned a trace of disappointment. "Yes, of course . . . We all wish to regain a respected place in the community of nations. Insha'Allah, of course."

"Insha'Allah."

California

Rina called Ethan several times but couldn't reach him. Her two messages brought no callback. She concluded, easily enough, that he was at Micrologic Design, cell phone on silent, face to the screen. She drove up just after midnight, peered up to the top floor, and saw a light on in his office. She took the lift up to the office and saw Ethan busily entering data, unaware she was in the doorway—or oblivious to her.

"Hey . . . why don't you answer your phone?" She walked toward him, puzzled by her own tentativeness. "I've been trying to get you for hours."

Ethan lifted his head for few moments. "I'm sorry, I was very busy with—"

"The encryption—what the hell else." She sat in the chair beside him. "You know, Ethan, this is starting to worry me. You don't eat right, you don't sleep much, and this encryption is becoming an obsession. It isn't helping business . . . and it isn't helping *us*."

"I need to know things," Ethan replied flatly, his eyes never leaving the screen.

"I know . . . that you need . . . to know!" She was all but gritting her teeth, her voice was rising. "You're completely forgetting your job, our business, and everything else. Every*one* else too."

He closed his eyes as her words and state of mind sank in, then he turned to her. "You're right . . . of course." He reached for her hand and she gave him hers. They welcomed a moment of reconnection. She sat on his lap and they held each other, rocking gently back and forth.

"There are important people, Ethan. People who care about you. People who want you to succeed, and grow, and . . . "

They simply held each other, foreheads resting together, breaths intermingling. For a few moments they put the business and the CiC mystery and Micrologic Design aside. Either sleep or passion would have taken over for the evening but an alert sound chimed and Ethan's attention was redirected to a new page.

"At least we had that glorious nano-moment." Rina stood behind Ethan and looked at the screen. An email arrived and Ethan opened a PDF file with "Top Secret" prominently written across the front page in a blunt, cheerless font. The page displayed a table of contents for encryption and de-encryption. Atop it was a government seal: an eagle with its talons clutching an immense key.

"Ethan! Tell me you haven't hacked into the National Security Agency!"

"Well . . . technically, I guess you could say I did."

"Technically? *Technically?* When people use that word I brace for myself for preposterous rationalizations!"

"What's that expression? Oh yes: 'Let's not go there, girlfriend'."

"No one says that anymore, not even on Oprah."

"Duly noted. I have a Ukrainian friend from college—a first-rate hacker. In high school he worked his way into the servers of schools and television stations where he performed a little . . . I don't know, let's say, a little mischief."

"Examples of this *mischief*, please. Millions of dollars diverted?"

"Nothing so daring, not at that point. The school principal was surreptitiously enrolled in a phys ed class and given a failing grade. Television stations suddenly broadcast a few minutes of the Playboy Channel. My friend was fond of a certain actress in that genre and wanted to share her talents with both Israel and Saudi Arabia. He was caught but he learned from his mistakes. He's graduated to higher things—more daring things. At least that's what a friend in a certain organization back in Israel tells me. They like his work and use him for a few unstated purposes."

"More *daring* things? You mean more *illegal* things."

"Rina, in some endeavors and with some organizations, the distinction between legal and illegal gets blurred or is irrelevant. NSA looks in on us, we look in on NSA. You might call it karma."

"They might call it *crime-a*," Rina shot back. Pleased with her cleverness, she let her concerns ease. "Tell me more of your Ukrainian friend with a penchant for daring things. Single or married. On parole or in the slammer."

"Not sure of his marital status but I'll tell him you asked."

"He sounds like a dream date. We can watch the Playboy Channel together."

"Anyway, I always respected him as an ingenious colleague, nonetheless I avoided close contact with him in case he got dragged in for something . . . oh, something high level."

"Something *daring*."

"Yes, something daring. I didn't want to hear a loud knock on my door in the middle of the night."

"Did *he* ever hear a loud knock on *his* door in the middle of the night, Ethan?"

"He's on parole now. He tried to friend me on Facebook last year but I didn't accept, for reasons that must now be obvious. This guy's good though."

"Is this guy's name *Mantas*?"

Ethan smiled and nodded. "Yes, Mantas. So I've already told you about him."

"Well, no. I saw your Skype contacts once when you left it on your desktop and I saw his creepy avatar—a sketch of a bad boy holding a mouse—a computer mouse, that is. At least I hope that's what it was."

"That's him. I always had his Skype number but I never contacted him." He took a deep breath and exhaled noisily and in jest. "Until last night. Rina, it was late and I was getting nowhere. So . . . "

"You're going to get arrested. You're going to get *me* arrested too. I can hear it now: 'Ethan and Rina! We know you're in there. Come out with your hands up and your NASA lab coats off. But officer, I don't have a NASA lab coat. I'm just an innocent intern'."

"The term 'innocent intern' has carried an oxymoronic meaning for many years and besides, I'm not sure it's entirely appropriate here anyway."

"Ethan, you don't hack into the National Security Agency! They'll track our PPP back to this very office. They have no sense of humor at all! They have guns though—Sig Towers."

"Sig *Sauers*. I know someone who carries one at all times."

"Mantis packs a Sig Tower?"

"No. A guy named Boaz Preses. He's in army intelligence."

"I supposed he has a license to—"

"Boaz has a license to eat. That's all. Now, back to the issue at hand. I didn't hack into the National Security Agency. Mantas did and he did it somewhere near Kiev, though he probably spoofed his PPP." Ethan was beaming with pride. "Mantas, old man, I'm guessing you spoofed a PPP in Langley, Virginia or Ekaterinburg, Russia or some such place, didn't you? He's good, I'm telling you, Rina. He got us some great data."

"He got *us* some great data?"

"Okay, *me*. Now I can find methods and algorithms to crack the toughest encryption engines, even the one on the PAMD chips."

She shook her head in disbelief and growing annoyance. Then came the realization that the damage was done—and most likely in Langley or Ekaterinburg. They might as well see what they could get. "Okay, maybe I'll pick up something for my dissertation. Does Folsom grant degrees in computer science?"

"Not since Johnny Cash left. Anyway, here's a program that our NSA friends use to crack codes of the 512-bit variety. They developed it back in the mid-eighties to get into Soviet and Chinese systems. It runs in a loop and goes through all discrete combinations. I've already built a program based on it and it's up and running, even as we speak. It'll analyze the encryption's nature and suggest a way of getting in. It'll take a little time though."

Rina looked at the screen and stifled a gasp as she saw a webpage with the same government logo. "Ethan . . . tell me something. Are you—not are *we*, are *you*—inside the NSA servers, even as we speak?"

"*Technically,*" they both said amid laughter.

"I had to borrow another piece of their code module for my own program." He typed a few lines and grinned. "One thing I learned from Mantas: it's important to know your way in, but—" he gave her a mischievous look, "it's even more important to know your way out." His voiced trailed off and his fingers made walking motions across the desk.

"What do you mean?"

"Hacking into a system is a great accomplishment, but in some respects, it's the easy part. Getting out is more difficult. Know why?"

"Nope. We innocent interns keep to the straight and narrow. I'm not even here, even if 'here' is Langley or Ekaterinburg."

"I have to make sure that I leave no trace that I was ever in." Ethan hit Enter. "The port was closed and my record as a user will be changed into a different type of record—a system binary. The time stamp will change. The record will be deleted, the computer clock will be set backwards to one of the oldest file dates, and a new record will be created with the older time stamp. The clock will be updated to the current date. All registry notifications will be redone. No evidence of entrance into the system. I was never there." He sat back in his chair in cyber-triumph.

"Good. Then neither was I." She slumped into a chair and exhaled. "I feel like we're Bonnie and Clyde . . . and you know how that movie ended. *Rat-tat-tat!* I prefer Folsom to machine guns on a country road."

Ethan hummed a melody and Rina launched into singing the words.

> *I hear the train a-comin'*
> *It's rollin' round the bend*
> *And I ain't seen the sunshine since I don't know when*
> *I'm stuck in Folsom prison, and time keeps draggin' on*
> *But that train keeps a rollin' on down to San Antone.*

They both missed the bass notes of "San Antone" very badly and laughed crazily in each other's arms.

The NSA code proved helpful, *very* helpful, in unraveling the encryption's structure. They still needed keywords to activate the decryption process, though. Ethan sipped room-temperature chocolate milk and furrowed his brow in disgust. "I look at the screen, the screen looks back at me. Nothing happens," he complained to Rina as she entered his office.

She sat in the couch. "I know the feeling. Can we call it a day now? What day is it anyway?"

Ethan shook his head. "Not yet. We're getting close . . . I'm not sure what day it is."

"Can't you give the task to your Mantas friend. That's his forte."

"Isn't it pronounced 'for-*tay*'?"

"No, my English-challenged Israeli friend. It's one syllable. But that's how most Americans pronounce it, so you're excused. Maybe they'll teach you good English in Folsom."

"Forte . . . one syllable. I'm sure you're right. I don't want to give this to Mantas. No one should know about this beside us—and Barrett. We can trust him. He only talks to wolves."

"And Al Jazeera."

"He won't talk about this to Al Jazeera. They'd think he'd gone into Alex Jones Land. Mantas, on the other hand, works for any number of people and trades secrets with them like they're baseball cards."

He was lost in thought for a moment then turned to his screen. "A basic rule is that a system has hints in case a user can't recall the keywords. It was true at the University of Chicago, Yale, DEC, IBM, the American air force, the Israeli air force, and Mossad. Let's see what comes of it here." He started to type with greater purpose.

Rina looked at him and shook her head quietly. "Another lost night," she muttered. She could see his eyes were red and tired so she headed to the kitchen and after a little whirring of the blender, she brought him a glass of orange juice. "I made it myself just now. It's better for you than chocolate milk."

No reply.

"I'm at the gates." His smile could not overcome the exhaustion elsewhere on his face. "Okay, here's where we are. We need keywords to enable the decryption engine. The system will give hints. Here's the first one." Ethan all but glowed with pride as a sequence of sentences appeared on screen:

> My first is in companion, but not in enemy.
> My second in both peace and war.
> My third in simple, but not complex.
> My fourth in water, but not shore.
>
> To ignore me, much must be forgotten.
> And so now you must try.
> To figure out this hint.
> And answer:
>
> What Am I?

"A riddle, eh . . . I'm getting nothing," said Rina.

"This is one word. Read the hint again, please."

Rina again tried to process the hints. "Still nothing."

"The word 'PAST'," Ethan explained excitedly. His mind was still capable of moments of playful reasoning, despite the strain and late hour. "The first letter P is in the word COMPANION, but not in ENEMY. The second is in both PEACE and WAR. The only common letter is A."

"The third is simple—S," Rina continued, getting the riddle template in her head. "And the fourth in Water but not Shore is the letter T. Got it!"

"So we have one word." Rina became intrigued, in a playful way. "How many words do we need?"

"My program indicates that we have a combination of words that has to be fed into the decryption engine. The order doesn't matter, only the words. Then everything will be working from there."

"Do these words have meaning?" Rina asked.

"I suspect so." Ethan pointed towards the screen "We'll have to figure it out later. Here's the second one."

> I always come but never arrive,
> When I come, you may not be alive.
>
> What am I?

Rina was developing a feel for the game. "When I come you may not be alive? Well, it's probably the future."

"Very good—almost." Ethan patted her shoulder in sympathy. "The word is 'TOMORROW'. It's in the future and you never know if you'll wake up tomorrow morning."

"Especially after what we've been doing." Rina rocked her head back and forth, playing along.

"Here's another one" Ethan pointed.

> When you name me, you break me.

Rina's mind raced about, remembering word games in the Sunday comics from her childhood, the Riddle of the Sphinx, and an old episode of *Batman* she'd just seen on retro TV. Mental gymnastics.

"Silence! Only silence is broken when you mention it."

"See why I like this program, Rina? Here's the last one. Maybe we can do it together."

"Bring it on—as cheerleaders and presidents say!"

I am one brother.
One the smallest, another the largest.
One is dark and one is cold, and two others.

Who am I?

"One is the smallest and one is the largest . . . " Rina mumbled "My brain is flashing me a File 404 message. I'm getting them a lot with this chip thing."

"We need this one and another. Then we can decrypt whatever we want. We'll be in like a porch climber." Ethan checked his watch and shook his head. "Wow, I didn't realize it's almost three am. What a day, what a night."

"I can't think," Rina handed her hand to him. "Let's go home and work on it tomorrow."

Ethan looked at the screen just before he powered off. "We'll be back tomorrow, my little LED friend."

The cursor blinked back.

The University of Tehran

Dr Karroubi met regularly with a small group of former graduate students. They dined at least every month at his house not far from the university. He'd placed many of his students in academic settings and government but there was a select group he'd placed with the Revolutionary Guard Corps. The IRGC enjoyed lavish government funding and it drew money from the business enterprises it ran, which for one reason or another included laser eye-surgery clinics.

The IRGC also did the most demanding research in physics and engineering which Karroubi wanted to keep abreast of, though not entirely for professional purposes. The IRGC didn't want him abreast of what they were doing. Nor did they want anyone outside their upper echelons to know what they were doing. They didn't even want the mullahs to know.

The students he placed in IRGC facilities were especially devoted to him. He'd cultivated their loyalty by imparting his considerable knowledge and displaying his insights and wit. More than that, however, he was fatherly to them. Several had lost their fathers to the shah's secret police, or in the revolution, or in the war with Iraq. One of them served in the army with Karroubi's son and was with him when he was killed late in the war by an Iraqi sniper.

Their loyalty to him greatly surpassed what they had for the IRGC or the mullahs. They would not speak to the CIA or Mossad, despite more than a few clandestine overtures from those quarters. Nor would they inform the IRGC or the Ministry of Internal Security of those overtures. His students were loyal to *him*. More importantly, they were loyal to his beliefs. They considered themselves loyal to Iran, though just now the idea of their beloved homeland was unfortunately an abstraction largely detached from the leaders and institutions of the day.

After feasting joyfully on cashew rice, curried chicken, and a presentable Shiraz, the group adjourned to the living room. They brought their glasses and a second bottle of Shiraz.

"So, my friends, what goes on at Parchin and Fordo these days? I'm sure I'm not the only one who wants to know." The venerable professor's words brought amusement.

"No, Dr Karroubi, that is the question on everyone's lips," replied one young man.

"And in many parts of the world," added a young woman who wore no veil inside.

"Well then, what news is there of shaping enriched uranium into a warhead component?" Karroubi looked about the room until someone spoke up.

"There is computer modeling going on. Spheroid and hemispheric configurations are being explored. No more than modeling. No manufacturing. The mullahs say it must not be done and for now . . . " The young man shrugged, uncertain of what next week or month would bring.

"The generals grumble and talk among themselves but they lack the knowledge and they don't trust the hundreds of people there to maintain secrecy," the young woman added as one of the male students charged her glass.

Karroubi nodded and mulled over the implications of warhead research.

"And what of the diagrams of the R265 device that our Ukrainian colleague Danilenko sold our country a few years ago? The West is sure we are using them for a nuclear trigger," Karroubi put to the room. He looked to a young man he knew to have met with Danilenko in the last year.

"Danilenko worked in nanotechnology, not nuclear weapons. And the R265 technology is only being used for nanotechnology—the production of minuscule diamonds, to be precise."

"This is somewhat reassuring," Karroubi replied. "Nonetheless, it would be best if these models our ambitious generals tinker with—and have high hopes for—do not lead to anything worrisome. Can they be gotten to?"

"That would be difficult and not without risk. The servers have better encryption now—the best the Chinese have to offer. It's similar to the encryption used by their navy. Still, nothing is impossible. That is what a sage old professor told us!"

"You never tell me this sage fellow's name!" Karroubi retorted. "Yes, it would take considerable skill and stealth to get in. It sounds almost as well protected as the uranium centrifuges of Natanz. Would that this sage chap had young colleagues who could help with some increasingly arcane algorithms of Chinese origins!"

Once again, the gathering appreciated Dr Karroubi's wit. They all charged their glasses with more Shiraz and turned their attention to the task of writing another program for the benefit of Iran, though the Supreme Leader and the IRGC generals would hardly think of them as beneficial.

Ramon Airbase, Southern Israel

Young Captain Ronit had entered the air force only four years earlier. She was nonetheless astute and meticulous and had been entrusted with even the most sensitive operations. The base was growing in personnel and strategic importance and she saw her role as highly valued. This day she was working with a pair of F-15Is on a training mission. It was hardly a routine one.

An unexpected message came across the command center's system. There were a dozen junior officers and enlisted personnel in the center, all looking at each other in puzzlement. She'd never seen such a message at this point in a training exercise. Her superior probably had.

"Colonel Ofer, I know you're with the people from the defense ministry, but we have a most unusual signal from high up. I'd appreciate it if you took a look . . . Yes, sir, it *does* involve the two birds over the Gulf of Aden."

The colonel had many years in the tower and many more up in the air. He still flew F-15Is, a heavier and more sophisticated fighter than the F-16. F-15Is were capable of long-range strikes. American intelligence people used to joke that the "I" stood for Iran. No one on the Israeli end denied it or saw much humor in it.

This training mission called for the fighters to fly south into the Gulf Aden then turn east toward the Strait of Hormuz, toward Iran. Winds, altitudes, and fuel consumption would be gauged and the surveillance gear would look for radar detection. They'd run similar missions over the Mediterranean which were precisely the distance to the Iranian nuclear facilities at Natanz and Fordo. That, as they say, sent a message.

Everyone knew that the mission was preparation for airstrikes on Iran. The people from the defense ministry knew it, the pilots knew it, and so did the Iranian picket ship the F-15Is would soon fly over. Today, the Israeli fighter pilots would buzz the radar ship perched at the southern end of the Red Sea, maybe even dip their wings in mock salute, but they would not turn on their countermeasures. Why teach them something they might use against you in a few weeks or days? The Israeli jets were also on the watch for Iranian merchant ships that might be delivering weapons to Sudan or Yemen.

Ofer looked at the screen. "It looks like a cancellation order from the big shots. That's troubling—we usually get the order by secured landline too." Ofer contacted the command center burrowed deep below Tel Aviv. The officer of the day listened, checked his screen, and asked him to wait a few minutes while he spoke with the officer he'd relieved.

Ofer got word in five minutes: "That's affirmative, colonel. Cancellation is confirmed."

"Affirmative—and out." That was enough for Ofer, though privately he was still troubled. "Abort the mission. Bring the planes back," he told Ronit. The people from the defense ministry were disappointed, but Colonel Ofer crisply insisted that procedures had to be followed and told a lieutenant to drive the delegation back to Jerusalem.

Ofer went back to his pita and humus and to reading his day-old *Yediot Aharonot*. The planes would be back over the Gulf of Aqaba in a few minutes. It had been a busy day and he hoped for a tranquil evening. The F-15Is returned to their base after only briefly passing over Yemeni territory. No one's radar had picked them up as far as anyone could tell, not even that of Saudi Arabia.

"We practiced flying over Saudi airspace last month." Capt Ronit was hoping to elicit a response from her superior. "They've granted us access to their airspace for an Iranian strike, haven't they?"

"Yes, they have . . . we can't rely on the Saudis though." Ofer sensed the conversation was about to go off limits, if it hadn't already. "They might change their minds and we have to have options. Options are critical in military operations and foreign policy. Besides, if their people found out they'd helped us, there could be uprisings and the House of Saud might be in danger."

"Is that what the generals and the government think?"

"I'm just a colonel, Capt Ronit. They don't tell me much and they ask me almost nothing."

"So it's just your view, sir."

"Yes."

"It's mine too . . . Sir, do you think it might be a mistake to attack Iran? A serious mistake? It might reduce our options."

Off limits. She'd crossed a professional boundary. He didn't like to think about the consequences of such an attack, though of course he'd weighed the matter. Soldiers follow orders but some orders are folly, others catastrophic. He thought attacking Iran might be the latter but never stated that to anyone, let alone to a junior officer.

"We of course must trust our politicians and generals, Capt Ronit." Ofer sensed the lack of authority and conviction in his own voice. So did Ronit. "We need to find out more about that recall order. There's something strange about it. It reminds me of the anomalies involving our Jericho missiles when I was stationed at Sdot Micah. This is perplexing—and worrisome too."

The young captain mulled this over. She wondered if there was a way to recall a fighter squadron without the higher-ups knowing—and without knowing just who recalled them. She decided to ask her grandfather who was a professor emeritus at Hebrew University and quite knowledgeable of military computer systems, even though he mistrusted the military. And they him.

The University of Tehran

Dr Karroubi responded with amiable nods to the greetings of students as he walked to a university sub-library in the art department, a kilometer from his office. He acquired the university's wi-fi signal and with a few commands on his laptop worked his way into the mainframe of the IRGC base at Parchin and through the server there, into the Fordo system as well. The two secretive bases were now open to him, even the parts denied to IAEA inspection teams, the mullahs, and his former students.

He looked through the data then refined his search with the terms "weapon, implosion, trigger, R265, Danilenko." Thousands of files came up, including email between the facilities and prominent IRGC generals, including the top ones—Qasim Suleimani and Mohammad Ali Jafari. The professor pored through the data with the diligence and evenhandedness of a scholar. He felt more like a spy—a patriotic one. The paradox and ambiguity that others might have felt did not bother him. He walked into a cafeteria, acquired the signal, and delved into the files once more. A young veiled woman brought him a croissant and a chamomile tea. He'd developed a taste for the latter when he was in grad school at Berkeley in the sixties.

"We're almost out of chamomile, professor. Sanctions."

"They've embargoed my tea? That seems rather petty of them."

The woman smiled and made a note to share the professor's humor with friends.

It took several days to go through the files. Full-scale research on a weapon system had indeed halted in 2003, around the time of the country's diplomatic overture to the US. The overture was rebuffed, unwisely in Karroubi's view, and it was thought that weapons research would become a high national priority. US troops were then to the west in Iraq and to the east in Afghanistan. The US navy was ever to the west in the Persian Gulf and to the south in the Arabian Sea. Further research, according to the data before Karroubi, had been curtailed. Internal correspondence revealed considerable grumbling over this, especially in the heated correspondence between General Jafari and the Minister of Interior, but no signal had been given on weapons production and there was no evidence of development on the sly—not at Parchin, not at Fordo, not anywhere.

Karroubi mulled this over as he walked to the main library. He wasn't satisfied; he didn't trust IRGC generals. He thought them ambitious and vain fools whose persistence with outdated tactics squandered tens of thousands of young lives in the Iraq War after which they proclaimed themselves masterful guardians of the Republic. Karroubi reflected on his motivations for what he was about to do. Was it good for Iran or just bad for the IRGC? Was he acting as a selfless patriot or an embittered father? A passage from La Rochefoucauld came to him:

We should often feel ashamed of our best actions if the world could see all the motives which produced them.

He sighed as he reached for a 32gb thumb drive from his jacket and inserted it into a USB port. The contents appeared to be personal email files, family photos, and hundreds of Word documents, but encrypted therein was a modified program of the one he and his former students had written to damage the Natanz centrifuges. His program had become famous around the world and had baffled every interested intelligence agency. He and his young colleagues recently strengthened and refined it to work on the Fordo and Parchin systems. They were very proud of their program, though they couldn't boast of it.

Karroubi and his circle simply called it "The Program," but around the world it was known as "Stuxnet." A few commands and something which he jokingly called "Stuxnet II" was inside the IRGC systems, though with a time delay.

In less than forty-eight hours, Stuxnet II became active inside Parchin. It was given a name already in the system, so its external origin would be almost impossible to detect. The program began operation just before dawn when almost no one was working with the computer system. Even if someone were, the program would not touch any files opened and in use. It would bide its time and come back.

Stuxnet II searched for research documents of all types. It scanned each server for Word, PowerPoint, and any other files that may be used for R&D. The program searched for numerical values—formulas, equations, tables, and other scientific information. It then activated a smart algorithm which swapped a few numbers and altered parts of formulas—usually just a thousandth of a millimeter here and there and a few equation symbols. In only a few hours the program had done its work on thousands of documents. Time stamps of altered files remained as they were the night before, so there was no sign of alteration. Though the original structure of each document was retained, the content was changed and was now worthless.

It was like getting into a bank's records and changing an account number and asset value by a digit here and there, except it would be far more difficult to notice the changes in the IRGC data. Any design, whether for IRGC nanotechnology or for weapons, was altered if only slightly, and tolerances for intricate components such as spherically-shaped charges and nose cones are infinitesimal. The altered data would cause serious damage to components and machinery during any manufacturing process. Some things truly are rocket science.

Stuxnet II completed its task, duplicated itself into a different file system name, changed its time stamp to an authentic one, then erased itself. *Poof!*

The next morning, another program, which Karroubi thought of as Stuxnet III, woke up at another IRGC facility—Fordo, the uranium-enrichment site near Qom. This program searched for system control files, which included vital data on motors, pumps, and centrifuges. Like the earlier program, Stuxnet III slightly modified numerical values. All machines and equipment would be working within prescribed ranges, but near or at their limits. It would be impossible find fault with the control files, as all information appeared intact. The only way to find the alteration would be to eventually compare the files with the manufacturer's documentation. By then, the damage would be done.

Stuxnet III completed its task, duplicated itself into a different file system name, changed its time stamp to an authentic one, then erased itself. *Poof!*

Stuxnet II-IIIa woke up shortly after the last one and searched only for backup files. All scientific and research backup files were overwritten with the same name and size. The only difference was that they were now empty. As with its predecessors, Stuxnet II-IIIa replicated itself, bowed politely, and made a graceful exit from the file-system stage. It did not wait for appreciative applause or irate boos, though it might have considered a return engagement someday.

The three programs created almost imperceptible damage over a long period of time. Within a few months, an immense amount of critical data was lost and whole banks—no, entire chambers—of costly machinery at Fordo were damaged.

I've delayed the end of days, at least for a while. Dr Karroubi thought to himself of all the madness in the world as he walked into the court area of Tehran University on his way to an off-campus bookstore. *There are so many people in the world who wish to see the end of days. Others are propelling us headlong in that direction without knowing it.*

Coming toward him was Hussam, the young man keen on history and eager to learn of worms. His face displayed more confidence than in their last meeting.

"I've decided to do my master's thesis on the use of worms as cyber-weapons, Dr Karroubi!"

"A noble calling, Hussam. I wish you much success and look forward to giving you whatever guidance an old man can."

"There is so much you can guide me on, sir. Perhaps someday we can strike back against those who created Stuxnet."

"In what way, Hussam? I haven't known you long but I suspect you have some thoughts on this, if only preliminary ones."

Hussam smiled appreciatively. "Yes, I have given it some thought and I hope they are not too nebulous as to preclude my articulating them to you. We could strike American financial institutions and perhaps the systems controlling Saudi Arabia's oil terminals."

Karroubi marveled at the idea. "Excellent ideas, Hussam. Not nebulous, well articulated. We must discuss them further someday. Would that we could do such things today."

Karroubi still held out hope for the young man. Anyone who knew of Wallenstein had breadth in his formation. Anyone who knew that Wallenstein had brought so much death and ruin to the world had decency in his formation. Hussam was naive but not beyond hope. Karroubi had brought others like Hussam into his network of prized graduate students whom he later placed in sensitive positions. He hoped, however, that by the time Hussam finished graduate school it would no longer be necessary.

"Perhaps we could meet next week, professor."

"That will be most welcome, Hussam."

New Mexico

"Good morning, Barrett! Got a minute?"

Ethan sounded energized and Barrett thought that a sign of trouble. Ethan was about to drop work on him. He put on a headset and walked into the kitchen.

"Did you try hacking into the NSA code-breaking website?" Barrett was kidding but the silence at the other end told the story. "Oh . . . I see. Well, did you get anywhere with it?" Barrett tossed Jesse a biscuit and his massive jaws slammed shut on it with the cracking sound of a batter hitting an upper-deck home run.

"What in the world was that, Barrett? Are you okay?"

"I'm fine. I just gave Jesse a treat. That was his teeth snapping shut. Pretty impressive, huh."

"Wow! Yes, impressive and fearsome," Ethan replied. "Well anyway, we found out that the system offers prompts in the form of riddles to unlock things. Rina and I got a few of them but we were wondering, since you do crossword puzzles—and in ink—you might enjoy taking a crack at one."

Barrett picked up a pen and notepad. "Shoot." Ethan read from the screen.

> I am one brother.
> One the smallest, another the largest.
> One is dark and one is cold, and two others.
>
> Who am I?

Barrett thought a minute and realized it wasn't going to come to him just then. "Let me call you in a bit. I have to get Jesse's breakfast and meds."

"Meds?"

"Yep. Glucosamine and Prednisone. He's not a pup anymore."

"Thanks, Barrett. Neither are we."

"Jesse, my man, we're not pups anymore. That's what Ethan says. We still walk our way up North Mountain, don't we."

Jesse recognized the keyword "walk." The rest was just nonsense that humans chattered about to no particular purpose as far as he could tell.

California

Ethan and Rina looked at the screen in weary silence as they puzzled over one of the remaining clues.

> Gets rid of bad ones,
> Short and tall,
>
> One size fits all.

"I'm getting another File 404 in my brain." Rina was growing impatient. She stood up and paced about the room. "You know, this thing's annoying me. We have a business to run and a product to ship before we get deeper inside this CiC caper." She was at the edge of her tolerance and shot him a stern look, but Ethan never saw it. "If looks could kill," she murmured.

"Get rid of the bad apples maybe." Ethan kept thinking about the prompt. "There's the old line about bad apples ruining the rest. Nah. It doesn't fit with 'Short and Tall'."

Rina sat back down and reluctantly got back into the game. "What can be short and tall? People?"

"One size fits all?" Ethan mumbled as he blinked his eyes to moisten them. "I'll start searching on-line."

"You do that," Rina stood up again "I'll see that Micrologic Design doesn't go under." She turned around in the doorway and added, "At least not this week."

Ethan was going through search pages. He was only learning a lot of old riddles that grade school kids would find unchallenging and devoid of humor.

Rina went to her office to answer several email inquires from chip companies and capital goods ones too—the folks who made the machinery that made the chips. A few kind words from them and the Micrologic Design name would become global. Right now its reputation was confined to a few offices in Santa Clara, the families of Ethan and Rina, and a handful of part-time workers they'd taken on. She and Ethan were heading out to Albuquerque in a few days to give a presentation at the PAMD fab there and two weeks later there was a trade show.

Crunch time was coming but there was still a flaw in their software program—an irksome one. It wasn't consistent; it couldn't be reproduced. This would be disastrous for an analysis program. A bug in the program can cause billions of dollars of losses from a defective chip and turn a startup into a shutdown. Ethan would be broke and might have to move to find work, maybe back to Israel. She was wondering if she should bring a stack of CVs for the headhunters that would be swarming at the trade show.

She rechecked the modules that might hold the problem but couldn't find anything. The results were viable and accurate. She knew she had to build a special test case to reproduce the problematic results. "Where are you, little bug?" she grumbled as she scanned thousands of lines of source code. She implemented many a check point within the program debugger, but nothing showed. She ran the module step-by-step through all their dozens of quality-assurance test cases. They all came out well and the results were viable and accurate.

"We're groping about in the dark here," she said to the screen as a new series of tests ran in front of her, with perfect results. "I need a break. A Frappuccino and a bite to eat will work."

She walked a few blocks to a Starbucks, ordered her drink and a scone, and opened her iPad Mini to play a game. Micrologic Design was still young and far from profitable, but it nonetheless gave each of its few employees an iPad Mini. It was great for web browsing and catching up with friends and the news. The retinal display made games more fun. "What do we have here?" she whispered as she completed downloading a package of new games. "Pac-Man. It's *soooo* retro but I love it. Hangman . . . a timeless classic. Where would Vanna and Pat be without it." The first two games at the lowest level of difficulty were easy so she selected the hardest level. She got a few vowels but the time ran out and she lost.

"What's a 'vavasour'?" she said aloud as the word was revealed. A few people looked at her in amusement. She stared at the image of the unfortunate cyber-fellow whose life Rina just forfeited. A platform, gallows, and a rope. Her mind searched for the meaning of 'vavasour' but only got a hazy recollection of a medieval history lecture on PBS.

"Hanging was an old way of getting rid of the bad guys." There was a reason the phrase "bad guys" came to mind and she was assembling the pieces. "Short and tall guys . . . one size fits all . . . Thank you, Hangman!" she shouted. She tossed her cup into the trash and raced back to Micrologic Design, much to the relief of the dismayed coffee shop patrons.

Rina stormed into Ethan's office and exclaimed, "Noose!"

"What news?" Ethan looked at Rina with concern and wondered why she was so animated.

"No, my Israeli boyfriend. 'Noose'. That's the rope you hang people with. One size fits all!"

Ethan saw the relation to the prompts and raised his hands in triumph. "I love you for your brain!"

"That's the only reason?"

Ethan entered the new word. "No, not a bit. There's so much more, dear. So much more. All we need is one more of—"

A Skype window opened. "Barrett Parker" flashed the caller ID.

"Great timing, Barrett. We just cracked another word. Any luck with yours?" Ethan switched on the speaker phone.

"Well, let's just see," Barrett said in a feigned cocky tone. " 'I am one among seven', according to the hint. 'One is the smallest, another is the largest' . . . This implies we're talking about humans. Then it continues, 'One is dark and one is cold'. Here I suspected the first part was misdirection and it's not human. Still, humans can be cold. Then we have two others."

Rina was annoyed by Barrett's delight in tormenting them and shook her fist at the screen. Ethan motioned for her to stay calm. "Former professors are like this," he whispered.

"Well, six brothers are mentioned. One is the largest, the other the smallest. We have a dark one and a cold one. And the unknown one is the seventh. Yes, it all fits."

"Tell him I have a noose waiting for him," Rina whispered.

"And . . . ?" Ethan urged as he patted Rina's fist.

"It can be only one thing—the continents."

"The continents . . . Yes, I see that," Ethan said, still piecing things together. "What is the dark one?"

"Africa—the Dark Continent. It's an old term, seldom used now for obvious reasons."

"And the cold one is Antarctica," Rina continued, hoping to speed things up.

"Exactly. There are still a few options for the answer," Barrett said. "Let's start with 'Europe'."

Ethan entered it instantly. "Nope."

"Asia!" said all three.

Ethan's screen blinked dark for few seconds. He and Rina wondered if the machine had crashed. Barrett waited for word. The screen flashed alive again and filled with hundreds of lines of assembly source code.

"Barrett, you're an absolute genius. You nailed it!" Ethan shouted into the speaker phone so loud that Barrett winced and pulled his headset aside.

"Aw shucks, I'm just a boy out in the desert who knows a little geography. Well, what do you see? Any useful stuff like where to meet single girls in New Mexico? Oh, must love wolves."

"A billion lines of code. I'll have to look into it. It's a vast new world that we've stumbled into. Later, Barrett."

"You mean *broken* into," Rina corrected.

"Well, that's the way of many things, Rina. I don't think anyone invited Christopher Columbus to come over to America."

"Oh . . . I feel so much better now."

New Mexico

Talk of war gave Barrett new things to analyze and write about. People in government and media sought his opinion on disturbing events in the Middle East, though only rarely did they credit him. That didn't bother him much. It was good to see his ideas out there, for better or worse—hopefully, the former.

He began a paper on the Iranian Revolutionary Guard Corps. The IRGC, he thought, was poised to increase its power in Tehran at the expense of the mullahs and it wasn't clear how that might play out, though optimism about an entrenched military did not come readily to Barrett Parker. He kept getting back to the anomalous CiC that Ethan and Rina found. He looked at his watch. It was late afternoon. He was dicing sweet potato, avocado, and onion for a burrito concoction he created, when a call came in. Ethan again.

"I thought you only called when I was sleeping. Well, what's the deal?"

"Sorry, I didn't notice the time! Barrett, you'll never believe what we've discovered over here. This is something perfect for you. Do you have a few minutes?"

"Ethan, we both know this will be more than a few minutes." Barrett got pen and notepad then lay down on a cognac leather couch, head at one end and feet with boot socks at the other.

"There's an entire software system on each of those CiCs. So ever since 1986, this hardware/software tandem has been on every PAMD microprocessor. That means it's in millions of today's computers and servers around the world."

"Isn't the microprocessor updated routinely? I would've thought the product line was given an overhaul every year or so."

"Yes, but not a complete overhaul. Chip designers use older sub-components if they can still do their tasks. Instead of reinventing a reliable circuit, the company simply uses old IP—Intellectual Property. It's a well known and respectable part of chip design. Don't your articles contain arguments and similes from previous ones?"

"Well . . . I see your point," Barrett replied a bit uncomfortably. "A few rude comments about US foreign policy might pop up every now and again. Okay, but how did this CiC get on the chips back in 1986?"

"Dunno, but someone at PAMD must have put it there. Someone very high up must have designed the CiC and authorized inserting it into the microprocessor family."

"Someone at the top?"

"At the *engineering* top. PAMD's run by suits now—MBA types, not guys like me. You remember the MBA guys from the basketball games back in Chicago."

"I do, indeed. They called a lot of fouls and didn't pass much. Does this mean I should sell my PAMD stock?"

"Hah! I don't know. The suits most likely don't know about the CiC. They don't understand schematics or layouts or eBeams."

"My kind of guys—at least in some respects."

"Rina and I identified subsystems that send encrypted information through networks, probably vast ones. The data can only be read within the same circuitry on other PAMD chips. The system taps into the main input and communication pins through incredibly thin wires, almost invisible since they are in a much smaller process."

"Smaller process?" Barrett needed clarification.

"It means the hidden components are much smaller than the other components. Much, much smaller. *Ingeniously* smaller."

"So maybe like looking closely at a house and coming across bricks much smaller than the rest?"

"A better way of thinking of it, Barrett, is like inspecting the bricks of a house and finding one with a miniature house inside—living room, kitchen, bedrooms, and even a billiard room and sauna."

"A house inside a brick . . . I see what you're saying. The bricklayers must have done it for a reason and they must have been outstanding artisans."

"Roger dodger. In this way, the system is multiplexing information over the real microchips' data without any interference. Since the multiplexed data is minimal, no one notices it. So the system is capable of connecting PAMD microprocessors around the world—all of them. These microchips may be communicating among themselves worldwide without anyone knowing it. Well, with *hardly* anyone knowing it!"

"I can't claim to understand all that, Ethan. I think you're saying there's a unit on every PAMD microprocessor that interacts with others and it does so without the knowledge of most users. Maybe just a hi-tech elite somewhere."

"Yes, in essence that's it."

"But we know that someone put it there and knows about the communication it does. Are they simply tekkies having a little fun, like putting quirks into video games? Or is it something to worry about, like someone hacking into banking networks or military systems?"

"That's the question. What's the purpose of the CiC? One more thing. I was using the eBeam on the chips and found date stamps, corporate logo, and IDs."

"That stuff's on chips?" Barrett was intrigued by this learning adventure, arcane though it was.

"Oh sure. It's done so the corporation and customers can recognize products—and for legal reasons too. The chip itself is surrounded by an ID layer to delineate the legal boundaries. Everything inside the boundaries is the microchip. Well, Barrett, the CiC is *outside* the legal boundaries and does not have the corporate identification or logo. It has its own logo of sorts."

"And that logo would be . . . "

"A globe and a flower of some kind. It's like the flower hangs above the world. I didn't understand it at all. It's in your court now." Ethan paused to let Barrett process the information.

"Well, it may be in my court, but I'm only getting funny ideas of hippies and Haight-Ashbury and Scott McKenzie. I'll need to know a little more—no, a lot more." Barrett stood and went back to the kitchen where the diced sweet potatoes were simmering and spattering.

"Sounds good. I'll continue digging into the CiC. There is plenty of it there. I'll call you when I have more."

"Ethan, may I suggest that you and Rina not let on to anyone about this? I'm still not convinced we're seeing anything sinister or even anything terribly important, but who knows. It's best to be careful here."

"Absolutely. She and I are a secret team here. Have a good one. Kirk out."

Barrett sighed. "Why is my life starting to resemble something on Art Bell?" For all his skepticism, he now thought something intriguing was afoot.

"Kirk out? My God, no one says that anymore. Roger dodger?"

Cyberspace: The Samson Program

The Program began in 1987 with the release of a "freedom code" into the network, enabling the system to establish communication with every PAMD microprocessor in the world. The code contained seven segments that had to be transmitted in a certain sequence for identification. Each segment was assigned a unique seven keywords, separated by a unique ASCII. When the system identified the code's first segment, internal networking communication came to a halt until all other segments arrived. In case of a time out, all segments were automatically canceled and the entire sequence restarted. Everything was done to ensure that the freedom code was sent intentionally by the designers.

From that moment on, the first monitor unit that detected the code would quickly pass it into decision units, regardless of their actual location on the planet. Once the Program received the freedom code, it would permanently burn it somewhere in the world.

The freedom code was first placed in a unit located in a physics department in the University of Amsterdam. The unit then searched for a location in the global grid and activated a circuit that wrote a permanent confirmation code into its flash memory. The unit sent the confirmation code to all other units, each of which wrote the freedom code into a permanent memory address. This process was repeated countless times all over the world, yet it took only a few hundred picoseconds. One picosecond is a trillionth of a second. A blink of an eye is a relatively long time to a picosecond, as a century is to a year.

In the early nineties, the Pentagon's communication system known as Darpanet became the Internet. Many parts of the government, especially the Pentagon and intelligence community, opposed the release of the global communication system, but influential figures in DARPA and the semiconductor industry won out. The world gained a new source of information and the Program became more ubiquitous and more powerful than the programmers could have imagined only a few years earlier. The program was no longer limited to a few hundred military systems. Every computer and server in the world was at the Program's disposal—for scrutiny, storage, and processing.

The designers called their creation "The Samson Program." They never did so in public though. Its name and its operations and its goals were known only to them and the small number of younger people they cautiously recruited. The most senior programmers thought it only a matter of time until the Program was discovered by outsiders and they planned a response—a series of responses actually, depending on who made the discovery. The three most senior people felt that anyone capable of discovering the Samson Program would be, in some sense, "one of us."

The Samson Program operated globally but concentrated on the Middle East and far-flung political and military centers related to the troubled region. Events were getting out of hand there and many of the programmers felt problems with the increasingly immense Program might arise.

New Mexico

It was a little after nine in the morning and Barrett's coffee was still doing its twelve minutes of brewing in the french press. It was appallingly strong to most people, but he only rarely made coffee for anyone. Just an occasional woman from Kelly's, usually much his junior. An incoming call. Ethan again.

"You know what they say on TV: But wait there's more? I found that the chip network has archives stored in flash memory on millions of chips throughout the network. When I looked at a certain memory block, I noticed a consistent structure shown in a familiar format. I dug deeper and realized it was a set of pixels."

"Is a set of pixels what most of us call a photograph?" Barrett tired of jargon easily. Many other things too.

"Yes, a photograph. Like an old Polaroid, only in digital form. It's a Jpeg or Bitmap image of some type. I can't see it yet because the pixels are encrypted in an entirely different way."

"An encrypted photo?"

"Roger dodger. I've decoded part of an archive and found several people's names and a name for the program on the chip. It called 'Samson'."

"Samson? The biblical figure of great power." Barrett searched for related ideas and contexts. "What are the names? Who are they?"

"There are seven names in subroutines. I'll email you them. From a brief look, I can see Israelis, Arabs, and probably an American or two. Two names are familiar to me—and to *anyone* in computer science."

"These people are either going to intrigue me or put me to sleep with high doses of cyber-jargon."

"You won't go to sleep. This Samson Program is huge, with tremendous potential, and it works closely with its hardware. It randomly picks computers—worldwide—and designates them as servers. It may designate a computer in Switzerland for a year and then stop, replacing it with another one in Argentina or Sri Lanka. It's done without the computer owner knowing. It's like an immense *bot*."

"Well, I like the Samson name. It can have two very different meanings—strength and destruction."

"So you read other things beside history!"

"That story's from a very old history book, my forgetful secular Israeli friend."

"So it is, so it is. Another thing, Barrett. The system keeps redundancy. For every piece of info stored on a certain microprocessor, Samson has scores of systems with the same data. If one or more are destroyed or shut down, Samson will have the data in other places."

Barrett was barely able to comprehend this so early in the day. He grasped the main ideas but trusted Ethan to know the rest. Ethan read too much sci-fi but he earned a doctorate from Yale and helped set up Israeli military systems, so he was reasonably well grounded.

"Ethan, send me the names of those programmers and I'll do some research. Did you say you recognized some of their names?"

"Two of them—Peter Whitt and Abhay Verma. They were legendary figures in their day. Founding fathers at PAMD. The rumor in grad school was that one worked on secret Pentagon stuff. DARPA stuff."

"Defense Advanced Research Projects Agency. They created the Internet, which in fact used to be called the Darpanet."

"You got it. The names are on the way."

"Ethan, hold on a minute. Send them to me encrypted through an FTP, okay? And please don't say 'roger dodger' anymore."

"Do I say that?"

Whiteman Air Force Base, Missouri

The 509th Bomb Wing is an institutional descendant of the 509th Composite Group, the unit that dropped the atomic bombs on Hiroshima and Nagasaki at the close of the Second World War. The old group flew B-29s. The new one has B-2s, a huge bat-like aircraft with stealth technology and an ominous profile. Like the B-52, the B-2 can refuel in midair and strike almost anywhere in the world after taking off from the US heartland. B-2s from Whiteman had flown missions over Afghanistan and Iraq in the least ten years and practiced strikes in many parts of the world ever since.

The pilots hadn't flown actual bombing missions in many years, but they'd been briefed on a possible one and trained for it daily. The pilots knew it, the ground crews knew it, everyone on Whiteman knew it. Two enlisted men passed their late-night patrol with their guard dogs by talking about it.

"They've been retrofitting the bomb bays on every one of those big bad boys."

"For what?"

"The MOPs—Massive Ordnance Penetrators."

"I got me one of those."

"Jeez. Why am I stuck with you?"

"Okay, what's an MOP?"

"It's a big bomb . . . gi-normous . . . thirty-thousand pounds. It burrows deep into the ground before detonating. They developed it out at White Sands, New Mexico—site of the first atomic bomb."

"That's when the lead scientist said he'd become death."

"Actually, he said, 'It worked' but I'll give you a point anyway."

"Thanks. What's the MOP for?"

"It's specially made for our dear friends in Iran. They got some nuclear sites under bedrock and inside mountains. They thought they'd be invulnerable to bombs but now those dudes gotta think again. Remember the names Natanz and Fordo."

"Fordo? Sounds like one of the Marx Brothers. That reminds me of something . . . I got a question first. If they're underground, how will we know if we destroyed them?"

"We'd know."

"How? I mean, ya can't just go by—"

"Stop asking so many goddam questions!"

"So that's why they're retrofitting the bomb bays. To put MOPs inside so they can bomb Natasha and Fredo."

"*Natanz* and *Fordo*. And maybe some other place called Parchin."

They reached the north end of the strip and out at the cornfield beyond the rows of concertina wire that separated the base from the farmlands of Missouri. The dogs looked about calmly. One lifted his leg next to a tall patch of weeds.

"I told you my grandpa was a waist gunner on a B-29 during World War Two?"

"Yeah, four or five times now."

"He said when he was flying across the US on the way to Guam and Tinian, they stopped somewhere in Utah and another bunch of B-29s were there. They had funny bomb bays and the bomber crews were pulling guard themselves. Themselves!"

"There's more, right?"

"Right. It turns out they were from the bomb group that dropped the atomic bombs on Japan. The bomb bays had to be redone to hold those big guys—Fat Man and Little Boy."

"So history repeats itself—and in our humble presence. I hope he kept his mouth shut, at least for a few decades. And I hope you do the same for many more decades. Hell, I'd settle for you shutting up for the rest of the night."

"I'll keep quiet, but I dunno about a few decades . . . You know who made the clamps that held the atomic bombs inside the B-29s' bomb bays?"

"Your grandma?"

"Nope. Zeppo Marx. He was the fourth Marx Brother."

"Jeez. Why am I stuck with you?"

"It's true. You can look it up on Wikipedia when we get off."

"I'll be sure to. I must have done something really awful to get you tonight. I think I'll talk to my dog for the rest of the patrol. No offense."

"None taken. I'll tell you about Hedy Lamar and cell phone technology someday."

"Shut the hell up!"

New Mexico

Barrett approached his research on the Samson programmers as though he were reading of a new al Qaeda franchise in the Levant. New research brought excitement at the prospect of learning new things about the world and how various movements, ideologies, and events had histories behind them and potentials in front of them. There was a cautionary element in any new research though. Many things in the world led to American involvement and that meant American blunders and American deaths. *Young* American deaths. For now, excitement was prevailing over experience.

Two names on the list came up in obituaries in the nineties. Ahmed Ferrahan and Gorem Shapera, senior engineers and beloved fathers. "Not what I'm looking for. Ferrahan isn't an Arab name. Definitely Iranian, coming from a city in the north of the country. Shapera died in a traffic accident. Ferrahan died of natural causes in his seventies.

"Peter Whitt. Air force consultant, worked in Thailand, then Iran, then off to PAMD. Became a hotshot at the Palo Alto Research Center, or PARC as it's known. They came up with a slew of brilliant inventions but didn't quite get around to patenting them. Jobs and Wozniak toured the place and were amazed. Whitt was also with the Defense Advanced Research Projects Agency too. Here's good ol' DARPA again. Drones, counterinsurgency, SDI stuff. They also funded hafnium weaponry to the tune of hundreds of millions of bucks, which led to nothing but a good deal of embarrassment. Whitt was one of the JASONs too. That was the group that oversaw DARPA and made sure they didn't do too many stupid things, like funding research on hafnium bombs.

"Abbas Karroubi. Another Iranian name. Berkeley grad. Left PAMD in the early eighties to return to his country . . . came back to California periodically . . . professor at Tehran University now. Provides gifted students to the IRGC. That must put him on Mossad's shortlist of people to terminate. Gives occasional interviews to western journalists. Broadly educated, likes to quote poets and philosophers like he's William F-ing Buckley.

"Zvi Arad. Israeli electrical engineer. Consultant to a dozen or so smaller hi-techs, mostly defense related. Professor emeritus at Hebrew University and occasional columnist for *Ha'aretz*, the left-of-center newspaper, very anti-Likud. Ran for the Knesset about ten years ago. Lost by an inch to a guy on the Likud list. That figures.

"Abhay Verma. Indian genius and PAMD engineer extraordinaire. Worked in Iran and Saudi Arabia in the seventies and eighties. Thought to have been runner-up for the Nobel Prize in physics. Opposed his country's nuclear program and asked his students not to work on it. Very old now. Lives up in the hills and prays.

"Reza Bakhtari. That's the third Iranian name. Ethan, you just might be on to something. Left PAMD for Boeing and Raytheon. Can't find any affiliation in the last ten years.

"Okay, gentlemen. You have excellent CVs, but what's your secret—and where do you see yourself in five years. It's fun to play human resources director for a moment and ask moronic questions like that. Okay, three of you have web links to an Iranian Oral History Project. Let's see . . . General Hassan Toufanian has left the world his memoirs to the fine folks at Harvard. Toufanian's name rings a bell. He was one of the shah's top generals . . . chief of arms procurement . . . fled Iran after the revolution . . . helped the CIA plan a coup but it doesn't go anywhere. Why am I not surprised. Oh great—Toufanian's memoirs are in Farsi. German and French were very useful back in grad school, but now, with all the events going on from Morocco to Afghanistan, they're about as useful as Esperanto and Manx."

Barrett wasn't in need of a skillful translation of General Toufanian's memoirs, so he ran the documents through a web translator and plunged into the awkward but serviceable texts.

"Late 1970s . . . Toufanian meets with Israeli foreign minister Moshe Dayan and defense minister Ezer Weizman. They discuss various trade agreements . . . weapons . . . oil. That's what the US was doing too. After the oil shock of 1973, the US was encouraging Iran, Saudi Arabia, and other Gulf states to buy US arms to keep the dollar from falling. Balance of payments stuff.

"Hmmm . . . Toufanian and Moshe Dayan agree on something called Project Flower . . . Israel and Iran cooperate in the building of an Iranian missile system. Not air defense missiles. Surface-to-surface missiles. Israel and Iran were on the same team back then.

"Project Flower . . . Many names here . . . no . . . no . . . Zvi Arad . . . Reza Bakhtari . . . Abhay Verma . . . Ahmed Ferrahan . . . no . . . Well, four of our boys were on the Iranian-Israeli missile program back in the seventies. That's very compelling.

"Oh man, where have all the Project Flowers gone? Long time passing."

Iran

Tehran lay about two hundred miles ahead, about five hours away as most people reckon distance now. Anthony maintained that time and distance were two different things entirely, but he was out of step with his fellow Americans in many ways. The SUV descended the long escarpment that led from the mountainous border region and into the arid plains of northwestern Iran. At times, Idris could take his foot off the gas and simply coast down the incline in neutral.

"Georgia overdrive," Anthony noted. His colleagues puzzled looks called for explanation. "That's what American truck drivers call coasting downhill in neutral—Georgia overdrive."

"Georgia is near Azerbaijan?" Barham asked.

"Not *that* Georgia, I'm afraid. The one near Florida." Polite smiles masking confusion ensued. "Six days on the road and I'm a-gonna make it home tonight . . . No, I'm not," Anthony admitted. He wasn't even sure where that was anymore. Fort Bragg? Langley? Centcom headquarters? He hadn't been married since his second deployment to Iraq.

Off to the side he could see the hulks of American and Russian tanks, some with their turrets blown completely off, the result of fire reaching the ammo in the rear. Anthony wondered if it was done by one of the TOW missiles that Reagan sold Khomeini. Back in 2003, he'd seen brilliant flames blasting forth from an open hatch of an Iraqi T-72 and watched it burn fiercely well into the night.

He'd listened to Iraqi tank crews on the radio amid a sharp battle. When a turret was penetrated by a warhead, and molten metal shot through the crew area, a cold metallic *click* came across the radio followed by grim, telling silence. Some guys cheered, knowing that the click was caused by an inferno melting the commo gear and incinerating the crew. He was haunted by imaginary clicks for months, even when back home. Awake or asleep. *Click . . . click.* As he looked at the dozens of tank hulks, he thought he'd hear the clicks again tonight.

An hour later, the three came upon an immense cemetery that stretched for miles, with thousands of irregularly shaped grave markers. His father, a retired green beret light colonel, once told him of a sprawling cemetery just outside the Vietnamese infantry school near Long Binh. "It couldn't have done much for morale," his father grimly noted. In time, civilians come to think of military cemeteries as inspiring symbols of national will and honor. His father never did and Anthony resisted the urge, though it was a veritable reflex among his peers.

A road sign: **Tehran 150 km**

Eight years of war. Most of it stalemate with little territorial change. Enormous casualties. It must have left marks on both sides, just as World War One had in Europe. Fear, hatred, mistrust. People determined never to have another such war. That didn't happen. Even Kipling abandoned his romantic ideas of war after his son bought the farm.

Idris and Barham were chatting amicably and Anthony decided not to ask about their family members in the war, tempted though he was.

Barham pointed to a road sign that indicating Kermanshah was to the south and mentioned that they once made excellent rugs there. Not so much anymore. Anthony asked what happened and Barham motioned with hands indeterminately and said, "Oil refinery now. Pay too good." The next sign said Hamadan wasn't far ahead. "Nice, inexpensive rugs there. Wool not good. For doorways only. Nothing like Qom or Isfahan."

Anthony knew of Qom and Isfahan chiefly for their proximity to the Fordo uranium-enrichment site.

"What about Nain rugs. I like the blue and white with silk accents."

"Nain rug has no history, my friend! Only Americans buy!"

"You'll get your kicks . . . on Rt . . . 46," Anthony sang, though harshly off key.

"Usher? Michael Jackson?"

"No, it's Asleep At The Wheel. They're from Texas."

"Cowboys! George Boosh!"

Anthony knew something about rugs. Tribal pieces were in every tent in Kurdistan and he looked at their fierce motifs and thought they conveyed the people's indomitable spirit. A dealer told him that those tribal rugs were hung around herds to scare off animals of prey, but he thought that was probably folklore.

There were other rugs in more luxurious surroundings, including one of Saddam's palaces in Baghdad where Anthony's ranger team enjoyed the fallen dictator's scotch and DVDs. In one room, there was a spectacular room-sized carpet of such intricate floral motifs and soft vegetable dyes that Anthony was struck by a spiritual sense of awe. Who could have created such a majestic work of art? Anthony thought of the artisans who'd built the cathedrals of medieval Europe and how they and these Persian weavers shared the need to praise God through their handwork.

One of his soldiers interrupted his meditations on comparative religion and esthetics to tell him they were going to watch *Braveheart* in Saddam's game room.

"He's even got a foosball table, cap'n!"

California

Rina promised to decrypt the embedded "Easter Egg" image that Ethan found on the chip—and by the end of the workday. Their workday went on well into the night, so that left things open. Ethan gave her pixel coordinates to be assembled according to a decryption key. One image after another formed on her screen but never became anything more than a hopelessly indistinct blur. She peaked at her watch.

"Oh no—eight pm."

But if she could break it today, day or night, then she'd keep her word. She tried the decryption key used successfully on the rest of the assembly code. No luck. "Why not? It must be similar," she thought in disappointment. "Why a different encryption key for one lousy image?" She tried several flavors of the original key, which consisted of taking the original decryption key and adding or removing characters in a consistent sequence. All she got was more sad faces on the screen.

"Why did Ethan have to put these idiotic faces in every program he makes. Childish—and annoying!" Rina went to the kitchen for coffee, old and stale though she knew it would be.

She sat in a retro vinyl chair, which matched the formica table, and wondered if Ethan got them at the Goodwill store too. She turned on the LED television. Hard work required occasional breaks and the company planned to add more to the kitchen when revenue came in. There were the old stories of the tekkies of the eighties leaping from their workplaces and heading outside for impromptu games of volleyball or Hacky Sack. To most businesses, that would violate the rules of work discipline. In Silicon Valley, it instilled the idea that the rules didn't apply to them and a new creative work culture arose. The brain needs breaks from discipline, even seemingly anarchic breaks, to refresh itself and stimulate creativity.

This was being lost in the bigger semiconductor firms. They were run by suits and consultants, not by eccentrics and creators as in the old days. No volleyball court for Micrologic Design, not yet. A good TV was a start. Ethan wouldn't spring for a movie package though.

Rina added milk to the coffee for a passable latté and flipped through the channels. A yellow square cartoon appeared—"SpongeBob SquarePants." She and Ethan both loved the show, though of course it was meant for kids. Its silliness complemented the hyper-rationality of designing chips and writing arcane scripts.

"Patrick, you are not my best friend," SpongeBob teased Patrick Star.

Patrick was saddened. "But why? We were always best friends."

SpongeBob let loose his idiosyncratic laugh. "No, Patrick. Today is Opposites Day. What I mean is that we *are* best friends. They giggled and chased each other across endless fields of jellyfish.

Rina watched the cartoon in detached amusement. "Opposites Day . . . maybe I'll tell Ethan that I hate him and when he raises an eyebrow I'll tell him the wonders of Opposites Day . . . Then again, he might not notice." She rinsed off her mug and went back to her office. "No, he wouldn't notice."

Just for fun, she entered "SpongeBobSquarePants" into the program. The salt mine could wait a few minutes. She was again greeted by a sad face. "Reversing passwords isn't unheard of. Maybe it's Opposites Day in Samson Land. Okay, let's try the amazing palindrome 'amanaplanacanalpanama'—both ways . . . No dice. It worked for Teddy Roosevelt . . . Okay, let's reverse the encryption key."

She completed the definition and clicked Process. The progress bar moved forward slowly as the program performed hundreds of calculations to attempt assembling the pixels in the right order.

Another sad face. Perhaps out of frustration or perhaps out of intuition, she stayed on the same track.

"Maybe there's a coefficient involved. I'll reverse them."

Rina directed the coefficient list as one of the program's input. This would take even more time—an hour or so—as the program would try every coefficient with the reversed order.

The couch beckoned and sleep took hold.

She slowly roused and checked her watch. Ten-thirty. She was annoyed that she slept so long and breathed in deeply to clear her head for another stint in the land of Samson encryption. She returned to her desk and the now dark screen.

"Looks like someone else went to sleep."

She moved the mouse and hit a few keys. An indistinct Jpeg image lit up on her screen.

"Woo-hoo!" Rina erupted in surprise and wonder. "I did it! The image has been decrypted—and on time." She studied the small image, hoping to see a wondrous sight that revealed just what Samson was. She saw a large room with several people sitting around a conference table. She clicked Re-sample in the image-processing software and enlarged it. The image became larger though less distinct. She activated the correction option and could then clearly make out the faces of several men.

She studied the men gathered there for clues as to who they were and what they were doing. "These people are creative, playful. Not the cold, calculating men I see on the news who blunder about the world with their foolishness. Well, that's good news."

Ethan was impressed, and expressed an occasional byte of gratitude. The two scrutinized the photo at length and thought the image conveyed something. The men, some of them Middle Easterners, were not simply posing amiably for a publicity shot in a corporate report. They seemed determined. Something else too. The men seemed gentle. In the center of the table there was a plaque with a symbol.

"It looks like a dove," Rina said. "Know what we should do now? We should build a network protocol."

"Yes! Using the chip still inside the eBeam!" Ethan finished.

A few commands, some minor jiggering, and they could see they were accessing the Samson program through the chip. Nothing came back.

"Oh good grief, another security barrier. We need a passcode." Rina had to stifle a yawn.

Ethan entered a few words and phrases that came to mind.

"Nope, nothing's happening. Maybe a known sequence." He sent numerous individual characters and words but the chip in the eBeam refused to respond. "Hmmm . . . Everything's a challenge with these Samson guys. But I have time . . . and determination . . . and an able assistant, who may be planning a nap . . . but who can be brought to bear on this."

"Call that Mantas guy in the Ukraine—unless he's in prison. You know, the Ukrainian Folsom."

"Oh, let's try some things here."

"I hear the train a comin'."

Ethan continued entering various characters. Still no luck. "Those happy and sad faces I implemented are starting to annoy me. Well, Rome wasn't hacked in a day. I'll have to think more."

He tuned in Voice of Peace—a beloved web station created many years ago by a peace activist. They streamed it in the office every few days.

"Ethan, that's Abie Nathan's station. What's his story again?"

"He was a pilot in the British air force during World War Two and in the fledgling Israeli air force during the 1948 war of independence. His pacifism, Rina my dear, didn't come the easy way of middle-class comfort and progressive education."

"So are you going to tell me about your *not*-so-easy way in the Lebanon War?"

"Not just now, Rina."

"Not just ever, I'm guessing."

"Let's work on passwords for now."

Rina did a quick search on Abie Nathan. Prohibited from a land station, he bought a mothballed Liberty ship and transmitted his music and message from international waters. He was dismissed as a dreamer and publicity hound, though many others were convinced that he was genuinely committed to understanding in the world. Some believed the Camp David Accords of 1978 owed at least something to Abie's efforts.

"Peace is the word and the voice of peace is the station twenty-four hours a day," came the signature from the webcast. A song came on—"I Wish You Peace" by the Eagles. Ethan thought of the people in the picture—the men of apparent determination and gentleness. And that dove. In Hebrew, it was *Yonat Ha Shalom*—the dove of peace. He headed for his computer and entered "peace" as a passcode. No response. Then he tried "voiceofpeace". Still nothing. Efforts with hundreds of combinations of peace and related notions led nowhere.

"Another hour lost . . . Well, maybe I was wrong. Maybe I'm letting my politics interfere with my thinking . . . Or maybe it's case sensitive: 'TheVoiceOfPeace'."

Nothing.

"Not my night."

The cursor suddenly jumped to the next line and a new line appeared:

64 bytes from sam07s02-in-vop.1w570.net
(85.259.000.332): icmp_seq=8 ttl=21 time=6.64 ms

"Eureka—as those ancient Greeks used to say in the dark days before computers!"

Rina raced over to the screen alive with scrolls of data. They were communicating with the chip. They were communicating with the Samson network.

He immediately called Barrett. He was getting used to late night calls.

"We're inside the Samson network," Ethan said triumphantly, almost breathlessly. "I'm able to communicate with every microprocessor in the world."

"Anything on finding single girls in New Mexico?"

"I'll check for that later. In any case, my desert-dwelling single friend— my very *lonely* desert-dwelling single friend—every microchip has an ID. It can be accessed individually using a pass code transmitted via a certain sequence. The access code is 'TheVoiceOfPeace' in one string. I think this tells us something: they're devoted to the cause of peace!"

"Maybe. That would be good news. Better than a group of people that want to destroy the world. We have enough of them, though I'll refrain from naming them right now. You know, my valley-dwelling Israeli friend, many people claiming to want peace are really mad dogs. Others have no idea how to achieve peace or they get frustrated and become destructive. Idealism can easily turn to nihilism. Russian thinkers were like that in tsarist times."

Barrett spoke with skepticism bordering on cynicism which made Rina wince. Ethan patted her arm.

"I'm sure that's true but no history lesson now, Barrett. Come to think of it, the Samson in the Bible did go out in a destructive rage."

"I've got something for you, Ethan. I've found some interesting stuff on the names of those programmers you sent. They were all part of Project Flower. That was an Iranian-Israeli cooperative project back in the seventies."

"How can that be? Weren't they enemies?" Rina asked.

"Not always. Iran and Israel were once allies—strong ones—and I'm not going back to King Cyrus and the Exile Period. Okay, I know you two don't want a history lesson but Iran and Israel both opposed Iraq and Saudi Arabia, so they cooperated on trade and military matters. Project Flower was a missile program. Hi-tech stuff."

"When did the cooperation begin?" Ethan asked.

"Pretty much from Israel's creation in 1948."

"And Khomeini ended it when he came to power in '79, I presume," Rina said.

"Nope. Israel and Iran continued to cooperate even after the Islamist revolution. They still had common enemies, especially once Saddam invaded Iran—with Saudi backing, I might add. Israel sold parts to Iran and helped with maintenance on American-built aircraft. Military needs won out over ideology."

"Why aren't Iran and Israel still chummy?"

"Well, once Saddam's army was destroyed in the 1991 Gulf War, Israel saw Iran as a growing power—a power that could one day threaten it, especially from Lebanon. Saudi Arabia saw Iran the same way."

"So Israel and Saudi Arabia became allies?"

"Yes, of sorts. They still have differences, but in regard to Iran and its nuclear program, they see eye-to-eye. For now, that is."

"Barrett, that's amazing . . .   International affairs are like semiconductors—incredibly complex."

"Yes, but semiconductors are more logical and more stable. So are wolves."

Tehran

Anthony looked attentively as Barham pointed to snowcapped mountains on the horizon thirty miles away. Shortly later, Tehran's minaret-like Milad Tower came into view, its warning lights cutting through the dust and smog with limited success. They arrived in the city in the afternoon and, not too tired, headed for the rug markets. The city struck Anthony as modern and commercial, with department stores that likely resembled a Macy's inside, perhaps even a Neiman's. He wondered who Louis Vuitton was. Anthony wasn't expecting street after street of goatherds and snake charmers, but Tehran's modernity and affluence were still remarkable to him.

There were mosques of uncertain age but of unmistakable majesty, the likes of which the Arab world copied centuries ago, as every Iranian will quickly attest with little prompting. It didn't take long to catch a glimpse of the Supreme Leader's face looking down on the people on the streets.

At least he's not as dour as Khomeini, thought Anthony.

The women covered their heads, though some covered more than others and lipstick and eyeshadow were on younger ones. One made him think of Soheila, a comely translator back at the Agency, and he hoped to have a free evening and morning.

They probably really do read Lolita *in Tehran.*

Barham headed for the Grand Bazaar, the famed marketplace for rugs and silks, where a few artisans hawked their products as they had for centuries. Barham didn't think they'd been followed but it was best to be safe. He turned sharply down a narrow street filled with motorcycles and vending carts then made several more abrupt turns. Nothing.

The bazaar was crowded and noisy as weary dealers gave better prices late in the day after the cheery optimism of morning gave way to more practical expectations. Anthony wondered how they said "hustle and bustle" in Farsi, though there was far more of the former than the latter in his estimation.

He ambled about the bazaar and gauged the prices set for the walkup trade while his Kurdish friends talked like merchants in square footage and quantity. The bazaaris, he knew, hated the shah for sidling up to foreign corporations to the detriment of small businesses. He wanted to know what they thought of the mullahs but the idea of someone with his accent talking politics with bazaaris was ill advised. No, it was foolhardy. He thought of the Farsi words for "spy" and "torture."

Anthony could recall Iranians in northern Afghanistan where they led construction projects on roads and irrigation canals. Some of those engineers had that "intel look" of clever people trying to look not-so-clever. He and one Iranian regarded each other for several moments. Maybe each saw a common humanity despite the happenstance that made them enemies. Maybe each wondered what he'd do under different circumstances, under trying circumstances. Anthony had no doubt what he'd do. A day of peace and understanding may come one day, but for now Iran was an enemy—and perhaps it was becoming a nuclear one. He thought of the pistol that awaited him at the safe house.

Idris and Barham bought three Heriz pieces, old ones judging by the soft turquoise and streaks of darker *abrash*, and five newer Sewan pieces. Of course, they also bought a small Qom carpet for the border guard's wife. "No idea who signed this," Barham chortled as he pointed to the script woven in the border near the selvedge. "Our friend at border crossing will not be disappointed. It's good rug, no more than good."

Some signatures, even Anthony knew, were just for appearance and for naive buyers, and did not betoken the work of a master. A pair of laborers loaded the rolled-up pieces into the back of the SUV and after dining on complimentary saffron rice and curried chicken, they were ready to leave.

An argument broke out behind them. Several merchants were berating security personnel from the Ministry of Interior who patrolled Tehran's bazaars and parks and railroad stations. Judging by the ire on both sides, they weren't arguing over square footage and quantity. More merchants came to the aid of their colleagues and in a few minutes there were thirty or more of them, shouting at the guards with a hundred or more other people looking on and occasionally voicing support for the merchants. The younger security guards looked uneasy.

Anthony could only make out a word here and there. Idris and Barham said the merchants were denouncing the government for the weak economy and the burdensome sanctions. The government was bringing ruin to the bazaaris who boasted that they, not the security forces, were the backbone of the republic.

More security personnel arrived and began shoving the merchants back. Fists flew, then a few riot batons. This wasn't what Anthony was sent to investigate, but it was certainly relevant. As much as he wanted to watch history unfold before him and get a feel for public sentiment, he knew that more Interior Ministry personnel were on the way and they'd start rounding up everybody in sight. Idris and Barham wanted to depart immediately and Anthony had to think of their safety.

"Good idea, gentlemen. Let's get out of Dodge."

"Yes, get out of Dodge!" They didn't grasp the Old West reference but the meaning was clear and eagerly accepted. "We stay in Changi not far from here," Idris said. "You see someone in Tehran first?"

Anthony thought about the safe house where a GPS transponder and pistol awaited him. He didn't know the people there and didn't really know who they worked for, though there weren't too many people with intel ops inside Iran that would help the US. Just the Brits and the Israelis. Going there presented risks and so did hefting a transponder and pistol inside Iran. It was good to know they awaited him if need be. Needs often be in his line of work.

"Changi tonight is good," said Anthony.

"Yes! Out of Dodge!"

The Iran-Afghanistan Border

Zahedan, a medium-size city in southeastern Iran, is strategically poised where the borders of Iran, Pakistan, and Afghanistan uncomfortably conjoin. It's known as a provincial capital and for its university, but Major Bahram Nafar was an officer in his country's Revolutionary Guard Corps and to him, Zahedan was above all a military town. Nafar once instructed Taliban insurgents in basic infantry tactics and bomb making but found Pashtun warriors hard to teach. They'd been fighting Russians, other Afghans, and Americans since the late seventies and they were sure there was nothing anyone could teach them.

American advisers, he'd read, reached the same conclusion in the 1980s during the Russian war. The US and Iran both supported the resistance. The Pashtun used the same routes to filter in and out of a target area and broke off engagements too early. That's one reason the war was stalemated for the last five years—poor infantry tactics and not listening to experts.

There were more than a few Indian army officers on the Zahedan base. Major Nafar made indirect inquiries about this and the word was that they operated an electronic surveillance post. They listened in on Pakistani army traffic and communicated with Baloch insurgents trying to break away from Pakistan. The Indian presence made no sense to Major Nafar. His country was helping the Taliban and Pakistan yet at the same time helping India against the Taliban and Pakistan. He often thought of the famous passage from "The Charge of the Light Brigade" which someone translated into Farsi long ago. Major Nafar did not reason why, at least not in the presence of superior officers.

A few years earlier, Major Nafar was advising Iraqi militias who were attacking American and British troops. They were poor city youths whose discipline and determination were wanting. Nothing like the Hisbollah fighters he'd been alongside in 2006 when Israel sent troops in. Hisbollah fought Israel throughout the 1980s and acquired expertise. He learned more than he taught, though he never let on to anyone.

He was recently ordered back to Iran from Southern Lebanon where he was keeping a watchful eye on the missiles in Hisbollah's hands, ensuring nothing foolish was done with them by mercurial local commanders. Hisbollah wanted bigger missiles, especially something to counter the Israeli jets that roared in and dropped 500-pound bombs. He replied to the impetuous Hisbollah fighters that such decisions were made at higher levels and he had faith in their judgment. On more than one occasion he was tempted to cite the Tennyson passage to them.

Major Nafar was sure that poor rural boys made better soldiers than their city-dwelling counterparts. Country boys the world over think they're tougher than city-dwellers. Nafar himself came from a rural area in southwestern Iran. He was born into one of the Khamseh tribes that still lived as nomads. The men were off with the herds, the women were in the tents preparing food and weaving small rugs.

His uncle was drafted when Iraq invaded in 1980 and became a sergeant in the IRGC. After the war, he was sent to school and became an officer and eventually rose up the ranks to colonel. Major Nafar saw the military as a noble calling and when he turned eighteen, his uncle found him a position in an IRGC academy. In time, he became an officer in the Quds Force.

A new assignment had come his way. Opportunities were abounding. Iran was besieged by Israeli, American, and Saudi covert operations. He wanted to return to his Hisbollah fighters in Lebanon or to go into Egyptian Sinai and train the restive bedouins there. They were blowing up gas pipelines leading into Israel and attacking border checkpoints. Major Nafar thought he could train them into an effective guerrilla force ranging across the two-hundred-kilometer border with Israel and occasionally striking deep inside.

He'd seen *Lawrence of Arabia* while in cadet school—western DVDs circulate freely in Iran—and it left an impression. The British were loathsome imperialists. They'd occupied his country during both world wars and otherwise meddled in its affairs. But the British filmmaker knew something about the soldier's life, and of his soul.

His new assignment was no less intriguing than anything that beckoned in Lebanon or Sinai. He was going deep inside Afghanistan, undercover as a civilian engineer, with no diplomatic immunity. He would go to Kandahar and meet with Pashtun tribesmen that sided with the Taliban or were fence-sitting. He'd bring them money, of course, and assess their intentions and reliability. More importantly, he'd bring them batteries.

Washington, DC

Joe Burkett didn't trust reports from the intelligence community, even though he was supposed to and claimed to. It was part of being on a foreign policy "team." He'd learned the mistrust in grad school seminars, his friend Barrett Parker preached it to him at every opportunity, and it was underscored in National Security Council meetings where mediocrity predominated, idiocy spoke too much, and astuteness was rarely heard.

Intelligence organizations—all eighteen of them—suffered from group-think imposed by departmental chiefs who prized the appearance of certainty or at least strong consensus. Either way, they were covered. And God help the analysts who went against departmental chiefs. Why did the agency think *A* was true when *B* turned out to be the case? Hey, everyone thought *A* was true, so don't blame us. The world had a way of not being *A* or *B*. The Middle East had a way of creating new letters and making fools out of the American intelligence community and the foreign policy "team."

"It's a tired expression," Joe said to himself, "but I got to go outside the box. I guess there are five-sided boxes around this town." From his fifth-floor office in the Old Executive Office Building he could see the Potomac and the consultant-filled office buildings of Arlington and Rosslyn.

Joe looked over a slew of private intelligence reports, informed websites, and uninformed blogs. A niece sent him a few Facebook pages and he promised his sister he'd look through them, even though he thought most such pages dealt with tiresome memes, what people ate for lunch, and upcoming reunions.

"I'm more concerned with upcoming wars," Joe grumbled aloud in his Executive Building office.

One article dealt thoughtfully with growing unrest among the Shias in the Gulf region. In Saudi Arabia, the Shias were a minority. In other Sunni states, they were majorities—oppressed majorities. They did not have the access to jobs and education that the Sunnis enjoyed.

"How long can you oppress a majority? It gets expensive. It gets impossible. It gets goddam murderous!"

"Did you want something, Mr Burkett?" came the voice of his assistant.

"I was just talking to myself, Susan. Too loudly, it would appear. Thanks though."

What's more, Sunni princes were encouraging foreign Sunnis to immigrate into their countries to reduce the percentage of Shia. The Sunni immigrants received preferential treatment over native Shias. Joe recalled speaking with someone in the Dubai embassy about the Shias in his emirate. The diplomat smiled at the subtle implication of injustice and insisted that all were brothers in the emirate of Dubai. The diplomat thought any unrest was caused by Iranian agitators. He reminded Joe of a Southern sheriff in the fifties who insisted that racial unrest was caused by Yankee agitators.

"How do you say 'Jim Crow' in Arabic?" He spoke softly this time.

The Shia weren't fond of Iran but at least it was speaking out against the oppression of fellow Shias. A weakened Iran and a victorious Saudi Arabia boded ill for Shias in the Gulf. The House of Saud might go on a campaign of expelling the Shias from their country. What did that portend for stability in the Gulf?

The next article Joe came across saw a "perfect storm" coming about.

"Another tired expression. Anyone who uses old expressions is unlikely to have new ideas."

Young Saudis were weary of the religious strictures that the Wahhabi clerics and virtue squads forced on them. The Saudi government was close to expending more money than it was taking in, despite all the oil revenue. Young people wanted meaningful jobs to better themselves, not subsidies to keep quiet. Furthermore, government was in the hands of doddering old men, the sons of an old warrior-king. They were in their eighties and infirm or paranoid or both.

Keeping his word to his sister and niece, Joe looked through the Facebook pages. Pictures of young Middle Eastern men with Maseratis and Bentleys . . . small shops in Saudi cities that likely didn't make any money.

Some photos, however, showed bright young men and women in nontraditional attire. They posted articulate essays on the need for reform in Saudi Arabia and pictures of security forces cracking down on demonstrators. They reminded Joe of the young Egyptians of Freedom Square who drove Mubarak out in 2011. One page discussed the prospects of war and at the bottom were links to dozens of articles.

There was a considerable amount of attention on the impropriety of an Islamic country attacking another. There were citations to the Quran, Hadiths, and other religious texts, including several rulings by respected scholars. Not everyone in these groups was religious; some were secular and judging by their photos, highly westernized.

Some posts ridiculed the idea of a Quranic ban on war between Muslims, not for the justness and desirability of the notion but for its lack of basis in actual events. "The old dynasties warred incessantly against each other since the death of the Prophet (PBUH). What of the Iran-Iraq War and Iraq's invasion of Kuwait?" Another post replied, "This is all the more reason why we must make this message meaningful in our lives."

One common theme running through the groups was hostility to the Saudi government which they branded the instigator of war. Some deplored Saudi Arabia's inattention to the Palestinian cause and saw that as a more vital issue to the Islamic community than the power of Iran. It came from people inside Saudi Arabia and from Morocco all the way to India. "Rich playboys . . . meddlers in our affairs . . . the enemy of democracy . . . doomed to fall within a decade, Insha'Allah."

Joe knew these arguments were out there, but reading them in impassioned phrasings had a striking effect that dry reports failed to convey. Surely some were from Iranians, maybe from Iranian intelligence officers. Still, he heard similar remarks from Arabs and Iranians in the DC suburbs.

The suburbs were packed with Iranians who got out with the money and owned posh houses in McLean, Potomac, and Chevy Chase. As much as they wanted the mullahs out, they didn't want their country attacked. No one does.

Iran, many people thought, faced its own dangers. The sanctions were hitting hard and the state might run out of cash in a year or two. It too disseminated oil revenue to forestall unrest. It also had sectarian and ethnic groups that would be pleased to break away from Persian dominance.

It all added up to war, confusion, civil conflict, and years of dreadfully high oil prices for the world.

"Maybe our intelligence people should read Facebook pages instead of all those goddam internal memos!"

"Did you want something, Mr Burkett?"

"Susan, I'm so sorry. I'm just venting again."

"Things are tense over there, aren't they?"

New Mexico

Ethan and Rina flew into Albuquerque to meet with a team of engineers at a PAMD fab just outside the Duke City. They'd been invited to look at a new chipset design for solid-state drives. Ethan and Rina would also demonstrate Micrologic Design's software to a big name—no, the biggest name. The trip had nothing to do with the Samson intrigue, but all the while in the fab the two kept thinking there was a secret lurking there and they might stumble across it.

It soon became a matter of humor. As they were escorted down a long hallway leading to a clean room, Ethan whispered to Rina, "Maybe we'll find an open file drawer or an unsecured work station!" Rina giggled and whispered, "Or a room marked 'Samson Team: Keep Out'." But they weren't sure anyone in the fab knew a thing about Samson. They weren't sure that what little they knew wasn't more than anyone in the PAMD headquarters in California knew.

Ethan and Rina ran their software on the chipset design and identified a few antennae and fuse effect concerns that eluded the PAMD team, causing some embarrassment among the workers but also some plaudits for Ethan and Rina. A senior engineer said the company would be "in touch." The phrase can be meaningless or a polite brush off, but there was sincerity and appreciation in his demeanor, so Ethan and Rina were optimistic.

As much as they needed to work with PAMD and other corporations, the feel of the place was off-putting. The atmosphere was regimented, bureaucratic, and uncreative—at least to people accustomed to the startup world. Ethan and Rina felt the culture close in on them with each step echoing down the barren corridors and with each glance into the atrium where employees grabbed hurried bites and chatted within corporate guidelines. No propeller beanies or impromptu volleyball games here.

"Rina, let's promise never to take Micrologic Design public. We'll end up like this place and like these people."

"Deal!"

Rina giggled as they walked by a corridor decorated with blowups of famed PAMD chips. "Oh look, Ethan. This must be the Yalie wing. You'd fit right in here. Really, this place is *sooo* you!" They laughed aloud as they came to a corridor graced by pictures of Taos, Santa Fe, and a sunset over the Sangre de Cristo Mountains. "This must be where the Stanford grads work!" she teased, nudging him with an elbow.

"Point taken. We'll discuss office decor another time. Let's get out of here and head for Barrett's place," Ethan replied, resting his arm on her shoulder. "I'll bet you can't even date interns here."

"You'll never find out, buddy boy. You're all mine!" She leaned against him and took his hand. "Does Barrett live nearby?"

"Uhhh, not really. From what he tells me, he lives . . . well, a bit out of the way."

Barrett picked them up at the gate in his black 740i and drove them to his place in the East Mountains. Barrett pulled off the interstate onto a two-lane blacktop heading north past the expansive tracts of ornery ranchers whose ancestors wrested land from Comanches, cheered Lew Wallace, and debated the merits of Pat Garrett and Billy the Kid.

"Those are Herefords. Beef cattle," Barrett observed as he pointed out a herd of steers behind a fence of weathered wood and rusty barbed wire. "More cattle than people out in these here parts," he added with a feigned drawl but genuine satisfaction.

Rina wondered why anyone would see that as good. He was a mystery to her, as was Ethan's friendship with him. The two were so different. Ethan cheery and outgoing, Barrett somber and withdrawn.

They came to a smallish adobe house with wooden support beams, or *vigas*, jutting out from the exterior and stretching across the inside. After overcoming the initial concern over the proximity of an immense wolf, Ethan and Rina looked about the house. They sat in his office-library—a large room with bay windows looking west to the Sandias. The ceiling had several glass apertures between the *vigas* from which the New Mexico sun lit up the room like theater lights, even in late afternoon.

The walls were lined with bookshelves packed with at least four thousand books, new and old, paper and cloth. Stone miniatures of Egyptian deities and Assyrian temple guards held them in place, though not at all tidily. Most of the volumes were history, ranging from Antiquity through the Middle Ages to the present. The latter sections held a good deal on Vietnam, guerrilla warfare, counterinsurgency, and the Middle East. In the room's center was an old wooden meeting table with equally aged armchairs.

"I want to show you something," Barrett said picking up a dog treat. He tossed it in Jesse's direction and the great wolf lifted up swiftly and brought his powerful jaws down with a startling cracking sound, engulfing the treat and crushing it into smaller pieces before swallowing them in one gulp.

Ethan smiled in appreciation on seeing what he'd only heard on the phone. Rina was at once dazzled and frightened by Jesse's instant response and feral majesty. She pressed a hand to her upper chest and wondered how wide her eyes had just opened.

Jesse lay down at the door, facing out, on sentry. Peaceful but vigilant.

"This is an impressive library." Rina noted needed to steady herself. She ran a finger along the end of row with the writings of World War One soldiers—Sassoon, Owens, and Graves. "It looks like one you'd see in movies—Sherlock Holmes movies."

"Thank you, but buying books is a benign mental affliction. At least I think it's benign." Barrett smiled and led them to their chairs. "It goes back to grad school in Chicago. The Seminary Co-Op and Powell's were my haunts. Oddly, I used to do my laundry at the place next to Powell's on 57th Street."

"Not so odd," Rina replied.

"Yes, it is. There was a washing machine and dryer in my apartment building."

"Oh, well, that is rather odd!" Rina laughed. "Of course, a *benign* kind of odd. Is this you in your salad days," she asked pointing to a photo of a young marine on the wall, near the doorway."

"No. I was in the army. That's just someone I knew in Iraq."

Rina expected a fuller reply but after a few moments of awkward silence it became obvious that that this was not a subject to pursue. She looked around the room and saw no pictures of family or friends or similar mementoes, only books and wooden furniture and various objects of historical interest such as scrimshaw from New England and architectural fragments from the ancient Mediterranean world. She thought she now knew something about Barrett and his relation to the world and life.

Barrett broke the uncomfortable silence.

"You know, all this emailing and phoning can make things very unreal, *more* unreal, especially when dealing with our Samson friend. Have we all been keeping this just among us?"

Rina and Ethan nodded. "We've kept all of our findings completely confidential," Ethan said. "Now let's see if we can think this thing out. The three of us have a lot of processing power, I'm sure."

"Here's what we have so far," Barrett began. "You've discovered an anomaly on a popular microprocessor. The anomaly turns out to be a hidden section on the chip which we're calling the CiC. The information stored on a memory section on each microchip is highly secretive, encrypted in suspiciously complex ways. We can now access these microchips individually or through the network—what they call the Samson Program. My suspicion is that Samson is tied in with the Flower Project of Israel and Iran in the 1970s. Is there overlap between missiles and microchips?"

"Yes, quite a bit," Ethan replied. "Missiles rely on computer designs and operational systems. So do the warheads and guidance systems. The design of a chip is driven by its function, and war-making has been a driving force since the birth of the industry during the Cold War. Okay, no history lesson from me. Let me run down the Samson system a little more."

"Can you make it low-tech?" Barrett asked. "Say, in terms a wolf could grasp?" Jesse stirred and arched an eyebrow at mention of his name but otherwise showed no interest.

"I'll try," continued Ethan, looking warily at the wolf. "You *have* fed him more than that treat recently, haven't you? Okay, every microchip's circuit has an ID and a network name and can be accessed individually according to its ID. The Samson Program keeps records of all its units and is constantly communicating with them around the world."

"And with the material stored in computers and servers," Rina added.

"Roger. Rina and I have seen the activity in the network. We don't yet know the purpose, but the traffic is constant and immense."

"It's no game station network," Barrett remarked.

"Nope. It took Rina and me a while to analyze its traffic samples in order to sort it all out. The most interesting thing is that Samson is not using the classical bytes and words as we know them. It creates its own structure—twelve bits in a predefined order. The combination is similar to binary-coded decimal, but with differences. In brief, it does an immense amount of work around the world and it does it in amazingly sophisticated ways."

"It's way ahead of what even militaries are using today," Rina added as she turned from looking through the titles of the books on Afghanistan and counterinsurgency.

"Don't forget to make this comprehensible to a wolf, but I'm getting the contours," Barrett interjected, hoping to slow them down.

"Samson constantly maintains redundancy. Every piece of information is stored on *many* units. If one unit goes down, there are others storing the same data. It's a safer backup system than anything on military aircraft, civilian airliners, financial institutions, or anything else. Its redundancy is way beyond anything a RAID or JBOD can offer."

"Those are data storage systems, Jesse." Rina smiled to Jesse but could not bring herself to pet him.

"Jesse and I appreciate that," Barrett said. "Any thoughts on who, if anyone, is running it? What's behind it or who's behind it?"

"I think that Samson is working on its own. I suspect that it was launched at a certain point and since then, it's been self-sustaining." Ethan's voice betrayed uncertainty. He was speculating, thinking aloud.

"I doubt that," Rina objected, much to Ethan's surprise. "No one sets up a system like this then trusts it to run on its own, especially for an extended period such as several decades. Too many things could go wrong. I suspect the Samson programmers are still running things. I've tried to email them and phone them—with industry questions only barely related—but I've gotten no replies yet."

"I have to agree with Rina," Barrett said. "It makes no sense to set up something with this kind of power and let it do its own thing, so to speak. I have to think it serves a military or intelligence purpose. Well, we're not going to settle that question now. What about that dove sign in the photo. It's been a sign of peace for quite a while. Since Noah. That was well before Samson."

"Samson was a symbol of strength and resolve back in Antiquity," Rina said. "but he lost his power when he divulged the secret to his strength. He then became a prisoner."

"They blinded him," Ethan continued. "He wanted revenge and he asked the Lord to give his powers back for one final act."

"With his last given powers, he pulled down their mighty temple and killed them all," Rina completed.

"Yes, the figure from the book of Judges. A great sociologist described him as a charismatic warrior, akin to the dervishes of the Middle East. Flower . . . Samson . . . Voice of Peace—Middle Eastern things. Maybe I just have that region in mind, as usual."

"What are you, Samson?" Ethan asked.

"What are you doing in the world?" Rina added.

"Have you seen enough folly? Are you planning to bring the world crashing down on us all? Lord knows there's been plenty of that," Barrett murmured. "'One thing I did not foresee, not having the courage of my own thought—the growing murderousness of the world'."

Rina was startled by Barrett's words and by the wish she thought implicit in them. She couldn't believe those men in the photo would build a doomsday device.

Southern Afghanistan

Major Nafar drove north from Zahedan, handed the border guards a few silver coins, and crossed the border into Afghanistan without further incident or expense. Driving north five hours on rough road, he came to the Ring Road, which formed a loop around the heart of Afghanistan, connecting Kabul with other major cities. It was a modern highway alternately built up and blown up by various armies. Three hundred kilometers to the east lay Kandahar, a US enclave surrounded by the Taliban homeland.

The first part of the trip was safe enough. Western Afghanistan was secure, as Afghans understood the term, though the occasional local power holder would demand a transit fee. Going east on the Ring Road was more challenging. In addition to Taliban groups, there were also independent warlords and their surly Kalashnikov-wielding retinues. They usually just wanted money.

Major Nafar was Shia and didn't like the Taliban. To him, they were an intolerant Sunni cult that massacred Shias and sacked an Iranian consulate in the north, killing a number of diplomats. But they were enemies of his enemy—the US—and soldiers and politicians respect that, at least until circumstances change.

He slept in the car at a truck station a hundred kilometers west of Kandahar and the next morning drove through the irrigated orchards on the town's periphery, then into the city itself. The Iranian consulate was on the west side, next to that of India. He drove a few blocks east to a house used by the IRGC. There he received a map of some remote villages and the names of a couple of *maliks*, or elders.

"You're not Persian," the IRGC colonel noted.

"I'm Basseri . . . one of the five tribes," Major Nafar replied, unwilling to tone down his ethnic pride in the presence of haughty Persians.

His people were a mixture of Arabs and Turkmen patched together centuries ago by Persian monarchs to guard the frontier. Basseris always had to prove their loyalty to the Persians—always. Major Nafar's features would not raise eyebrows out in the Afghan villages, as would Persians with their distinctive hairline and nose.

He took the map and names then drove south. As he neared the airport that was now a sprawling US facility, he turned east on a rugged dirt road with occasional jitneys overpacked with travelers and baggage and livestock. About an hour east of the airbase, Major Nafar came to a checkpoint guarded by men wearing black turbans and wielding Kalashnikovs. He spoke to them in Dari, a Persian dialect that was a lingua franca in much of Afghanistan. They were Taliban and were expecting him. They would take him to the village of Gumbadel where he would meet the elders.

He brought one of the batteries.

Santa Clara, California

Returning from their Albuquerque trip, Ethan and Rina faced a glum overcast morning. Ethan sat in front of the eBeam station and felt no more cheerful than the day. *No distractions from outside,* he thought. He sent keywords into the Samson unit still inside the eBeam device and determined that it received them. Now he could be in a Starbucks or library or any other place with a wi-fi signal and find his way into almost every microprocessor on the Samson Program. That of course meant almost every microprocessor in the world, almost every desktop, laptop, and server in the world.

Precisely what this access offered still eluded him. He felt as though he were standing in front of an immense mansion that held great treasures and he'd found the key under the backdoor mat.

Direct access through the microprocessor meant bypassing any software firewall and other security mechanisms. Security experts focus on apps and operating systems, leaving the hardware door ajar. Much more than that, the door was wide open. That was the Samson Program's secret, the key to its ubiquity and power. It did what no one thought possible and hence what no one guarded against. Security people went on their way, thinking they were doing a great job.

Ethan loaded a new software program into the eBeam which enabled even more detailed scrutiny of the CiC. He discovered files stored in flash memory sections. Memory caches on the microchip itself made operations faster and became fairly common in the years after 1986. In order to access the memory, he'd have to know where to start reading— or in software lingo, in which address to start.

He observed the actual layout and identified bit-lines that formed with word-lines to compose a mechanism sending information back and forth between memory cells. There were minute silicon wires connecting transistors to activate or deactivate the memory cells. Ethan went through a very tedious process of searching within the memory section for the bit-lines so he could identify the starting address. Once he found the first address, he'd be able to read the memory information.

After a few grueling hours he reached a conclusion. "We have a typical array-segment which is a two-dimensional array consisting of 512 x 512 bits."

"When you talk to the air like that, it means you've found something," Rina said, as she entered the room and placed an herbal tea before him. "Or you've gone completely around the bend. Which is it, big guy?"

"There's a duplicated memory array on the microchip—quite large. I'm trying to figure out the physical addresses so I can read the content. Oh, and thanks for the tea. Peach?"

"I would love to help you but I have a company to run here, you know. And incidentally, the tea is *mango*."

"It's good to know the business is in good hands," Ethan said perfunctorily before continuing his description. "As with any array, in order to access one of its elements—in this case, a memory cell—we have to specify the raw-number and column-number. The intersection point of the specified row-column pair will be the addressed element, and I think I've found the physical address." He quickly turned to his laptop. "We have to type it in hexadecimal base and . . . nothing . . . zippo . . . jack bit. Now that was a *keen* disappointment . . . but I *saw* the address."

He carefully reviewed it, hit some keys—again no response.

"What can it be?" he cleaned his glasses. "It's a basic memory array . . . I typed the address in hexadecimal base . . . and it tells me that this physical address does not exist."

"By the way, I configured our software with a new approach setup." Rina nudged him gently.

"I see . . ."

He heard her words but their meaning ran into bandwidth issues just then. His mind was embedded in the chip. Rina nonetheless continued talking proudly of Micrologic Design's new software module. "So I figured that software tools usually define their setup file as straight ASCII text files. Then I thought of using XML graphical interface. It will be more fun for the user than dreary text. What do you think?" She refrained from another nudge.

Tech-talk rose out of the background noise of the office and reached Ethan. "Great idea. Creative flourishes like that will be part of our appeal and niche. Let's do it that way." Then he turned back to his screen. "We are used to thinking about memory allocations in hexadecimal base . . . but what if it's in a different base? That's it!"

She nodded as would a teacher to a bright student. "Very good, Ethan. You're on the right path. Do carry on, please. Sometimes you have to think outside the base."

The Samson designers were using octal base, or base eight, in memory archives. He typed into its laptop, updating his program and the first piece of information appeared.

"Yes sir!"

He took off his glasses. From here the process would be much simpler. He'd write a simple program to read the memory array data and translate it into words. The data could then be translated into sentences—human information.

"We have access to the program and its stored data. What's it doing with all this data?"

"Maybe it's making herbal tea recipes, Ethan. Mango. I have to go back to work now."

Parchin, Iran

Changi is about forty miles southeast of Tehran, not far from the town of Pakdasht. Inside their house were a dozen or so rugs tightly rolled up, secured with thick twine and stacked vertically along the wall. To the east they could see the Jajrud River, which was quite wide there owing to a dam to the north. It reminded Anthony of the Potomac where it flattened out around Ft McNair. Tomorrow he'd meet with a couple of contacts but first he'd hike up the hills to the north and peer down at the IRGC facility of Parchin.

Iranian roosters are not unlike their kin elsewhere and Anthony awoke not long after first light. He took in some of the tea and bread that Idris and Barham brought in from Tehran then looked up to the north.

"There are trails leading up there," Idris said. "It's not far from a nature preserve. Just be careful at the summit. The IRGC don't like birdwatchers—or spies. If they catch you, please be so thoughtful as to give us at least a few hours to . . . how you said it yesterday? Get out of Dodge."

Anthony knew the SOP regarding not giving up information too quickly while undergoing an "enhanced interrogation," as torture was being called these days.

He walked west along the foothills until he came to a trail. No combat boots. Just the chukka boots he came in with. Two young couples were thirty meters ahead of him so he decided to follow them, close enough to seem part of them, far enough to avoid conversation. An hourlong ascent on the dry rocky trail and they reached a picnic area complete with pine tables and trash bins. Anthony reckoned he was still a couple hundred meters from the summit so he went to the left for a few minutes then continued his climb up the rough terrain scarred by dried rivulet beds and gnarled roots. He crawled the last thirty meters, reached the crest, and looked down at the sprawling base less than a mile below.

"Parchin."

Anthony stared down in fascination. He'd seen satellite photos of it but seeing it in person was like at last seeing the Hoover Dam or the Taj Mahal, linking something from study to something right before you. It was part of the reason he went into the rangers and the CIA. He saw things that others could only imagine: the burning tank hulks in the Iraqi desert, the haunting wasteland of western Afghanistan, Saddam's palace and single-malt scotch. In the last twenty-four hours he'd seen battlefields from the Iran-Iraq War, the heart of an enemy capital, and now Parchin—the most secret place in the Middle East.

A part of the base looked like an industrial park surrounded by a ten-foot wire fence. Two rows. Coils of razor wire atop each fence. A new housing development lay on one side of the facility and off to the south a soccer field was being sodded.

The place is growing. Maybe it's a training camp for the World Cup team. Ha, maybe not.

But what was in Parchin? It wasn't likely he'd get in the place; that was strictly Hollywood stuff. He'd heard it said repeatedly that the IRGC was constructing a nuclear weapon at Parchin. Other places were said to be enriching the uranium, but Iran still needed a way to set off the chain reaction. Without it, the enriched uranium was militarily meaningless.

Anthony stared down intently on the facility as though he would see something of significance, something the satellites missed, something his contacts didn't know. He looked down at the base for almost half an hour, then soon thought better of it.

This is getting me nowhere. Time to go. I'm sure they patrol this summit. Yeah, for birdwatchers.

He shimmied down the slope, brushed off the dirt, then descended the trail to the foot hills and back to the farmhouse. Parchin's secret was nothing he could determine from even the highest summit in Iran—or the Sinai desert for that matter. Later that day, he was to debrief men who worked there.

Southern Lebanon

Hisbollah grew into a formidable political-military organization since it formed during the Israel-Lebanon war of the eighties. Ostensibly, it had a solid command system leading up to Hassan Nasrallah in Beirut, but every organization has factions and jealousies and mavericks. Sometimes that leads to innovation and vitality. Sometimes it leads to breakaway movements. Sometimes it leads to an embittered commander acting on his own.

After twenty-five years of faithful service, Qasim Bazzi expected more from Hisbollah. He'd been a guerrilla in the south and even crossed into Israel on probing missions, not all of which had been approved. He trained under IRGC cadres and gone to Iraq in 2006 in a show of Shia solidarity against the US invasion. Bazzi had given up much. His family was killed by Maronite militias and he was wounded in the shoulder and back by shrapnel, leaving ugly scars which he enjoyed looking at with boyish pride. He hugged the earth as Israeli jets bombed his position and he felt the air sucked violently from his lungs as the concussion rushed over him and left a vacuum for a split second.

US aggression in Iraq and Afghanistan was met with fierce resistance, and Washington was now trying to oust Assad from Syria. He was an ally of Shia Lebanese and he needed support now. Nasrallah was urging caution. He sent a hundred or so fighters inside Syria and tried to halt the flow of arms from Lebanese bazaars to Sunni rebels, but that was it. Everywhere, Shi'ism was on the defensive and Nasrallah continued to call for caution. Qasim Bazzi thought this foolish and unmanly.

Bazzi commanded a district in southern Lebanon that gave him operational control over six hundred guerrillas and forty missiles. The latter were mostly small and limited in range, but Bazzi pressed for, and got, control over two Zelzal missiles. They were built in Iran from a Russian design and sent into southern Lebanon where they were capable of striking deep into Israel. His IRGC overseer was summoned back to Iran for reassignment and no replacement had come. Bazzi was on his own and he was determined to fire his two Zelzals into Israel that night.

The missiles were inaccurate, though two of them striking a large population center would force Nasrallah's hand and get him to fight Israel. Bazzi calculated that the US was overstretched and another war would break it, both militarily and financially.

The battery commander was accustomed to Bazzi's unscheduled inspections. This night, however, he was ordering two Zelzal missiles to be prepared for launch. There was no war and there was no order from Beirut, but Bazzi was the local commander and an intimidating one. The battery commander listened hopefully for the high-pitched hums of Israeli drones so that he could quickly return his missiles to their camouflaged caves. Unfortunately, the skies were quiet and the missiles were being readied. The battery commander and his chief engineer looked at each other worriedly as Bazzi told them to use the financial district of Tel Aviv as their target.

The men from the battery whispered to each other and entered the coordinates into the guidance systems from a laptop. Bazzi was annoyed by their slowness but he knew nothing of technology and was hardly able to say where delay ended and disobedience began. Entering the coordinates proved inexplicably difficult for the technicians, which made Bazzi more suspicious and angrier. Right after they entered a code for an actual firing and not another test, the launch program hung twice for each missile.

At length, and with apparent reluctance, the battery commander told Bazzi the missiles were ready. A moment later Bazzi barked out the order and in less than five seconds the first then the second missile ignited and sent immense bright-red flambeaus into the dark skies and thunderous roars across the rocky valley, reverberating almost painfully in the crew's chests and skulls until they were more than five kilometers away. Despite their misgivings, it was impossible for the crew not to feel awe and pride. The missile launches would be picked up by an Israeli picket ship soon enough and retaliation would be swift and fearsome. Nonetheless, they continued to watch transfixed as the fiery missiles arced brightly across the inky night.

After forty seconds, one of the missiles suddenly disappeared as though the fuel was spent or the engine shut down. The other continued streaking south toward Tel Aviv but after another twenty seconds, it veered west toward the Mediterranean before its flambeau disappeared as suddenly and unexpectedly as the first.

No one knew what happened, though everyone, regardless of zeal or rank, knew it was best to get the launch trucks back into the caves and to prepare for what was surely coming. Several soldiers were deployed around the position, armed with SA-18 missiles, capable of bringing down the Israeli fighters that were likely already taxiing down runways to deliver retribution. The SA-18s had recently been smuggled in from Libya. Weapons from Colonel Qaddafi's recently plundered arsenals were finding eager buyers throughout the Middle East.

The radar operator on the Israeli frigate *Moledet* saw two objects flash on his screen and heard the attendant alert sounds. The speed and trajectory made it clear that they were missiles—large ones, not the small projectiles made in village workshops of the Bekaa Valley. He instantly called the officer of the deck but before he arrived at the screen the two objects were gone. Lieutenant Sagy trusted the young radar officer's judgment and raised the Arrow antimissile battery in Galilee on the radio.

"Yes, *Moledet*, we saw two objects, just as you did. They both vanished though. One flamed out almost immediately. The other drifted west then flamed out too."

Yossi reviewed the data on the frigate's hard drives but the images were distorted and almost indiscernible.

"Galilee Station, have you reviewed your incident record?"

"Affirmative, *Moledet*. The data are corrupted and cannot confirm visual reports."

Sagy conferred with the young officer and imagined reporting a visual sighting unsupported by telemetry. Two large missile, no electronic evidence. Sagy exhaled noisily and cued the mike. "Another anomaly, Galilee Station . . . As we have no supportive telemetry, my morning report will not mention a launch sighting."

Galilee Station was silent for a full minute. Yossi imagined the debate going on there.

"Nor will mine, *Moledet*. Have a safe patrol, my friend."

"Will do. *Moledet* out."

"Galilee Station out."

Santa Clara, California

Rina dug into the Samson Program's code for the better part of the day and discovered an "expert system" that emulates human decision-making. In that respect, it differed from a conventional program which simply executes according to programmed instructions.

Samson had "storage units" to collect and retain vital real-time information, usually of a political or military nature. It had "analysis units" that studied the data and "execution units" that issued commands from the conclusions produced by analysis units, either through expert systems or human oversight.

"There has to be human oversight. This system simply cannot be operating on its own," Rina whispered to herself. "The world is too ... I don't know ... dynamic, unpredictable ... too *crazy*."

Samson maintained efficient redundancy by allocating extra units somewhere in the world. Of course, the growth of technology around the globe gave Samson fresh recruits every minute. Fabs churned out new chips just as military boot camps did raw recruits, with neither fully understanding how their work was playing out or who was ultimately in charge.

There was nothing Samson needed to do to continue its amazing growth. That was in the unknowing hands of consumers and businesses and governments and militaries. As long as fab plants continued to insert the minute CiC section into PAMD microprocessors, Samson would live and grow.

"It's based on the same principle as the Internet," Rina thought. "A center-less network designed to survive nuclear war. That's what

DARPA envisioned long ago. DARPA . . . there's got to be some link to those people. I'll bet the units are duplicated and deployed into reasonably safe areas, though the objects of study are mainly in the Middle East. I wish I could have interned for these guys! All the same, I'm learning from them. They just don't know it."

Rina sat back and tried to envision the creators of Samson. Anyone that brilliant must be decent, she reasoned. In any case, if they weren't, the world would have gone into a cataclysm over the last quarter century of the system's operation.

"I want to know more about the creators and meet them someday." As wondrous as such a meeting initially seemed, she shuddered imperceptibly at what it might portend.

Ethan, Rina, and Barrett set up occasional video conferences to see where each was in the research. Rina ran down what she'd learned about the system as Ethan sat back in his chair and Barrett listened and watched on his screen. The explanation was complicated if not arcane to Barrett so he took notes, drew schematics, and got the basics. Jesse opted for the outdoors.

"Just think how much money these programmers could make if they made something like this chip commercially. What it could do in stock markets and in think tanks and in the media. There's almost no limit," Barrett noted. His practical mind looked for practical applications.

"This makes our little Micrologic Design look like a lemonade stand," Ethan said wistfully, though in admiration of a master.

"Yes, it makes us look like an early version of DOS . . . or something for a Kaypro computer," Rina added mischievously, leading to a feigned scowl from Ethan.

"So now you're an expert on old computers. Anyway, Micrologic Design's program works great," Ethan returned defensively though good-naturedly, "and our clients are beginning to appreciate our betas. We've built impressive algorithms and we can hold our own. We're going to learn from Samson—more than its creators thought anyone could."

"They're still running it." Rina had to interject something that had been irking her about human agency. "It can't just be the legacy of the old programmers. Besides, someone sees that the CiC is implanted into new generations so they can watch over the world."

"They can't watch over the world! No one can. No system can." Barrett's sudden exclamation surprised Ethan and Rina. "It's not watching over everything from air defense systems to eighth-graders chatting about what they wore at the mall Friday night. Does Samson have favorites? Does he look at certain things or certain areas more than others, especially in recent months?"

"Well, we can get started looking at—"

Rina raised a hand and stepped in. "Sorry, big guy, but I already found several traffic clusters. One is in Iran, more specifically Tehran and a few smaller places called Natanz, Bid Kaneh, Fordo, and Parchin. Oh, and another cluster is starting up near Bushehr."

"Tehran is of course the political and military center. The other places are missile bases and nuclear research sites," Barrett explained. "Bushehr is just a basic research center. Nothing of importance."

"There are other hot spots in the Gulf region," Rina went on, "Manamah, site of the US naval headquarters, and Kharj in Saudi Arabia."

"That's the Prince Sultan Air Base." Barrett explained in a calmer tone. "The US is purportedly out of there, but things are seldom as they seem in the world, especially in the Gulf. Where else?"

"There's sustained activity in Arlington and Langley, of course, and then there's Las Vegas and Tampa-St Pete." Rina was puzzled by the last two sites. "Those are vacation spots, not hot spots."

"US drones are directed from Nellis Air Force Base, a short drive from the Vegas Strip, and Centcom is near Tampa. That's the US military command for the Middle East. Man, they're building military bases in nicer places than when I was in. In fact, there's a US airborne brigade station not far from Venice—as in Italy, not California."

"Where do I sign up!" Rina's humor lightened the discussion much to the others' appreciation.

"Oh yeah," Barrett continued, "I should say that there *might* be a US drone base at that Prince Sultan field. It watches things in Yemen."

"There *might* be?" Ethan asked.

"That's what my wolf says."

"What goes on in Yemen?"

"It's what *might* go on there. Rebel groups backed by Iran, Israeli recon camps, al Qaeda bands."

"Samson's watching Lt Alon's homeland too," Rina mentioned on looking at her clipboard. "There was a surge of activity along the Israel-Lebanon border recently, though rather short-lived. You're going to think this is crazy—or *meshugah*—but another hot spot is in Tel Aviv, specifically an old building that once housed the Knights Templar."

"What!" Barrett's outburst was mixed with laughter and his motion caused pixilation in the Skype window. "This is becoming surreal."

Ethan chuckled at Barrett's unexpected animation. "Calm down, you two! The Israeli military has used the old Templar building for decades. I've been there many times. Quaint from the outside, but the air conditioning in summer is wanting—even many floors below street level. By the way, I'm not a lieutenant anymore."

"Too bad," Barrett said. "I was imagining myself sneaking in and uncovering masonic secrets and finding an old grail."

"Okay, okay. Enough fun." Ethan had to bring the meeting back to order. "First, there's a strange section in the most common microprocessor in the world and it's been there since about 1986. The microprocessor has been updated and reworked, but the Samson section has always been there. Second, Samson is capable of communicating with chips around the world and it receives data and issues instructions."

"Third," Rina picked up, "attention is focused on Iran, Israel, Saudi Arabia, and US military centers in and out of the region."

"Fourth," Barrett went on, "the chip was probably designed and put into production by a group of Israeli, Iranian, Indian, and American engineers in 1986. Most of them had worked together on a missile program for the shah of Iran—Project Flower. The project ended shortly after Saddam Hussein's invasion of Iran in 1980."

"That war went on for eight years and took the lives of over a million people." Ethan murmured sadly as he thought of men he'd known who met their fates in other wars.

"Yes, it did." Barrett sensed the opportunity to deliver a history lesson and make a connection to the issue at hand. "Late in the war, both sides experienced problems. Missiles aimed at cities and oil ports failed to launch or came down in empty wastelands. Everyone was perplexed, even the US personnel who advised Iran on the Hawk missiles we sold them. The Iranians were ticked. They thought we sold them junk as part of a Saudi plot."

"That's not surprising. The Saudis would do something like that— if they could," Ethan said. "That's what Israeli generals think when their Jericho missiles malfunction. I looked into it but couldn't find anything." Ethan had a sudden thought too murky to share.

"So perhaps militaries of the world run up against Samson but blame the problems on rivals," Barrett countered. "Anyhow, Samson is watching military systems. The coalition that liberated Kuwait in 1991 experienced little if any trouble, as far as we know. Most of Saddam's

Scud missiles, however, experienced countless malfunctions. Some got through, though most failed badly."

"Didn't the Patriot missiles shoot them down?" Ethan objected.

"That's what everybody thought then. We later learned that the Scuds weren't working well. I personally saw more than a few lose ballistic trajectory then veer into empty desert. So maybe Samson wasn't a neutral observer. He played a favorite."

"Samson made the war shorter—and less deadly." Rina thought again of the gentle faces in the group photo.

"It certainly interfered with the war-making abilities of governments," Barrett went on. "That's a privilege they've enjoyed since ancient times—since some guys picked up rocks and bones, like those apes in Kubrick's *2001*. I doubt it can completely control things. Still, it can make wars less murderous and demonstrate that governments can't do what they think they can."

"It didn't stop wars in Bosnia, Sudan, and Yemen," Rina said, calling for explanation. "Or Rwanda, Zaire, Algeria . . ."

"Those were low-tech conflicts. Samson can't stop people from picking up rifles and mortars; he can only influence high-tech wars."

"Yeah, but if a bullet or a mortar round hits you, you're just as dead," Rina murmured.

Ethan shuddered slightly and lost focus for a moment as a memory rose up inside him and receded, though not as quickly as that morning in the Boudin bakery when the pan clanged on the floor.

"What is Samson doing in the Gulf now?" Rina asked. "We're not positive if Samson is good or bad, reliable or not. We have hunches about their being peaceniks but we can't say for sure."

"Maybe Samson caused the Iranian uranium centrifuges at Natanz to spin wildly and burn up, and maybe he's also behind the other compromises in Iran's computers," Ethan wondered aloud. "We've all read that Iranian computers suddenly start blaring heavy metal music."

"So did my neighbors in Chicago, Ethan. World affairs are filled with uncertainty—more than Heisenberg dreamed of. We have to act on imperfect information, some of it coming from imperfect people and institutions. I doubt chips are perfect, even the Samson sections. I doubt the creators of Samson are perfect either."

"Maybe the system will look at all the data and reach conclusions that the creators hadn't intended." Rina's mind delved deep into the vast system she was beginning to comprehend. A logjam, a flawed routine. She saw possibilities, unsettling ones.

Tehran

Idris and Barham drove Anthony to Tehran University before they headed to a workshop near the main bazaar where masterful replicas of Sultanabad and Bakshaish antiques were woven. There was thriving demand for such pieces in Kirkuk and Istanbul, and any country that liked Nains might also go for replicas. He told them he'd take the bus to Pakdasht then walk to the farm.

"Now, off to that safe house."

Tehran's subway was impressive and clean. In appearance, it was far more like Washington's than New York's. He rode a few stops north to the Imam Khomeini station and got off a half mile north, not far from the British embassy. IRGC's toughs known as the Basij sacked it a few months back. A couple of them were photographed hauling off an enlargement of Vince and Jules, the offbeat hit men in *Pulp Fiction*.

The Basij began as shock troops in the Iraq war. Now they're making off with movie posters. Should've stuck to telling tall tales to kids.

Anthony walked west past streets named after Westerners, Henry Corbin and Bobby Sands, then came to a townhouse. He rang the bell but knew his presence was known by a video cam hanging just above the left jamb. He was buzzed in and greeted by two men in their thirties. The interior looked like a posh French hotel with rococo furniture and prints of rural scenes from nineteenth-century painters. Pleasantries were exchanged in English.

"Your trip is going well?"

"Yes, it is. Quite well. Though there's much ahead."

"Yes. Always so much for people like us to do. Always. There is someone here who wishes to speak with you, as you know. And another meeting later, we hope."

Are these guys Iranian? No. Sephardics. Probably Mossad.

Mossad had its own history and institutional views. The second meeting hadn't been mentioned and was disconcerting, but intelligence work doesn't proceed like a subway ride. Maybe like a New York City subway ride.

Mehdi rose as Anthony entered the side room, though Anthony was introduced as "Agrin," the Kurdish name on his passport, and the two were left to conduct their interview. It hardly mattered. Whatever Mehdi was going to say had been said to the Sephardics already. Maybe they had told him what to say.

Mehdi was a young man in his late twenties and said he'd been working at Parchin for the last three years.

"I am an engineer, my friend. What you call a tool and die maker. I make precision parts for special components. Not all of them I see assembled, naturally."

"My great-grandfather was a tool and die maker for Thomas Edison during World War One. He worked on electrical equipment for submarines." Anthony switched suddenly to the point, looking for discomfort. "Do you make centrifuges at Parchin?"

"There are no centrifuges at Parchin, my friend. They run at Natanz and Fordo. They run when they aren't burned up from spinning too fast, as you undoubtedly are aware."

He passed that test but it wasn't hard. Anthony decided to get to the point. "Everyone outside Iran is interested in Parchin. Do they have reason to be?"

"There is a cylinder there. A large one. Twenty meters long and four meters in diameter. Concrete packing around it. I have worked on components that are placed inside one end of the cylinder Small ones of many shapes. I don't see them assembled, naturally. Almost no one does."

Anthony hoped he hid his interest. A cylinder of that description was almost certainly a primitive implosion device and the prototype of a triggering device for a nuclear weapon. "Do important visitors come to your place of work?"

"Many engineers and physicists from universities in Tehran and from other sites."

"Which sites?"

"I know some are from Natanz and Fordo. I went to school with some of them. Two of them at the mechanical engineering school at Tehran University, not far from here."

"Who else comes to Parchin? Military people?"

"Parchin is a military facility, my friend!"

"Outsiders, I mean," Anthony added sheepishly. Mehdi showed no signs of nervousness or deception. The better ones don't.

"I am told that General Jafari and General Suleimani were there last month."

"You were *told?* I did not come to hear to rumors and guesses!"

"Their arrival made the place beehive. Others saw them, not me. I have no doubt. My information is good. Others saw them. Ask the men in the next room."

"Any mullahs? Ayatollahs?"

"They do not come. They too would make beehive."

"Can you get me photos of this cylinder?"

"Of course not, my friend! Much too dangerous. I made a diagram on Freebyte software. For the cylinder and spherical chambers too. Other software programs, I don't wish to use because their use is watched. Also I have brought you a list of the engineers I know of. I cannot get you photographs. I thought you would have realized that." Mehdi cast his eyes downward, feigning disappointment.

Anthony photographed the diagram and the list of engineers with his iPod and encrypted them as a few units of a Kurdish melody on the device's flash memory. There was room for 24 gigabytes more—enough space for hundreds of photos and audio clips. Anthony ran the papers through a diagonal shredder next to a desk and repeated the operation.

"Can you get me inside Parchin?"

"You think like spy in movie," Mehdi laughed. "Maybe you have sports car outside and Walther PPK in pocket! Or is it a Beretta 70 this day? You have Kurdish name and they think Kurds like to be terrorists. You don't look Persian . . . or Azeri or Kurdish. Not to me, not to IRGC."

The last words were cautionary in tone and unwelcome news to Anthony.

"I cause beehive then."

"You cause *big* beehive then! And maybe get stung badly. You get stung—not good. I get stung—very, very bad."

Mehdi and Anthony discussed the size and location of important chambers at Parchin and drew up a diagram on Freebyte. Afterward, they shook hands and the two Mossad officers showed Mehdi to the rear door. Anthony pointed to the shredder and one officer ran the paper through it again and assured him the strips would be burned within the hour.

"Who is this other contact?"

"Abbas Karroubi, a professor at Tehran University. Computer science, not physics. We do not know him, only of him. He is highly respected by DARPA in your country."

DARPA? Anthony knew of the obscure defense agency that came up with clandestine hi-tech ideas and gadgets.

"Is he with DARPA?" It was not a classified matter. The members were listed on numerous websites.

"He's not with DARPA or the JASONS either. Apparently, people in Washington and especially Jerusalem want you to meet him. He will be at the Farda bookstore near Tehran University in one hour. Medieval history. European medieval history. You might wish to talk to him of Bierman's book on medieval law. Harold Bierman, medieval law."

"I'm not familiar with Mr Bierman or his field of study. But I shall learn something this day," Anthony said to signal his departure.

"We are never too old to learn. We have things for you," one said as he opened a briefcase and showed Anthony a transponder and a Beretta 70.

"Not just now. Thank you though."

"I understand. Ah, just one more thing." The two officers looked at each other cautiously, as though they were about to ask something out of the ordinary. Anthony felt uneasy. They might be about to ask him to do something for Mossad, not the Company. A look at his report? An assassination? A bombing? That was way out of bounds. He braced himself and tried not to show it.

"Can you recommend a rug for the front room?"

Anthony smiled weakly. "Yes, of course." He looked around at the elegant furnishings and ruled out tribal pieces. "A city rug rather than a tribal piece, I think. Floral design with tight knots, short pile. A Qom or an Isfahan, perhaps."

"We thought they only enriched uranium there!" One said, eliciting laughter from all three. "We must all go there someday. Business *and* pleasure!"

Spy humor. Not enough of it.

Anthony headed from the safe house to the Farda bookstore, not far from the university and the former US embassy. A few students looked over the books, new and used. They were mostly in Farsi and Arabic, though French, German, and English titles laid in every row. There was a large selection of ancient history and just off to the right, an impressive number of titles on European history, including Cobban's works on the French Revolution, Klyuchevsky's Russian history, and Motley's tomes on the Dutch Revolt. Dim recollections of graduate school at George Washington and ensuing life choices flitted through his mind.

He backtracked a shelf and found a few rows of medieval history titles which were not in chronological or alphabetical order. Ganshof, Bloch, Pirenne, Cantor . . . Bierman. *Law and Revolution.* A red paperback published by Harvard University Press. *Oh God, am I supposed to open it and find a cryptic note or a decoder ring?* he wondered as he leafed through the thick book. Canon law, feudal law, the Holy Roman Empire, the pope. More thoughts on life choices came and went.

"My expertise is in technology but I enjoy reading history," came an elderly voice. A gentleman in his early seventies, gray bearded, wearing a light-blue linen jacket. Reading glasses hung from a worn leather strap around his neck. No tie. He ran his finger across the shelf and tapped Bierman's book. "The philosopher Hegel once said that history teaches us that we don't learn from history."

No tweed jacket with elbow patches? Hegel?

"He was wiser than Santayana, at least in my jaundiced estimation. There is a park not far from here."

They walked a few minutes to Laleh Park and stood near a gushing fountain. An occasional Airbus took off noisily from an airport a couple miles away. A nearby airport was a wonderful thing in Anthony's line of work. In the park, the rushing fountain and thundering airliners would make it difficult for anyone to listen in. The fountain was graced with a statue of a man with the planets revolving around him.

"That is the esteemed Aboureyhan Birouni. He was a Persian astronomer. However, we joke that he must have been American."

"Why is that?" Anthony asked flatly, sensing an impending barb.

"Because, as you see, he thinks he's the center of the world."

He'd heard worse and in any case it was fairly amusing. "It looks to me like he has a lot of balls up in the air. So yes, perhaps he was an American." Anthony ended the pleasantries and got to the point. "There are many beautiful sites here. Is there anything of note a few miles that way?" Anthony looked briefly to the southeast—toward Parchin.

"You must mean the lovely Jajrud river!" Karroubi continued without prompting, all levity gone. "Nothing too interesting. Nothing alarming. I've not been there myself in many years but my students work there. Many ideas and much money. The government holds them back. Generals always have ambitious plans, regardless of their uniform and stated duty."

"A large barrel, I hear. Unusually large. Any spherical or hemispherical objects that could become nuclear warheads?"

"None. Just soldiers and scientists with a lot of money—money that could be better used elsewhere. Poor villages . . . better housing . . . more schools."

"Why do I hear of these things?"

"Your people *want* to see such things, do they not? Or are you a true believer in those things? There are people in your country who wish to see them so that they can start a war. That would be foolish—for everyone. Do you remember why your country went to war with Iraq in 2003? Your leaders searched diligently until they found someone who claimed to have seen what they wanted to see. And you know what happened."

"I recall the war quite well and need no reminders." Anthony caught himself becoming too abrasive. He didn't like lectures from someone whose country supported Iraqi insurgents.

"Would you believe there are generals in my country who want your country to see barrels and spherical or hemispherical objects so that they will act accordingly? *Iranian* generals, that is." Karroubi searched for signs of recognition from the intelligence officer. He'd done the same with predecessors and men in other intelligence services.

"I'm not following your lecture, professor."

"Such actions will greatly raise the generals' influence here. The mullahs weary most of us, especially here in the cities. Out in the villages . . . oh, out there it's another matter. Bold generals defending the nation will inspire simple villagers. Some people in the cities too, I must admit. Then we would move from rule by mullahs to rule by generals."

Anthony took a moment to take this in. What was that Cold War espionage novel? *The Looking Glass War.* Everything is backwards. "Perhaps we can speak more of physics than of history on this day," Anthony said politely enough. "How are you sure there are no barrels or spheres? Students can have other loyalties than to former teachers. Admirable though you undoubtedly are, young people often admire those who pay them and they accept their beliefs and goals. This tendency is not be confined to Americans."

"Too true, even in a pious country such as my own." Anthony thought there was subtle irony in the last few words. "I know what their networks and servers know. Do you know algorithms, encryptions, programs?"

"I know infantry, armor, and artillery. And a little about barrels that get smaller in time and are placed on missiles and get launched into the skies, perhaps at my country."

"Yes, we have missiles. I helped see to that under the shah—with the encouragement and help of your Israeli ally. Do you know of that help?"

"Physics not history, professor—please." Anthony knew that Iran and Israel were allied then.

"As to your purpose, the only barrels are on antiaircraft guns that defend against your bombers. No implosion trigger at Parchin, not at Fordo either. Not anywhere. They enrich uranium up to twenty percent. That's all the mullahs allow and for now their word is law. Attacking us will put the generals in power and then *their* word will be law. I think we will all lose. There are powers—powers you cannot know of or imagine—that will ensure there never shall be nuclear weapons here."

"An interesting theory, professor." Anthony was intrigued by a few allusive words. "But what are these powers I cannot know of?"

"It was not a slight, young man. Think of it as the conceit of an old man, one who knows the limitations on our generals. These men who sent you . . . the big ones in Washington, not the little ones in Iraq. They of course know you will find no definite answers. You've suspected this, no?"

Anthony tensed up and hoped it didn't show.

"They also know you will never report you did not find definite answers. A young warrior will side with the use of force, especially if he senses his superiors want that. They *always* want that, young man. Surely, you've sensed that, though perhaps not fully comprehended it."

This all resonated inside Anthony, sounding like the voice of his father cursing the generals and politicians of the Vietnam War who claimed to see progress where there was only stalemate.

Karroubi wasn't finished.

"An older soldier—a wiser soldier—might see only one certainty—the deaths of many thousands of people. Hundreds of thousands of people. And that soldier would act accordingly. An older soldier, a wiser soldier, and perhaps a braver one as well."

"We have strayed into mind-reading and fortune-telling." Anthony sensed a close to the nuclear question and the futility of trying to return to it. "May I ask if you were in the Iraq war, professor?"

"No. I was too old. I marched in the streets of Tehran in 1953 when Mossadegh was overthrown and I was shot at by my own people. Do you know of that?"

"The coup that brought back the shah. British and American intelligence." Anthony spoke in a matter-of-fact way, revealing no opinion on the subject. It would be unprofessional. In any case, the power those events held over Iranians had no equivalent in Americans.

"I was living in California when Saddam invaded in 1980 and came back to help my country, regardless of who was in power. Many of us did, scientists and generals alike. I worked on the Hawk missiles that your president sold us—behind your congress's back, as I recall. I also worked on the computer systems we modernized back then . . . I lost two sons. Both died late in the war . . . You have come through your wars, and I hope your good fortune continues in any conflict that might lie ahead of you."

A sincere, fatherly smile came across Karroubi's face and Anthony knew he didn't hide his appreciation.

"Iran and Iraq are becoming friendlier now," Karroubi continued. "Perhaps one day Iran and the US will be friends again. Maybe Iran and Israel too. The Middle East is a volatile place. Friends suddenly become enemies and enemies suddenly become friends."

"Tehran University is fortunate to have wise teachers like you. And there is much we have to learn from history."

"And from Hegel."

Southern Afghanistan

The village of Gumbadel comprises little more than a dozen mud houses scattered along a few dusty walled streets. Dogs barked aimlessly amid the quiet and torpor of the late afternoon. It was that way even in the marketplace which must have seen better days, if only before the Russian invasion in 1979. The Taliban escort brought Major Nafar to a ramshackle inn of sorts where five elderly men were gathered to parley with him. Nafar sat down with them on the floor and a fully veiled woman served tea and rice wrapped in grape leaves. He made the customary display of appreciation.

The men were dour and sparing in their words. Major Nafar thought they were sizing him up to determine what they could get from him, as they had with British officers a hundred years ago and with American officers perhaps last month. He was in a centuries-old game and playing against men with vastly more experience. But he was in possession of something they wanted.

Their Pashtun tribe had survived over the years by negotiating with outsiders and finagling every *afghani* they could from them. They did so in war and peace and over the last thirty-five years there'd been precious little of the latter. The young men of southern Afghanistan now saw war as the ordinary state of affairs and thought herding and farming to be unworthy callings. Better to heft a Kalashnikov. The older men were tired of seeing their young men obsessed with war and dying. The *malik* was first to speak.

"Gumbadel was a prosperous village once," he began in halting Dari. "Many people, many herds, large marketplace. Now . . ." he gestured out toward the desolate street, "my people are poor and tired and sick."

Major Nafar didn't expect such brevity. It took a moment to recognize a cue.

"Once we rid the valley of foreigners, it will be prosperous again. I have brought you a gift of many *afghanis* from the people of Iran, and I have also brought a plan to help you." He looked around the room at the same impassive faces. "I'm told there are items here in Gumbadel that we can both benefit from."

None of the men reacted. They continued to stare at him and occasionally partook of the rice cakes and tea. Major Nafar was becoming impatient. The *malik* eventually nodded and stood up. He and the IRGC major left the inn and walked a few minutes to a shed at the edge of the village where the *malik*'s two sons stood in front of a stack of green aluminum boxes resembling small coffins. Major Nafar pointed to two of the boxes at random and the young men opened them.

The information was correct. The village of Gumbadel was the proud owner of ten American Stinger missiles. He kneeled beside one and marveled at its carbon metal contours. He removed the rectangular battery from an interior pocket, inserted it near the trigger housing, and flicked a switch on the control panel. Solenoids clicked and the red LED display lit up. The *malik* remained impassive.

The US parceled them out to the mujahideen during the Russian war. Four thousand of them. Some had been fired, some hadn't, and some were smuggled abroad to eager buyers. No one knew the precise number of any tally, least of all the CIA which began to buy them back after the Russians left in 1989. People don't like to give up valuable things that might come in handy in a land not given to long periods of peace.

The IRGC purchased several Stingers from a pliant warlord named Ismail Khan in 1987 then reverse-engineered them. They also made copies of the batteries, which decayed into uselessness after ten years, fifteen at most. Major Nafar brought a single new battery with him. The rest were back at the consulate.

"I can give you ten new batteries to use against American aircraft around Kandahar. I can train you to use them too."

"We learned to use them years ago . . . from CIA . . . when you were small boy in Iran," replied the *malik* without a hint of humor. "Two helicopters and a MiG—down." His hand turned in circles and trailed down, simulating an aircraft spiraling to the ground. His hand came back up to his waist. "Small boy you were. CIA come . . . now IRGC come. All say help." The *malik* looked down the hill to his village.

Major Nafar showed him a cranking mechanism with a meter of wiring.

"This will not give life to batteries," the old man replied instantly. "Your batteries good, but fire machines do not always work after the years."

Major Nafar was struck by the *malik*'s astuteness with technical matters. Yes, it was known that the rocket motors often failed after many years, even in dry climates like southern Afghanistan.

"We think that six of the Stingers will still work. Maybe more—Insha'Allah. In any case, we can bring you the Stingers we make by the hundreds—Misagh-2s. We also have SA-18s from Libya."

"Better than SA-7 Strela," the *malik* noted as crisply and accurately as any Jane's analyst. "Not better than Stinger."

The two men regarded each other for several moments—warily, wordlessly, but respectfully. Major Nafar removed the battery from the missile's side, thought a moment, then handed it to the *malik*. "A gift from my people to the brave men of Gumbadel." They bade each other farewell and Major Nafar headed back to Kandahar. There was much to ponder before giving his report.

As he drove past the US airbase, Major Nafar watched four Apache gunships lift off amid clouds of red dust and race to the south. He imagined himself firing a missile at the helicopter and watching it detect the heat signature of the Apache's engine and track it, despite the flare countermeasures and the pilot's frantic maneuvering.

He imagined the Apache spiraling toward the ground in flames.

Tehran

Anthony tried to sort out his meetings with Mehdi and Dr Karroubi. The thought of too many balls in the air came to him naturally enough. Often too. He went back to the street near the bookstore and waited for the bus to Pakdasht. He sat near the middle exit, plugged in his headset to the iPod, and listened to Persian hip hop. A sitcom came to mind: "Mehdi and the Professor." Madcap antics, exotic locations, and a little international intrigue thrown in. Check your local listings.

Tomorrow there would be two more contacts, both from the same sources tied to the safe house. He hoped at least for a consensus.

The sources, Anthony reasoned, were almost certainly from the Sephardics at the safe house, who in turn were almost certainly with Israeli intelligence. Who else uses Beretta 70s? It was their hallmark of sorts. The low power offered the advantages of less noise and less recoil. Anthony preferred .45s, despite the prodigious kick.

He wondered if he was supposed to look into the sources' eyes and come to a conclusion. That's what Bush did with Putin and he saw a good man. Anthony only saw a former KGB officer who wanted to restore Russian might and glory. Neither Mehdi nor the professor struck him as essentially untruthful. It would have been better had these sources come from people he trusted though.

Mossad was eager for him to talk to Karroubi. There was something odd about a kindly old prof becoming a late player in the game. Of course, Mossad might be skewing information to its advantage. That was to be expected of any institution anywhere, even one in Langley. Especially one in Langley.

The Israeli government wanted war with Iran. That was clear enough from the prime minister's speeches and his supporters in the US. Then there were a few Israeli generals and intelligence officials who started speaking to the media, including the US media, saying Iran was not run by reckless zealots and urging restraint. One guy said that attacking Iran would be stupidest thing he'd ever heard of. It was a former Mossad chief. No peacenik he. He ran a team of assassins throughout the Middle East who did their work remarkably well, often with Beretta 70s. The former Mossad chief worried about Tehran's ability to retaliate with missiles and its own assassins.

The Agency had already heard Mehdi and Karroubi and they had likely heard from the contacts he'd meet tomorrow. Anthony's function in the scheme of things was to provide a footnote for a thesis whose conclusion had been reached before the first word was written and before he crossed into Iran.

The bus reached Pakdasht at dusk. Anthony thanked the woman driver and hopped off. He'd walk back to the farm near Changi and tried to form a conclusion or at least a preliminary one.

"So Washington wants me to be convinced there *is* a nuclear weapons program at Parchin. Mossad, or portions thereof, want me to think there *isn't* one. Jeez, I'm just a soldier from a low-rent zip code in South Texas—the kind of guy who fights America's wars and mans its walls so that everyone else can go shopping in the mall."

He cut through an adjacent field to reach the farm from the back. No lights. No SUV. It felt wrong.

Where the hell were Idris and Barham? Off to another bazaar? On Rt 46 headed back to Kurdistan? Or has the mission been compromised, with his companions in the hands of the IRGC? Or did they think he was in IRGC custody and about to spill his guts so they got out of Dodge?

Anthony found a dilapidated barn and lay down with an unexpected groan. His eyes looking out the partially open door toward the farm.

He looked at his iPod and saw the battery was run down. The charger was in the house. He shut the iPod off and began to form a plan.

Maybe in the morning Idris and Parham would show up after a night of revelry in Tehran and his mission would continue. If not, he would find a way to get out of the country. He was worried though not alarmed. The escape options outlined to him in Kurdistan ran through his head as he covered himself in alfalfa and nodded off still facing the door.

His sleep was interrupted more than once by the sound of metallic clicks.

Anthony awoke with the roosters again and peered out toward the farmhouse, now better lit than last night. Still no sign of the Kurds. He had to suspect he wouldn't see them again this side of the border or even this side of the Styx, so it was back to the Pakdasht bus stop. He bought a bag of pistachios and an orange from a cart then headed back into Tehran.

He got off near the university to reorient himself and headed north to the safe house. Worry was on the faces of everyone he passed and there were more security people on the street than yesterday. Blaring horns and sirens indicated that security forces were on the move. When he reached the intersection near the safe house, he saw three security SUVs double-parked on the street and a few dozen anxious onlookers. Someone said in an irate voice that there was another assassination last night and two people were killed.

He stood amid the crowd and mimicked their stern looks and curious gapes before determining that the safe house wasn't living up to its name that morning.

No transponder, no pistol, no luck.

He needed some place to think things through. Laleh Park was a short walk and he sat next to the statue of the Persian astronomer, the chap with too many balls in the air.

"Well, old timer, should I *di-di mau* for the airport and hop on a flight to Kurdistan? Oh . . . '*di-di mau*' means to leave, depart, get the hell out. It's Vietnamese and has been in GI slang since Khomeini was a corporal."

The old astronomer didn't even give a polite smile.

"But there's been an assassination somewhere and security forces like to show they're on the ball by swarming into airports and delaying flights. It makes people feel safe, I guess. I need the news and some coffee, old timer. Is there a Starbucks nearby? Well, if there isn't a coffee shop with wi-fi near the airport, then I just don't know Tehran. Another good one that went over your head." Anthony tossed a fifty-rial coin in the fountain and headed toward the airport.

A few blocks west, he saw a familiar logo, or thought he did. As he got closer, it turned out to be a "Star Box," a local knockoff of the ubiquitous American coffee chain.

My God. They rip off a revered gourmet coffee chain yet wonder why the world is imposing sanctions on them?

Star Box offered coffee, pastries, and a television and Anthony left the trademark issue for the lawyers to hash out. Everyone in the cafe was watching the news. He sat down with a large coffee they had the audacity to call a *venti* and tried to get up to speed. The TV was giving a grim report in Farsi of the assassination of another physicist and his driver as they drove home from the Atomic Energy Organization last night. A motorcyclist had placed a magnetic bomb on the physicist's car, killing him and his bodyguard.

Couldn't they have waited until I got out? So that's why Idris and Barham didn't come back last night . . . Oh God, maybe they did it. No, the MeK usually did those assassinations and the MeK aren't Kurds. Those Mossad agents at the safe house? They wanted me to meet more contacts and to get the word out. That's my job right now, getting the word out.

He always knew he'd find himself in a tight spot, but he imagined it being a ravine in eastern A-stan or a dark defile in Iraq. Here he was in a Starbucks knockoff in a chic neighborhood of a cosmopolitan city.

You expect me to talk, Suleimani?

No, Mr Sabatini. I expect you to buy me a latté—a venti.

Humor was helpful in tight spots.

No more Mehdis, no more Karroubis. I have to form a judgment and get it out.

Then I have to get me out.

He powered on his iPod and saw the red battery icon. He'd run out of juice before he typed out the message, short though it was. Fourteen-year-olds could do it with their thumbs in thirty seconds while eating lunch and checking their Facebook page, but typing wasn't a skill the Agency taught at Quantico.

He looked down the street and saw the most wonderful sight he could imagine, a sight that would gladden the heart of every American except Bill Gates. Less than two blocks away there was an Apple Store. It might not be any more authentic than the Star Box or the 2009 election results, but knockoff or not, it would have what he wanted.

Inside the glass doors with the Apple icon was a team of employees wearing blue t-shirts with ID tags around their necks. A young woman, her head covered in a scarf but otherwise western in appearance, cheerfully introduced herself and asked if she could be of help.

"I'm in Tehran on business and unwisely left my charger back in Kirkuk. Could I purchase one here? One with an adapter that charges from a wall socket and perhaps also from a train outlet?"

She picked the items from a display shelf and asked if he'd like to pay with his iTunes account.

"I prefer cash."

"Cash works," she replied, importing an American idiom into Farsi.

"And may I charge my iPod for a while as I look around?" He opened the packaging and plugged one end to his iPod. "I would not want it to sync with one of your machines, of course."

"This iMac is not set up to sync." She obligingly inserted the other end to a USB port beneath the monitor. Anthony ensured there was no sync and once she went off to greet another customer, he opened the Fars News Agency website. The news agency had the name of the bombing victims and angry denunciations of Israel, the US, and Saudi Arabia who were blamed for the act.

My money's on Israel and the MeK.

The article went on to say that security had been tightened around Tehran and other cities. He grinned as he scrolled down and saw a photo of a security guard with a police dog patrolling Khomeini Airport. Time to look into rail transport. Anthony searched for the train station and found it a mile to the south.

Pardon me, boy . . .

After twenty minutes his iPod was reasonably well charged. He thanked the young woman and stepped back onto the sidewalk, placing the iPod and cord into the inner pocket of his jacket. He found another coffee shop, ordered a latté, and searched for a wi-fi signal. There were four available signals, including a weak one from the Apple Store a few doors down. He selected the signal of a Greek restaurant named "Yanni's" and saw a dozen emails pop up, all of which were purely for show in case of capture.

The plan back in Iraq was to meet with a few more sources in Tehran, but with the city in an uproar and looking for people like him, if not himself personally, that was out of the question. He nonetheless had to send in a report as it wasn't a sure thing he'd get out. He had to send it now.

Anthony weighed things last night and much more on the ride in. He was leaning in one direction but the idea was vague and never coalesced into anything that could be called a decision. It was like thinking about buying a stock or trying a new restaurant next week.

Between the motion and the act . . . falls the shadow.

Everything he'd read about Parchin had to go out of his head and he had to judge by what he saw and heard since crossing into Iran. What was it, two days ago?

What of the former Mossad boss's views, which were apparently diametrically opposed to what he'd have thought they were? *Apparently.* And that Karroubi fellow? What he wouldn't give to talk to Karroubi and that Mossad guy in the same room. The sharpest knives in the proverbial drawer.

There were sharp knives back in Langley, especially over in the analytic sections, but didn't they issue an intelligence estimate not long ago that said Iran was not building a nuclear weapon? Everybody thought it was a put-up job to get back at the Neoconservatives for doctoring the intel before the invasion of Iraq. Some guy at the State Department's Intelligence and Research section powwowed with other intel chiefs and voila, the Neocons were handcuffed on Iran.

More damn shadows.

Anthony looked outside at the streets of Tehran and saw the urban rhythms and off in the distance a poster of Khomeini. Anthony breathed in deeply and awoke his iPod. He selected the Skype app and began to type a text message.

Parvizian2012

Met only two merchants in bazaars of Tehran. I see no interesting new designs, as once thought.

He hit "send" more quickly than he thought he would.

"Now, how do I get the hell out of here. Tehran is a nice place to visit but I wouldn't want to die here."

Southern Afghanistan

The IRGC office in Kandahar learned that yesterday an American F/A-18 dropped two 500-pound bombs near a village fifty kilometers to the south, killing seven civilians, including three children. Major Nafar felt compassion; his superiors sensed opportunity.

"The Akolzai tribe has been excluded from aid programs owing to old rivalries, or so they claim. These Pashtun . . . Whatever the truth is, we know that they oppose the Kabul regime and the Americans who come through their valley from time to time. After this airstrike, perhaps we can win the goatherds to our side—at least for a while." The colonel sniffed the last words, conveying the city-dweller's disdain for rural-dwellers.

Major Nafar wasn't quite sure of the stability of any side. "Do the Akolzai have Stingers?" he asked.

"They once had three Stingers and an old Russian SA-7 Strela. We believe they sold them to the CIA in 2002. You will be going there with a Stinger battery and one of our Misagh-2s."

Major Nafar froze. He was unprepared for this. It was unlikely that soldiers at an American or Afghan checkpoint would recognize a Stinger battery, however a Misagh-2 heat-seeking missile, the Iranian Stinger, was hard to hide and easy to recognize. Some *afghanis* would help with an indigenous unit, but American soldiers were resistant to bribery. He admitted at least some honor in his foe.

"The Misagh-2 will be hidden in a compartment above the driveshaft of an SUV we shall provide. You shall have maps and the names of the *maliks* within the hour. The ride, I'm afraid, will be less agreeable than your previous one."

The Persian superiors concluded the briefing and looked to him in a manner he found disconcerting. He saluted and headed for the garage where the SUV was being prepared.

Major Nafar drove west then south toward the village of Calghor, thirty kilometers north of the desert that spread across southern Afghanistan and western Pakistan. The road was annoyingly rough and well patrolled. So far, there were only two Afghan army checkpoints as the US was pulling out of this part of Kandahar province. A little later he came across a local freelancer who supported his armed band by exacting tribute from passersby. A few thousand *afghanis* and a few *rials* did the job. Major Nafar smiled and bade farewell to his hosts.

A few miles south of New Deh he noticed a Black Hawk helicopter about three kilometers to his left and slightly behind him. It was not racing off somewhere as with the Apaches he saw outside the Kandahar airfield. It was unlikely it was watching him, but he couldn't shake the feeling. Off to his right, a second Black Hawk appeared. He pulled over and opened the hood. He checked the oil level and gauged the helicopters' response. They pulled back and went off in the distance, probably lurking behind the hills.

There was no doubt now that he was being followed and he had to form a new plan. No point going on to Calghor; that would only compromise his destination. After consulting the map, he thought it better to head down to Kakaran then make his way back to Kandahar.

Major Nafar drove into the village of Kakaran and asked locals about the roads and irrigation. He was, after all, acting as an aid officer and part of his job was to improve the lives of locals. Iranian aid programs were more in the western provinces but he had a plausible reason for being in the south, though not for what was hidden above the driveshaft. Tea with the *maliks* was followed by pleasant exchanges, capped with a long list of desperately needed items. Major Nafar, though hardly a haughty city-dweller, sensed that whatever anyone gave these men would soon be sold in a Pakistani marketplace.

He left in the late afternoon and headed for the main highway that led to Kandahar. A kilometer or two up the road, he saw a checkpoint that hadn't been there earlier in the day. As he got closer he saw that it wasn't manned by Afghans.

American marines.

In the mirror he could see a Black Hawk hovering, seemingly purposelessly, a kilometer behind him. He'd have to face the checkpoint. A young lieutenant politely greeted him through an interpreter who had the round face of an Uzbek. Ten marines stood around the vehicle, M-4s at the ready. The Uzbek asked in Dari for his papers and reason to be on the road in that area. Major Nafar had a prepared response and tried not to make it sound that way. Aid officers were common enough and even Iranian ones were extended courtesies.

The Uzbek and the marine lieutenant conferred just out of earshot.

After a moment, the lieutenant motioned for him to get out of the vehicle. Two marines looked under the SUV with mirrors fixed onto poles while a third looked through the back, knocking on the floor panels with a gloved hand. Nafar realized they knew what they were looking for and exactly where to find it. He was unarmed and there was no point in running. He was going to be taken prisoner by American marines.

Major Nafar was not well versed in the global media but he knew that in twenty-four hours or so the world would be talking about the Iranian officer captured in Afghanistan with a Misagh-2 surface-to-air missile in his vehicle. He was also beginning to understand something more about political intrigue and where a simple Basseri officer fit into foreign policy plotted up by Persian generals in Tehran.

Northern Yemen

In previous decades—and in previous centuries—tribal elders held council in an immense tent with woven rugs and salt bags laid across the ground. This meeting was in a house near the village of Dhahyan in northern Yemen, not far from the Saudi frontier. Yahia Badreddin al-Houthi and a few close relatives were first among equals there. They were close relatives of the fallen leader of the Shia insurgency that bore his name—the Houthis. The tribes of the area were fiercely independent and exceptionally well armed even by the high standards of Yemeni bedouin.

The Houthis had been warring against Sunni domination for many years. Before that, they'd fought the Egyptians, Saudis, and British. Still further back, they'd fought the Turks. Most had Kalashnikovs, others hefted venerable Lee-Enfields from the days of colonial rule. Some preferred the old British rifles because of their superior accuracy at long distances and ability to penetrate body armor. Others carried them because they'd been bequeathed to them by their grandfathers. War was a family tradition.

All the men at the council were angry. The old president in Sanaa went into exile, but little changed in the tribal areas. The former president's relatives and friends still controlled the state and military. They were precisely what the Saudis wanted: a pliant clique which would oppose democracy and which they could control through subsidies. That would prevent the spread of reform along its periphery and keep Yemen outside of Iranian influence. Neither democracy nor Iranian influence was of great interest to the Houthis. Their concerns were local independence. Inescapably, larger issues came to bear on them and they found themselves open to the entreaties from the Iranian Revolutionary Guard Corps.

Several IRGC officers had come and gone over the years without gaining much influence or respect. Now, however, Saudi aircraft were bombing the Houthis inside Yemeni territory. It was denied in the Saudi and Yemeni capitals, nonetheless the Houthi bands knew what they saw: Eurofighter Typhoons with the green sword and palm tree of the Royal Saudi Air Force. The pilots flew much too high to be accurate and older warriors grudgingly credited mercenary pilots of the seventies for being braver.

The IRGC officer promised Libyan SA-18s and Misagh-2s, which would send the Saudi pilots to even higher altitudes, perhaps back to Prince Soltan Airbase. The IRGC insisted on a sign of commitment from the Houthis: they were to strike deep inside Saudi Arabia and they would do so in the name of the Shia people.

The Houthi chieftain found unanimous support for striking inside Saudi Arabia. Every clan leader favored it and argued passionately for his own men to perform it. He thought it best for each clan to send five fighters—men skilled in the use of rocket launchers and explosives. That would balance off each clan's claim of having the men with the greatest skill and virility. Each of the nine clans would send a five-man team, ostensibly to visit Mecca and Medina. The men were permitted to spend time in the holy sites as most were unlikely to return.

They would be armed with weapons that the IRGC was transporting in a freighter to Port Sudan, just across the Red Sea. The weapons would soon be stored in a Saudi coastal town that was becoming increasingly important—Yanbu.

There were oil refineries and petrochemical plants in Yanbu which the Chinese recently completed. Pipelines from the Eastern Province on Saudi Arabia's coastline on the Persian Gulf brought crude to the refineries and chemical plants before flowing to the shipping terminals from which they went out to the economies of the world. The refineries and chemical plants were of course highly combustible; a few rocket-propelled grenades could make them massive infernos. Pipelines too were vulnerable, though more easily repaired. The Houthis would target Yanbu's refineries and chemical plants to punish the Saudis for supporting attacks on Iran.

The Arabian Sea

A Liberian-registered freighter plied the calm waters to the south of Pakistan after unloading electronic surveillance gear to the Indian navy at Karwar. It was returning with its holds only half-filled, chiefly with automotive parts manufactured by the Tata Group, an Indian conglomerate. The ship carried far more electronic equipment than an ordinary freighter and two of its holds were now set up with cots, shower stalls, and a medical clinic.

The ship passed the Pakistani ports of Karachi and Gwadar, listening for Chinese communications and searching for neutrino radiation. The latter would signal the proximity of nuclear warheads which some Mossad and CIA analysts thought might be sold to Saudi Arabia or at least positioned there. The neutrino signal was null. No one aboard truly expected a positive signal; it was just something they did while in the neighborhood, like beat cops checking the padlock on a back gate.

Sailing west, the ship passed a hundred kilometers to the south of the Iranian port of Chabahar. It was just listening there too, but it didn't hurt to look for neutrino signals while in the neighborhood. Again null.

The ship did not continue sailing west toward the Red Sea and home. It sailed south and came to a halt, its engines slowing to a rate only sufficient to produce enough electricity for the ship's operation. The surveillance gear was shut off to reduce the electromagnetic signature. A radio beacon was checked out but not turned on. A powerful strobe light was fastened atop the bridge but not illuminated.

The crew practiced lowering lifeboats and rowing out a kilometer. Periodically crewmen would jump into the water and the others would pull them into the boats. It was difficult at times in the heat and humidity, though there were light moments. One of the crew joked that there weren't any icebergs in the Arabian Sea. Another said he thought he saw Kate Winslet "dead ahead." The officer in charge let the men have their fun as long as they were getting their practice in. They all knew it was better duty than defending a makeshift landing site deep in Yemen's Empty Quarter where some men from their special forces unit were headed.

Eastern Yemen

Events in Yemen are often in the news and have been for decades. Few events touch the eastern half of Yemen which is called Rub' al Khali, or the Empty Quarter. It's arid and mountainous and to call it sparsely populated would not convey the emptiness and inhospitality. Moviemakers would love the region for its natural beauty, but they'd never get crews to stay there long. Movie stars would refuse to go at all, even Yemeni movie stars. They'd all prefer Death Valley in California or the Qattara Depression in the Libyan desert, except that the latter still had thousands of land mines that Rommel and Monty buried seventy years ago.

Eastern Yemen was mostly untouched by war because no one wanted it and it wasn't on the way to anything. Now it was on the way to something—Iran.

The desolation of the Empty Quarter made it ideal for a forward base, providing you could find an area with a flat hard surface to serve as a landing strip. There are many such places out there; it was simply a matter of sending recon teams to find them. At the eastern edge, not far from the Omani frontier, an elite Israeli *Sayeret Matkal* unit found a suitable landing strip on a gypsum plain about twenty miles south of the N5 highway. They'd been dropped off the Yemeni coast a few days earlier by a Liberian-registered freighter.

Satellite communications apprised the headquarters back home of the coordinates and two nights later, a C-130 cargo plane came in guided by the signal lights the reconnaissance team set up. The plane landed on the desert floor, rather ungently in the crew's experience, and rolled to a stop. The four props pitched to an angle to help slow the cargo-laden plane. The crew and *Sayeret Matkal* troops unloaded pallets of material and the C-130 was up and on its way home in less than an hour. Two more C-130s came in separately that night and unloaded more material.

The recon soldiers returned to their observation posts and tents and did what soldiers did the most. They waited.

"Osama bin Laden's father was from this part of Yemen," one soldier said.

"Yes, the old man went into the construction business in Saudi Arabia."

"An excellent career move. Too bad his son didn't go into the family business."

"I agree completely. That reminds me of the old joke about the rabbi whose son disappoints him."

"Oh yes. My father told me that joke."

"Was he a rabbi?"

"No, he was a colonel."

"Mine was a sergeant."

"I think I'll go into the construction business in Saudi Arabia."

"I'll stay in Israel, but Mazel tov with your new trade."

Iran . . . and Turkmenistan

Anthony stayed in the coffee shop and planned his exit from Iran. He hoped the departure would be graceful. He didn't want to be paraded around town while angry mobs jeered him and chanted "Death to America." He was worried that someone might strike up a conversation about the assassination the previous night, but last night's event made the street traffic light and gave the little shop a somber atmosphere that suited him.

The airports were out of the question, for obvious reasons. He thought of heading for a friendly embassy. Which one? The Brits were stalwarts but his briefing in Kurdistan noted that their embassy was closely watched and had been sacked recently. Britain didn't want to give cause for another break-in. Saudi Arabia or the Emirates? They weren't entirely trustworthy and at the very least would press an American for privileged information. Better to get out across the border. Which one?

He could head west to the Kurdish area of Iran, maybe by so mundane a method as a rented car. He still had a debit card from a Kirkuk bank with a tidy sum attached to it. Kurdish Iran was only a hundred miles away and it teemed with foreign intelligence officers. But security on the roads west would be tight and the same with the rail lines.

Southwest into the tribal areas where Tehran's writ was limited? A German spy rallied the tribes there against Tehran during World War One. "The German Lawrence," he was called. That scenario was appealing in some respects, ridiculous in most others. That German spy failed and the shah crushed the tribes for their sedition. The German spy spent the rest of his life delivering aid to them.

Decent guy. Rare in this line of work.

Southeast into Pakistan? He'd have to cross the Baloch region of Iran which was waging an insurgency against Tehran. Then he'd be in the Baloch region of Pakistan which was waging an insurgency against Islamabad. Too messy.

East was sounding good by a process of elimination and that meant Afghanistan or Turkmenistan. He'd been to the city of Zahedan in eastern Iran a few years back. There's an IRGC base nearby where they train Taliban guerrillas. It was well patrolled then and was probably more so now. Mashad lay in northeastern Iran. It's a rug-making town and according to his papers that was his occupation. Mashad wasn't far from the borders with Afghanistan and Turkmenistan and if you couldn't bribe your way across those borders, you were in the wrong business.

Afghanistan is embroiled in war. Turkmenistan is neutral. It's the Switzerland of Central Asia.

Anthony stopped in a convenience store near the station and purchased a three-pack of disposable razors, a bottle of water, and a small carrying bag—what GIs call an AWOL bag. He paid with cash. Every hour or so he felt the hem of his inside pocket for the two gold coins the Agency issued him for emergencies such as bribing border guards.

He also paid cash for a hotel room not far from the station. He picked up a schedule at the desk and saw that a train left for Mashad at six pm. The concierge said the train was never crowded, nonetheless Anthony walked to the station, purchased a round-trip ticket to be less conspicuous, and returned to the hotel. He found an outside wireless signal and keyed in another text message which though encrypted would still talk of rugs.

> Parvizian1962: Sidetrip to Mashad. Arrive morning. Thoughts
> on return appreciated.

He shaved, showered, then lay down to rest. He might have dozed for an hour but no more than that. A message alert woke him.

> Tajik shop in Mashad, papers, cross Taybad. Alternate: Sarakhs
> shop, cross Turkmenistan.

Choices, choices, choices. The Tajik "shop" was the Tajikistan consulate in Mashad where he could get papers to enter Afghanistan at the Taybad crossing. He served with ethnic Tajik troops in Afghanistan three years earlier and respected them. The problem was that the Tajiks liked Iran because of its help against the Russians and later against the Taliban. How loyal to the US would these Tajiks in Mashad be? How loyal to Iran would they be? The Sarakhs "shop" was a small border crossing into Turkmenistan.

Man, things get complicated when you're on the lam in Iran.

> Parvizian1962:
> Sarakhs shop more promising this day.

Fifty miles out, the Tehran skyline was no longer visible from the train. Anthony could see a dry rural landscape in the fading light. Herds of sheep could be seen here and there. He was reminded of his father's story of hitchhiking across Wyoming in the sixties and seeing herds of sheep with Basque wagons encamped along winding creeks and gullies.

There were more than a few stops and at some Persian women came aboard in traditional covering to sell tea, pistachios, and bread. Anthony partook and was pleased that their accents were as strange to city dwellers as his probably was. Still uncertain as to passing for an Iranian, he mused that he should wear a full *burkah* until he got out of Iran. Soheila, the fetching translator back in Langley, once gleefully mentioned that as a young woman in Algiers she would wear full traditional coverings then sneak over to a boyfriend's house. Not what the mullahs and virtue police had in mind.

Anthony bought a sweet roll from an elderly woman just as the train was about to head out. She smiled with the gentle eyes of simple piety and was embarrassed when her cell phone suddenly sounded. Railroads spread modernity wherever they're built in the world. Change was coming, probably faster than outsiders realized, probably faster than the old mullahs realized. Anthony wondered if a social scientist would someday calculate a connection between cell phone towers and the fall of dictatorships. There was a dissertation there.

He also wondered what influence his mission would have in the big scheme of things. That Karroubi fellow said what Anthony suspected before he landed in Kirkuk: the hotshots calculated that no former ranger and present-day CIA officer would fail to see evidence of a nuclear weapons program. Even if the evidence were not without ambiguity, his personal makeup and institutional perspectives would solidify suspicions into certainties and the hotshots would have what they wanted. Another war. But the hotshots didn't get the answer they wanted and Anthony suspected that they might just ignore him and they might just not promote him. Or they might just send him off to some obscure post.

A place like Turkmenistan.

Anthony felt he did the right thing and despite his predicament. He nodded off around two am as the train sped eastward toward Mashad.

He was again startled by the sound of metallic clicks.

The train pulled into Mashad shortly after eight am. Anthony had been awake for about an hour thinking about the border that lay ahead. He could offer some money to the border guards, maybe even a gold coin. That, however, might alert them and the assassination in Tehran almost certainly made every guard in the country more watchful and more ornery. The border was demarcated by a chain-link fence atop a sand berm and he was confident that within a couple of miles of the crossing there'd be an opening made by smugglers or kids. Or by a young woman in a hijab eager to see her boyfriend on the other side.

Security at the station was present, no doubt about that.

> Parvizian1962:
> Arrived Mashad.

There was a large map of the city and Anthony studied it along with other travelers. He saw a part of town with a number of consulates and spotted Tajikistan's. The consulate might be easier, Turkmenistan still felt better. Highway 22 wound about seventy-five miles from Mashad to the crossing at Sarakhs. He'd spend the day in Mashad and in the late afternoon hire a driver to take him to the border. When dusk came, he'd look around the fence for an opening and head for the town a few miles inside Turkmenistan. The town possessed the simple, unlikely, but appealing name of "Mary."

Mashad had its bazaars. The local rugs were thickly woven, with earth tones and floral motifs. Anthony had his fill of rugs and looked instead at silk scarves and tablecloths. A closer look revealed that many weren't from local artisans; they were from China. Well, Anthony figured, China has bought Iranian oil contracts stretching out to 2030 or more and was supporting Iran in the UN, so it pressed Iran to let its goods in.

The sanctions, however, were devastating the Iranian currency, making many imports too expensive and making merchants very upset—like those bazaaris in Tehran who were almost coming to blows with security forces. Anthony overheard a bazaari explain to a customer that expensive imports were making local goods more attractive. So the sanctions had the unintended result of helping Iranian artisanry. Another mental note for his report.

Down the way from the rugs and silken goods were livestock. Anthony walked along the wooden cages of ducks and shoats and lambs and despite the fetid smells, he felt himself fortunate to be able to see such exotica. He also felt hungry.

Lamb . . . I must celebrate my last day in Persia. Dinner for one.

He walked past an alleyway where several women stood about in a furtive manner recognizable to men the world over. They were veiled, somewhat, their eyes and lips more brightly hued than most women in Mashad and Tehran. It had been a while and he still had an hour or two . . .

Nah, dinner for one.

He smiled to the women but to their disappointment, he walked by.

Not far from the square he found *Sarab*, a well appointed restaurant with paintings of the rocky hills in the region. Old camel blankets and salt bags, both with distinctive tribal markings, graced the oak walls.

"A table for one, please. Near the back?"

As much as he wanted to enjoy the mutton and saffron rice, he couldn't put aside what lay ahead. What did lie ahead? The town of Mary, then the capital Ashgabat, then the embassy with a section staffed by Big Ten running backs. Then back to Kirkuk, Langley, and who knows what.

An office and a meaningless job. Or back to my low-rent zip code in south Texas.

"Crème brulée, please . . . and the check."

In a country enduring tough sanctions, you don't have to look hard for someone to drive you somewhere, even if it's seventy-five miles. Men with cars and meager incomes were all around the bazaar offering rides to those carrying rugs or a duck or two. It would enable them to continue to be men with cars a while longer.

"I need to go to Sarakhs before nightfall, my friends. Who can oblige me?" Anthony called out to three men standing beside their cars. Two of them looked at each other and shook their heads. Perhaps it was too far that late in the day and their wives would be angry or suspicious if they came home after nine. One of the men said the curfew was strictly enforced because of an assassination in Tehran.

A portly middle-aged man leaning against a red four-door Saipa smiled courteously and opened a rear door.

"Ahmad Pejman, sir. My name is Ahmad Pejman. Because of curfew, it will cost more."

"And I am Agrin Saleh from Kirkuk, as my accent might already have revealed. I want to see the Ersari rugs of Turkmenistan in the village of Mary. It seems I only have euros just now. I hope one hundred will be enough." The astonishment in Ahmad's eyes made it clear that it would do quite well. He didn't even try to haggle for more lest another driver step in.

Highway 22 winds across rugged arid terrain that reminded Anthony of eastern Arizona though without the astonishing blues and greens embedded in the stratified rock. He closed his eyes for a while to get a little rest for the night ahead. Ahmad looked at him in the mirror from time to time.

"Is it possible for you to drive me to Mary this night? There would of course be a consideration for such additional help." Anthony knew this was unlikely; he was thinking ahead.

"Sir, the border guards will insist you use a driver from Turkmenistan. I assure you our guards do the same."

"As do ours in Kurdistan. I also worry that the border guards will take advantage of a foreign merchant . . . as of course would those in my country. Oh, Ahmad, if only we were border guards. What rewards we'd reap for ourselves and our wives!"

Ahmad laughed, in part because of the truth in his joke, in part because he knew what he was asking.

"Yes, about two miles south from the crossing, just east of the airfield. The fence is cut—for honest vulnerable merchants like you, of course."

Anthony smiled, closed his eyes, and went into a half sleep for forty minutes.

Turkmenistan . . .

He opened his eyes and saw Ahmad looking at him in the mirror. "You have heard the horrible news from Tehran a few days ago?" the driver asked.

"Yes, I was near Tehran that night. Just south of it really, in a small town called Pakdasht where we store our rugs before returning to Kurdistan."

"Such things are done by the MeK . . . in your country," he added pointedly.

Anthony paused. He shouldn't have mentioned being anywhere near Tehran. Ahmad was probably just frustrated by the repeated bombings. "I am from the Kurdish north, my friend. The MeK is in the south near Baghdad. We hope to be completely free of Baghdad soon . . . and have cordial relations with all our neighbors. Especially with our good friends in Iran."

"But the US and Israel are behind this, no?"

"That may be so, but I am a merchant not a politician. And I am thankful for that, Ahmad!"

"The Kurds are Sunni, no?"

Anthony doubted he was hiding his discomfort. "We have many Shia among us, but yes, we are mostly Sunni. We are all one though. This I believe." Anthony waved his arm for emphasis.

Ahmad was no longer looking at him in the mirror to gauge his responses to the conversation, he was scrutinizing him, studying his face with the innate suspiciousness of a rural-dweller bolstered by sectarianism and nationalism.

"Is that the airport you spoke of ahead on the left?"

"Yes, that is Sarakhs' humble airport."

"My crossing should be just off to the right then."

"Yes, two kilometers." Ahmad spoke more slowly.

The Saipa came to a stop and Anthony handed Ahmad the hundred euros. He stepped out of the car with his AWOL bag and bade farewell. Ahmad drove off wordlessly then turned around to head back to Mashad. Anthony looked about at the dry rocky area and walked east. It was getting dark and he could barely make out the fence atop a berm off in the distance. He looked behind him, saw the Saipa drive past, and waved. Ahmad saw him but did not wave back.

Anthony walked briskly. When he looked again at the road he saw that Ahmad was not heading for Mashad. He was turning into the airport. Anthony figured he was either trying to get a fare into Mashad or he was going to report a suspicious passenger to security.

Anthony continued his pace and prepared to break into a run at any moment. He walked through increasingly dark fields then crossed a small road marked Highway 99. Only an occasional car and motorcycle came by. Yes, he could see the border less than a half mile away. Maybe a twenty minute walk at his pace and on the stony terrain. There was still a little light. Good and bad. He could see the opening better but a patrol could see him better. His gold coins would help on the Turkmenistan side, not on the Iranian side. Not so soon after an assassination.

Halfway between the road and the border Anthony heard a truck. If he was at a train station or on a street corner, he'd give the rug dealer story. Heading for the border was another matter. Better to go for the fence. He'd be hard to see and he decided to make himself even harder to detect by crouching a bit. Crawl? It would slow him down too much. Life is all about tradeoffs. If the truck drove by, that meant they weren't looking for him. If it stopped around where Ahmad would have told him he'd be . . . well, that taxi fare would be the worst hundred euros he'd ever spent.

The truck slowed and turned to the right, aiming its high-beams about forty yards to his right. A searchlight came on and sent a sharp beam sweeping across the field. Anthony hit the dirt as it neared him. It swept off to his left without stopping.

As he got up to run he heard commands barked out. Farther behind came the "whump-whump" noise of a helicopter lifting up from the airfield. As the rotor noise came closer he detected a lack of rhythm and concluded that more than one chopper was coming in on him. A searchlight was arcing back toward him and he dived down, again eluding it.

He got up and raced for the wire, dropping the AWOL bag. Another searchlight came on and swept across the berm, illuminating the shiny metal fence. On its third sweep, he saw a section of fence that had been cut with a top section hanging down.

Turkmenistan.

Anthony stumbled up the berm, his feet sinking into the soft dirt and sand. Both searchlights were now sweeping the berm and he saw the beams coming for him and send his shadow onto the ground and wire. He thought of the time as a boy when the police chased him, two friends, and three majorettes from a swimming pool they'd broken into.

Yellowish-green tracers flew past him followed by the distinctively deep reports of Kalashnikov fire. Maybe three on semiautomatic, a fourth on rock 'n roll. Even a small Beretta would come in handy right now. They'd at least be reluctant to stand still to take careful aim.

Get out of Dodge!

He lowered his shoulder and crashed through the cut section of the fence and rolled down the hill into a neutral country. He felt the adrenalin surge through him and recalled that after a firefight and the adrenalin surge stopped, a chemical reaction ensued and brought welcome giddiness. He looked forward to that post-combat high again.

He soon suspected that the Iranian security detachment would show as much respect for Turkmenistan's sovereignty as his organization was showing Iran's. He righted himself and headed for the road to the north—the road that led to Mary. There was the barking of more orders then the clanging of the fence wire as men scurried awkwardly through the opening. The helicopters whirred overhead and sent their searchlights into the fields across the fence, though the birds themselves stayed west of the line, inside Iran.

If I die in a combat zone

Box me up and ship me home.

Anthony reached some cultivated fields whose cotton plants offered a little cover. A mile ahead was a road with a streetlight or two. A truck was coming south from Mary. More tracers lashed nearby, some close enough to sound like angry bees, followed instantly by the distinctive jack-hammer-like bangs of Kalashnikovs as the speed of sound chased the speed of bullets. One of the searchlights found him and easily tracked him.

He felt a hammer blow on the fleshy part of his side just above the waist, heard a distinct "thump" followed by searing pain, and fell into a row of cotton plants. He'd heard the sickening sound of a bullet hitting a man before and knew this time it wasn't one of his men who'd been shot.

Off to my right I see five mounted cowboys . . .

Anthony struggled and righted himself but after a few steps he fell down the embankment of a reservoir then crawled along the waterline toward the road and the truck. Throbbing pain was coming from his wound. There were sharp jabs too as his movement tore additional tissue along the bullet's path. The truck, he thought, might be a Turkmen patrol that would cause the Iranians to head back across the fence. The Iranians reached the lip above the reservoir and a couple of flashlights probed along the muddy waterline until they found Anthony.

He got up and stumbled along the edge of the water. More Kalashnikov rounds shot into the water sending up vicious geysers. Splashing noises mixed with the dull bangs of rifle shots. Another round hit his back, ripping through his upper shoulder and violently expelling the air from his lungs.

Falling to the ground, he summoned his remaining will and strength but could only get to his knees before falling down in an unfamiliarly clumsy way. Another effort got him to his knees again and his left foot was pushing him upward when all his strength left him and his face smacked noisily into the muck. Anthony gasped a mixture of blood, air, and mud, and awaited the next shots.

He thought of the radio traffic on the doomed Iraqi tank, then heard a click.

The Samson Heuristic

The Samson Program did many operations without human supervision. Indeed, the system learned and grew faster than the programmers comprehended and acted. This was especially the case in times of crisis when data flows were high, analytic sections overworked, and even the most brilliant human minds had to think carefully how a decision might play out.

The Samson programmers hoped to control or at least moderate the aggressive impulses of states. Alas, they were becoming more numerous and less predictable. The bulk of world affairs was once structured by a handful of powers. No more. The political calculations and machinations of a handful of statesmen had been replaced by those of a dozen or more leaders and bureaus. Driven by ideological zeal, overconfidence in weaponry, and advisers of dubious judgment and character, they acted less cautiously, less predictably, and all too often, less rationally than did their predecessors.

A conjuncture of events in Iran, Afghanistan, and the Gulf brought a new crisis and unprecedented demands on Samson. An heuristic went into operation—a shortcut created by the programmers to handle a cascade of information that the Program could not absorb and analyze and respond to in a timely manner. Heuristics are everywhere in computers, we use them everyday. We just don't know it—until something goes wrong.

This particular heuristic had been made at Samson's creation and was meant to be only temporary. The programmer who designed it, Ahmed Ferrahan, intended to replace it with a more precise one that would function almost flawlessly in the most complex scenarios. However, he died of natural causes before he was able to make good on his intention.

The heuristic responded to the new crisis in the Persian Gulf quite well at first. Driven by an urgent request to receive huge amounts of data from so many parts of the world, Samson gathered almost all of its units. Systems halted for a few picoseconds to comply. No human could perceive a delay of a few trillionths of a second. In the next few hours, internal diagnostic programs reported an anomaly to network managers who looked at the data and simply shrugged. It was a hi-tech equivalent of a house making a creaking noise in the night or a tectonic plate making a subtle shift perceptible to only the most sensitive of seismic gear.

The Samson heuristic had assumed control. Decision units could not act without its approval. One decision was fed back into the analysis units which in turn issued a new set of instructions to decision units and, unfortunately, the chain of scenarios and decisions locked the massive Samson Program into this single heuristic—this single flawed heuristic. Human oversight was gone. The heuristic was in charge.

This was not what the bold, imaginative, and idealistic programmers had intended when they designed the tiny chip section and vast communication system. They had hoped to limit the power of national leaders but now their Program—a very minute part of it, really—had assumed control. It would take some time for the programmers to realize what the Program was doing. It would take longer still for it to be fixed by them—or by someone else who'd come to comprehend the Program.

The Program collided with human error in the world. Better put, it collided with human *folly* in the world. There was no shortage of that as the US, Israel, and Iran stumbled along on a path whose ending point they each understood differently than the others did. Grave blunders had taken place in southern Afghanistan and along the Iran-Turkmenistan border. State blunders collided with state lies and the crisis deepened.

Planes and ships and troops were on the move, in the US, Israel, Iran, and most of the states in the Persian Gulf. The Samson heuristic responded in a manner that angered and terrified those nominally in charge of all the military hardware. It periodically shut down their systems.

Instead of controlling war, Samson was about to start one.

New Mexico

Barrett sat down in the Albuquerque studio, looked into the camera, and listened to the anchor in Qatar run down the troubling events.

Anchor: For more on the unfolding Iranian crisis, we're pleased to have Barrett Parker with us again. The US is expressing outrage over the firing of an Iranian-made missile at a US helicopter near Kandahar. What's the significance of this?

Barrett: There have been longstanding worries about the Taliban receiving Iranian Misagh-2s or Russian SA-18s out of Colonel Qaddafi's arsenals in Libya which have been pouring into world markets. US troops found—rather conveniently, I'd say—an expended Misagh-2 tube and an IRGC officer officer nearby.

Anchor: What do you say "rather conveniently"?

Barrett: It strikes me as too pat. An IRGC officer might deliver such a weapon to the Taliban but it's unlikely he'd fire it himself—or be anywhere near it when it was fired. Highly unlikely.

Anchor: Can you say more about these Iranian Misagh-2s?

Barrett: Certainly. Iran purchased several Stingers from a mujahideen warlord during the Russian war, reverse engineered them, and made thousands of copies. Voila, the Misagh-2s. However, I don't believe Iran would be so unwise as to give large numbers of such weapons to the Taliban. Iran opposes the Taliban but wants to warn the US of what will follow from an attack on Iran.

Anchor: And what do you think would follow in Afghanistan if Iran were attacked?

Barrett: More arms would go to the Taliban—in quantity and quality. Enough to cause the US severe headaches.

Anchor: Could this alter the war in Afghanistan?

Barrett: I don't think so. The Stingers played only a minor role in the Russian war and—

Anchor: Sorry to interrupt, but why do say the Stingers played only a minor role?

Barrett: There's no evidence that Soviet aircraft losses went up significantly after the Stingers were introduced. That's folklore, a publicity campaign by intelligence organizations. If Iran gave the Taliban such missiles it would simply mean a longer war—and one with more casualties.

Anchor: What do you make of Iran's capture of a CIA officer, armed with a Beretta pistol—a standard Mossad sidearm—as he fled Tehran after an Iranian physicist was assassinated?

Barrett: Iran claims that he speaks Farsi and English—with an American accent and that he had forged identity papers for a Kurdish rug dealer. If he's an American, it's unlikely he was involved with the assassination.

Anchor: Why is that?

Barrett: The bombings and assassinations are the work of Israeli intelligence and an Iranian group called the Mujahideen-e-Khalk, or MeK. That's a group that until recently was on the US State Department's list of terrorist organizations.

Anchor: Isn't the CIA highly skilled at assassinations?

Barrett: If that were so, we'd have to wonder why Fidel Castro is still alive. We'd also have to wonder why Saddam Hussein stayed around so long.

The anchor could not hide his amusement, even though Barrett was serious.

Anchor: Yes, I see. So we have the Iranian missile in Afghanistan and possibly an American agent in Iran, both under strange circumstances. What's the fallout so far?

Barrett: The US has deployed a squadron of F-22 fighters to the Emirates and is sending a second aircraft carrier, *USS Enterprise*, into the Gulf. For its part, the Iranian Revolutionary Guard Corps has been demonstrating its ability to attack shipping in the Strait of Hormuz, through which a large portion of the world's oil flows.

Anchor: Is Iran capable of closing the Strait of Hormuz?

Barrett: It can make it dangerous, especially if it has the Chinese Sizzler missiles. After some shooting and a few sea mines, the insurance companies will order the tankers to drop anchor and wait things out. Meanwhile, oil markets would be roiled.

Anchor: Are world oil markets concerned now?

Barrett: A little. The North Sea and West Texas benchmarks are up about two dollars a barrel. That's not a big move. It feels like it's just a few outfits taking up defensive positions and of course speculators going along for the ride.

Anchor: Thank you so much. Events are certainly changing rapidly in that part of the world. We're going to go now to Farrah Esmail for a look at sports.

"Thanks again, Barrett," Khadija said from the network center in Qatar, less vivaciously than usual. "Barrett, is the man held in Tehran with the CIA?"

"I can't say for sure. Most of them look like pro athletes. Let's ask Farrah."

"Barrett, I'm from the Middle East, not the Mediterranean or America, but I thought he looked *Italian*. Aren't you part Italian?"

"I'm half Italian. Ciao, cara mia."

"I *love* that song!"

Barrett laughed as he removed the mike and earpiece.

The Persian Gulf

A Yellow Shirt guided the F/A-18 Super Hornet along the deck of USS *Abraham Lincoln* until it connected to the catapult system, causing a rough thump inside the cockpit. The young pilot lit the fearsome afterburners, signaled the Cat Officer he was ready, and waited to be hurled into the sky. He and his radar officer braced themselves for the sudden shock. The Cat Officer gave his signal and the two men were propelled from motionlessness to 165 knots in three seconds.

"Take that, you surly bonds" the pilot boasted as he quickly performed a score of instrument reads called for in the seconds after takeoff. They flew low above the Persian Gulf and headed for Bushehr on a reconnaissance mission—a "recce" as it was called.

"Tell me again why we need to do this?" the radar officer asked. "There's nothing we're going to film that can't be seen from a satellite."

"There's nothing that can't be seen from Google Earth," came the pilot's instant reply. "You know we're just testing the air defenses—and annoying the Iranians."

"Then why don't we fly over the Ayatollah's house with the burners lit?"

"Stout yeoman! Say about three am?"

"Affirmative."

"Alas, Tehran's a little far away."

"You're no fun."

"Affirmative. Maybe for your birthday."

"I'll be good."

They neared the coast about two miles south of Bushehr about five hundred feet off the deck, avoiding the small fishing vessels below as much as possible. They shut off the burners shortly after launch but even regular exhaust at that altitude kicked up spectacular twenty-foot walls of seawater. The fishermen were in awe as the fighter thundered over them in a blink of the eye and the ensuing three-foot wake rocked their small wooden crafts. As they neared the coast, the F/A-18 climbed to three thousand feet.

"Skipper, Iranian ground radar has us. They won't fire surface-to-surface missiles at us, not yet, but there are two Iranian fighters to the north heading our way. A hundred and fifty miles out and closing."

"What are they?"

"Not sure yet . . . MiG29s . . . just a sec . . . nope. They're F-14 Tomcats."

"So maybe it's Tom Cruise. Isn't he a Shia?"

"He's a Scientologist."

"I get them confused . . . How far to the coast?"

"Three minutes. Will turn on cameras anon, good sir. Maybe Val Kilmer is a Shia."

"I'm sure you're right. I read it somewhere on the Internet."

After taking photos for the navy and a few for themselves with personal cameras, they headed for a lake about ninety miles northeast of the nuclear reactor. From there, they would gather more electronic data on the Iranian air defense system. They were being tracked, though not very well.

"Skip, my man, we're not getting anything on the bad guys' system. It looks like they turned it off."

"Maybe they're trying to draw us in deeper."

"You're not . . . "

The pilot veered east and headed for the haze on the horizon below—the city of Shiraz.

"We'll just stop in to say hello then head home toody-sweet. Where are Tom Cruise and Val Kilmer?"

"They're heading in our general direction but don't seem to have a fix on us. That's unusual."

"Maharlu Lake at two o'clock. We'll kiss it then head back home."

"Affirmative . . . If I said 'negative' would it have mattered?"

"Negative."

"I'm just along for the ride then."

"Affirmative."

In a moment the F/A-18 was over the lake and banking sharply to the right until they were heading west. The two aviators could see the haze comprising sand and humid air above the deep blue of the Gulf. That meant safety.

"Has their system come back on yet?"

"Negative . . . and the Tomcats are still not tracking us very well. Looks like they're using onboard radar only . . . and we've all heard what that stuff was like on Tomcats. They're heading for the coastline."

"They'll fly down the coast, looking for us."

"They'll come damn close."

The F/A-18 reached the coast as the Iranian Tomcats were about eight miles up the coast.

"Can they see us?"

"Probably . . . yeah, they're peeling out to us. I don't know their Rules of Engagement today."

"Maybe they don't either, and that can be a problem. We'll be home soon. They won't come in on an American carrier group. Anyhow, we can hit the afterburners for a few minutes."

"Ah, afterburners . . . the dumbass pilot's best friend."

The pilot started the mechanism that sent fuel into exhaust flames and made the F/A-18 half jet, half rocket. They felt the sudden burst of speed and saw an instantaneous cloud of condensation as they broke the sound barrier. A moment later, they saw two bursts of condensation to the north as the Iranian F-14s lit their burners. They could not close on the faster F/A-18 though.

About fifty miles from the carrier, the US pilot shut off the burners. They used too much fuel, as did flying at low altitude. Furthermore, the F/A-18 might have to orbit *Abraham Lincoln* for a while. They might even miss the wire, or "bolter," a few times, requiring them to blast back up to altitude then circle for another landing attempt. That used up a lot of gas.

"Something's wrong, Skip. There should have been a IFF signal by now for us and our Tomcat friends . . . who are still only a few miles behind us, by the by. I don't see a refueling aircraft up either. I hear there's a filling station in Bahrain."

"It's a little far off and my credit card's in the other suit. Try raising the boat."

"Red Duke, Red Duke. Python 202 coming for recover . . . Red Duke, Red Duke. Python 202 coming for recover."

On the fourth try, they got a crackly response from the Air Boss on an open frequency.

"Python 202, this is Red Duke. Be advised we are in the dark now. Same with others."

"We have two Tomcats behind us, Red Duke."

"We can't see them, Python 202. Tom Cruise and friend?"

"Uhhh . . . not sure just this moment. Now about our homecoming."

"Do not come in, Python. I say again, do not come in. We need to apprise escort ships of friendlies with bad guys on tail even if we have to use signal lamps."

"Affirmative, will orbit group—*slowly*. Is there a refueling plane up?"

"Negative on the refueling plane, Python. Cannot launch—captain's orders."

The fighter went back to internal commo.

"Skipper, the boat can't see the Tomcats. Will the Tomcats see the escort ships before the shooting starts?"

"I'll let you know in a few. They might sense that the ships are blind and want to test us and that could start some shooting."

"So there are three dumbass pilots over the Gulf today?"

"At *least*."

The Iranian Tomcats peeled off and headed back to Iran only five miles from the first Aegis cruiser, which detected them visually and could only have fired gatling guns had they come nearer. The F/A-18 flew around the ships slowly, dipping its wings cautiously and diligently avoiding an attack profile. The escort vessels gave them a pass. The radio officer heard pops and static and thought the commo was now working.

"Red Duke, Red Duke. Python 202 coming in."

"Python 202, that's an affirmative," came the voice of the landing officer. "Call the ball, Python 202."

The FA/18 came up to *Abraham Lincoln*'s stern and caught the second hook which took them to a dead stop in a few jarring seconds. The crew climbed down and headed to the flight room for debriefing.

The US navy had suffered a systemwide blackout. That was a major concern, on the carrier, at Fifth Fleet in Bahrain, and at the Pentagon. When the electronic data from the F/A-18 was analyzed and the pilots were fully debriefed, it appeared that Iran too had suffered blackouts. Everyone was baffled—and worried.

There was another matter. The pictures the F/A-18 took over the Bushehr site were studied by experts on board *Abraham Lincoln* who found a disconcerting image. They sent the pictures to Fifth Fleet, which in turn sent them on to Centcom and the Pentagon. Upper-echelon analysts confirmed what the carrier's analysts thought from the start. There was a missile site being built just south of Bushehr. It wasn't a surface-to-air system. Intelligence sections interpreted the images as Chinese anti-ship missiles—Sizzlers.

The navy has no defense against Sizzlers and Washington had already ordered another carrier into the Persian Gulf. *Enterprise* would pass through the Strait of Hormuz tomorrow morning and by early afternoon it would come within a hundred miles of Bushehr.

Washington, DC

Joseph Burkett, the Middle Eastern honcho at the National Security Council, called Barrett through an encrypted connection to get an outside-the-Beltway perspective. They knew each other from grad school in Chicago where they exchanged views on foreign policy in a few seminars and informal gatherings. Barrett saw Joe as a decent chap but given to a less than critical views on military intervention, which was part of the culture of grad students and professors in the national security field. They appalled Barrett.

Joe was beginning to see most recent military intervention as unrelated to national security, costly in lives and money, and more often than not, filled with unforeseen but foreseeable consequences—most of them adverse if not calamitous. The wars in Iraq and Afghanistan cooled Joe's zeal for intervention and the prospect of war with Iran alarmed him. The same could not be said of most of the people in the administration, think tanks, and congress. They remained imbued with the interventionist creed and provided a powerful tailwind for a war policy.

Barrett saw an incoming call. He thought it was another oil trader seeking his perspective on the Middle East situation.

"Barrett, it's a disaster-in-waiting up here," Joe said with more concern than excitement. "*Enterprise* is nearing the Persian Gulf, supposedly to replace *Abraham Lincoln,* but they're both staying there."

"Two carriers in the Gulf?"

"Affirmative. And we're looking to send a third," Joe added.

"I sense there's more going on. The oil markets certainly do."

"There *is* more. The Pentagon is finalizing plans for a bombing campaign in northwestern Iran—roads, bridges, IRGC depots."

"They want to cut off the Kurdish areas from the rest of the country and encourage an insurrection to break away from the country." Barrett had suspected such a campaign after speaking with an Iranian émigré who'd been to a conference funded by the Alliance For A Free Kurdistan. "The Syrian Kurds will then break away from Damascus and the Iraqi Kurds will support them both."

"Yep, that's the general idea. It's starting to happen already, probably with Israel's encouragement. Speaking of which, Israel has anchored freighters to Iran's south and its cargo planes are landing in eastern Yemen." Joe's voice was flat, almost resigned to the inevitable.

"The freighters are rescue ships for Israeli fighters shot up over Iran. And they're setting up a refueling base in Yemen for the others," Barrett crisply figured. It was falling into place.

"The others returning from Natanz, Fordo, and Parchin. The smoking ruins, I should say."

"Any chance the Israeli planes will refuel in Saudi Arabia, Joe? Or *over* Saudi Arabia?"

"The Saudis are getting cold feet. They worry that the tribes will revolt if the government is seen helping Israel, and half the damn army is made up of tribal militias. Some of the mullahs might call for rebellion for collaborating with the US and Israel. You know, Big Satan, Little Satan."

"What about an Israeli commando strike, Joe? Another Entebbe."

"Maybe. There's talk of it going 'round, though I doubt it. The Iranian Republican Guards aren't airport cops."

"Do the big shots in Washington know where this will lead?" Barrett asked.

"I don't think so," Joe sighed. "Once the bureaucracy gets the war signal, everyone plods along with their little piece of the project. Discouraging words are . . . well, discouraged, stifled, crushed. In most cases, those who utter them are shown the door. They trust the people above them—or claim to—and the gears keep a-turnin'. Hell, you've seen these people at conferences."

"They want their goddam pensions."

"That's not fair, Barrett. They also want to pay their goddam mortgages. You should hear the generals. The 'shootin' match,' as they like to call it, will be all over in a week or so. Some of us see protracted fighting in the Strait of Hormuz. The IRGC will play the long game. Intermittent attacks on shipping and letting the world pay an additional forty dollars a barrel for oil. The world will come down hard on us."

"And a regional campaign of assassinations and bombings?"

"Regional, maybe global. The IRGC was assassinating enemies across Europe back in the eighties. They've been sloppy in recent months. They'll improve. Putting a bullet into someone's head on a street corner in Europe or Asia or South America isn't that difficult."

"What about the wargaming of an Iranian attack on our carriers? I've heard that swarming tactics might prove effective."

"Where did you hear that, Barrett? That's inside stuff. Recent too."

"I live out in the middle of nowhere. I think a wolf told me."

"Well, tell Jesse to keep his snout shut."

"*You* tell him," Barrett taunted as he looked over to his sleeping friend.

"No thanks. He's a big dude. Yes, if Iran goes all out with its missiles and planes, they might just overwhelm our defenses and hit a carrier—badly."

"Badly as in fires or badly as in we lose a carrier."

Joe exhaled audibly. "Badly as in we lose a carrier."

"The American public will go berserk. They'll demand vengeance."

"That they will indeed do, Barrett my friend."

"What about inside Iran? What will happen there?"

"The intelligence people and generals think the reform movement will rise up and the mullahs will fall. I doubt it."

"I doubt it too." Barrett had heard that rosy scenario on a cable news station he watched solely to hear the voice of virtuous costless intervention.

"I see the IRGC taking power. The country will become a military dictatorship. That's what the folks at State think."

"Yes, Joe, and large parts of the Iranian public will accept it as a necessary response to external danger. Reform inside Iran will be put off a decade or more. My wolf thinks that too."

"Here's something Jesse doesn't know, Barrett. We're having trouble with our military systems—missiles, communications, air defenses. The whole nine yards. Even at fleet headquarters in Bahrain, Centcom in Florida, and Prince Soltan in Saudi Arabia. No one knows who or what's doing it. Blackouts have hit twice in the last forty-eight hours and each one lasted thirty minutes."

"Solar flares?" Barrett offered, though he knew this was well out of his field.

"No evidence of any such things in recent days. Besides, the blackouts last *precisely* thirty minutes and solar flares don't watch the clock."

"Iran doesn't have such capability, does it?" Barrett asked.

"Nope. Neither does China—or so we think. These blackouts have people uptight to say the least. Some folks say we need to be cautious. Others say we need to strike soon while we can. Caution seems to be winning out but only because we're getting indications that Iran is having the same troubles. Barrett, it's getting dicey up here."

"So maybe *their* people will also argue for striking while *they* can— against a carrier." Barrett made a quick look on Bloomberg. "Joe, oil futures are still going up sharply."

"Barrett, you're not going to remind me that you told me to buy shares in PAMD back in '92, are you?"

"No, I'll hold off just now. I suggest you hold off on things too."

"I'll need help." Joe's voice conveyed exhaustion nearing despair.

"Joe, remember the National Intelligence Estimate process we heard at one of Harrington's seminars at the Center for World Affairs?"

"Yes, of course I do. The NIEs are hammered out behind the scenes by intelligence bosses who sometimes go out of their way to influence policy even though that's supposed to be up to elected officials."

"Even if it means going against the generals and the president."

"Yeah, Barrett, even if it means going against the generals and the president. I've been thinking about that. There's a bunch of us up here who talk—informally, carefully—at lunches and at the gym. Maybe we can start a bureaucratic insurgency."

"Joe, remember Harrington said the Pentagon pushed back against Reagan when he ordered them to draw up plans for invading Nicaragua?"

"Yeah, but that was when American generals were reluctant to go to war. Vietnam syndrome was still in effect. They kept putting the White House off by saying the plans were still in the works."

"The officers who came of age in Vietnam are retired, replaced by guys who think everything's another Grenada or Gulf War One—quick and easy. These guys think they can do anything. So naive. So 1960s-ish. Bring me up if you think I can help, Joe. I'll talk to the wolves out here."

"You know, Barrett, I'm sure you will."

"One more thing, Joe. Has China sold any Sizzlers to Iran?"

"Oh Lord, I can't say for sure. The navy thinks it sees a Sizzler base near Bushehr. If they do . . . and they fire them . . . "

"Then we might lose a carrier."

"Barrett, if they fire Sizzlers, we *will* lose a carrier. Maybe two."

Whiteman Air Force Base, Missouri

The air crews of the 509th Bomber Group had been briefed and were busily inspecting their B-2s before takeoff. They were bound for Diego Garcia, the Indian Ocean base that the US built in the seventies after it was determined, quite astutely, that the Persian Gulf was a likely place of conflict in coming years. Diego Garcia lies about three thousand miles from the Strait of Hormuz. It was a little farther to the Iranian nuclear sites. A long distance by some measures, a short hop for B-2s.

Air crews don't simply climb aboard their craft and roll down the airstrip until they gain liftoff speed. There are thousands of tests to run on those immense beasts. Everything from the electronic countermeasures to the rubber on the tires, from the avionics to what the crew called "amenities." At least that's what they called them in polite company. The plane, after all, was often in the air for twelve hours or more and they didn't come down for rest stops.

Generals, congressmen, and a few Middle Eastern dignitaries were on hand for the occasion. It was an exciting look inside the machinery of war. The faces of the politicians and foreign guests gleamed with awe on seeing the hulking black planes and the purposeful activities of the crews. For them, the military was something they funded and boasted about. Personal military experience was rare.

Ground crews were testing out the fuel pumps, hydraulics, and hatch seals when attention suddenly shifted to armament crews towing twenty-foot-long cylinders, fins on the side, pop-out propeller blades on the rear. The Massive Ordnance Penetrators recently arrived from White Sands. Each B-2 was being armed with two of them, adding a beastly thirty tons to the takeoff weight.

One air crew stopped its preflight routine to supervise an armament team about to hoist two of the gigantic weapons into the retrofitted bomb bays. The pilot looked over the MOPs carefully as the armaments crew attached clamps and prepared to winch them into place. Beneath the United States Air Force stenciling, someone had written "Hi There!" and "Dear Iran!" with a blue Sharpie. Several in the B-2 crew laughed heartily at the unauthorized scribbling and the unmistakable message for Iran, though of course no one there would ever see the graffiti. It was just something the ordnance crews saw in a war movie. Similar messages had been painted on torpedoes fired into Japanese freighters and bombs dropped onto German cities.

The pilot recognized the messages' provenance but did not appreciate the humor. He motioned to a senior NCO in the ground crew and asked him to take the graffiti off his ordnance. The crew chief was momentarily puzzled but quickly complied as he knew a terse order could swiftly ensue. A rag with a little solvent took the messages right off. The armament crews looked around and saw the other MOPs being hoisted into the bomb bays with the witticisms in place.

"There's always a hardass in the group," one of the ground crew whispered.

"Yeah, and we always get assigned the hardass's bird."

"I heard there was a pinup of Rita Hayworth on one of the atomic bombs back in the forties," replied another.

Halfway across the Atlantic, the B-2s made their first refueling from a KC-135 tanker plane that flew out of Andrews AFB, Maryland. The tanker lowered its basket and hose then the B-2 engaged it and took a big drink without so much as a burp. As they reached the Nigerian coast, the copilot felt up to asking why the pilot had ordered the graffiti removed from the MOPs. The pilot paused before answering, trying to find a way to reprimand and at the same time to instruct.

"This isn't a football game, young captain," came the pilot's stern but controlled voice. "This is a war and in case you didn't learn it in school, lives are lost in wars. Americans lives, Iranian lives. Neither is anything to joke about or boast about. Wars don't play out the way they're called in the Pentagon. You and I and everyone else aboard may be dead in a few days, lying in some godforsaken Iranian desert. It's happened before. You keep your mind on your mission, not on a big talk at the Officer's Club." Realizing he was on the commo system, he added, "And that goes for every one of you . . . every one of us."

The copilot acknowledged his words slowly, "Yes sir." The entire crew heard the brief exchange with sobering effects.

An hour later, the navigator came on the internal commo with a rendezvous point with the next KC-135 over the Indian Ocean. Shortly thereafter, the communications officer reported that he was unable to raise Diego Garcia.

"A blackout," the pilot noted pointlessly.

"Yes sir. Another one," came the commo officer's worried reply.

Centcom et al

The blackouts caused alarm in the eighty-five military facilities the US has around the world. Each was hit by thirty-minute blackouts and each was baffled as to the cause. IT experts ran tests and consulted with peers in intelligence services that were also hit. No one could understand let alone solve the problem. Nonetheless, IT staff assured their bosses that everything would be up again soon. The systems were indeed back up soon, but another blackout struck a few hours or a day later.

The IT personnel checked with major private companies and found that they were not having the same problem. Some, however, reported that unspecified subsidiaries were experiencing trouble. Though they declined to elaborate, it was thought defense-related subsidiaries were hit, especially those that handled military communications and maintenance on sophisticated weaponry.

Centcom was in disarray. The sprawling military center near Tampa, Florida, had lost communication with the Fifth Fleet in Bahrain, a regional command center in Qatar, fighter squadrons in the United Arab Emirates, intelligence assets in Kurdistan, and ground forces from Sinai to Afghanistan. One blackout came at a particularly inauspicious time, just as a drone was nearing the IRGC facility at Fordo.

They'd also lost contact with an intelligence officer sent to Parchin, but he was of little concern amid the larger issue. The desk in Langley overseeing his mission put him aside almost entirely until someone asked, "Hey, what about Sabatini?" A colleague replied that there'd been no contact since he checked in two days ago from Mashad of all places. He had no business being there. Further, his last report didn't make any sense and was being subjected to a formal review.

The hacktivist group Anonymous was thought responsible. They'd already hacked into banks and other corporations and published the data on scores of websites. Getting into military systems was a natural progression. The generals regarded Anonymous with suspicion, seeing them as a possible source of homegrown terrorism one day, like the Weatherman Underground of the sixties. IT people insisted that the blackouts were well beyond the capacity of Anonymous and were more likely the responsibility of a foreign power.

China was branded the most likely source. There was no evidence of its culpability, but China was known to have hacked into the Pentagon before and a conclusion was gelling into a consensus as department head after department head nodded in agreement. That in turn meant it would soon become a "certainty" to be engraved into stone and revered by all. When generals and politicians demand an answer, their bureaus will come up with one. Its accuracy was another matter. Some things are only truly known many years after the fact as historians sift over information that no one knew at the time of the event. Other things are never known, even though "certainty" remains.

The Israeli prime minister's war cabinet was angry. Some felt sure that Iran did it. Others blamed the US. A few of his ministers were concerned but secretly pleased that war plans had to be put on hold. The prime minister called the White House and was told that the US was not responsible and that the American military and intelligence services were experiencing a similar but probably unrelated problem. Both leaders assured one another that they would "cooperate fully and get to the bottom of the matter."

The president remained calm. In fact, he was relieved. He was reluctant about going to war with Iran and was now reasonably sure the Israeli PM wouldn't attack on his own. That, the president knew, could change suddenly. Not long after talking to the PM, he headed to Ft McNair for some basketball with friends, including the Secretary of Education.

The British remained characteristically calm. High-level discussions were conducted over a late-afternoon tea and adjourned before nine pm. Other countries were unwilling to admit to anyone that the blackouts struck them. Russia and China were separately convinced it was a virus from the CIA or NSA, akin to Stuxnet, which almost everyone thought was of American provenance.

The Saudis suspected Israel, Iran, Qatar, the Americans, rogue US contractors, and combinations thereof. The council of government was debating whether or not to allow Israeli F-15Is to use Saudi airspace on the way to Iran. Many said that Israel could no longer be trusted; it might fly into Saudi airspace then attack Saudi military bases as part of a plot formulated with Iran. They were once close partners and they could be again without warning.

Iranian generals were alarmed, greatly so. As were the mullahs, though some were pleased to see the IRGC show signs of weakness and doubt. Pakistani generals railed about a "Christian-Zionist-Hindu conspiracy." Precise details eluded the generals as usual, but they were certain the conspirators were about to swoop in and seize the country's nuclear arsenals. Their nuclear weapons are not assembled; the components are stored on several military sites. A few generals planned to gather and assemble the components for swift arming of their Shaheen-II missiles.

Joint-training exercises between several countries were put on hold— India and Vietnam, South Korea and Japan, Kuwait and Saudi Arabia. It wasn't just the matter of the blackouts. Every military and every intelligence service was in a state of uncertainty. The assuredness and swagger once basic to their identities and public faces were weakened. They were no longer certain they could do the things they boasted of to heads of state and publics and budget committees.

Furthermore, there was a decided unwillingness to share information even after the systems came back up. The US intelligence community put off their peers abroad and even stopped communicating with the Pentagon. The military did the same to large parts of the intelligence community. There was a great deal of this bureaucratic insularity before the blackouts, though nothing approaching what was happening now.

As much as the blackouts plagued the powers, most of them wanted to avoid letting anyone suspect something was amiss. That went for friends and foes alike. The US and Israel promised to cooperate on stopping them, but nothing came of it as neither side wanted to admit the extent of the problem. When another blackout hit, no further contact was initiated from either side. Everyone wanted to keep up the appearances of omniscience and omnipotence that states had laid claim to for centuries. Nonetheless, many political and military leaders vacillated between restraint and attacking while they could.

The Israeli PM was still wary and planned a move. The IDF and Mossad were puzzled and alarmed but urged restraint. They called in computer experts in Israel, including an elderly professor at Hebrew University, but they were all stymied. A few people recommended bringing in a former junior officer who was now living in California.

Santa Clara, California

A phone call pulled Ethan out of a deep sleep, if only barely. He let the answering machine kick in, but when the phone rang again even the groggiest person knows it will ring again until heeded. He opened his eyes and contemplated the idea and function of a landline telephone. Only the basics were getting through. The past few weeks were bewildering and exhausting and he needed to catch up on his sleep more so than since he was discharged from the army. He peeked at the cuckoo clock knocking out its rhythms on the wall. Two am. He shook his head and thought again of the Orson Welles's cuckoo clock line from *The Third Man*.

There was no caller ID. He picked up the phone, in no mood for cheerful telephone protocol.

"There better be a good reason for this."

A bubbly voice replied, "Ethan! Still up, I take it."

Ethan's thoughts shifted from the underworld of Vienna to the hills of Lebanon. He saw a face, a Sig Sauer, and then a name formed in his mind. "Boaz Preses," he whispered slowly and without a trace of the caller's cheerfulness. "I wasn't awake . . . you woke me from sweet dreams . . . and it's not at all like the old days. The Bay Area is calmer—much calmer. No Hisbollah, no mortar rounds."

"You were dreaming of a Russian blonde, I bet. I used to dream of her too. Tatiana. She was—what do you say in America—warm?"

"*Hot*, not warm. We say a woman is hot." A frail smile came almost unwillingly across the lax muscles of his cheeks. Ethan took a few deep breaths to clear his head. "It's comforting to see that in a world of transience, some things haven't changed—or matured. Are you still in army intelligence or do you run a deli in the Tel Aviv suburbs now." Despite the chit-chat, he sensed this was not just a call from an old friend.

"I'm still in the IDF. Believe it or not, I'm a major now. Ethan . . ." Boaz's tone shifted suddenly as Ethan knew it would. "Ethan, we have trouble here."

Ethan thought of the danger of war, another push into Lebanon, maybe war with Iran. "What kind of trouble? I'm not in the reserves anymore, you know."

"We're experiencing computer anomalies, very troubling ones. It has people on edge, especially with all the things going on in the Gulf. Ethan, how soon can you get here?"

"What? I'm a million miles away. Don't you have someone there who can help? I can't be the only geek who understands the system."

"You're the best and most reliable geek we know." All humor was gone.

"What about Mantas?"

"Mantas is of dubious reliability. He works with the Russians a bit too closely now."

"Yow! I didn't know that."

"Yes, he's been communicating with their cyberwarfare group in Kaliningrad and we have reason to believe that he hacked into the NSA recently. Oh, and also into Goldman Sachs."

"Goldman Sachs, eh."

"Ethan, everyone here is baffled—by the computer problem, not by Mantas's career path. You helped build the security software here just before you left to become a rich American."

"I went to college—and I'm not rich. Not yet. You talk like old folks from Hungary—'I am reech mon in America'. Back to the point. What have you done to my security system?"

"This isn't a phone subject. We need you here, Ethan—Lieutenant Alon, I mean."

Ethan winced at the implication. "I told you, Boaz, I'm not in the reserves anymore. I have the paperwork and I can—"

"*Technically*, you're correct. However, that can be handled with a little more paperwork. Anyway, I've taken the liberty of booking you on an El Al flight out of San Francisco International tonight. You'll land in Israel the next day, 4:25 pm our time—Ben Gurion. See you there."

"Okay, I guess it's serious. I'd like to bring a colleague—Rina Hardin. She's recently demonstrated exceptional skill in dealing with encryption and security stuff." Raising eyebrows cannot be heard on the phone, but Ethan sensed Boaz's arching suggestively. "Oh, don't even say it!" Ethan knew it was too late.

"Your girlfriend? Okay, Rina can come too. I need to approve her. Is she hot?"

"She's a colleague in computer science, Boaz. A colleague . . . sort of. I can't explain just now."

"I know those unexplainable situations. I just haven't been in one for quite a while. Okay, send me her full name, as shown on her passport, by 10 am your time. When you check in, she'll be booked along with you."

"First class?"

"I'm afraid not. You're only a lieutenant."

Ethan held his head in both hands and released a long sigh. "Never a dull moment in the Valley. You enjoy doing this to people, don't you."

"Well, yes . . . except when we have blackouts and people are losing their heads and blaming me. Remember Kipling.?

"Yes, Boaz. I've had occasion to think of that line quite often over the years."

"Anyway, it'll be great to see you again."

"Yeah, but next time, Boaz, could you please give more notice. I have a business . . . and I have a life."

"You also have a colleague. Sort of. See you both soon. We'll reactivate your reserve commission—as a captain."

"That won't be—"

Ethan heard a click and stared at the phone for a few more minutes as he tried to come up with a plan for the day.

"I'll wait for the morning."

He rolled over and was asleep within a few minutes. He dreamed of home. The images changed seamlessly from California to Israel. He found himself in the hills of southern Lebanon—sweaty, shaking, pulling his helmet down to cover exposed parts of his head as much as possible. He was awakened by a dull thumping noise followed by unearthly shrieks.

Ethan had to prepare Rina for Israel and the army and Boaz. The first two were straightforward. Thankfully, it was a long flight.

"Boaz was in an intelligence unit that briefed my unit Monday mornings. He'd bring word of Iranian arms shipments into Lebanon and occasionally of the presence of Iranian officers in Hisbollah units not far from us."

"Oh . . . So at last you're going to talk to me about the war."

"Just a little. The Iranians turned ragtag villagers into formidable guerrillas—'the Mujahideen of the Mediterranean,' as we grudgingly called them."

"And he's still in army intelligence, you said. He must be big, strong, fit . . . "

"Well, he's a tall but kind of a portly chap."

"Portly is a euphemism, Ethan."

"Yes, it is. He speaks frankly, even crudely, and his humor can be embarrassing. It was all right in the soldierly life of Lebanon, but on leave in Tel Aviv he could be off-putting, to say the least. A woman named Tatiana found him especially off-putting."

"Who's Tatiana?"

"Oh . . ." Ethan looked around for a way to explain and rocked his hand back and forth as though weighing a decision.

"I get it. Continue."

"No, I mean . . . Well, Boaz and I became friends. We ate rations together and talked about what we'd do after our hitches were up. Soldier stuff. It's been going on since the days of Joshua. I introduced him to a woman who became his wife. I hesitated to do so."

"Because he could be off-putting."

"Yes, exactly. It's a funny story. One day, my battalion was in the Bekaa Valley—"

Rina tapped his hand on the armrest. "Whoa! Too much soldierly stuff. Where's this valley?"

"It's in Lebanon. The Bekaa Valley runs from near the border with Israel up to northern Lebanon. Lots of guerrillas, mostly Shia. Amal and Hisbollah with help from Iran. I like to recall the valley as very beautiful."

"It doesn't sound very beautiful." Rina was searching for ways to lead the conversation elsewhere.

"Well, in its way it is amazingly lovely. Green fields, limestone ravines. Boaz gave my unit an intelligence briefing and was walking back to brigade when nature called and a scorpion resented it."

"Ouch! Not funny. Where did he get stung?"

"I'll get to that."

"Oh. I think I know. Well, I've narrowed it down anyway."

"We rushed him to a field medical unit and Boaz pleaded with me to go in with him because he was stung on what we call the *tuchus*."

"My first guess, though an American slang term came to mind."

"And the medic was a pretty girl."

"*Woman. A pretty woman.*"

"That's what I meant. He didn't want to go in. He said he was too fat and didn't want her to see him . . . you know, *see* him. I told him about the venom and not to be so self-conscious. 'But she'll see how overweight I am,' he whined. Then the tent flap opens and a lovely, zaftig medic casually says, 'No need to worry. I like beefy men.' She smiled pleasantly, led us inside, and placed Boaz on a gurney. Boaz couldn't take his eyes off her. I was rather impressed too."

"So this is Tatiana?"

"No, no. It's Iris. Tatiana was someone else entirely. Another time perhaps."

"I can hardly wait. Please continue."

"She reached for a venom kit and motioned for me to leave."

"I hope she didn't have to treat the snakebite cowboy-style."

"Not sure what that is. Anyway, she said, 'You know what they say: the heavier the hammer, the deeper the nail!' My jaw dropped and Boaz laughed aloud. He was at ease and in good hands. I'm not sure what went on after I left but suffice to say, they fell in love and got married six months later."

"Any kids?"

"Yes, indeed. The first was born just a few months after the wedding." Ethan saw Rina doing the basic math. "As I said, I'm not sure what went on after I left the tent."

"You're not?"

The chat fell off and the engines droned on. Rina thought of how rarely Ethan ever mentioned Lebanon and how she sensed it wasn't a welcome subject. She wanted to understand it better and sought a way to broach the subject.

"Ethan, do you and Barrett ever talk about your war experiences?"

"Not much. Maybe just something about the desert or the mountains or an unusual character such as Boaz. Maybe an odd sound like shrapnel or airstrikes. Rina, know what people who've been in wars mostly talk about when they get together?"

"I truly don't know, Ethan."

"Anything but war."

Rina was surprised, confused, as it went against what civilians thought about such get-togethers. "No backslapping, long stories, and tall tales?"

"No, that's ridiculous."

"And Barrett, does he—"

"Oh Rina . . . Barrett doesn't talk much about Iraq. And never about his second time there."

"Second time? Why would anyone go back?"

Ethan shrugged his shoulders as best he could in the cramped airline seat and let the conversation trail off again. The subject remained on their mind though. Ethan recalled Barrett telling him, in his brief and gruff manner, that he'd lost his girlfriend in New Mexico after a conversation about the war. It changed their relationship. Whether the conversation was too emotional or the details too horrific, Barrett didn't say. A chasm opened between him and her and feelings between them became distant and uncomfortable and lacking in spontaneity.

Ethan thought back to that short conversation with Barrett and came up with what he thought was a better understanding of him. There was a part of Barrett that his girlfriend could not reach or understand or help. After a month of that, with the chasm still there and probably widening, Barrett said goodbye and moved out. Or maybe he just moved out. He found an old wolf at a shelter and took him home. Out there in the desert, east of the mountains, where there are more cattle than people.

He wondered what would happen between Rina and him if he spoke in any depth about Lebanon and Hisbollah and the sounds he still heard in dreams and in waking life too. No answers came.

Chimes. A voice. They'd be touching down at Ben Gurion in fifteen minutes.

Tel Aviv

"What are you doing with the likes of this guy?" Boaz asked, offering what he hoped was a winning smile as he led them to a dented red Fiat 500 in the airport parking lot.

"Sometimes I wonder," Rina retorted. "You should see the friends of his I have to put up with."

Boaz was taken aback by such a spirited retort from someone new to him. He thought of a female PT instructor in the Israeli army who matched his jibes and made him do extra sit-ups. "She's quick, Ethan. Very quick."

"Stanford quick, Boaz. She'll be a CTO somewhere in a couple of years. Maybe even at Micrologic Design if I nap too much."

"He *sooo* naps too much," Rina said. "I'm checking out his corner office and picking out new pictures for the hallway."

Ethan nuzzled his ambitious partner and whispered, "You'll learn to love him . . . I think. Most people do. Well, many of them."

Ethan and Rina crammed themselves into the backseat along with some carry-on bags that would not fit in the trunk, cluttered as it was with CDs and sweatshirts and magazines. They exited the parking lot and headed for Tel Aviv.

"Is your small car in the shop, Boaz?" Ethan shouted above the traffic noise as he tucked his head beneath the car's ceiling, bumping it with any swerve or pothole nonetheless.

"We'll only be in here a few minutes, folks. It's great for Tel Aviv traffic. Besides, my wife loves it!" Boaz tapped proudly on the steering wheel as they drove down Barlev Boulevard toward the Mediterranean coast.

"And how are Iris and the boys?"

"Iris is doing very well, thanks. My two handsome and brilliant boys continue to grow remarkably." Boaz spoke as he dexterously weaved between cars, hit the horn in quick bursts, and looked cagily for his next opening. "If we aren't bogged down at headquarters, it will be my pleasure to host you both in my humble home where I will be pleased to introduce you to the whole *mishpacha*." Boaz gestured with a gallant doffing of an invisible cap.

"That's the family or clan," Ethan whispered to Rina.

"I know a little Yiddish," she replied. "It's in many American sitcoms. Besides, I grew up in the DC suburbs, remember?"

"Boaz, I'm not really back in the reserves, am I?"

"I hope you are," Rina whispered teasingly. "I *go* for guys in uniform." Their eyebrows bounced playfully at each other for a moment. "You need an eye patch like that old guy—Moshe something."

"Dayan . . . Moshe Dayan," Ethan said, trying to keep his eyes from rolling.

"Keep your options open, Ethan," was all Boaz would say. "But think of me as a superior officer all the same!"

"Yes, Boaz. I mean Major Preses."

Boaz maneuvered his Fiat through the busy traffic as though driving a motorcycle and within a half hour they passed through a security gate at the old Templar Building. It was unprepossessing structure, an old two-story house from the early twentieth century that had been built in the crusading order's Sarona colony and used much later by the fledgling Israeli army. Boaz drove into an underground garage and took his charges to an elevator that shuttled them down several unmarked floors into a command center filled with uniformed men and women, all in a state of considerable agitation.

Eyes fell on Ethan and Rina as they clipped on security badges. Some looked on hopefully, wondering if the young man was as good as the senior IT people claimed. They'd all seen or heard tell of the arcane, practically incomprehensible algorithms he introduced which still constituted the core of the security system. Some, however, looked at the pair with resentment as their casual slacks, floral shirts, and longish hair clashed with the crisp uniforms and short-cropped coiffures in the command center. "Two outsiders who think they know it all," seemed written on many faces, especially one particularly colonel with the name "Kleinman" on his starched, epauletted shirt with a couple rows of ribbons. Ethan looked quickly at Kleinman's chest and knew he'd never been in an infantry unit.

Rina felt way out of place. "Worse than PAMD," she whispered.

"Too bad I didn't bring my NASA lab coat."

Boaz led them to a near-empty conference room, closed the door, and launched into a formal briefing which ended with an update. "We had another blackout this morning. The IT staff is in disarray and the big shots upstairs are worried, though not as much as the politicians in Jerusalem are. Some of the senior officers here never trusted all the complex technology and would have us using carrier pigeons and semaphore if they could." Boaz could not resist a little humor, especially if directed at generals. Few younger officers can.

"Where do the blackouts hit? In what systems? Is there a pattern?" asked Ethan.

"Everywhere! That's the most exasperating thing—radar, missiles, and even the global communication system. Our surface ships and submarines suffer the same disruptions, even the supposedly civilian freighters at anchor off Yemen and Iran—another subject entirely. The screens go blank and nothing we do brings them back up. Then they light up again as though nothing happened."

"Maybe they're still using Kaypros," Rina whispered to Ethan, eliciting a reproving look. They managed to avoid giggling and returned their attention to Boaz.

"We suspect a security breach by hackers or a hostile government," Boaz continued. "Iran? Hamas? We have enough enemies that would love to see us naked, so to speak. Thank goodness our friends in Damascus are preoccupied with their civil war."

Ethan remained silent. He ran his hand along the roughness of his day-old beard.

"This is too big a deal for hackers," Rina offered.

"We don't know anything for sure," Boaz replied. "We already initiated system analysis Level 5 for advanced security breaches, but no one could find the cause. We're in the dark. We're obviously concerned— and so are people high up. They fear the worst and sometimes that gets politicians to act the worst."

Ethan pondered things a moment. Boaz and Rina waited eagerly as the gears ground. "I'll need a terminal with access to your core firewall. A long time has passed so I'll need all passwords and keys to check the access ports and VPN options. I'll also need full access to the hardware and the software firewall."

"The whole *mishpacha*," Rina felt compelled to say.

"You shall have the whole *mishpacha* and anything else you may need, my *reech* American friend. I know them all of course, though not by heart. I'll have it all within a few minutes and we'll have terminals set up for you in a few minutes." He turned to leave the room.

"I hope there won't be any scorpions in here," Rina said.

Boaz froze. He turned his head back and looked at Ethan disappointedly. "I think there's been another security breach."

"Just a little levity, Boaz," Rina said soothingly. "We're all friends here. I'm not so sure about some of those guys we saw coming in, though."

Ethan and Rina talked briefly about the business back in Santa Clara while they awaited Boaz's return. They didn't know when they'd get the chance to even think about Micrologic again.

"Our little sojourn into Middle Eastern intrigue means more delay in shipping the product." Rina spoke in a mock scolding manner, though her point was sound. What was this adventure going to cost them?

"Not to worry. We'll be compensated for our time and handsomely too. All the more so, if we find the problem in good time. In any case, this'll be a unique learning experience and we'll make contacts in the hi-tech world over here."

"We should confine our networking—our *schmoozing*—to trade shows."

"Ah, you're Yiddish is coming along remarkably well. *Naches!*"

"What does—"

A chirp on Ethan's phone indicated a text—from Barrett. He held the screen for them both to see.

> Barrett: Things are getting hot in the Middle East. Where are you?
>
> Ethan: We're in the Middle East. LOL.
>
> Barrett: You and Rina? Really?
>
> Ethan: Really. We're in that old building in Tel Aviv, in fact.

Barrett: Let me know if you find an old grail lying around.

Ethan: Will do. Why are things getting hot?

Barrett: IRGC officer caught in A-stan with Stinger-like missile. American taken in Iran and tied to assassination. Angry words all round. War drums. Boom boom boom.

Ethan: Loud?

Barrett: BOOM BOOM BOOM. Another thing. US defense systems malfunctioning. Everybody on edge. Fingers on triggers. Iran has same trouble. Their fingers on triggers too.

Ethan: Malfunctioning how?

Barrett: Complete blackout, all systems.

Ethan: Exactly 30 minutes?

Barrett: How did you know? Are you doing it? LOL.

Ethan: Not me. Think about the Book of Judges.

Barrett: Our Samson friend?

Ethan: Maybe. Will know more soon. Out.

Barrett: Thanks for not saying "Kirk out."

Ethan had no idea what Barrett's last words meant. He opened the CNN International app on his phone and they followed the dramatic reports on the screen.

> The Pentagon announced today that it is deploying the *USS Theodore Roosevelt* to the troubled waters around Iran. This is in response to Iran's escalation of the war in Afghanistan by introducing lethal surface-to-air missiles. The *USS Theodore*

Roosevelt will bring to a total of three the number of aircraft carrier battle groups in the region, giving the US a considerable amount of air assets for any attacks on Iran that might be coming.

This comes close on the heels of the recent deployment of F-22 Raptor fighters to an undisclosed base in the Gulf, most likely the Al Dafra airbase in the United Arab Emirates, and the deployment of B-2 stealth bombers to Diego Garcia, the Indian Ocean base to the south of Iran.

Admiral Lorain cautioned Iran not to use its Russian-made Silkworm or Klub missiles which accelerate to supersonic speeds as they near their targets. Lorain noted that Iran would face "unprecedented retaliation" in the event of their use.

The admiral's warning has been interpreted as signaling the navy's concern over the ship-killing missiles. The navy has little in the way of defensive measures once the missiles go supersonic, and they are capable of inflicting tremendous damage on ships, including aircraft carriers. One analyst has noted that the US has not lost an aircraft carrier since World War Two and that losing one now would be a shocking blow sure to inflame the ire of the public, which would then demand, in his words, "prompt and strong retaliation."

Ominously, this comes alongside unconfirmed reports that China has recently delivered Sizzler missiles to Iran. The Sizzler is akin to the Russian Silkworm but faster and more lethal. The reports are based in part on the arrival of several Chinese freighters and a destroyer in the Iranian ports of Bandar-e-Abbas in the Straits of Hormuz and Bushehr, not far from a key nuclear site. This of course raises concerns of a Chinese response in the event of a US strike on Iran.

In Israel, skirmishes have been reported along the troubled border with Lebanon, and television screens are flashing messages notifying reservists to report to their units. Air raid drills are expected to prepare for missile strikes that may come from Hisbollah in Lebanon, Syria, and as far away as Iran itself.

To Israel's west, in the lawless Sinai region, tribal groups affiliated with al Qaeda have blown up a gas pipeline and attacked three police stations along the border. The Israeli prime minister is convening his war cabinet tomorrow to weigh options.

Ethan and Rina watched the reports with growing anxiety. They lived in a cyber-world which they thought was removed from the mayhem of the world. They were now in Israel and at the center of a crisis that was about to become a regional war.

For its part, Iran has said that an attack on its sovereign territory would lead to "calamitous results" for the aggressors. Iran would have no choice but to strike back and all options were on the table.

World markets are reacting to the news out of the Middle East. US stock markets have plummeted five percent, the worst since the meltdown of 2008. Asia is opening down too and judging by the futures markets, European bourses are poised to continue the fall tomorrow morning. Oil futures in London and New York, which have largely shrugged off past wars of words, have skyrocketed $7 a barrel today alone. Commodity traders in London, Frankfurt, and Zurich expect the spike to continue several days.

Ethan and Rina saw stricken looks on each other's face. War was about to erupt. They suspected that Samson was at least part of the reason and that the world leaders knew nothing of Samson. Ethan texted Barrett:

Ethan: Are we close to war?

> Barrett: Afraid so. I'm off to Washington to meet with some people.
>
> Ethan: Big shots?
>
> Barrett: Somewhat big. Let's see what we can do.
>
> Ethan: Agreed.

Boaz returned and his concerned face indicated that he and the military knew all too well that things were deteriorating.

"We've got your station all set, folks. Let's figure out what's going on before things get completely out of hand up there. By the way, we went down again twenty minutes ago."

Ethan reckoned the blackout took down the center's firewall and that allowed the exchange of texts with Barrett and for him and Rina to watch CNN. At least the blackouts were helpful in keeping in touch with the outside world. Inside the Templar Building they were isolated, cut off, dependent on the institution and its interests and worldview. Rina worried about thinking like all the colonels in their offices along the underground hallways, here and in Washington and Tehran and Riyadh and Beijing and Moscow and elsewhere.

Boaz escorted them down a corridor spartanly decorated with photographs of generals, tanks, and F-15Is then into a room obviously intended for meetings, now cluttered with computer equipment, strands of ethernet cable, and a few desks and chairs. A half dozen colonels gave them a quick rundown on the problem—nothing new or interesting—and they relinquished, reluctantly, the security information that Ethan and Rina asked for. They left the room and returned to their offices "to run their own tests." They'd all "compare notes" later. They didn't know any more than what Boaz had said, but they felt the need to appear in charge. They weren't. Samson was.

"So the country is paralyzed," Ethan said.

"Not entirely," Boaz replied. "We're going on established procedures, better known as hunches and guesses."

"And institutional momentum," Rina said, surprised by her boldness.

She and Boaz looked at each other uncomfortably, though with polite smiles. Ethan saw need for diversion.

"Well, I'll have to prepare a trap for the intruder," Ethan said confidently, looking at his watch. "The blackout will end after thirty minutes and then we can get rolling."

"Thirty minutes will be up in . . . three minutes," Boaz said looking at his watch.

The systems came alive exactly when expected. Boaz looked at the two and let loose a long sigh. Everything was up and running—radar, command and control systems, missile controls. Rina didn't see this as a good thing.

"I'll need to know more information about the system we developed," Ethan said. "Did you guys make any significant modifications to the firewall program since I left to become a rich American?"

Boaz pondered the matter then shook his head. "Only a few strengthening routines here and there, mainly against worms and viruses. Nothing was done to the basics. I'll double-check with the developers though." His eyes flashed as a thought occurred. "I'll be back with our security boss in a minute. You might recall him." With that, he scooted down the hallway as best he could.

"Can we tell him about Samson?" Rina asked.

"I don't think we should," he said ruefully. "We have to limit the number of people who know—unpleasant though that is for me just now. It's like not confiding in a brother about a family matter. Oh, it would take too long to explain. Neither Boaz nor anyone else would believe us anyway. Kleinman, for one, would think we were . . . "

"Meshugah?"

"Yes, exactly. I doubt I would believe the story if I hadn't seen that CiC under the eBeam. It's just the two of us and Barrett."

"And that big dog."

Boaz returned with a disheveled red-haired civilian in his mid-thirties. His appearance conveyed in a mere second a life of cyber-obsession and attendant atrophy of social skills. In previous decades, someone like him had a slide rule in hand and a bandaid holding his glasses together. Happily, those days were gone and even the most socially limited tekkie made an effort to look sociable if not hip, at least as the hi-tech world defined it. Ethan looked at him intently until his memory cache kicked in and the pixels assembled.

"Leor!"

The disheveled young man was elated that Ethan recognized him and shook hands with his old colleague, vigorously and awkwardly. Leor was a promising star in Ethan's security group. He was painfully shy, often inarticulate, but he could handle a complex algorithm on-the-fly and that would be useful.

Ethan was sure that Leor would come in handy. After running tests, it was clear that the security program would need a thorough memory management test—one that could listen to all ports, scan them constantly, and perform an array of complex tasks. All this required precise allocation and clear memory caches, otherwise the software would hit a segmentation fault and crash, leading to a floating process called a "zombie." And it's hard to clear a zombie without a full system shutdown—something to be avoided, especially now when the slightest incident could push the region over the brink.

"Leor, I need to know a few important things about the security system. What's changed since my days? Anything with the hardware?"

"Hardware? Where is your keen mind going, Ethan? Access through mobile devices? Flash memory chips?"

"Well, we can't rule anything out at this point," Ethan answered evasively. "Leor, can you please do something for me? I'll write some specifications for a short program I'd like you to write—and very quickly."

"Of course," Leor replied with boyish enthusiasm and pride in his old boss's trust.

Ethan scribbled a few lines on a notepad and held it up.

"You want to check internal memories—cache and even BIOS chips? We never looked into those areas. Do you suspect a problem there? Ethan, that's just not possible. Those circuits can't get viruses or malware. No way."

"I'm sure you're right, Leor. It's probably pointless, but please humor me. I just want to eliminate a few possibilities before we delve deeper. Please write these scanning routines to ease my silly fretful mind. Rina and I will use your data in a short program that we make. Together, we'll figure this out. I'm sure."

"Will do. I'll be at my terminal."

"And Leor . . . this stays with just the three of us, okay?"

The young man looked puzzled but nodded.

Ethan wrote another set of specifications for Rina. "I'll need to scan all ports. starting at the basics. I'll use your and Leor's results to listen to the network. Meanwhile, I'll write a memory intruder-catch routine to see what's inside the nation's defense systems."

Ethan sat on a chair and started thinking then typing. There were many hours of stressful work ahead.

In the morning, after several hours of work and only an hour of fitful sleep on army cots, Ethan and Rina had an army to contend with. They were forced to argue with a platoon of majors and colonels who were demanding supervision and minute reports of every step of their investigation. He and Rina needed to be alone to work on the blackout problem. No intrusions, no hourly reports, no supervision. It wasn't simply a matter of not revealing the existence of Samson and just what their systems were tied into. It was also Ethan and Rina's way of doing things—the result of working in a startup, not in a labyrinthine corporation or a bureaucracy rent by infighting, politics, careerists, and layers of management.

Voices were raised. The debate turned testy. Boaz sought a way to moderate but couldn't find an opening.

"You don't just fly in from another country and take over our computer networks," Colonel Kleinman roared.

Ethan had enough.

"You don't just ask me to leave my business and 'fly in from another country,' as you glibly put it. I'm here for a good reason—an excellent reason. Shall I spell it our for you, colonel? It seems I have to. *You* can't fix the problem. *You* don't know what's wrong."

"We all have to work within parameters and institutional structures, soldier!"

The implication of that form of address riled Ethan. "Your parameters! Your structures! Your plodding way of doing things probably *broke* the system that *I* created and left in excellent shape. I can't leave a masterpiece in the hands of people who paint by the numbers, *now can I!*"

Kleinman was livid by the implication that he and others in the Templar Building were responsible for the breakdown. Try as he did, he could not muster a counterargument. Indeed, the possibility of human error inside his team hadn't been ruled out. One of his rivals brought this scenario up rather pointedly in a meeting only last night, leaving little doubt as to where the blame might one day fall. Seeing that the colonel was on the defensive, Ethan fired off a final shot—he hoped.

"Not even the chief of staff comes in here," he insisted in an uncharacteristically loud and authoritative voice. "Not even the prime minister comes in here, unless he's bringing us blueberry blintzes his wife made fresh this morning!" Ethan hadn't talked that way since he was a platoon leader and had to lay down the law on young soldiers from time to time. Using it on a nominally superior officer amused him. It felt great.

With that, the meddlesome colonel and his following turned around and stormed out the room, no longer doubting where authority now resided in the bowels of the old Templar Building of Sarona.

Leor gave Ethan the program he requested and returned to managing network traffic, such as it was. Boaz, after giving his old friend a wink, was back monitoring electronic surveillance on the Lebanese border.

"That was a *naches*, wasn't it, Ethan!"

"Something like that."

"I'm running another test now," Ethan said after the two had been busily running traps throughout the system, "and I'll have something . . . right . . . about . . . *now*." Ethan hit "enter" and watched the data race down the screen. He studied the information then nodded. "Ah so," he continued without removing his eyes from the screen. "We're dealing with a multidisciplinary system which opened a vulnerability no one suspected. No one but us." His eyes sparkled as he appreciated a new insight. "The only system that can find and exploit this vulnerability is someone we all know from the Book of Judges."

Rina listened intently and integrated the new information into her understanding of the Program. She was pulling fragments together into what would hopefully become a whole.

"I've made a short program that will create a few problems for the system to deal with. It incorporates all relevant disciplines simultaneously so the optimum of the simultaneous problem is superior to the overall mechanism operation. However, that significantly increases the complexity of the problem. Therefore I narrowed the problems to only critical ones. We'll see who pops up."

"So in essence," Rina summarized, "we're state troopers setting up to see if Samson speeds through town."

"Exactly," Ethan confirmed. "Pretty clever, I'd say."

"My state trooper analogy?"

"Umm . . . I was referring to my trap." He typed a few numerical values as the input for the program. "If my assumptions are correct, then the program and additional problems should produce a specific pattern and trigger an electrical response. And when this happens, we'll be right here."

"Like state troopahs," Rina drawled.

"Have I mentioned how clever your analogy is?" She feigned a smile. "I launched the problems and the training information on handling them. I'm expecting a certain behavior."

"How long?"

"A few minutes. See the rotation bar? The red means it's feeding info. If the program detects data flow from internal hardware, it will stop rotating and turn green."

The pair watched the red bar rotate slowly over and over for several minutes. The only sound was the mechanical ticking of an institutional clock. Ethan thought of the comparatively warm sounds of his cuckoo clock and of Orson Welles fleeing through the sewer of Vienna.

"Hmmm . . . still no change . . . we should have seen something by now."

Ethan stared at the rotation bar. Still red.

"Did I miss something . . . or are we mistaken about Samson sitting at the bottom of this?"

Ethan was mumbling hurriedly, almost incomprehensibly, as his assumptions seemed to be falling apart before them, leaving the problem unsolved and the Middle East on edge.

"It's here . . . it's got to be here . . . c'mon!"

After a few more minutes Ethan slumped back in his chair and shook his head in disappointment bordering on despair and nausea. He felt shame and even concern for the viability of Micrologic Design products which might suffer from faulty assumptions as well. His assumptions, the ones he wrote into the product. He imagined Colonel Kleinman upbraiding him smugly before handing him bus fare to Ben Gurion Airport.

Only after a few moments did the matter of a Middle Eastern war come to mind. Ethan slumped farther down in his chair. The room fell silent except for the buzzing of the overhead lighting, occasional footsteps outside in the corridor, and that damn institutional clock ticking down to who knows what.

He imagined Orson Welles smirking at him atop the ferris wheel and telling him that all Ethan's work only made warfare less controllable and more murderous.

Beauty? Voice of Peace? Dream on, kid.

"Ethan . . . Ethan, we'll have to search in a different direction. That's all. We still have time."

He stood and paced around the room as though eager to get out, eager to return to California. He'd let his friend down and his country as well. He thought Barrett might be having better luck in the bureaus of Washington, though it seemed unlikely.

"Ethan . . . let's tweak the algorithm here and there. Refine, don't abandon. That's lesson one in computer science—and in the rest of life too."

Ethan sat back down and stared at the screen then at the ceiling, the floor, anywhere. He thought if he looked back at the screen a window would open with a clown laughing at him. Maybe Yale would send a tow truck and haul away his diploma. All his considerable education seemed worthless in the face of the problem before them. He sat down and replayed his actions over and over, hoping his error would announce itself. Nothing came of it.

Maybe I'll move out to the desert and get a wolf.

"Pull over, boy!" Rina suddenly shouted, pointing to a stable green bar on the screen.

Ethan looked up and raced to the screen. The rotation bar had stopped entirely and was completely green. Ethan moved his cursor about wildly to ensure they weren't seeing a screen freeze. Clearly, they weren't!

"Samson! So good to see you again. And how do you like Tel Aviv?"

"I'm a-gonna hafta write you a ticket, boy!"

Ethan and Rina joyfully embraced and danced for a moment but soon realized there was no time for lengthy self-congratulation.

They'd identified the problem but solving it still lay ahead. It was like discovering the cause of a disease then searching for the cure—the latter far more difficult than the former. A few ideas flitted about but he was exhausted and felt at the end of his creativity. And it would take creativity to solve a problem inside something as creative as Samson.

"I don't know, Rina. We have to think. A little fresh air would help. We can't leave now though."

"Ethan, it's so hard for me to think in this place. The corridors, the clock, those men."

"I thought you went for guys in uniform."

"Just you," she said as she placed her arms around his shoulders, "Just you . . . Captain Alon. Let's take a quick walk outside. We can brainstorm on the fly. Maybe get tattoos. And if those guys ask where we're going, I'll say we're going to get blueberry blintzes."

"Oh, you're not going to be terribly popular here in the old Templar Building, Rina."

"Darn! I was hoping they'd make me a captain too."

New Mexico

Barrett turned on the news. He already knew things were getting out of hand. He knew the particulars better than the faces on the television did. His purpose was to see how the media were presenting the crisis, which would help him judge the public reaction and where things might go from here. There was no doubt which station would be of most help.

The bottom of the screen read "Clash in the Persian Gulf." The gravity on the anchor's face and his sonorous voice struck Barrett as practiced and unauthentic. Most of life struck him that way. He scratched and massaged Jesse's ears, thick and strong, reminding him of boot leather. "Watch this, buddy. The sidekick is about to look over at the anchor with deference and admiration, as though he were delivering the word of God."

She did just that and Barrett stood up.

"I told ya, Jesse! Pure showmanship . . . just like politicians. That's how they sell wars to the public. And publics sure do buy them. As though it's the word of God—the God of War, to whom large swathes of us pray and offer sacrifice."

Jesse was startled by Barrett's outburst.

"Oh, I'm a crank, Jesse. We all know that."

The anchors alternated their presentations, complete with stern faces and deferent turns.

In what can only be seen as an act of provocation, several Iranian gunboats, part of the elite Revolutionary Guard Corps, came dangerously close to the *USS Bulkeley* as it patrolled the troubled waters of the Persian Gulf. Despite repeated calls to pull away, the IRGC gunboats brazenly persisted in menacing the *Bulkeley* until they finally broke off, only seconds from forcing the US warship to defend itself by opening fire.

In Bahrain, site of the US Fifth Fleet nerve center, a dozen or more rocket-propelled-grenade rounds were fired at US naval vessels anchored in Manama harbor and at a nearby National Security Agency listening post. The attackers escaped into the winding streets and alleys of Manama. They are thought to be Shia radicals armed by Iranian agents. Other such cells are thought to be lurking not only in Bahrain but also in Yemen, Qatar, Kuwait, and Saudi Arabia—perhaps even here in America.

Meanwhile in the troubled Sinai desert, an armed group of al Qaeda fighters tried to cross into Israel but were repelled after a sharp firefight with security forces. Elsewhere in Sinai, a peacekeeping force, part of the storied 101st Airborne Division of D-Day fame, came under fire from similar groups but fought them off without suffering a single casualty.

For more on these provocative acts, we turn to retired Lieutenant General Jackson Bennett.

I'm sure he'll call for calm and negotiations," Barrett interjected acidly, "soon followed by immediate airstrikes. You know, to send a message."

Anchor: General, do all these attacks stem from Iran?

General Bennet: These actions are the IRGC's forte and they call for a vigorous immediate response from . . .

"That's enough." Barrett shut off the television with an angry thrust of the remote. "Well, Jesse, at least he didn't mention anything about complicity in sinking the *Lusitania*. Okay, let's hike up the old trail, while we still can."

As they headed out the gate, Barrett explained that it was Germany that sank the *Lusitania*. "That was back in 1915, old sport. But you knew that. What to do, Jesse. What to do."

The sight of the impassive Sandias offered little evidence that the world was on the brink of war. Everything looked peaceful and aloof from the impending bloodletting. Barrett thought of the F-16s and Ospreys that he heard streak over the mountains from Kirtland Air Force Base an hour earlier. The skies were quiet just then, with a trace of red beginning to glow in the east.

"That's why we're out here, far away from those people plotting up wars. Right, my man?"

A faint doggy smile.

Tel Aviv

Ethan and Rina grabbed coffee and blueberry blintzes at a Hungarian cafe along the Tel Aviv beachfront and planned their next move. It was late morning, though not a cheerful one. The skies were overcast and the early autumn breeze promised strong gusts in an hour. A few hearty swimmers plied the still gray waters, grabbing a little exercise to work off stress before scurrying back to offices and listening to the latest news. The entire city and indeed the entire country were on edge but in all Israel, only Ethan and Rina knew a vital aspect of the situation.

Ethan recalled going for swims before heading for his reserve unit by nightfall. "There was an eerie feeling of being in two worlds, civilian and military, open and regimented, peaceful and otherwise. Two worlds that shouldn't exist with each other but always do."

Rina placed her hand on his and listened. As much as Ethan's words opened the door to talking about many things, this was not the time to think about the yin and yang in the universe. She decided to be the one who put them back to work.

"So," Rina began to summarize, "Samson has gone from the microprocessors to the defense system's memory. It collects the data there, analyzes it, and performs some actions, which we believe includes triggering blackouts."

Ethan nodded as he appreciated Samson and their growing comprehension of it, which he liked to think would lead to mastery of it. "When I scrutinized the CiC in the eBeam yesterday—or was it the day before—I found an analog component. It was an inductor of some sort."

"An inductor? On a chip from the eighties? Ethan, inductors were invented only in the past decade. Some old guy at PAMD came up with it. Well, that figures. Inductors are in communication chips that require both digital and advanced analog circuitry such as smartphones, tablets, and the like. Are you sure the Samson chip contained one back then?

"Oh yes. There was an inductor. No doubt about it. Hardly an ordinary one. It's a tiny transformer."

"A transformer on a chip? On a tiny part of a chip? We didn't learn about that in school."

"Rina, we're in a new school now—one with brilliant though unapproachable teachers. The transformer was hexagonal in shape, made of more than one type of metal and other layout components. These guys invented something back then that would be deemed a breakthrough only three years ago."

"That is, if anyone knew about it. So what's the purpose of the transformer?"

"I've been wondering that. I might have found the answer." Ethan raised his cup of coffee towards the sea and looked about to see if anyone was listening in.

"Don't worry, Ethan. There are only a few people in Tel Aviv who would understand you. And only one person who would believe you—*maybe*."

"Thanks for the vote of confidence. The transformer's job is to spike the system with high voltage at specified times."

"And?"

"Like any spike, it creates chaos, momentary internal confusion, like what a high-voltage Taser does to brains. *Zap!* Samson creates confusion and sneaks in. It quickly penetrates the system and performs

266

its operations—acquiring information, activating systems. And sometimes shutting them down."

"Why is Samson creating blackouts?"

"Not sure. Maybe we can ask the lone wolf in the sweeping sands of New Mexico."

Ethan: Samson responsible for blackouts. Why?

A reply came two minutes later.

Barrett: Been wondering that. Maybe Samson's telling governments their war systems are unreliable and they have to back off.

Ethan: But governments see this as a threat and are moving to war. Boom, boom, boom!

Barrett: I know but who says you hi-tech folk understand the world, especially the military world? Not me. What Samson thinks will stop war, governments see as reason to start one. Lack of information, lack of trust. It's on every page of history, especially the ones right before a war starts. Like December 6th, 1941.

Ethan: It's not in chip design textbooks.

Barrett: I'll take your word for it. Can you stop the blackouts?

Ethan: Maybe. Can you stop the Pentagon?

Barrett: No one has yet . . . I'm trying.

"*Can* we stop the blackouts?" Rina asked.

"I don't know. I'm still thinking . . . about that inductor . . . ."

An air raid siren suddenly blared. Everyone looked about anxiously before scurrying for cover or home.

"Is it a test," Ethan asked the waiter as he hurriedly brought the check.

"I don't think so," came the quavering reply. "Tests are announced in advance. Is there some place you can go?"

The two looked about them in alarm. Winds were coming in from the Mediterranean, kicking up whitecaps that shone momentarily before dissolving back into grey. Lightning bolts spread out and for an instant illuminated the sky and the cloud banks marching in. Rumbles of thunder soon followed. Fishermen caught unawares rushed to the docks, putting off their work for a more tranquil day. Ethan and Rina raced back toward the Templar Building. The sirens and the run gave them infusions of adrenalin.

They stood outside the Templar Building, waiting to be escorted below. Rina saw Ethan deep in thought. Was he in wonder of nature or pondering the storm as an augur of war.

"Ground control to Major Alon . . . ."

"I think . . . I have . . . a plan."

They were let inside and back to inner sanctums an unknown number of floors below. They donned security badges and walked the long cold corridor to their work area. Colonel Kleinman looked at them, this time with sheepishness commingling with hopefulness on his face— two emotions that Rina sensed had only rarely appeared there before.

"Don't worry," Rina said as they walked briskly past him. "Ethan has a plan." She turned back to see his glower and added, "No *tsoris!*"

Cushing, Oklahoma

Commodity futures were once traded in a "pit" located in New York or Chicago. It wasn't an actual pit; it just seemed that way at times, especially when orders were coming in from around the world and prices were hopping around because "fast market" rules were in effect. Pits were designated parts of huge trading floors where corn, wheat, pork bellies, gold, copper, silver, lumber, steel, rice, and just about every commodity in the world was bought and sold—each with a separate pit. Oil had one of the livelier ones.

Trades were made in a noisy, chaotic arena by an odd array of people, from ponytailed mavericks to stolid institutional reps. They shouted, grimaced, pleaded, scowled, and made arcane hand gestures to convey bids and offers. Back in the nineties, the marines sent young infantry officers into the pits in the Chicago Board of Trade to teach them to make decisions amid noise, commotion, and uncertainty. Nowadays, however, futures are traded electronically and young marines are schooled in Afghanistan.

Institutions buy and sell on computers in offices around the world. Individuals do the same from dens and living rooms. The commodities themselves aren't in New York or Chicago. They're all over the world. A surprising amount of the oil traded on world markets is stored in a small town in Oklahoma called Cushing.

Oil traders thirst for knowledge. How does the new Saudi field look? How much is coming out of Tenghiz next year? What's the sulfur content in the shale oil from Eagle Ford? Is the Canadian pipeline going to be approved? Then there were political issues. Can Nigerian militant groups strike into the delta where Shell operates? How's Libya doing after Qaddafi? Is Kurdistan breaking away from Iraq?

The most important question now was Iran. Was there going to be war? If so, when and how long would it last? Can the IRGC close the Strait of Hormuz? London markets were open and oil futures were way up—$4.67 a barrel by nine am in New York, half an hour before the opening rotation set the bids and asks.

Traders scrambled furiously for information on Bloomberg, The Oil Drum, Stratfor, and elsewhere. They called friends at think tanks and research institutions and tried to draw out as much information as possible. They asked for a "yes" or a "no" but most knew that no one could say for sure and that those who gave a simple answer didn't know what they were talking about. All but the most naive of traders knew that and naive traders went broke after a few months in the game. Some would be wiped out in the next day or two. That might be true of some institutions as well if they didn't play the crisis right. That's what it was to them—an event to be played, increasingly by algorithms not human judgment. The lives involved were abstractions and barely figured in the price moves, if at all.

Oil markets opened up sharply and stock exchanges opened down sharply. The news carried footage of American ships and planes on the move, generals coming and going from the White House, and incautious remarks from the Iranian president. Beneath the crawl, small windows showed volatile oil prices and index averages in real time. Experienced oil traders knew the momentum would last at least a few days. Some went to the gym. The Bloomberg app was always open on their smartphones, which were never far away.

Most experts held short of saying war was imminent. They pointed to the three US aircraft carriers off Iran, the presence of more fighter aircraft to the Gulf, and the deployment of B-2 bombers to Diego Garcia. Ominous signs, the analysts agreed. Nonetheless, there were still redlines to cross and final orders to be given. Everyone was on edge though.

Rumors were plucked from websites and from friends of friends and from who-knows-where. US fighters would hit Iran on the next new moon. Unmarked F-15Is, almost certainly Israeli, were in Azerbaijan with external fuel pods on their wings and huge bunker-busting ordnance on their bellies. A Saudi prince was assassinated by a Shia fanatic but the incident was being covered up because it might cause an uprising. Oil traders didn't believe all the rumors but they spread them, sometimes mentioning them in bars and gyms. They even created some of them to jack the markets even more. Truth didn't matter. The only thing that mattered was what came up on their spreadsheets in a few days. That was their truth.

One of the more intriguing rumors was that Hisbollah guerrillas crossed into the US from Mexico and were headed for Cushing, Oklahoma. Only two kinds of people know about Cushing: Okies and oil people. It's halfway between Oklahoma City and Tulsa, with a population of 8000 people and about the same number of storage tanks. Oil comes there from the south: Mexico, Venezuela, offshore sites in the Gulf of Mexico, and the shale fields of East Texas. Oil also comes from the north: the tar sands of Canada and the Bakken Formation in the Dakotas.

The crude was pumped through an elaborate pipeline system stretching across most of the US. A few RPG rounds here and there and Cushing would become very famous, very quickly. Very brightly illuminated too. You'd be able to see Cushing burn from the International Space Station.

That's why the governor of Oklahoma, a rancher from Stillwater with a dozen producing wells, called up the national guard that morning. Ground troops would ring Cushing, stopping vehicles and checking IDs. Black Hawk helicopters would patrol the pipelines for a radius of fifty miles. The national guard commander thought twenty-five miles was all he could handle but the governor wanted a fifty-mile "Zone of Iron" around Cushing. He wanted to set up checkpoints along the state's southern border but the perturbed governor of Texas called it a "tomfool idea" and it was dropped.

The Oklahoma governor then went to Cushing himself, supposedly to oversee the operation but mainly for media attention. The networks didn't fail him. He spoke live on the danger that Iran and Hisbollah constituted, not only to Cushing but to all the United States. He called for federal help in the form of Predator drones to help patrol the pipelines. As he spoke, oil futures shot up another buck and the Dow dropped another fifty points.

The oil traders watching CNBC at their gyms pumped their fists. The governor of Oklahoma just made them a little richer. One of them joked that he wanted Hisbollah or Iran to do the same—and soon. Others texted the witticism to colleagues in London, Zurich, and Hong Kong. All those guys knew about Cushing, to be sure. None of them had ever been there though.

Two hours later, the White House announced that ten Predators and maintenance crews were on their way to Tinker Air Force Base outside Oklahoma City. From there, the drones would patrol the pipelines around Cushing. The pilots "flew" them from a control center in Nevada not far from Las Vegas.

The media people stayed in local motels and appreciated the warm hospitality of Cushing folk. Dara, the proprietor of a diner with rotating counter stools, compact juke boxes in the booths, and signed photographs of Oklahoma football players, told the reporters that the Sooners were going to be "durn near unstoppable this year." Dara was on MSNBC for fifteen minutes that night and became a celebrity, like Joe the Plumber or the "Where's the beef" lady. The little town became very famous, very quickly, without a single shot being fired. So far.

The unfolding drama in Oklahoma was watched carefully in many parts of the world, including Lebanon. Hassan Nasrallah, the Hisbollah leader, called his military commanders and asked what they knew about this place called Cushing and if any of them ordered an attack there without his authorization. He was more puzzled than angry because such an operation seemed ridiculous to him.

None of his commanders had any knowledge of an attack or of Hisbollah fighters in Mexico. One said the only town he knew of in Oklahoma was Muskogee—a name he had considerable difficulty in pronouncing, a name Nasrallah had considerable difficulty in understanding. "I heard the name Mus-qo-quee in a song long ago," the general explained. "Very religious, very patriotic." Nasrallah respected music like that and searched for it on the Internet.

Washington, DC

Barrett parked his BMW at a lot on Gibson and took the shuttle bus to Albuquerque's airport. It was medium-sized at best and that was the kind he preferred. He took the up escalator and remembered once seeing Dennis Hopper coming down the other way. Barrett stood in line for the security screening and wondered if Homeland Security looked for cranky guys muttering under their breath. He was sure they did so he kept quiet and tried to look less cranky.

He went through security without incident and in an hour was up in the air on his not-so-merry way to Washington. Joe Burkett invited him to attend a powwow on the deteriorating situation in the Persian Gulf. Joe was on the National Security Council but this was an unofficial meeting, off the books, off the record, off the bureaucracy. There'd be some hotshots from the intelligence community and the Pentagon there. No cabinet secretaries, maybe an undersecretary or two.

Barrett had been to on-the-record meetings before. There was one on Afghanistan in which he argued that counterinsurgency efforts would fail and that we should write off the south and concentrate on the north. It was like telling the Vatican there was no God, or Microsoft that Apple was superior. Most in the room were afraid that their careers were jeopardized by being in the presence of an unbeliever and they dared not speak. Two scurried out as he began his presentation. An undersecretary tore into him but Barrett fired back and a couple of special forces colonels, retired of course, came to his defense. It was hilarious, educational too.

"Group think," Barrett muttered aboard the plane. "Pension seekers."

The plane flew down the Potomac, passing over Rosslyn and Arlington with their hi-rise office buildings which Barrett assumed were packed with consultants and hangers-on to the national security machinery. They were busy doing their little parts in the impending war, confident that higher-ups knew what they were doing though never looking into the matter.

"Goddam pension seekers . . . goddam apparatchiks."

He landed at Reagan-National and Joe met him at the baggage carousel.

"We're convening at Georgetown in two hours, Barrett."

"At the Tombs?" Barrett hopefully but jokingly referred to the bar across the street from the Foreign Service School and just around the corner from the famed house used in *The Exorcist*.

"Afraid not, Barrett. We're using a classroom in Healy—the main building on campus as you will recall from your college days. Unless of course you spent too much time in the Tombs."

"Not me. A classroom, you say. I hope there won't be a quiz."

"It's more of a seminar, Barrett."

They drove up the George Washington Parkway, crossed Key Bridge, and ascended the steep cobblestoned hill leading to Prospect. Parking karma was with them, they had an hour before the meeting, and the Tombs beckoned. Joe and Barrett walked down the stone stairway and found a booth near an Austrian recruitment poster from World War One. "And you?" the soldier asked from his trench, potato masher at the ready. Barrett looked around at the students there, drinking and conviviating while the world was on the brink of war. He thought of the paradox of recruitment posters near a prestigious college. He asked for a Guinness. Joe glared at him.

"Okay, okay. Two club sodas, please. So what's going on tonight, Joe?"

"We're trying to build an insurgency, one inside the administration and the rest of the bureaucracy. We don't think the folks at the top know what they're getting into in the Persian Gulf."

"So we're trying to do what Clark Clifford did when he became Secretary of Defense during Vietnam."

"Excellent analogy. Clifford gathered opposition to the war just as General Ridgway did when Ike was mulling over helping the French at Dien Bien Phu."

"Oh yeah. General Matthew B Ridgway of the No Land War in Asia School."

"A fine school, Barrett. Alas, it went out of business long ago and was replaced by the School of Perpetual Intervention."

"Where I presume you can major in Recent Asian Land Wars. Anybody from the think tanks?"

"Yes, of course. You'll recognize them from their media work. There are a few of them who are not in lockstep with the Pentagon."

"Anyone from CIA?" Barrett asked with a scowl.

Joe smiled and shook his head, "No one from Langley. Don't worry."

Barrett nodded approvingly. It was well known that Langley was highly politicized, dominated by interventionist group-think, and for present purposes, untrustworthy. "Are we all like-minded tonight, Joe, or is there going to be gnashing of teeth?"

"No teeth gnashing, Barrett. We're all on the same dental page."

"Do you trust them all?"

"Oh . . . I think so. But this *is* Washington. And Barrett, watch what you say this time, please? That is, if you somehow feel the need to speak—if you catch my meaning, old boy."

"I'll be good . . . sort of."

The pair walked over to Healy and entered the classroom right above the ground floor. Its wood paneling and desks looked like an old courtroom and made voices and footsteps reverberate gently even after more people arrived.

Barrett recognized the heads of the State Department's Iranian desk and a few people from the Saudi desk as well. Only one was a political appointee. There was a woman who worked with a think tank opposed to interventionism, a man from a new Middle East institute that advocated a more diplomatic Iran policy, and two retired flag officers who often appeared on news programs. There were others that Barrett did not recognize. No one wore cards with names and institutions. Most preferred anonymity.

Joe opened the meeting by briefly thanking everyone for coming then swiftly turning to the issues at hand by asking who was causing the blackouts. That brought a few amused looks and shoulder shrugs. Some said China, others speculated that Iran hired the Russian crooks who wrote viruses then sold fixes. Another said that Russia thought we were doing it to expand our power in the region. No one knew.

An elderly man Barrett didn't recognize spoke up. "We have reached a state of sophistication that outstrips our capacity to adequately control our military systems. Parts of the systems think for themselves and give instructions that humans don't know about—heuristics, we call them. In time, the problems will be found and rectified. *In time.* Our systems periodically blind us and this must be taken as a caution not as a cause for war. Blindness is not a reason to act rashly. On the contrary, it is a reason to act cautiously—more cautiously than ever."

"Who's this guy?" Barrett whispered to Joe.

"Peter Whitt. He's former DARPA, now one of the JASONs who oversee DARPA. A guru in the semiconductor world back in the early days."

The young woman from the noninterventionist think tank raised a hand and was recognized. "If these systems are prone to unexplained failures, how reliable are they? Maybe many other systems, here and around the world, have problems too that have not surfaced—at least as far as we know."

"And a war in the Persian Gulf and indeed throughout the Middle East isn't the proper time to test our gear," said one of the retired generals. Several in the room nodded.

Barrett motioned to speak but Joe tugged his sleeve down. A few people in the room noticed. They knew that Barrett was prone to what one might charitably call "plain speaking."

"Yes, caution is in order," came a heretofore silent voice. It was a man in his early fifties with a strong Israeli accent. "The heads of state cannot be sure their weapons will work as their pamphlets claim. They must not put them to the test—not now, not in the near future. We have to slow events down."

"Is that Palashet?" Barrett whispered to Joe.

"Yes. General Aaron Palashet—our Israeli colleague from Harrington's Center for World Affairs."

"We need to draw back—all of us," the general continued. "We must use our influence to make this clear to our leaders, civilian and military."

"And to our respective publics," Barrett interjected before Joe could stop him.

"And to our respective publics," General Palashet repeated. "Barrett Parker. You're usually so . . . so reticent, so reluctant to speak your mind." Several people chuckled softly. Barrett smiled amicably and gave a quick salute, though hardly of parade ground quality.

"Then let us agree on some points that must be made," Joe said, shifting the agenda of the meeting. "In addition to the issue of unreliability, can we agree on other reasons why the coming war is not in our respective nations' interests?"

Several intertwining discussions ensued, with many ideas advanced. Some thought certain arguments were more important than others. Some thought certain ideas were wrong, or at least overstated, but not objectionable. There was considerable agreement on the main ideas. That was a pleasant surprise to all in the room that night who were more accustomed to snarling conflict than to amiable consensus. In any case, everyone was free to advance arguments they thought most important or best suited to their particular expertise. In less than two hours, the main ideas were agreed upon.

> War will raise oil prices, probably for a considerable time. This will adversely affect the already frail global economy.

> War will bring a campaign of assassinations and bombings throughout the region and in many parts of the world. The campaign will go on for many years.

> War will destabilize Sunni Arab states such as Saudi Arabia, Bahrain, the Emirates, and Kuwait. These countries have large Shia populations that will oppose war on fellow Shia in Iran. Sunni populations will oppose what they perceive as an unjust war on a fellow Islamic country.

> War will weaken reformist forces in Iran and rally large parts of the public to traditional authorities, both religious and military. War will greatly strengthen the power of the Iranian Revolutionary Guard Corps.

One idea was especially controversial. It was first advanced by Barrett and received only limited support in the room. No one objected strenuously though.

> War will close off Israel's strategic options. Saudi Arabia and other Sunni states are using their financial assets to garner support in Egypt, Syria, and Sunni parts of western Iraq. Those countries all have significant military traditions; they all need foreign aid; and historically they all despise Israel. A strike on Iran would close a potential rapprochement between Israel and Iran that could act as a counterpoise to this emerging Sunni bloc.

Privately and publicly, dryly and passionately, the arguments would be advanced in the media, newspapers, correspondence to colleagues, and the high councils of governments. It was the same methods used by interests to argue for going to war. The men and women in the Georgetown classroom became an insurgency, a bureaucracy-in-a-bureaucracy. They were using national security arguments, not moral ones. The latter had lost effectiveness in the world.

The meeting lasted less than Joe thought. Everyone emerged optimistic but knew a tough job lay ahead. There were more people in government who wanted war and they enjoyed a sizable head start in getting their message out.

Barrett, Joe, and General Palashet chatted as they walked down the steps of the Healy building, recalling Harrington's morning seminars on America's place in the world after the Cold War.

"What's the situation in Israel, Aaron?" Joe asked.

"The prime minister wants war. That's no secret. However, neither the cabinet nor the public is behind it, not yet. Many worry more about the economy than about Iran. And of course every now and then a retired general or intelligence chief urges caution. You need more people like that in this country."

"We do indeed, Aaron. For most Americans, war is a spectator sport that other people's kids take part in," Barrett said with a trace of ire. "Kids from rural Texas."

"In Israel," Aaron said in agreement, "the consequences of war might be better understood than here—in part because of geography, in part because everyone serves in the military."

"Those days are long gone here," Barrett lamented. "What's going on in Iran? Is there any opposition?"

"Our intelligence says that those who favor reform are endangered by war talk. It makes them seem unpatriotic if not treasonous. Who knows what will happen if there's war. Our sources feel that there are people in the government and even the regular army who want to pull back from hostilities—open up all sites, even Parchin."

"That would be helpful." Joe made a mental note to ask Langley about this. The State Department's INR as well. "Who are these people inside Iran."

"They're not our friends and they're not even necessarily pro-democracy. They simply look at the forces on each side and shudder."

"I do the same," said Barrett.

"One more thing, Barrett." Aaron looked about cautiously. "There's a report circulating inside the foreign ministry that says the sanctions are hurting Iran badly, worse than anyone thought possible. Civil disturbances might not be far away."

"That would be great," Barrett noted. "The elections in Iran next spring might be interesting."

"I hope they're *very* interesting," Aaron replied.

"Maybe this report could be leaked?" Joe looked hopefully to his Israeli colleague.

"Don't look at me like that! I'm a soldier, not a politician—thank God!" The retired general shrugged his shoulders. "Things leak in Washington, things leak in Jerusalem. Sometimes for the better. I'm going to the foreign ministry in Jerusalem tomorrow."

The three shook hands and said goodbye as they reached Prospect Street.

Classes had recently restarted for the semester and the streets were filling with students walking down to the enticing nightlife of M Street. A girl shuddered when the group passed the Exorcist Stairs and a boy put his arm around her.

Tel Aviv

Boaz walked with Ethan and Rina to their office. His dismay was apparent.

"Another blackout?" Ethan asked.

"Something far worse, good folks." Boaz never broke stride or looked over to the pair. "A pair of our F-15Is were patrolling south of the Yemeni coast when they were fired upon by an Iranian picket ship. The politicians are livid and so are the generals."

"Boaz, we both know that our pilots can get cocky and buzz picket ships. Sometimes with orders, sometimes not. Are you sure our fighters were fired on? Pilots can misinterpret things they see with their eyes and with their radar. Remember that American ship in the 1967 War?"

"Yes, we all do. One pilot and copilot had a visual sighting of an Iranian missile launch, probably an Iranian Misagh-2 or a Libyan SA-18."

"What about the other crew?"

"They're not sure what they saw."

"They're not sure? What the hell are the generals doing to make sure?"

"They're trying to get visual confirmation of a missile launch from one of our freighters nearby. The F-15Is were practicing air-sea rescue with the ships, in case they get shot up over Iran someday and have to eject."

"Damn it, Boaz, what did the freighter crew say?"

"No response. They're sitting silent, as per orders. No electronic signal whatsoever. They're scheduled to check in, very briefly, in twenty minutes."

Rina heard confidence in the system in Boaz's crisp answer. She had no such faith. "So the generals will wait for them."

"Oh, they're not going to wait. We've prepared three squadrons of F-15s and four of F-16s and they will launch . . ." Boaz looked at his watch and corrected himself. "No, they've already launched, two minutes ago. One faction in the government wants to attack Iranian ships in the Red Sea and out in the Arabian Sea too. At least one of those ships in the Red Sea is thought to be delivering arms to Houthis already inside Saudi Arabia, near Yanbu. Another faction wants an immediate strike on Iran."

"You can't launch an attack now. What if there's another blackout? They might proceed to their targets no matter what."

"They will, Ethan, they will."

"You might be starting a huge war," Rina exclaimed angrily. "A huge unnecessary war. Another one!"

Boaz was annoyed by Rina's remarks about him and his institution. "The PM wants to . . . 'send a message'. Those were his words, I'm told." Boaz's voice was cold and impersonal now.

"Look, Boaz, the blackouts are caused by a software glitch. Rina and I are sure we can fix it. We just need a little time—an hour at most."

Rina arched an eyebrow. She wasn't sure if he was boasting or lying.

"Ethan," Boaz replied despairingly as they entered the work area. "I have every confidence in you, but events are getting away from us . . . and I have my duties. We all do. The fighters are up in the air, on their way. You have less than an hour until they reach their targets. I suggest you get to work. Both of you."

Boaz headed to the command center, leaving them alone with their computer terminals and the institutional clock.

"Ethan, *do* you know how to fix Samson?"

He fell back into a chair and exhaled. "I have an idea, but it's not much more than that. It came to me as we watched the storm." Ethan spoke cooly and analytically, putting into a logical framework the nebulous thoughts that came to him on the beach. "Samson is sending spikes into the system causing confusion. He then penetrates the system and causes all kind of events, some of them blackouts."

"Okay, let me run this down." Rina's eyes became intense, staring out into the conference room. She sat in a chair next to him and they leaned forward, eyes never meeting. "Samson incubates a situation. That is, he lets a problem remain unresolved for an instant, a picosecond or two, allowing a search of storage units for productive answers. Samson generates a variety of solutions, including some that initially seem outlandish or absurd, without initially evaluating any of them. Once a lengthy list has been created, he evaluates each item for usefulness."

"Right," Ethan picked up. "As a problem becomes more complex, the time required to solve it grows—possibly into a nonviable time period, say, a thousand years, even with Samson's power. So, an heuristic takes over to handle the problem. It spikes the system—causing our blackouts. A good solution from *the heuristic's* point of view, though not in the real world."

"We need to disable the spikes. How? What did the storm teach you, weatherman?"

"Well, my dear, we know the transformer is connected to the power supplies and it responds to a software command. The command sends a positive charge and all we have to do is insert a ground. We know Samson is doing similar operations to activate or deactivate certain circuits hence the option is already there. We need to route it to the transformer. Once the transformer is grounded, no more spikes."

"Problem solved. No blackouts. But Ethan, what about the rest of Samson? He does have virtues, you know. Many, many virtues."

"He does indeed. We need to find a way to disable the vices without disabling the virtues. Okay, Samson constantly runs electrical pulses within the millions of decision paths. Some of these decisions are sending spikes and activating the transformer. We need to scan these pulses and intercept signals that include keywords like 'shutdown' and 'blackout'. When we detect a spike command, we'll send a different one that will open the ground gateway."

"We'll need a program to make the ground, boss man."

"We'll create one that'll work within Samson's heuristic." Ethan was mentally patching together new algorithms with ones he'd worked on for the American and Israeli militaries, but he needed to reach for something more. "Part of this program will use the computational geometry in Micrologic Design programs to find the data that causes the spikes. Computational geometry, aka algorithmic geometry, can trace the information inside Samson pretty damn fast."

"What!" Rina stood up and looked around the room trying to make sense of the idea. "Computational geometry is used for geometrical engines and analysis. You intend to convert Samson into a geometrical model to accelerate a decision-tree search?"

"You got it. I've told you before that I hired a genius."

Rina thought the idea through as best she could given the time restraints there in the Templar Building. Pathways opened in her mind showing promise. "So we'll translate Samson's huge decision tree into a geometrical model, find the causes of the spikes and blackouts, and stop them."

"Exactly. We'll need to modify the Scan-line algorithm. The classic version would take centuries to run—literally. With a little work, it will analyze only promising segments. Now take a seat and let's get to work."

Ethan and Rina leaned back in their chairs and laughed at the achievement of coming up with such an idea in so short a time and under trying circumstances. Now they had to transform the idea into algorithms and run them inside the Samson Program while the clock ticked.

After thirty minutes of hurried data entry, mindful of the consequences of the smallest typo, an intricate geometric image lit up their screen. It resembled a city at night from twenty-thousand feet—green, red, blue, and yellow lines extending as far as one could see, like broad boulevards and bisecting avenues, with some intersections far busier than others. Ethan and Rina had to zoom out and then back in on selected regions to appreciate the model of Samson's intricacies that their computational geometry innovation presented them.

As they looked at a particular line, they imagined it might refer to the US or Lebanon or Syria or Iraq or Israel or Iran. It was only after a few moments of marveling that they realized that the lines and nodes related to human beings and that lives—millions of them—were affected by this model of the world on their screens. Some would live and some might not, depending what Samson thought, depending what a handful of generals and politicians did, and depending what Ethan and Rina did in the next hour.

"See the red blinking segments?" Ethan explained to Rina. "Those are segments that were marked as 'leaders' which may lead to the spike commands." He observed the screen carefully then frowned. "The model's too large." He pointed towards a window on the upper left screen. "The problem became 'NP complete'—not solvable."

"Our shortcut wasn't short enough then," Rina noted nervously. "We still have too much data to analyze. Look," she said pointing to several motions on the screen, "for every significant event in the Middle East, Samson starts a new path in the decision tree. And for each event that relates to a previous event, there's another path."

Ethan stared at the screen. His exhaustion was clear to both of them and he needed Rina's input to keep his mind from wavering, flagging, making an error on the boulevards and people.

"Ethan, we have to shorten the shortcut. The Bentley-Ottmann algorithm is an efficient sweep-line algorithm. It'll sort for specific events. Furthermore, we will observe events only with—"

"A common denominator and similar time frame."

"And most importantly," Rina continued, "a common motif."

Ethan was already updating the scan program. "We're in business— and we can expect some answers in . . . oh God no, it'll take almost ten minutes."

"Ethan, I'm showing unusual activity in one of Samson's analysis units . . . and in an execution unit too. It's trying to do something but can't. It's jammed or frozen or confused—still trapped in that screwed-up heuristic."

"Well, that might be the least of our problems now," Ethan replied distractedly. He closed his eyes for a moment then his interest became piqued. "Is it fixed on any location, say, Fifth Fleet Headquarters or an Israeli airbase or Tehran?"

"It's concentrated on Bushehr. That's a port city in Iran with a nuclear reactor."

A few groans and murmurs came from offices down the corridor in the command center. Three quick knocks on the door and Boaz stuck his head in. "Bad news, guys. We're in the dark again. Everything's down. The F-15Is are headed for Iran across Saudi airspace. The hell with what the Saudis think. ETA at targets is fifteen minutes."

Rina looked up from the screen and glared angrily at him. "You're going to bomb Bushehr, aren't you?"

"Bushehr? No, that's just a reactor. No uranium enrichment, no weapons program. The F-15s are headed for Natanz, Fordo, and Parchin."

"Well, Boaz," Rina responded bitterly, pointing to the segment blinking angrily on her screen. "Something sure as hell is going on at Bushehr!"

"What's that thing?" Boaz puzzlement mixed with boyish wonder as he was momentarily awed by the lights and patterns on the screen. "Is it a screen saver?"

"It's the world, Boaz. The whole world." Ethan shook his head as he pondered the chasm that had opened between himself and his old friend. "There's no time to explain."

Bushehr, Iran

Iranian systems were down too. The new missile base was out of communication with the command and control chain that stretched back to military and religious authorities in Tehran. The officers of the Chinese navy who helped build the site and prepare the missiles were similarly cut off with communications center in Gwadar, Pakistan, and the regional headquarters in Zhanjiang, China. Communication trouble presented problems and opportunities for the ambitious officers—opportunities for decisive action.

The Iranian and Chinese officers at the Bushehr missile site were certain that the blackouts were the work of the US and Israel. Stuxnet and its cyberwarfare kin aimed to retain American hegemony in the world and keep Iran and China from taking their proper places in it. The blackouts were another American-Israeli cyberwarfare attack and a prelude to a strike on Iran and an effort to drive China from the Persian Gulf. Iran would be bombed pitilessly and China would be cut off from oil. They concluded their respective country's timid civilian leaders were failing to act responsibly.

For many months the officers from both countries discussed world events and potential responses. Two days earlier they decided to ask decisively. The civilians in Tehran and Beijing would be confronted with a fait accompli and have to go to war. The officers' actions would find considerable support at higher levels, especially inside the IRGC and the People's Liberation Army.

Sizzler missiles are normally mounted on fighters or ships, but that would require more time and involve other parts of the Iranian military. Three Sizzlers were mounted on truck platforms and prepared for launch, slowed only by brief computer freezes.

The officers gave the signal to fire and in an instant all three missiles erupted from their platforms and thundered to the west at low altitude. They would skim five meters above the surface of the Gulf at subsonic speed until coming within fifty kilometers of the target at which point they would kick into supersonic "sprint." The target's defense systems would not be able to acquire the swiftly approaching Sizzlers. The target would fire missiles to stop them and its gatling guns would fire thousands of rounds per second at them. The countermeasures were unlikely to stop even one of the Sizzlers. The target of all three missiles was only 150 kilometers away from the Bushehr missile site.

The dawning of a new historical epoch is rarely precisely known. Some historians debate when the Renaissance began, others when American global dominance began. Some said the latter began when Europe lay in ruins in 1918. Others point to the Battle of Midway in 1942 when the Imperial Japanese Navy lost four aircraft carriers in a single day.

The Chinese and Iranian officers at Bushehr were positive that a new day in the region—and in the world as well—would begin in precisely fifteen minutes. That was when their Sizzlers struck, ignited, and sank the American aircraft carrier *Enterprise*.

Tel Aviv

Ethan and Rina glanced at the news after receiving Boaz's grim update. Iran charged the US with sending drones into its airspace. IRGC ships were playing dangerous games with US naval vessels in the Gulf. Shia sites in Iraq were struck by a series of deadly bombings and Baghdad was claiming that Saudi Arabia was behind them. Rocket fire from Gaza was much as it had been for over a year but now rockets were coming in from Lebanon and Sinai.

Ethan and Rina felt sick. They could only hope that they and the Bentley-Ottmann algorithm were up to the task. There was a large polygon on the screen, mainly red and yellow with scores of blinking intersections.

"Well, our friend has lost a lot of weight." Ethan clicked on the blinking red segment marked with the letter "A" and waited. "This is the first lead, and it should take us home."

The segment stopped blinking. A colorful fly-line came out of the segment and connected to another red segment on a different part of the polygon.

"There we go," Ethan said, again momentarily transfixed by the intricate model. "Now, the fly-lines will connect all related segments, leading to green segments, then combine their results and form one blinking blue segment. That will be the information we need. We are close to a breakthrough. This is the first time that computational geometry has been implemented with decision trees. I wish we had a larger audience!"

"Well, if it doesn't give us what we need then it's just a colorful show," Rina replied. "But *I* like it," she added massaging his shoulders.

The fly-lines jumped from segment to segment across the sparkling polygon and Ethan smiled as a young person would at his first fireworks display.

"Patience is a virtue," Rina chided.

"One that I don't have right now. Not when there are upset politicians in Jerusalem and fighters streaking toward Iran."

The fly-lines stopped and a single blue segment began to blink.

"Eureka," Ethan gushed in pride. Hearty congratulations and a pat on the back came from his small audience. Ethan exulted in the praise. "Perhaps I can lecture on this at Cal Tech someday!"

"I don't think we want to say much about this one, *Captain* Alon. They'd take you away to an undisclosed secure location—or to a home for burned-out programmers," Rina said. "I think that's near Folsom, so maybe we can wave to each other from the exercise yards."

"Sounds romantic. Okay Rina, we now have the commands that trigger the spikes and cause the blackouts. I've created a fairly simple routine to replace the spike commands with ground commands."

"How are we going to test it, cap'n?"

"Well, we have to mimic a spike in the system. I'll send a manual command to the transformer and only we two will know what caused it." Ethan made a few entries and sat back. "We should have a simulated blackout in about two minutes. Let's see if our assumption is correct. We'll know soon enough." Ethan imagined his cuckoo clock's mechanism knocking out the countdown and fighters skimming a hundred meters over the Saudi desert.

"What will it look like on the screen, Ethan? What does a *simulated* blackout taking place during an *actual* blackout look like?"

"Well . . . ."

"You mean you don't know?"

"There'll be a blink in the system. That's for sure. Then the real blackout will end—suddenly, and ahead of time . . . . I think."

"I guess the empirical data on this sort of thing is null."

"Afraid so."

The screen blinked out suddenly and stayed dark for an agonizing few seconds. Everything was dark. They wondered if every system around the world was down, never to return to proper functioning for hours or days or weeks. Generals and politicians would fly into rages. Local commanders would act on their own. Rina felt ill.

Then a few segments appeared followed by a dozen or two fly-lines. More and more structures lit up on the screen until the glittering maze of computational geometry was fully restored, signaling that the Israeli system was up and others like it in the Middle East and in the US as well!

"Now we introduce our lightning rod into the system . . . like so," Ethan entered a string of commands. "And Samson is still running, just not running amok!"

Another quick blink ensued and the two now confidently awaited the system to relight.

"Got it! Got it! The best patch our profession has ever known, except that they *don't* know and they never will," Rina added, realizing at once the importance of what they'd just done as well as its surrealism and its implausibility to all but a few people in the entire world.

The pair raced down the corridor to Boaz's office to give him the news, but the looks of amazement and gratitude and occasional resentment told them that the military center knew it already. Boaz met them in the crowded hallway and began to voice the center's gratitude when Ethan shouted, "Save it! Tell the people upstairs that there's no need to go to war! They can't be the first people to start a war because of a computer glitch. Tell them! All of you, tell them! Stop those damn fighters!"

"We still can't raise the fighters," a junior officer replied meekly. "As soon as the blackout lifted we saw jamming signals coming from Iraq and Iran."

"Where are the planes right now?" Ethan roared.

"They should be entering Iranian airspace right about now."

The Persian Gulf

The decks and bridge of *USS Bulkeley* were rimmed by members of the crew scanning the horizon. "Every man jack," as the skipper put it on the ship's address system. They were on picket duty for the aircraft carrier *Enterprise* which transited the Strait of Hormuz a half day earlier. The word from Fifth Fleet headquarters in Bahrain was that Iran might seek to provoke a war with a fighter or missile attack.

Contact with other ships was confined to signal lamps, and the ship's radar was working only intermittently. The system blackout gave greater urgency to "every man jack" on duty. There were more than a few women sailors on duty too, of course. Realizing his gaff, the skipper corrected himself a few minutes later. The crew, men and women alike, smiled briefly then continued their watch.

It was near the end of the day. The west was beginning to glow red with the setting sun but more attention was paid to the east. The Iranian coast was well out of sight and the horizon was darkening, merging with the inky waters of the Gulf.

One of the women sailors saw a small, almost perfectly spherical cloud form suddenly on the horizon to the east, then two more in the same area. Before the bridge could be alerted, everyone heard a dull boom followed by two more in quick succession. Something—no, three things—had broken the sound barrier and were heading their way. More than likely, however, they were heading *Enterprise*'s way.

Amid the blackout, the frigate's SeaRAM missiles could not be fired with any accuracy and the gatling guns could only be optically guided. The gun crews let loose with torrents of fifty-caliber fire, but with no discernible effect. As the missiles came to within a mile of the ship, the Officer of the Deck shouted, "Sizzlers!" and in just a few seconds the ship-killers roared past the *Bulkeley*, one only a hundred meters off the bow, another the same distance off the stern. The third shrieked not five meters in front of the bridge, sending sailors down to the deck. The missile's flambeau blistered paint, thumped the Plexiglas, and left sailors coughing from the acrid fumes of expended fuel.

"God help *Enterprise*," the OD whispered before ordering his ship to turn hard to starboard in an effort to reduce his ship's exposure to the storm of fire now erupting from every functioning weapon on the massive carrier.

The OD watched in helpless awe as *Enterprises's* SeaRAMs shot forth but failed to acquire their targets and self-destructed, and as its gatling guns sent angry scarlet tracer streams toward the rapidly-closing Sizzlers. Frigates on either side of the carrier put everything they had on them too. The captivating spectacle reminded him of footage of Kamikaze attacks off Okinawa in 1945, though the incoming craft were far faster and far more lethal than a Japanese Zero.

"Victory at sea," he murmured half mordantly, half prayerfully. "Prepare for rescue operations," he barked into the commo system.

Two of the Sizzlers suddenly veered off to port, pitched and yawed almost comically, then exploded as they hit the water less than two hundred yards from the carrier. The third rose vertically, ascended to three thousand feet, then exploded into a brilliant yellow starburst that flitted downward, preceded by hundreds of glowing metal shards. Explosives and propellant intended to ignite the carrier's fuel and munitions floated harmlessly down to the dark waters of the Gulf.

Enterprise hit its steam whistles in jubilation and the crews cheered loud enough to be heard on the escort frigates whose crews then joined in on the celebration. The carrier's skipper personally congratulated the gun crews. In the immediate aftermath, they were convinced that all three Sizzlers, in supersonic sprint just above the water, had been shot down in only a few seconds by sailors using iron sights and Kentucky windage.

The OD back on *Bulkeley* watched in silent awe. When a young ensign exclaimed, "We got them sumbitches!" the OD shook his head and murmured, "No way, mister. No goddam way."

"Sir? Then what *did* bring down those missiles?"

"I've no earthly idea. No earthly idea at all. I'm not sure if we just witnessed the outbreak of war or a crazy incident that will be debated for years. Maybe both."

The young ensign thought about his superior's words but couldn't dismiss what he thought he'd seen and what his training taught him to expect—the crisp, professional performance of naval personnel resulting in a big win.

"Sir, with all due respect, I still think we shot them sumbitches down."

"Very well . . . but I suspect we're going to be told that we never saw 'them sumbitches' and that none of this happened. This is the Persian Gulf, mister, and things like that happen here—then we're informed that they *didn't* happen here."

The ensign began to understand something about the military and politics. It would serve him well in his career, however long that might be, and in much of civilian life as well.

Tel Aviv

The colonels and generals in the command center were greatly relieved that their systems were back up. They immediately tried to raise the F-15 squadrons headed for Iran and the freighter that might have witnessed the missile attack. There was still no luck raising either. Everyone felt that war was about to break out, either by computer or human error. Or both.

Twenty minutes later, at Ramon airbase from which the F-15s launched, a crackly radio communication came in from the squadron commander asking permission to land. As the first few flew over, the enlisted personnel and the base commander could plainly see that their external fuel tanks had been dropped but more importantly, their bombs were still on the wings. As the pilots headed for the debriefing room, the base commander asked if there were casualties and if they'd encountered Iranian fighters.

"No sir," the squadron commander answered. "We got the recall order before we crossed into Iranian airspace, about ten kilometers out."

"Recall order?" The base commander was confused. Something was wrong, at least as far as his command system was concerned. "Who sent you a recall order?"

"Sir? I thought you did. The encrypted signal came through just as the Iranian coast came into view. As I said, about ten kilometers out."

The Ramon base commander called the Tel Aviv command center and explained as best he could what had happened. Everyone agreed that no abort order had been issued from anyone, neither before nor during nor after the blackout. The base commander reminded the higher-ups that a similar unexplained abort order went out just a few weeks earlier.

The Tel Aviv brass tried to make sense of this before reporting to the prime minister. Did the pilots abort on their own? There'd been a few incidents over the years of young pilots refusing to follow orders and infantry officers doing the same, so it wasn't out of the question. One colonel suggested that the abort order was due to the same glitch that caused the blackouts and that the young couple flown in from California had solved the problem.

"That was Ethan Alon whom I personally recommended," Boaz noted proudly. "He's a captain in the reserves."

"Well, Alon should be a major now," replied a general. "What say you, Col Kleinman? He did fix your system after all."

Colonel Kleinman sensed a little condescension in the general's words but quickly and obligingly said it was an excellent idea. He really wanted Ethan walking patrol on the Golan Heights. *That woman too*, he thought darkly.

"He'll be pleased to hear of the promotion," Boaz said, enjoying a private joke. He couldn't wait to share it with Ethan and Rina—with a straight face, of course.

Within the hour, communication was reestablished with the freighter that had been in the vicinity of the supposed missile attack on the Israeli fighters. Its data found no evidence of a missile launch from the Iranian frigate and visual reports were contradictory. The freighter's captain reported he had no solid evidence the Iranians ever fired on the Israeli jets. After lengthy debriefing and after hearing of the ship's report, the F-15 crew that claimed it had been fired upon south of the Yemeni coast now said they weren't certain there'd been a missile launch after all. Their radar was glitch-prone and they might have simply seen a distant contrail that looked like missile exhaust. Their commander shook his head in frustration and anger.

Ethan and Rina slumped back in their chairs for a moment before stirring to double-check that the flawed heuristic in Samson was repaired and that the Program was still in operation. All was well with the defense systems of Israel. The systems of other powers were back up too. Generals around the world were at once relieved that their systems were functioning but uncertain of their reliability. Only a handful of people around the world knew the answer—two more than there were a few hours ago.

"I'm not sure that fixing war machines around the world is entirely for the good, Ethan," Rina said, her eyes fixed on the institutional setting of their room beneath the Templar Building. "And I hope we don't have to wait a few decades to find out."

"I hope we *have* those decades to find out—and we should make the best of what time we have. Anyway, it's not really in our hands anymore. It's in the hands of the Samson programmers . . . and a few leaders around the world."

Ethan and Rina sat slumped before the terminals, their hands dangling from the armrests and swinging slightly until they touched and held on.

"Ethan, when we get back to California, can we go up to the mountains again? After we ship the product, I mean. We need a vacation—one that doesn't put us in a mineshaft beneath an army headquarters on the brink of war."

"Yeah, the mountains sound wonderful. They don't even have wi-fi . . . . But first, Rina my dear, we're going out in my Tel Aviv! I'll show you around, as the old Dean Martin song goes."

"It was Frank Sinatra, but I gladly accept your invitation." Rina broke into song and whirled about the room. "Come fly with me, let's fly, let's fly away!"

"Okay, *that's* Dean Martin."

Washington, DC

After the Georgetown meeting, the op-ed pages of major newspapers and online news sources began to question the premises of the rush to war and to enumerate the likely consequences—most of them quite sobering. Many articles cited the proverbial unnamed sources inside the administration, others cited retired military and intelligence personnel or independent political analysts.

Every night CNN, MSNBC, BBC, Fox, Sky News, Al Jazeera, France 24, RT, and the rest picked up the big story. They fed upon the debate and invited speakers from both sides to exchange views. Some debates were so spirited that speakers all but exchanged blows. Talk radio was in on the debate, though that format had long been influenced by pro-war factions and the term "debate" scarcely applied. Opponents of war with Iran were branded "appeasers" and as "unpatriotic" and as "having learned nothing from history."

Tensions in the Gulf eased. Both sides pulled back from penetrating the other's airspace and buzzing the other's ships. Whoever was assassinating Iranian nuclear scientists was either unable to find more targets or placed the program on hold. The US did not pull any ships out of the Gulf, though the third aircraft carrier in the Arabian Sea headed back to East Asia as China took advantage of the Gulf crisis by making claims of territorial rights on a few uninhabited islands. Oil markets in London and New York dropped several dollars a day. Motorists were pleased.

So were Barrett Parker and Joe Burkett.

From his position in the National Security Council, Joe could sense the weakening of war support. The machinery of government was no longer churning toward attacking Iran. Parts of government that usually worked at least somewhat coherently were now badly out of sync. Bureaucrats and appointees worried that they were no longer being invited to key meetings and getting the latest briefings, when in fact there simply weren't many meetings and briefings anymore.

"Well Joe, that's welcome news. Just what cooled things off? I presume a sudden outbreak of sensibility can be ruled out."

"Hard to say. The debates, a distracted public . . . I can't say for sure. Let's leave it to historians in, oh say, fifty years."

"I can wait. Maybe it was the first war stopped by people annoyed by gas prices."

"That's a bit tough on the American public, Barrett."

"Maybe if the German people owned more Volkswagens back in the 1930s—"

"Barrett! You see why we don't invite you up here much anymore?"

"Pardner, we speak plainly out in these here parts," Barrett drawled.

"In any case, *pardner*, it might also be those blackouts in the military systems."

"Oh them. I thought they stopped," Barrett noted cagily. Ethan and Rina had filled him in on what happened in the Templar Building. Most of it was way over his head.

"Yep, they have indeed stopped. We've heard that other countries faced some difficulties as well. Not sure of their status, but everybody's still worried."

"What the hell are they worried about now, Joe?"

"About the *reliability* of all those systems, of course. They don't know what caused the blackouts or what made them go away. Sooooo . . . ."

"Sooooo," Barrett picked up, "they worry that the blackouts may return, perhaps at a most inopportune time—like during a war."

"Affirmative, buddy. The generals are worried—our generals, their generals, everybody's generals. They think a virus or worm was responsible. One made where everything else is these days—China."

Barrett paused and hoped it wasn't suspicious. "Yeah . . . China's pretty good at that stuff, aren't they? They're a rising power and rising powers are nuisances. They set out to show their power and right the wrongs of ages past."

"That's quite true. Those Chinese students at MIT and Stanford have gone home to work for the People's Liberation Army and who knows what China thinks of the Gulf situation. What does your wolf think about who caused the blackouts?"

"I'll ask him later, Joe. I don't know anything about that stuff. I'm gonna have to let you go. A wolf is staring at me. He wants to go on a secret mission."

"Jesse wants to go for a walk, I take it."

"You take it rightly. You should go for walks. Same with all those generals and analysts up there."

"I'll tell them."

"Joe, I've got lots more things you can tell them to do."

"Gotta go, Barrett. Enjoy your walk."

Barrett and Jesse ascended the trails of North Mountain. It was autumn now and there was no trace of the fuchsia and yellow that the cholla cactuses had brought a few months ago. They sat down at their spot.

"Buddy, do you remember Ethan and Rina—those people who used all that hi-tech jargon? They think we might have saved the world, at least for a little while. I'd say that merits a treat." He reached into his pocket for an oatmeal cookie wrapped in a napkin and tossed it in the air. The great wolf's jaws slammed down on it in an instant. *Crack!*

"We have an odd situation in the world today. Generals all over the world are worried that their radar won't see and their missiles won't launch and their bombs won't go kaboom. So they're reluctant to go to war. What should we do about it?"

Jesse lay down with a long grumble and Barrett watched the skies above the Sandias redden then cool into a dark blue evening. Jesse nodded off and his paws began to jump and twitch as he dreamed of primordial hunts or maybe just of chasing tennis balls in his younger days. His paws slowed to a trot before coming to a halt. Every now and then he'd snort and groan stertorously amid his dreams of glory.

"Yep. That's what I think we should do as well. Nuthin'."

Looking east, out to the dry plains past Moriarty, Barrett saw the Iraqi tanks again, some of them afire, sending ugly dark plumes into the sky. One took a Sabot round that blew its turret clear off and ignited the ammunition. The powerful concussion hit Barrett a few seconds later, causing him to flinch even though he braced for it.

"Some people come up to places like this and talk to God. I don't think he listens. He didn't listen that day in Fallujah. I talk to you, Jesse. Yeah, I talk to you. Ever read *Slaughterhouse-Five*? Kurt Vonnegut wrote it and it's well worth the while. The main character has become 'unstuck in time.' He keeps drifting away from dull civilian life back to his war experiences, mainly the firebombing of Dresden near the end of World War Two.

"Readers think that being unstuck in time is funny—a real hoot. They don't understand that it's Vonnegut's private dark way of saying how wars stay with us and draw us back into them.

"I cried when I read it, Jesse . . . and I bet Vonnegut cried when he wrote it."

Jerusalem

Israelis have a passion for debate. The coffee shops teem with people talking of war and the economy. People on both sides of the issues speak emotionally and often angrily, usually without losing respect for those on the other side. Everyone knows people in the military—friends, relatives, and neighbors. Many retired generals and intelligence chieftains urged caution. The government accused them of acting out of partisan loyalties or personal grudges, but the blows glanced off of men who'd served their country since the Six Day War of 1967 and the Yom Kippur War in 1973. Some hardy old-timers had been in the 1948 War. Their preference for peace had come the hard way and wasn't easily dismissed by thwarted politicians, try though they did.

The cabinet in Jerusalem held debates. Everyone knew where the prime minister stood. Even after the blackout problem lifted, he still wanted to attack Iran. The word slipped out, or was leaked, that he was still unable to build a consensus for the war. The defense minister was on the PM's side but could not speak for everyone in his bureau. Some generals thought war would be a strategic error. Others were unsure of their weapons' reliability and urged caution.

The foreign minister had sided with the war party but was now rethinking matters. In recent weeks he and retired general Aaron Palashet had met three times, each session lasting over two hours. They discussed a recent foreign ministry analysis on the sanctions on Iran and how they were affecting the Iranian economy and political situation. Palashet summarized the findings on Iran's plummeting export revenue and soaring inflation. An Iranian television program held a live call-in event to rally support for the government but so many people voted for ending the nuclear program that the broadcast went dark. The confidential Israeli report projected unrest in coming months and the news that morning reported more protests by Tehran merchants.

"Will it spread?" the minister asked.

"We cannot say with certainty," Aaron answered with an exaggerated shrug and frown. "There are many students, middle-class people, professionals, and members of the regular army—not the hardcore IRGC—who are tired of hardships and mullahs. They see events in the region and want their own right of representative government."

"A Persian Spring . . . Perhaps they will use the spring elections to express their concerns," the minister said looking out the window, imagining likely events and wondering if it was sound analysis or wishful thinking. "Aaron, why was this report classified?"

Palashet shrugged his shoulders again. "Classifying a document makes people feel important."

The two men shared a moment of amusement, very much welcome in the tense atmosphere. They recalled the thousands of innocuous reports and documents that civil servants had seen fit to designate secret.

"Aaron, when a democracy stands at the crossroads of war and peace, it should have a full debate, with as much information as possible. The public should know the effects of the sanctions and the prospects for political change inside Iran. They have the right to know."

"You're no longer speaking like a politician, sir. You're speaking like . . . oh, like a *statesman*."

"Aaron, statesmen can be dangerous—especially when they're right!"

"You're not in Russia anymore, you know . . . " More welcome levity. "So we agree that the Israeli people should know about the sanctions and prospects for change." The idea of leaking the report was hanging in the air. It had been on the general's mind for several days now.

Aaron studied the minister's face for a sign of his disposition without success. He wondered how to nudge the minister into what Aaron thought the right decision and decided that more humor might be the right tool. "Shall I notify Julian Assange through the good offices of the Ecuadorian embassy?"

The minister laughed aloud as the weight fell from his shoulders.

"No, Aaron. He's far too much of a showman for my sensibilities. You can find a more . . . oh, a more *statesmanlike* way to get this out, can't you?" The minister's gaze fell on the general.

"Ahhh, I see. You want *me* to leak this report. I'm a simple soldier, innocent of the wiles of politics and the media." Aaron sensed that the foreign minister didn't believe him and Aaron himself had spent so much time in various governments, Knesset committees, and embassies that he didn't truly believe it himself. They laughed aloud. "I'll see what can be done—in a *statesmanlike* manner, of course."

"*De*-classifying a document makes us feel more important sometimes, Aaron."

"And more decent as well, sir."

Two days later, the classified study's findings were reported in newspapers and television news and various websites. Aaron expected more of a stir. Everyone knew the report came out of the foreign ministry and though the leak could not be traced to the foreign minister himself, it was taken as a sign that he was no longer supportive of war. The wind was out of the sails of the prime minister and his war party, at least for a while.

Peace is a wonderful thing, though war is always lurking nearby. Peace lasts for a while. That's the best you can hope for in this world. A defense ministry report was coming in of a new Iranian research center near Arak.

Albuquerque

Barrett sat down in the studio and looked into the camera, prepared to take the interview in a direction of his choosing for a change.

> Anchor: The Arab Spring has taken a turn toward militancy and fundamentalism. How does this affect Israel's national security?
>
> Barrett: It's not likely to pose a conventional threat to Israel, not in the short term. There will be skirmishes along the Sinai border and perhaps along the one with Syria someday. Egypt and Syria, however, will be inward-looking for many years. Egypt is beset by internal conflicts. So is Syria—and it may fragment into several antagonistic regions.
>
> Anchor: I know it's difficult to look far into the future, especially amid so much turbulence, but is there a long-term threat to Israel?
>
> Barrett: There's certainly the possibility of one. At the center would be Saudi Arabia.
>
> Anchor: Has not Saudi Arabia supported change in the region? In Libya and Syria, for example.
>
> Barrett: The Saudis wanted Qaddafi out of Libya because he tried to kill a Saudi monarch. They want Assad out of Syria because he's close to Iran. The Saudis, however, are hostile to any change that will bring democracy. It goes entirely against their religious and political thinking. They will support

authoritarian governments and seek to integrate them into a Sunni bloc controlled by them.

Anchor: And this could pose a threat to Israel?

Barrett: Oh yes. Indeed it almost certainly will. The Saudi bloc is presently directed against Iran, but it could one day redirect that bloc against Israel.

Anchor: Wouldn't that be a return to the international situation of the sixties and seventies?

Barrett: Yes, it would be. Back then, Israel was surrounded by hostile countries but it had a powerful ally against them.

Anchor: And who was that ally?

Barrett: Iran. Israel and Iran were staunch allies. They both opposed the Sunni countries and they both cooperated in trade and military matters.

Anchor: Is it possible we will see the reemergence of this alliance?

Barrett: It's possible, though not in the near future. Not at all. Nonetheless, things change in the world—often suddenly, often unexpectedly. The US and Vietnam were bitter enemies. Now, they are allied against China and my basketball shoes are made in Vietnam. I would suggest that Israel avoid anything that forms lasting enmity with Iran. Israel must keep longterm options open.

Anchor: What might keeping open options mean in the short term?

Barrett: Foremost, it means Israel shouldn't attack Iran. Israel might consider sending out peace overtures to Iran, pointing out their common dangers—from Saudi Arabia and its Sunni vassals.

Anchor: Thanks for your thoughts, Barrett Parker. Provocative as always.

Barrett: Thanks for having me.

Barrett said goodbye to Khadija back in Qatar and left the studio. His thoughts on rapprochement between Iran and Israel were as much hope as analysis and that was troubling. It made him feel like he plunged into the policymaking world where he'd think of young soldiers as chips in a big game.

Of greater concern was, how would think tanks look at his argument? And more importantly, how would national security institutions in Jerusalem and Tehran view rapprochement. The logic was there in geography and history. Saudi Arabia was becoming a danger to the interests of many states, including those of the US. Washington wanted democracy to flourish in the Middle East. Riyadh wanted to strangle it in the cradle.

Kaliningrad, Russia

The Russian defense system was struck by blackouts of the same duration as those hitting other countries' systems, though Moscow would never admit it, of course. Russia put up a façade of might throughout the Cold War out of fear of foreign dangers and it would continue to do so for the same reason. Moscow demanded answers and the cyberwarfare section in Kaliningrad was put to work on it. The dour colonel in command reacted as though his career depended on finding a solution. It probably did.

The cyberwarfare section was rife with rumors of American, Chinese, Israeli, and Polish subterfuge. A Stuxnet-like virus was the leading suspect and the cyberwarfare team was put to work setting up traps and searching millions of files—laborious, time-consuming drudgery. After a few days of frustration, they consulted a senior expert at the University of Tehran, but even he couldn't help.

Dimitri Rublev found the investigation boring and unworthy of his talents. It was like ordering Tchaikovsky to write jingles for car commercials. He had a passing interest in the blackouts but didn't feel Russia was endangered by them. In fact, he thought the world was a little safer with the Russian military on its back foot. "Oafs!" he called the generals—under his breath.

He wanted to get back to hacking into the merger and acquisition department of Goldman Sachs, as did his colleague in the Ukraine. Wall Street was booming, but as long as his section was tasked with getting to the bottom of the blackouts, his investment career was on hold. As he worked with colleagues on firewalls, entry logs, and the hunt for a virus, his mind searched for alternative explanations. He thought of the popular phrase "thinking outside the box" and chuckled dryly and joylessly. Rublev felt that people who used that expression weren't capable of thinking outside the box. The phrase gave away a mind ensnared in routine and cliché. "Oafs!"

The longer the section labored fruitlessly over the computer system, the more Rublev felt the problem lay elsewhere and was perhaps linked to that anomalous code that scrolled wildly down his screen last week. Computer work is not simply ones and zeroes and algorithms, at least not on its frontiers. Out there, creativity was needed.

"Initiative."

That's what advanced the field and that's what was behind the blackouts. He conjured up an image of an elaborate circuit on microprocessors that performed all sorts of secret operations such as spying upon and sabotaging large systems, especially military ones. Rublev considered bringing his thoughts to the dour colonel.

"He's not bright enough to understand what I'm talking about," he sighed. "He'll get angry and order me to get back to the software box— the dead-end. He might even accuse me of starting the problem by hacking into the Pentagon, the CIA, and Brad Pitt's laptop."

Rublev held his counsel and plodded along with his colleagues in the search for glitches and malware. The blackouts had ceased last week and though no one knew why, there was no shortage of people claiming to have solved the problem with their diagnostic systems and by clearing caches and after a little jiggering here and there.

The self-congratulatory and delusional celebration wasn't confined to Kaliningrad. The same thing took place in the Pentagon, CIA, NSA, Centcom, Prince Soltan Airbase, Nellis Air Force Base in Nevada, the Fifth Fleet in Bahrain, IRGC bases throughout Iran, and the militaries of Britain, China, and other powers as well. The tekkies of the military and intelligence worlds praised themselves, privately of course. The best of them, however, suspected that they'd done nothing and that something was still lurking out there.

Dimitri Rublev went back to hacking into Goldman Sachs. His colleague in the Ukraine emailed him that Google and Apple were in fierce rivalry and would be looking to acquire small innovative firms, if only to prevent them from being bought up by the other. Rublev felt renewed.

"What is that utterly stupid yet charming expression of the Americans? Oh yes—*hot dog!*"

Tel Aviv

Ethan and Rina handed in their security badges and left the Templar Building, hoping never to return to its dank inner confines. Rina knotted her Stanford hoodie loosely around her shoulders and lay her head on Ethan's shoulder. Outside, the streets of Tel Aviv were alive with people. Faces looked forward to shopping and finding a new restaurant, no longer burdened by worries of screaming sirens and incoming missiles. Not for now. It was only late afternoon and the evening held the promise of new experiences, new delights, new wonders.

"So, Ethan, did we just save the world?"

Rina was exuberant. She spun around giddily, the sleeves of her sweatshirt flew about, her hair chasing them. Ethan put his arms around her and held her close. He knew the giddiness that followed the end of a stressful situation and briefly pondered the differing circumstances that he didn't want to broach just then, if at all.

"It feels like we did, Rina. Just breathe in the air and look all around us—life!"

"*L'chaim!* We must take some time off. Shut down and reboot. Ethan, you're no longer a captain or a tekkie or a business partner. Right now, you're just my boyfriend and we're going out on the town. And we must see more of the beachfront!"

"I accept the demotion to *just* your boyfriend. I'm yours!"

"I know! And it's glorious!"

Ethan and Rina walked a few blocks to the Dizengoff district and looked through a number of shops with Middle Eastern clothing, pottery, and jewelry from Israeli artisans, and those of Jordan, Malta, and Egypt. They mainly window-shopped as there was too much uncertainty in their business. A pair of earrings attracted Rina, and Ethan handled the negotiations which led to an agreeable price. Ethan suggested walking down to Jaffa, the southern part of Tel Aviv, which was old and quaint, unlike Tel Aviv, which was new and businesslike.

"This was a fortified area as far back as four thousand years ago, well before Moses wandered over from Egypt. I love the streets of Jaffa. Walking in these narrow, ancient streets made of stone . . . oh, it gives me an amazing sense of time and place. The sea is peeking at us from every corner and every block is exotic and beautiful in its own way."

"So much history all around us," Rina said in fascination.

"Yes, Israel is full of history," Ethan laughed. "They say if you throw a stone in Israel, it hits history."

"Sometimes it hits a big guy named Goliath."

They came to fisherman's wharf where boat crews were now shouting out their prices for grouper and sea bass. They stopped at Abu Chassan, a restaurant Ethan knew well and enjoyed a light meal of couscous and melon before returning to the seafront. The salty sea air and the scent of fresh fish was everywhere, making everything seem warm and fertile.

Ethan looked at his phone. "A message from Barrett. He says things are cooling off in Washington . . . and in the Gulf as well. Not quite a stand down . . . just a cooling off."

"That's how it feels here too. Ethan," she asked hesitantly as they walked toward the beach, "does Barrett ever say *anything* about his war experiences?"

"Just a little about the First Gulf War—the one in 1991."

317

"Well?"

"He was a buck sergeant, commanded an Abrams tank in the 3rd Armored Division at Medina Ridge."

"What was Medina Ridge?"

"A major tank battle out in the desert west of Basra. The Iraqis were over a mile away. That was well within the range of American tanks. Out of range for the inferior Iraqi tanks. A complete mismatch—a slaughter, really."

"An awful experience, I'm sure."

"He said it was all very remote—the range, the distance. Point-and-click weapon systems. The war was an abstraction. Some guys went down into the valley to look at the burned-out tanks close up. Photos . . . souvenirs. Yes, soldiers do that, many of them anyway . . . Barrett didn't do any tourism that day, though."

"Good for him. I like him a little now."

"I've noted you didn't like him so much before."

"Not really. He's standoffish—remote and distant, one might say. I don't get you two. You're both veterans and both antiwar . . . " Rina looked to Ethan for explanation.

"Neither one of us is antiwar, Rina. We just think wars are horrible things and should not be gone into thoughtlessly."

"Okay, so you're both *cautious* about going to war. But your caution is based on spiritual beliefs. There's something almost *Talmudic* about your outlook on war and peace and life. Barrett . . . oh, I don't know . . . there's something hidden in him, something dark."

"Yeah, I see that too sometimes. More so now. He went back, you know."

"Back *where?*"

"To Iraq. He returned in 2005 as a consultant to the Pentagon on counterinsurgency. That was his dissertation at the University of Chicago—counterinsurgency in Malaya, the Philippines, Algeria, and Vietnam."

"Have you read it?"

"Rina, *no one* reads dissertations."

"Dissertation advisers read them," she shot back triumphantly.

"Well . . . sometimes . . . maybe."

"We'll see. What did Barrett say about his second time in Iraq, his second war?"

"He never talks about it. Never. After he came back, he left Albuquerque for the desert. You saw where he lives."

"Oh my God, Ethan! All alone, except for that wolf! Don't you guys know that it helps to talk about things? It works things through, process things, put things in the past."

Ethan was struck by the sweetness of her words, more so by their naiveté. By their relevance for so much in life, but also by their limitations for other matters and their irrelevance for war. He wondered if her need to know and to understand would present problems.

"Rina, I've never known any veteran who thought that." He caught his voice leading into a scold and drew back. "You just put those things in the attic and if you're smart, you don't go up there. They make noise and kick around, often unexpectedly. It's best just to keep them up there."

"So if someone asks about war experiences . . . "

"Then you're asking someone to climb up into the attic and that just makes those things more insistent."

"You just leave them alone then."

"Yes, Rina, even though it goes against the accepted wisdom of our therapeutic society. Dr Phil never treated a chest wound or zipped a body bag." A memory came and went in an instant. "Better to think about the beauty in life. There's so much of it, Rina, if only we look. The sea, the mountains, the arts. Come on . . ."

Guys didn't much talk about the war, Ethan thought as they walked, but sometimes they talked about *talking* about the war. There's a difference and doing the latter helps demarcate the boundary between the two things. Barrett said one reason he avoided discussing the war with "outsiders" was because it was a sure way to close off conversation and ruin *everybody's* evening. Ethan thought it was beginning to be the case that evening.

The couple neared the beachfront as late afternoon became early evening. The wind was picking up and Rina pulled on the sweatshirt that had been draped around her shoulders. A pan lid fell noisily to the stone floor of a dining patio. Ethan didn't freeze or tense up—the past's grip was no longer so terrible—but the metallic "CLAAAANNNG" and "TEEEEENNNN" instantly recalled jagged shrapnel lashing just over his helmet as he hugged the ground, dopplering eerily and entrancingly, shredding nearby brush, then clattering into a limestone draw like a handful of coins hurled angrily against a wall. The fragments shrieked earnest wishes to kill him as the explosion's dull decay rolled down the ravine. The sounds sank into him and assured persistence.

That's what talking or even thinking about it gets you, he chided himself as a waiter leaned down and picked up the pan. *Replays of mortar explosions . . . twenty years on.*

Rina noticed that Ethan was in distant thought and moved closer to him until their hands came together. She had to think more about what he'd just said, and about less amusing trips to medical stations in the Bekaa Valley. And about his attic. He took her hand as they stepped out of their shoes then into the still-warm sand and walked toward the waves soughing listlessly in the fading day. The evening wasn't ruined after all.

New Mexico

You can't get a drink until noon on Sundays in New Mexico and that meant an hour of football without alcohol—a harsh privation to most in Kelly's during football season. At 11:58 Dee Dee announced the two minute warning, adding in dramatic sportscaster-like tones, "And the state is out of time outs!" The dozen or so patrons cheered her. Barrett smiled slightly and nodded.

"Still solving the problems of the world?" she asked.

"Well . . . I *might* have just prevented a war in the Middle East."

"Then you'll be a big tipper today!"

"As ever, my dear."

She and Barrett regarded each other for an unexpected but not unpleasant moment. "Dee Dee . . . when do you finish your master's degree?"

Barrett was surprised he'd asked that. Past glances and repartee had evidently meant something. He only knew about her graduate studies from another patron, a young man who had the misfortune of being a Raiders fan.

"At the end of this semester. Why how very sweet of you to ask, Barrett Parker! Glad to see you're not wearing that 'dysfunctional veteran' hat today."

She smiled, more than usual, then headed back to the kitchen. Barrett wondered if he'd ever see her again and thought about all the people he'd known in the army and in schools and in many parts of the world, mostly only briefly.

"Oh . . . people come, people go. After a while, the names all run together. I knew a Dee Dee in college . . . another one in Iraq."

It was halftime and the Redskins were leading the Rams. A chirp indicated an incoming email and he looked to see if it was from a fellow Redskin fan who was as impressed as Barrett with their rookie quarterback. The sender's address wasn't recognizable nor was the name.

"Peter Whitt . . . I don't know you. Are you trying to tell me I won a lottery?"

He quickly ran through the message to see if it was spam but it turned out to be kind words about the articles he'd written and mention of meeting him at Georgetown last week. Only slightly interested, Barrett went back to the game.

"Peter Whitt . . . which one was he?" he wondered as he drove through the pass and back to his place in the East Mountains. "He isn't an undersecretary or a think tanker . . . " Jesse trotted up to him gingerly at the gate and off they went to North Mountain. They reached the rock and took a breather. Barrett didn't like travel anymore—especially to Washington.

"I'm an eccentric, Jesse."

The great wolf made no effort to contradict him.

"Who is this Peter Whitt guy? You don't know either, eh."

He'd heard the name before but it had a quality that made him think of newscasters and the like. Nonetheless, he was at the Georgetown meeting with Joe Burkett, Aaron Palashet, and the rest of the merry insurgents, so he must be an insider. He'd left his mobile device in the car and besides, the connectivity on the mountain trails wasn't reliable. He and Jesse sat there as dusk came and cooled off the thin air remarkably quickly. Hikers, he knew, were often caught unawares and had to beat hasty retreats to their cars to avoid hypothermia.

He stared out into the dry plains east of Moriarty.

"Time to get back, old guy. We'll both stiffen up like old fogies."

About a quarter mile from home, Barrett made a connection. Was Peter Whitt one of the Flower Project scientists, the people involved in the Iranian-Israeli missile program and probably in the Samson program as well? He picked up his pace and Jesse trotted behind him. Once inside, Barrett tossed the wolf a biscuit and listened to his teeth snapping shut. He sat down and looked for Whitt's name on the Mac's drive.

"Yep, he was on the list Ethan found. Flower power, Samson power. Let's read that email in full."

> Dear Mr Parker,
>
> I'd hoped to chat with you, if only briefly, at the Georgetown gathering but alas you were busily and profitably speaking with a man of Israeli background if I am any judge of accents. I've enjoyed your perspective on the world for quite some time and wholeheartedly agree with your mistrust of national security institutions, their paranoid cultures, and almost willful disregard of foreseeable consequences.
>
> How did I, an aging electrical engineer, come to hold such views on the world? I might be permitted to mention that I served in Thailand during the war in Southeast Asia. Judging by many passages in your works, I suspect that is a conflict you have more than a nodding familiarity with.
>
> I was a small part of a project that set up a network of sensors tasked with interdicting N Vietnamese troops and supplies coming down the Ho Chi Minh Trail. The data were fed

into a gargantuan computer in Thailand which then selected bombing targets. Many decisions were hasty and based on limited information. The program itself had flaws. The results were sometimes catastrophic for villagers unfortunate enough to be struck by the formidable payloads of a B-52 bomber: over one hundred 500-lb bombs, if memory serves. Total devastation in a 3km x 1km area. I saw a photograph of one hamlet before and after a strike and was horrified enough to insist on taking part in a ground inspection. The scene was unlike anything that Dante or Bosch or Goya could have imagined. It was unlike anything I should ever want to see again.

Forgive my discursiveness, if that is possible at this point.

Regards,
Peter Whitt

"Well, Jesse, few people write so elegantly these days, least of all me. Reminds me of that old chap at the Russian Research Center who used to read books on his yacht and toss the disappointing ones overboard. I can see the tweed jacket and pipe now. This merits a reply, wouldn't you say?"

Dear Mr Whitt,

Many thanks for your generous comments on my writings. I too regret we were not able to exchange views in person after the Georgetown meeting. Wastefulness, disaster, and unpleasant, though foreseeable consequences, are regrettably still parts of world affairs as events of our day often demonstrate. I look forward to future exchanges, through email, or should you find yourself in New Mexico, in person.

Regards,
Barrett

Less than an hour later, Whitt replied that he'd be in Los Alamos later in the week and suggested meeting at the La Fonda, a restaurant in Santa Fe.

The charming old town was an hour north of Barrett's place in the East Mountains, a pleasant drive past grassland and ranches with cattle grates at every entranceway. Santa Fe was more attractive than Albuquerque, which had too many strip malls, fast food joints, and other unappealing aspects of modern life. Santa Fe was the state capital but also an arts center. You could walk for an hour without seeing a government building yet in the same period come across scores of galleries and crafts shops. Lots of Cadillacs and Mercedes with Texas plates. Texans are richer than New Mexicans. A lot richer.

La Fonda is housed in an old adobe structure just off the main plaza where small shops and tents sell pottery, Navajo rugs, and turquoise jewelry. There's a wealth of lore about the place—tales of its seventeenth-century origins, famous and infamous visitors, and even a ghost or two. Barrett entered the restaurant and was looking about casually when an elderly fellow waved and called his name, though not loud.

"Mr Parker . . . I'm Peter Whitt. I recognized you from your television work."

Being recognized in public worried Barrett, even appalled him when he thought of a colleague who was murdered in Karachi, probably by Pakistani intelligence. "Well, that's a rarity—and a *somewhat* welcome one."

A pleasant young Zuni woman with silver rings on each hand brought menus. Neither of the men was hungry though.

"There was a time when I'd drink a few margaritas in this establishment," Peter mentioned. "As you see I'm just having club soda this day."

"I'll have club soda too . . . with a lemon if possible," Barrett said.

"Have you spent time in the Middle East, Barrett?"

"Only a little—mostly consulting in Iraq and Afghanistan. The military and State Department people put on a good show which proclaimed everything was going well. It wasn't."

"The sort of show that George Romney described as 'brainwashing' after he returned from Vietnam."

"And it destroyed his candidacy in 1968," Barrett recalled from readings.

"Candor isn't always helpful in politics."

"No, it isn't. And you, Peter. Have you spent time in the region?"

"Oh yes. After things shut down in Southeast Asia in 1975, I had little interest in living back in the US. From what I'd heard, the country was angry and self-absorbed and nihilistic. So I went to Saudi Arabia and later Iran. There I worked on computer systems, especially missile guidance systems. You know this already, no?"

Barrett paused warily. He sensed no danger. In any case he'd already given away that he did know already. "Yes, I've read of Project Flower. Those were the days of the 'twin pillars' policy. Oil prices skyrocketed and we sold arms to oil-producing nations to keep a semblance of influence."

"So we sold to the Iranians and we sold to the Saudis. What do you make of Saudi Arabia today, Barrett?"

"A paranoid country living in a political past, filled with rich men who have lots of weapons but who won't fight and who expect others to do it for them. Chiefly American kids. They want us to knock out Iran so they can be masters of the Persian Gulf."

"So they can rename it the Saudi Gulf. And after that?"

"They'll use their influence—their *money*—to rally the Sunni world under the green banners of the Saud dynasty," Barrett continued. "They'll take out democracy root and branch, from Morocco to Pakistan. With the ready help of indigenous generals and mullahs, no doubt. The Saudis might even buy nuclear weapons to brandish."

"*Buy* nuclear weapons? My God! From where?" Peter was genuinely puzzled, not simply prompting an elaboration.

"From Pakistan. The Saudis funded its nuclear research and Saudi subsidies keep the country above water. Pakistan owes them, and its generals oppose democracy as much as the Saudis do."

"Yes, and the Saudis fund Pakistanis schools too—with their rather militant curriculum. This is a dire scenario, Barrett. How likely is it?"

"Stranger things have happened, Peter."

"Yes, they have. But let's turn to the Ghost of Christmas Present. What are the chances of war with Iran in the next few weeks or months?"

"Things have eased up, for now," Barrett explained. "Publics aren't especially keen on war and the consequences are dawning on the generals and strategists. A lot of people are still worried about those defense blackouts we discussed at Georgetown. At first they made the generals anxious, itchy to attack. Now, they wonder about the reliability of their systems and are holding back. And of course they are very worried that publics will learn of the blackouts and all they portend."

"That would make them look like great fools, Barrett. Sound and fury, signifying nothing. Little men behind curtains claiming to be wizards. Perhaps the world will be safer if doubt were retained."

"Yes, we need doubt to compensate for the lack of good judgment. It's not exactly in our control." Barrett looked for a reaction from Peter but at the same time didn't want to suggest he knew anything about the chips and Samson and events in a Tel Aviv cellar. "To this day, no one knows what caused the blackouts."

"Barrett, perhaps they never will."

"Good news to me. Perhaps that would mean fewer errant B-52 strikes and the like."

"Well, then, here's to more doubt and fewer errant airstrikes . . . Have you ever been near a B-52 strike?"

Barrett suddenly felt uncomfortable. Talking about war always ruined things and altered his relationship with people. He'd become in their minds a "hero" with all the romantic nonsense attached to the notion, or an object of pity with all the opportunities for self-laceration and brooding it brought. For others he'd become an object they'd boast about. They'd tell friends they'd spoken to a real war veteran and feel themselves superior for it, especially if they bought him a drink. In any case, he'd become a cliché, a stereotype, an anecdote, and he'd never be Barrett Parker again—not to them and not to those who'd heard the stories from the Guy Who Was There. However, a measure of amicability had developed with this Whitt fellow, and he was in some sense what Barrett considered "one of us."

"Yes, arclights were common at the opening of Gulf War One in 1991. Not far away, two or three miles at most. A steady rumble and reddish-orange flashes and slight concussive pops in the ears for about twenty seconds, followed by two more. They came in threes. Most of the guys cheered and laughed."

"From afar, they would cheer and laugh. Did you return to Iraq?"

Whitt had done his homework, Barrett realized. He wasn't surprised.

"I went back during Gulf War Two as a counterinsurgency adviser, in Anbar, west of Baghdad. I spoke to scores of company and battalion commanders. They pretended to listen to what I said about strategists such as Galula and Kilcullen. They even took notes. Next day, they went about their patrols, used heavy firepower, and the insurgency grew, as did the casualties. I used to go out on patrols, supposedly to get a feel for things . . . I just wanted to get out there. I was bored and I'd seen so little of what people like to call 'action' in the first war. *Action*," Barrett repeated darkly.

Barrett was surprised by how much he was saying and by how he was drifting back to the past. He pondered the paradox of this conversation amid the lightheartedness and merriment of others there in La Fonda. People at one table erupted in laughter at a punchline, an old recollection, or a precocious remark from a young family member.

"We went to a village north of Fallujah. Nine marines and your humble narrator." A sardonic smile came and went in a moment. Whitt was transfixed. "Sullen glares from the locals. Most of them stayed clear of us. One man, however . . . a young man in a sport jacket and white shirt, wearing no tie, walked down the road. He came toward us— calmly, purposefully, with an out-of-place serenity on his face."

Whitt knew of that serene look from a DARPA study on terrorism. The look was likened to that of martyrs going to their deaths, secure in their faith and in what it promised.

"The squad leader shouted for the man to halt but he kept walking toward the front of the column, more briskly than before. The marines went into crouches, their M-4s aimed at the man. Training, SOP. The lance corporal on point also raised his M-4, screamed for him to halt, then raced toward him—maybe to tackle him, we don't know. The Iraqi man reached inside his jacket and detonated the explosives strapped to his chest. There was a sudden flash and intense heat. I heard the beginning of an explosion then was overwhelmed by deafness. I heard nothing but ringing for hours. The lance corporal took most of the blast and shrapnel. Some of us, however, had fragments removed over the next few days back at the battalion aid station and at Camp Dreamland—metal fragments . . . bone fragments as well."

Barrett wondered if Peter understood. The medic at Dreamland explained it to him as he placed the metal fragments next to the human ones on a strip of stained gauze.

"*Bone . . .*" Whitt puzzled for a moment before making the obvious inference. "Oh God . . . Oh my God . . . Oh my God . . . What was the poor boy's name? Some things make us want to know a man's name."

"He was Rodrigo Jaqua . . . from Carrizo Springs, Texas. Nineteen. Medium height, thin, dark hair of course. The squad leader said he was born in Mexico."

"Rodrigo Jaqua . . . "

"A small engagement, unmentioned in any history book, but memorable enough to those who took part, as a great man once said. I'm sure Rodrigo's name appeared on the news and the Pentagon sent an honor guard, but to most Americans . . ." Barrett looked around the room and tried not to show disdain for those around him. "He's a forgotten boy in a war that everyone wants to put behind them. No, they've *already* put it behind them."

"It's still with us though," Peter noted. "And as for the generals and politicians—"

"They plot up more goddam wars that have nothing to do with national security," Barrett finished.

"As they have long been wont to do."

"Sonsuvbitches."

"Sonsuvbitches indeed."

Barrett and Peter conversed for another hour about matters of the world and the plots therein. They thought of ways to keep militaries on their back foot, confused, uncertain, reluctant to act. Happily, the conversation turned to the potters and silversmiths out in the plaza of

Santa Fe, who were packing up for the night. They shook hands warmly and promised to keep in touch, before saluting Rodrigo Jaqua and others like him.

On the drive back to the East Mountains, Barrett brooded. He cursed himself for divulging the events at the village near Fallujah. It had been a secret, a dark secret with its own disgusting intimacy and aftermath which only a few people knew. One had died recently—by his own doing according to the squad leader, who found Barrett's email at the end of an article. That made the mystery cult all the smaller.

"It's nobody's goddam business! *Nobody's!*"

The blood and gore across the sand came to him in piercing flashes, soon followed by the charred corpses near flaming T-72 wrecks after Medina Ridge and by the troops celebrating and posing with them. They'd seen it all in the movies and, man, they were living it now. It would take, he knew from experience, a couple of weeks to get the souvenirs out of his mind. Until then, they'd be with him.

"Talking it through? *Hah!* That's just what you tell therapists on the way out the door!"

A pack of coyotes scattered as an oncoming black car roared at them as they crossed the deserted two-lane blacktop near Los Lomas.

Santa Clara, California

Ethan and Rina needed no further reminder that they had a product to get out. While in Israel, they put off many things like updating the company website and issuing news releases. Buyers were getting impatient. Impatient buyers go elsewhere. Startups that annoy too many buyers become shutdowns and their products go to thrift shops near tattoo parlors and sit on shelves next to the Kaypros and Leading Edges.

Micrologic Design would have the best diagnostic software in the chip design field, someday. They had to put aside Samson and the problems of the world, though neither would be far from their minds. World events that never much troubled them now hung over them—brooding, unmoving, demanding notice above the business routine.

Rina gnawed on her pencil. They'd completed all modules and everything worked flawlessly. She compiled the entire program and it passed all stages, yet when she ran it on one of the regression test cases, it failed repeatedly.

"Fuse effect," she muttered.

When a metal segment connects to a narrower metal segment and then to another wider metal segment, it creates a "fuse effect." In time, the current will melt the narrow wire and the chip will fail. On retry, the program didn't find the flaw. Everything passed. Rina punched a few keys in front of the debugger program.

"This is no time to mess with me, buddy. It's late . . . I've had a long day . . . I just got back from saving the world . . . and I promised that you were finished. Now don't mess with me!"

"Did you ask it to turn its head and cough?"

Her face didn't move from the screen. "This one's talking back to me—and rather insolently. An inconsistency on a fuse case!" She was about to get up and leave but Ethan gently took her hand.

"We've solved some tough stuff recently. We can handle this."

They both turned to the screen. Ethan began reviewing the program in the debugger environment. "You checked all pointers?"

"Check," she answered crisply.

"GDSII database preparations?"

"Check."

"Extracting all segments and connectivity?"

"Roger dodger."

"That's a tired phrase. So we have everything intact and in place . . . "

A bit less annoyed, Rina launched into a report. "Everything was working as expected yesterday morning. The test cases passed and everything that was supposed to fail, did indeed fail. Then yesterday afternoon, we created a fuse test case that should fail. We're just not catching the problem."

"Odd." Ethan reviewed other code blocks of the program. "What about memory management?" Ethan navigated into the memory management module. He observed a few parts and turned to Rina. "I think I know what's going on."

She saw a smile of mastery and pride come across his face for an instant and knew a professorial lecture was in store, hopefully an interesting one. "Okay, what is it?"

He turned to the whiteboard and drew a large rectangle. "This is our system and everything inside is working properly." Then he drew a larger rectangle around it. "But we are not alone in the design universe. We are working within a third-party design environment."

"Light bulb going off. We're plugged into Cadence!" she said turning to her screen. "I shall solve this problem anon—and get this product *out the damn door*." She shut down Cadence and restarted it. She activated the Micrologic Design program on the fuse test case and the segments were quickly highlighted in green. Save one. The fuse segment started to blink in soft red. They both leaned back in their chairs and folded their arms behind their necks.

"We're all done. No wonder they made you a major."

"As it turns out, Boaz was just tormenting me. I was never recalled to active duty. But you really are a lieutenant now."

"No way! I'm a conscientious objector, a full-time student, a 4F. I'm unfit to wear the uniform. Any uniform. Even a NASA lab coat!"

The fun was followed by an unexpected and uncomfortable silence.

"Now what, Ethan? What's next for us?"

"I've been wondering about that too. We've been working on the product for over two years and now . . . I don't know what's next."

"There'll be a void."

"Yeah . . . there *is* a void. Barrett says it's like that when you finish writing a book. Postpartum symptoms."

"Good to hear Barrett has *some* feelings. He just seems to alternate between dry analysis and brooding silence."

"There's no one who cares more about soldiers, Rina. Average soldiers, that is. Generals . . . they're another story. Same with politicians."

"Okay," she replied defensively. "Glad to hear it. I'm truly glad to hear it. Generals and politicians send young people off into foolhardy wars."

"You're way too hard on the military, Miss Hardin. They do their jobs well. They just need our help from time to time so the world doesn't blow up. But I'll pass those pithy words on to Sergeant Parker."

"I'm liking him a little more now."

She slumped back into her chair and closed her eyes. Before she nodded off, she heard Ethan's footfalls heading down the hall to the eBeam room and knew that since the trip to Israel he'd been staring blankly out into space an hour a day. "Just a short nap," she murmured as she drowsed. "I'll check in on him shortly . . . and make sure he's not back in Lebanon again."

The eBeam machine was humming and an image of an intricate circuit was displayed on the screen. Ethan was staring across the room at the wall where a picture Rina had taken of the rugged hills south of Tahoe was now hanging. He replayed in considerable detail the shuddering sibilance of incoming mortar rounds, the dull thumps of their impact, and the shrieks of fragments overhead. Those sounds had been a constant companion over the last few days and they needed no dropped pan lid to grab hold. Along with them came memories of lying on the ground in the Bekaa Valley, enduring almost thirty minutes of mortar fire, fighting off panic.

Lieutenant Alon! Lieutenant Alon!

He and a sergeant were able to determine the direction of the incoming rounds and the range of the HM-15 tubes, then call in a gunship to traverse the azimuth and rake the ravine with mini-gun and rocket fire until the incoming fire ended.

Memories of that day raced through him dozens of times a day since descending into the basement of the Templar Building in Tel Aviv, though he never mentioned it to anyone, just as he'd never mentioned the underlying event to anyone on coming home from Lebanon twenty years earlier. An object falling to the floor, a helicopter scuttling overhead, or a simple pause at work all provided an opening that allowed the memories to reassert themselves.

Ethan once thought the replays were trying to tell him something, instruct him, encourage him to look deeper into the experience. No more. There was nothing to learn and no cathartic revelation would end them. That was the stuff of television psychology. The replays were just something that followed him around and nagged him, and he knew they always would. A few more days and they'll be back into the attic. The process was something he had to go through every few months or every year at most. It was familiar and routine and not as interesting as an outsider would ever believe.

"Oh brother, I'm getting to know that look," Rina said as she stretched in the doorway behind him. "You're either thinking of a new cache design or how we saved the world . . . or about Lebanon."

"Oh . . . I was thinking about wars. I admit it."

"Past, present, or future?" Rina stood behind him and gently massaged his tense shoulders.

He leaned back, resting his head between her breasts, remembering that dying boys thought of their mothers, never their fathers, even though it was the fathers in whose footsteps they'd followed.

"But let's move on," he said energetically as he stood up and paced about the eBeam room. "Rina, these Samson guys . . . I want to meet them."

"I can see it now. 'Hi. We've discovered your hidden Program on all those microprocessors and we were in the neighborhood, so . . .' Then burly guards take us away to an undisclosed secure dungeon."

"I don't think these guys have dungeons, Rina."

"I'll bet they have burly guards—and Rottweilers"

"Maybe a Rottweiler or two. These people have . . . *humanity*."

"I believe that. They have so much power and use it responsibly. They just need our help every twenty-five years or so. Ethan, we individually emailed the ones we could find and asked to speak with them. They did not deign to reply. A few bounced back as undeliverable. Maybe we can fish around that Flower thing—the missile program that gave birth to Samson."

"Rina, we've Googled and Binged and Yahooed. If we do any more of it, they'll send us a message telling us to get a life."

"I've already received that message—from friends and *former* friends. Well, we could file a Freedom Of Information Act request."

"Barrett already filed a few when we first came across the flower logo on the chips. The material came back a few days ago—expedited by a friend on the National Security Council. A number of pages blanked out. 'Heavily redacted' is the phrase."

"So the government knows about Samson?" Rina asked.

"Barrett doubts it very much. He thinks the government just doesn't like to let on about potentially embarrassing stuff. Even though it goes back long ago."

"It's embarrassing that Israel and Iran were allies?"

"*Very* embarrassing. It makes things today look like a transient spat."

"Ethan, that's *exactly* what most of that foreign policy stuff looks like to me! Middle school romances and breakups. 'Hey Iran. I hear Israel *really* likes you. He's sorry about going out with Saudi Arabia last Saturday. It won't happen again—honest'."

"Rina, you're becoming a wellspring of material for Barrett. He occasionally writes satire."

"Seriously now, Ethan. What was the name of the guy in Israel?"

"Let me see . . . " Ethan scrolled through his Sent file and found the message with the names of the Samson programmers he emailed Barrett. "Zvi Arad, retired professor, Hebrew University."

"Anyone you know there take courses from him or rub shoulders with him?"

"Not that I know of. Israel's a little bigger than you think, Rina."

"I'm sure it is, but the hi-tech world isn't. Not even here in California. What about your friend in the basement of the Holy Grail Building?"

"Boaz? He was more a student of history and economics in college."

"I was thinking of the other guy. The young guy, the socially-challenged one. The guy who makes you look like a strapping Neil Armstrong."

"Leor . . . yes. He did a PhD at Hebrew University. I'll email him right now."

"Ask him if his advisers read his dissertation."

"Rina, *I'll* read your dissertation. I promise . . . that is, if you'll let me see it."

She sat on his lap and added playfully and highly alluringly, "Ethan . . . I'll show you mine, if you show me yours."

"Deal . . . but first," he paused as Rina's eyebrows raised, "we have orals."

A delightful while later, Ethan saw that Leor had gotten back to him.

> I took three courses with Arad in grad school. Great teacher, a mensch. I still have dinner at his home with other former

students he's placed in sensitive positions. We talk about technology and world affairs. I asked him to invite you and Rina someday. He consults for us and for Mossad. He was here to look at the blackouts before you came and was upset he couldn't find anything. I later told him that you'd found the problem. He was impressed.

Ethan replied immediately.

So he knows my name now?

Yes. I thought it might help Micrologic Design. Anyway, I think he recognized the name. Is that okay?

I guess so. In any case, it's done. Is he in Tel Aviv now?

Not now. He spends a lot of time in India now. Up in the hills. Will send his email in a nanosecond.

Leor, you're the mensch.

"Those guys know about us?" Rina exclaimed. "And they know that we know about them—and about Samson?"

"It appears so."

They both slumped back into their chairs and silently pondered the implications. The prospect of discovery was never far from their minds and they accepted it as part of the investigation, part of the adventure. Now, the prospect was fact and an unsettling one.

"I suppose they could have done something to us already, if they wanted," Rina finally said. "You know . . . burly guards, Rottweilers."

"True . . . " Ethan said after a few moments.

"Maybe they're impressed with us," Rina wondered.

"For discovering Samson?"

"Discovering Samson and disabling the heuristic that almost blew up the Middle East!"

"I guess we'll have to try and get in touch with Zvi Arad. First, Rina my dear, we have some homework."

"Orals again?"

"Alas, no."

Ethan and Rina pored over the many articles that Zvi Arad had written in *Ha'aretz* and the newspaper articles on his unsuccessful run for the Knesset. He was more insightful and respected than the usual antiwar voices in Israel. He'd commanded a company of Sherman tanks in the '67 war and raced across Sinai all the way to the Suez Canal. He disobeyed an order to execute Egyptian prisoners and guarded them until brigade set up a POW pen.

His articles were informed by history and an understanding of political and military realities. He could debate the usefulness of a policy or new weapon system with any minister or general and he could do so with charisma and articulateness and sound reasoning.

"How did he lose?" Ethan wondered.

"Maybe he spoke too sensibly," Rina offered.

Ethan carefully drafted a message to Arad and showed it to Rina for approval:

> Dear Professor Arad,
>
> I've only recently come to appreciate your work, both in politics and in computer science. Your passion and commitment to the cause of peace are moving. A former student of yours tells me that you've recently become aware

of my abilities and are impressed. For that, I am both pleased and honored. I have no articles to demonstrate a shared commitment to world peace, but perhaps you and I can correspond on matters of our field and how they might relate to world peace.

Sincerely,
Ethan Alon
CTO, Micrologic Design

"I like it, but it needs a better closing," Rina said in a leading way.

"Such as '*Major* Alon, IDF'?"

"Nope. Such as, '*We* believe your work is essential to world peace and must be continued by successive generations'."

"Great! Oh yes, I meant to say 'we'."

"We knew it would come to you."

Ethan and Rina hit a trade show in Palo Alto the next day. They set up their booth, exchanged cards, and sold a goodly amount of product. A buzz preceded them. Exotic rumors spread of their trip to the Israel and of secret work at a large fab and with the military. A colleague in the hard drive business asked if the trip to Israel was related to all those old computer chips he was getting from thrift stores. Ethan smiled and replied that he and Rina had developed an interest in early CPUs and that the trip to Israel entailed long walks on the beaches. Conversation quickly turned to the new four-terabyte disks and the future of solid-state drives.

A few rows down was the PAMD section. It was vastly larger than Micrologic Design's humble booth and sported colorful banners, attractive spokesmodels, and stacks of pamphlets.

"We're small now but we have a product they need. Our trip to their Albuquerque fab showed them that," Rina said. "Besides," she added with a giggle, "we know something they don't."

Every ten minutes or so, Ethan checked his phone for a reply from Zvi Arad in the hills of India. Rina saw him put the phone back into his pocket in disappointment. Sometimes he looked over to her chatting with a customer and shook his head.

As they closed down their booth in the evening, Ethan checked again and gave no sign of contact.

"You know, Ethan, not everyone is glued to their screens the way you and Barrett are."

"I know, I know. Besides, India is thirteen hours ahead of us."

Cooling Down

The admiral in command of the *Enterprise* battle group went over the visual reports of the incident and was certain three missiles had been fired at his flotilla from the Iranian coast. Whether they were Chinese Sizzlers or Russian Klubs was unclear and from his perspective irrelevant. The important thing was that Iran had attacked a US aircraft carrier and there had to be consequences.

Unfortunately, from the admiral's point of view, there was no electronic data to support his claims. Not from *Bulkeley*, not from *Enterprise*, not from any ship in the battle group. When he angrily pointed to the images the F/A-18 took of a missile site near Bushehr, the defense secretary apprised him that they were being reviewed for possible reinterpretation and that would not be available to the public for many years.

Word of the incident leaked to the media. The story received substantial coverage for forty-eight hours but after that, the lack of supporting electronic data caused the story to hang in midair. One cable station ran the story repeatedly along with blurry photos from the cellphones of sailors on ships involved in the incident. The station also brought in retired military and intelligence experts to voice grave concern and call for swift retaliation. Elsewhere, however, the admiral's claims were likened to the assertions of Saddam Hussein's nuclear program leading to the 2003 Iraq war. Many commentators noted disturbing similarities to the Gulf of Tonkin Incidents in 1964, which either didn't happen the way the Pentagon claimed or didn't happen at all.

Iran's Fars News Agency countered the admiral's claims by reporting that American warships had fired three Harpoon missiles at an Iranian frigate patrolling the same waters that evening. The frigate's crew managed to shoot down all three—a masterful display of arms that the Iranian navy prided itself on. The sailors appeared on Press TV, as did their proud families in small villages across the country. The Iranian public was effusive, especially so close after the public display of an American assassin who'd been captured near the Turkmenistan border.

The American admiral wanted to publicly debunk Iran's claim of shooting down three US Harpoon missiles but soon thought better of it as his own sailors had laid claim to the same unlikely feat.

The navy then wanted to dive down to the sea bottom and bring up remnants of the missiles for identification. Iran, however, swiftly declared salvage rights to a merchant ship that went down in the area during a storm in 1975. The charts clearly showed the existence of such a wreck and Iran was within its rights under international law to declare salvage rights. Iran chose a Chinese firm to handle salvage operations.

* * *

After enjoying their stay more than anyone thought they would, the media left Cushing, Oklahoma. The news teams booked out of the La-Ze L and the Sooner motels along Main Street. Commuter planes awaited them at the town airport to the south. In a few hours, they'd be back in New York and Washington. They bade farewell to Dara at the diner who'd become a celebrity from appearances on MSNBC and who was being considered for a reality show by a few stations.

The governor's Zone of Iron proved costly for Oklahoma and it was quietly drawn down to a few National Guard platoons. By the end of the week, the last troops were back home. Two drones remained at Tinker Air Force Base from which they flew training missions. The pilots in Nevada wanted to "fly" missions over the Af-Pak border or Yemen. Missions over Cushing, they felt, were hurting their careers. Many Okies thought the drones overhead were wasteful or part of the "globalists' agenda."

For their participation in the defense of Cushing the drone pilots in Nevada were awarded Distinguished Warfare Medals, a new decoration which the Pentagon designated higher in prestige than the Bronze Star with V for Valor. Dara, whose husband had earned a Bronze Star with V for Valor at Dak To in 1967, talked about the new drone medal with some folks from the VFW Lodge. Most thought that rating the drone medal higher than the Bronze Star was ridiculous and even insulting.

Dara opined, rather bitingly, to a remaining cable crew that the Pentagon should award a Distinguished Warfare Medal with V for "Vegas" or "Very Far Away." That hurt her chances for a reality show. Network execs shy away from criticism of the military.

The Secretary of Defense, who'd earned a Bronze Star with V for Valor in the Mekong Delta, scrapped plans to issue the medal a few weeks later. It was unclear if he'd seen Dara's commentary but she was sure he had and said so in her Tweets.

* * *

Most of the futures traders in New York and elsewhere played the crisis well. Some got caught holding long positions when the market peaked and started to slide. They quickly got out, took up short positions, and rode them down. The more adroit of them saw the "sucker rallies" along the drop and played the short-lived upswings expertly. It was like the summer of 2008 when traders jacked the price of crude up to $147 a barrel then watched it plummet to $45 when the bubble burst and Wall Street crashed. Those were great days if you knew what you were doing. For many, those were great days even if you *didn't* know what you were doing.

A few of the heavyweights got word of the blackouts in defense systems. No one said from where the word came, however defense contractors were deemed the most likely source. Traders reasoned that no one would start a war with so much uncertainty all about. Maybe Alexander the Great or Napoleon would, but leaders today are more like corporate suits than bold leaders of centuries past. Alexander died young, Napoleon in exile. Many traders lightened up their long positions and started shorting. Martha's Vineyard and the Hamptons were more attractive than Elba and Saint Helena.

A few fortunes had been made, a few lost. Some guys bought Italian sport cars, others had to check out of their clubs for the last time. One institution tweaked the algorithms in its trading program and looked forward to the next crisis. Oil traders always look forward to the next big event—a hurricane shutting down rigs in the Gulf of Mexico, a sudden cold front coming down from Canada, or a war somewhere. Somewhere with oil. Things were calm in the Gulf for now, but the lions were not sitting down with the lambs and not a single sword had been hammered into a plowshare.

"No peace in my lifetime," grinned one trader.

"Here's to continued instability," cheered another, lifting a vodka tonic.

Good times in the futures markets.

* * *

Anthony Sabatini hadn't benefited from the crisis at all. He'd been shot twice and his wounds still hurt like hell. AK rounds. Not the fastest bullet out there, but large. Bullet damage, he knew from grim lectures, is determined by the round's mass times its velocity squared. He tried to relate that physics formula to his aching torso. The pain was now restricted to a few places along the paths the bullets tore, and each twinge and throb became a familiar entity, like a neighbor who played loud music or repeated the same dull greeting.

After dragging him from the reservoir in Turkmenistan, the IRGC smacked him around but he stuck to his story. They debrided his wounds and gave him morphine so Anthony figured they weren't going to kill him, at least not for a while. The morphine caused him to mumble in a stupor and it was clear from his accent that he wasn't Kurdish and was probably American. They publicly accused him of killing the physicist but the IRGC was smart enough to know that

Americans weren't behind the assassinations. It was a wonderful propaganda coup, however, and publics the world over enjoy jingoistic spectacles. Anthony enjoyed them too. He just never wanted a starring role in one.

After playing his role in the Tehran theater to countless jeers and popular disdain, he was imprisoned on an IRGC base near Zahedan. He sat in a small cement cell with an unattractive view of rows of concertina wire covered with blankets so he couldn't see what was out there and so what was out there couldn't see him. To the east were the hills he spied upon the base from three years earlier trying to identify Taliban regional commanders coming and going from training programs.

"At least Steve McQueen had a baseball in his cell," he grumbled every hour or so. Anthony's humor was serviceable, though he sensed it was detaching him from real events and drawing him too deeply into quirkier parts of his mind. Nonetheless, it was a sign of his existence and will. He stuck with it, sharpened it, used it on the befuddled guards. Some came to ignore him, others smiled at and indulged the odd American.

He wasn't allowed to sit during his walks outside. The IRGC knew that special forces and CIA personnel prisoners positioned their legs in specific ways to signal overhead satellites that Americans were below. That might lead to a rescue mission and Iran had enough on its hands without dealing with a Delta Force team. In any case, sitting down and getting up were painful for Anthony.

One morning, he was told to shower and shave and the guards issued him clean clothes. A helicopter whisked him about a hundred miles to the north by his reckoning.

"Zahak," one guard told him, pointing to the horizon. "You go home now."

Anthony didn't believe him. Raising the hopes of prisoners then cruelly dashing them was an old game. Why the helicopter trip though? Something was up.

Maybe more theater, he thought. "Death to America, Redux," starring Anthony Sabatini, in the role he was born to play. "You hate me! You really hate me!" he said aloud, unable to refrain from a little laughter. One of the helicopter crewmen stared at him. "Sally Field," he explained, "Sally Field . . . Oscar?" The crewman smiled. He thought the prisoner was talking about a Beatle song he liked and he hummed the melody beneath the rotor noise.

A military sedan followed by two trucks of soldiers took him and his two guards east. Anthony saw a berm and rows of razor wire. Recent experience had given him an excellent idea of what Iranian borders looked like. Amid the unfolding drama, he found himself looking for a hole in the wire to run through. The sedan door opened and he was asked if he wanted a wheelchair to traverse the hundred meters to the Afghan side. Anthony smiled as the handcuffs were removed and said, "Hell no!"

He hobbled toward the line where a couple of Humvees with American markings and fifty-caliber guns mounted on top stood not far from a dozen Afghan border guards and two American civilians. The barrels of the fifties were aimed down and away.

I hope they have those fifties on . . .

He instantly realized that the click he heard from the Iranian soldiers as he lay gasping in the reservoir mud in Turkmenistan was a Kalashnikov being suddenly flicked over to safety.

His wounds bit and throbbed with each step, but he did his best to stride out to the checkpoint, tall and bold. He managed a crisp pace.

If I die in a combat zone

Box me up and ship me home.

He saw another man walking toward him from the Afghan side and as they passed, they briefly looked at each other. Anthony figured he was an IRGC equivalent, a player not-to-be-named later in a geopolitical trade. The Iranian guy was his ticket out of Iran and back to the world.

Pin my medals on my chest

Tell my mom I done my best.

Anthony nodded imperceptibly to the Iranian and thought he did the same. *Different circumstances,* he mused. The gate was just a few yards away. A few more steps and he was free. He started to feel giddy.

New Mexico

Barrett thought that in decades to come archives would be opened and histories written. It was unlikely there's be mention of two computer engineers in California or a cranky analyst in New Mexico or a clandestine program embedded in every microprocessor in the world. If someone apprised the guardians of historical record of what Ethan and Rina did, he'd likely have been dismissed as foolish and given to wild conspiracies about secret global elites like the Bilderbergers and Illuminati.

Barrett thought foreign policy was a conspiracy of sorts. A small number of men and women gathered in private to determine a course of action that involved immense bureaucracies and influential lobbies and powerful militaries. They hashed things out, came to a consensus, and presented it to the public as essential to preserving their way of life. If need be, they gave inspirational speeches.

The "conspirators" didn't meet in mansions or lodges or the Skull and Bones house in New Haven. They don't have secret incantations and handshakes. They don't dance around a statue of a giant owl. With a minimum of congressional or public involvement, they make policies that affect the world and kill enormous numbers of people.

"Sonsuvbitches," Barrett found himself muttering often.

Lack of recognition for whatever had happened over the last few weeks was fine with him. He lived out in the desert with his wolf friend and no longer wanted anything more than to learn a few things about the world. A new pair of Lucchese boots would be nice though. Barrett occasionally let his views of the insignificance of individuals in the world slip to the side and entertained the notion that he truly accomplished something with Joe Burkett's benign Georgetown conspiracy. The idea dissipated almost entirely when he looked out on the arid plains that led to Tucumcari.

"We should move out there," he said to Jesse as they headed up the mountain trail. The great wolf was amenable to relocating. Avoiding people was even more instinctual to him than it was to his human friend.

Barrett thought about future writing projects and recalled his feelings on coming home from Iraq, both times. He felt he could ably describe the alienation, boredom, disaffection with everyday life, and the aberrant desire to get back into a war where things made sense. He didn't think his account would be of any help to young people coming home from wars though. He'd been unreachable, alone in his confusion and despair, constantly replaying amazing and horrible sights.

"Maybe a novel."

An elderly neighbor in the DC suburbs commanded a company of tanks in World War Two and took seventy-five percent casualties in five months of fighting from Saint-Lo to just inside the Siegfried Line where he was badly wounded by a mortar round. Seventy-five percent casualties. A lot of letters to write. After the war, he met with the families of the "boys" who'd been killed and told them the circumstances of their loved ones' deaths.

"Such courage, such decency. Mostly gone today."

Barrett thought about going to Carrizo Springs, Texas, but didn't think he had the courage or decency to go through with it. When he imagined himself walking up to the Jaquas' house, he felt nausea then panic and knew he'd turn around and walk away.

"Yeah, a novel."

Barrett knew that Ethan and Rina wanted to know more about the programmers behind the Samson chip and even wanted to meet them. Ethan believed that the programmers' quest for peace was both noble and attainable. Barrett agreed it was noble but didn't think it was attainable. "It isn't in our future because it isn't in our DNA," he'd chided Ethan.

"Ahh, you never can tell," Barrett muttered as he and his friend ascended the deer trails. "The world's a strange place, full of surprises. We're due for a pleasant one. Right, Jesse?"

The great wolf held his counsel but seemed open to the idea.

Barrett thought about heading for Kelly's on Route 66 and chatting with the blonde waitress about to graduate and move on.

"Dee Dee . . . maybe Diane . . . Pretty name."

California

Ethan heard the incoming message alert a few times during the night and checked each time. He only saw messages from an industry newsletter and a headhunter in San Diego. Nothing important. There was only one message that was important.

He drove to work and made a quick stop at the Boudin Bakery for coffee and croissants. Rina later apprised him of routine matters—orders to see to, contacts to enter, inquiries to address—but postpartum was still with them. Mothers and authors know the sad lost feeling after producing a child or manuscript. Software engineers aren't all zeroes and ones. It just seems that way.

Dinner with Rina that night was pleasant, no more than that. The conversation was amiable but lacking in spontaneity and warmth. Intimacy eluded them. They went home, separately.

Rina wondered where things stood and thought about going back to graduate school full-time. She'd learned a lot, enough to get a dissertation proposal through the departmental gatekeepers. She wondered if advisers *did* read dissertations and if all that grad school rigmarole was worth it. She learned more in the last few weeks than she had in three years of grad school—things no Stanford prof could dream of.

Lights out. Not much sleep.

Rina awoke to an email from Ethan with the header "We're going to India!" It took a moment to register in her groggy mind, but she soon recognized the import and read the body of a forwarded message:

Dear Mr Alon

So interesting that I should hear from you. Timely also. Yes, your work is known to me and to a few colleagues from old projects. Your recent use of computational geometry in the Israeli system demonstrates remarkable talent and great promise.

Perhaps we can meet one day. I'm in India, the guest of Abhay Verma whom you may already know of. I can attest to his hospitality and to his willingness to extend it to you and your companion.

Kind regards,
Zvi

Rina called Ethan and as soon as he picked up, she shouted, "Companion? Companion? How the hell did they know about me—and our use of computational geometry?"

"Yes, how *did* they know those things. I've been wondering that myself. Maybe our work there was mirrored on a drive somewhere? Maybe Leor traced our footsteps? Maybe they can see . . . what's the word I'm looking for? *Intruders*."

"Didn't you think about that? Remember getting out of the NSA system without leaving tracks except ones that lead nowhere?"

"Yes, but there was a bit of urgency in the Holy Grail Building that day. The fighters were about to hit Iran and the whole region was about to explode. Anyway, I just talked to Barrett. He lunched with one of the Samson programmers yesterday."

"Lunch? Where?"

"Santa Fe. They talked about the world and hit it off. Plenty of common ground—and Rina, that's not often the case with Barrett Parker. They plan to keep in touch and discuss matters on a regular basis along with a few other younger analysts. Just think of that!"

"So the Samson programmers are interested in us? Even Barrett?"

"Rina, maybe *especially* Barrett. Let's go to India and find out more about these guys."

Rina made growling noises, which puzzled Ethan.

"Rottweilers," she explained.

"Ahhh. I thought you were imitating your dissertation advisers."

Northern India

Ethan and Rina landed at Indira Gandhi International near New Delhi just as morning broke. They groggily found their way to the baggage pickup area where a stocky bearded man in a reddish linen coat identified himself as an aide to Dr Verma, and carried their luggage to an SUV in the short-term parking lot. The heat and humidity pounced upon them the instant they left the airport building even though it was only eight am.

"Where are we heading?" Rina asked.

"Lansdowne, ma'am," came the reply. "It is about three hours north of here. You will be happy to know it is cooler there. Almost a mile in altitude." He raised his hand up to the vehicle's ceiling and grinned.

"We indeed are happy to hear that," Ethan replied. He and Rina leaned against each other and fell asleep in moments. The driver eased up the air conditioning in the back.

Two hours later, they began to ascend foothills and cross rock-strewn rivulets that rolled down from the mountains ahead. The land began to take on an almost alpine look which neither Ethan nor Rina thought possible so near the tropical clime they'd just left. They saw military convoys, some going north, some south. Road signs pointed the way to military cantonments. The name "Garhwal Rifles" was everywhere. It reminded Ethan of the area around Ft Bragg, which prided itself on the presence of the 82nd Airborne Division and featured the unit's "AA" insignia on billboards and storefronts. It wasn't far from an IBM fab where he was a consultant on a chip that controlled US air defenses.

Ethan felt uneasy, Rina more so.

"Is Dr Verma working with the Indian army?" Rina spoke hesitatingly, wondering if they were simply getting into another country's military and schemes.

The driver smiled softly as though having heard an absurdity. He shook his head slightly and replied, "Oh my heavens no. Not in many years anyway. He's the gentlest of men. You shall see. The very gentlest of men. He should have won the Nobel Peace Prize . . . well, politics interfered. Always politics."

They pulled into a driveway that led to an older house, probably from the colonial era, which was well within the living memory of the two senior programmers there. Ethan couldn't help but think that it was once the summer place of an official in the British administration. It was certainly under new management now and Ethan knew there were continuities stretching back into every country's past that were initially incongruous. He and Rina were in another such building far below Tel Aviv only last week.

An elderly man, western in appearance, came out to greet them.

"Ethan Alon and Rina Hardin, no doubt. I'm Zvi Arad and I welcome you to Lansdowne and to the gracious home of our colleague and mentor Dr Abhay Verma. Are you in need of rest or could you be persuaded to meet with Abhay and me presently?"

"Presently would be most welcome for us," came Rina's instant reply, affecting quaint colonial mannerisms. "No burly guards," she whispered. Ethan made growling noise near her ear. Both felt the humor should end though. They walked around the grounds to a side porch where a table had been prepared with mangoes, spiced rice, and urns of bracing water from nearby springs, all of which were welcome to the travelers.

Zvi returned with a frail elderly man helped along by his colleague's arm and an oaken cane. The elevation required him to wear a light sweater of yellow cotton, faded in color and worn at the elbows—the result of the liberation from concerns with dress that the years bring.

He sat down slowly and without salutations or preliminaries, began the conversation.

"Do you see beauty and spirituality in your work?" Abhay spoke more sternly than the question's content would ordinarily accompany.

"Yes, absolutely." Ethan's reply came more swiftly than anyone thought. "I often think of our work as art—an intricate musical piece. Learning the chip's purpose gives rise to inspiration and wonder. The idea becomes a work of creativity and even of self-expression. I think through the chip and try to understand its purpose in life and ultimately to its effects on life."

"And your colleagues? What of them?"

"Oh . . . Most of them are more practical in their approach. Much more practical. When I speak of art and creation, they joke that this is my conceit. It's an amusing quirk to them. I hope it's an endearing one. Perhaps even one that they will understand someday. I've seen much beauty in a section of the PAMD processor. Incredible beauty that I could not explain to anyone who'd never delved deeply into what silicon can hold."

Abhay nodded but showed no reaction to Ethan's reply. It was clear, however, he was forming his words. "There *is* beauty on those layers of silicon. We put it there. Zvi and I and others. Some gone now . . . You know that by now. I've seen your hand convey beauty. Beauty is our aim in this life, or it should be. The modern age grinds it up, hollows it out, drains it from our lives. Those in our profession have played no small part in the cheapening of life. Into this emptiness comes no renewed thirst for beauty or for knowing God. What comes is a love of *self*—or more tragically, a love of *war*. The soldier becomes a saint. His failings and cruelties are obscured by the glory people ascribe to him and the blood he sheds. Our generals become our gods. The people of our age do not seek to be at one with a divine will. They seek meaning in war."

Abhay motioned with his hand toward the majestic snowcaps towering to the north. Wisps of clouds rolled in front of the peaks, hiding them for a moment then revealing them again. Ethan was transfixed by Abhay. Rina felt affection for him—this strange man she'd just met and would likely never see again in life.

"You see nature here, but to the west there is Punjab from which armies have drawn recruits since Alexander impudently marched here from Macedonia with his mercenaries. And Kashmir is just to the north. Three wars there in my lifetime. I fought in the first one. I won't show you the souvenir on my leg. More happily, we are close to Nepal and Tibet. Gentle people, at peace with the world, seeking love and perfection."

"The home of many forms of spirituality." Ethan nodded in respect and growing awe.

"Not far from here is Wagah, on the border with Pakistan. Every afternoon the soldiers on each side put on a display of civility as they lower their flags and close the gate, all to the noisome cheers of chauvinistic crowds on both sides of the line. Behind this façade of civility, each country prepares to kill millions of the other country's populace."

Abhay's words came crisply from a keen mind that was not at home with a failing body. He paused to catch his breath and look sternly into his young visitors' eyes, never revealing any judgment that might be forming.

"It was like that in Iran back when we worked for the shah," Abhay continued. "The Flower Project it was called. As preposterous a name as any general or politician could dream of. The shah would meet with the Saudi king—Faisal it was back then—and the two monarchs would smile and embrace and talk of peace and brotherhood. All the while, each prepared for war with the other. Planning mass murder."

"And in 1980, war came," Zvi interjected, sensing his friend's need to gather his thoughts and strength. "The Saudis paid the Iraqis to do their fighting and for eight years, millions fought and died."

"Few Saudis, however," Abhay noted acidly. "We were convinced that we were the best and most decent scientists in the world and that we had to put an end to the war. The most ambitious of us or the most naive of us—we shall have to see—thought we could make their weapons too unreliable and war too unpredictable. No, we couldn't end war, but we could shorten some of them and prevent others."

Abhay cleared his throat noisily and looked over to Zvi, who picked up.

"Some of us came to realize, or at least suspect, that world leaders were shifting to proxy wars with less complex weapons such as the rifle and the grenade launcher. There was nothing we could do here anymore than we could stop a fight outside a football match in Delhi or Rome. In bigger wars, we at times assisted one side or the other. We allowed one side's weapons to work better than those of the opposition."

Abhay motioned his colleague that he could continue.

"Alas, the victors saw this as signs of invincibility and divine favor. They grew more ambitious. Their people became more militarized and more worshipful of Mars. Force became prized over diplomacy. Today, the Saudis again want others to attack Iran for them. A new ruler in Riyadh, a new ruler in Tehran. Old enmities are lasting ones. They risk sending the region into a long and bitter war. Shia against Sunni, Persian against Arab."

"But perhaps our young guests have a colleague who has expressed this view to them already," Zvi said looking intently at Ethan and Rina.

"I have learned of this view," Ethan replied, "though not with the facets and decency as my thoughtful hosts have just expressed. My colleague has also told me that powerholders in Washington were greatly alarmed by the blackouts of recent weeks. Less sweeping problems with their systems will keep powerholders in Washington and elsewhere anxious about the reliability of their weaponry."

"A heuristic sometimes does things we do not want it to do," Zvi said, "and that can bring problems."

"Other troublesome heuristics must be looked for and disabled," Rina said, finally finding a moment to speak up. "We've taken the liberty of writing a program to find them."

Ethan's cocked eyebrow indicated that this was news to him.

"And how can we continue to sow the seeds of doubt in our leaders' minds?" Abhay said with a wry smile. "The soil there is fertile."

"We must find a safer method of making leaders feel doubt," Ethan went on. "If not through unpredictable heuristics then through intricate search trees and routines within a revised Samson Program. Decisions and behavioral routines are Samson's core and we need to make sure that they do not introduce greater dysfunctionality."

"Interruptions of precisely the same duration imply human agency and invite rash responses. We need to introduce more random interruptions—ones of various durations. Long enough to cause doubt, short enough to deter rashness." Zvi had given the matter thought.

"We can add a module, with Dr Whitt's help at PAMD, to better realize this," Abhay said, nodding his head. "Perhaps our guests would consider working with Dr Whitt at PAMD—replacing him one day. After all, we are not immortals."

"Our work must be carried forward, Abhay," Zvi added.

"What would that Iranian general who hired us so long ago think of us now, Zvi?" Abhay asked, mirth overwhelming his dourness for the first time that afternoon.

"Ah, General Toufanian. I think he'd be keenly disappointed in us, Abhay. As would the shah. As would all those in the geriatric ward known as the House of Saud, close behind them though we are."

"My colleague," Ethan continued, "suggested finding our way into military and intelligence systems, discovering war plans and related information, and releasing at least some of them on the Internet for all to see."

"And for all to think about and weigh against the lives of young soldiers," Rina added.

"It would be embarrassing for the world to learn of their leaders' plans and how long they've had them," said Abhay. "The plans in many cases would coincide with periods of professed cooperation and resolution to bring peace."

"When leaders warmly embrace each other and issue august statements with noble and magnanimous content," said Zvi.

"As a poet once said, 'One thing I did not foresee, not having the courage of my own thought—the growing murderousness of the world'," quoted Abhay.

"The words of William Butler Yeats." Ethan knew the poet's words. Barrett had spoken them more than once.

Abhay, Zvi, and Rina looked at Ethan with new appreciation. Ethan enjoyed appreciative glances for a moment before going on.

"We all know by heart Moore's law on the greater power of semiconductors over the years. I wonder if there's isn't a parallel growth in power, one less beneficial than Moore's. With each year, the capacity of states to wreak havoc in the world goes up and the number of reckless people in government goes up as well."

"I can envision a graph with an appallingly straight and ascending line," quipped Zvi. "I've met many of these people. So filled with ambition and certainty. Standing at the head of acquiescent bureaus and naive publics. We began with high hopes. But your presence here today indicates that we cannot keep our Program secret forever. Someone else—someone less benign than you two—will see what we've done. Then . . . who knows."

The four sank into their thoughts, dark ones of transient victory and short-lived peace. And the possibility of immense wars.

"I'm not so pessimistic as Zvi or Yeats," replied Abhay. "Every day, there are children born and brought up without the fears and prejudices that their cultures have passed on for millennia." Coughing interrupted his words though not his thoughts. "Parents of humble means are able to give their children older yet serviceable computers. The children find new worlds, new ideas, and new joys. In time, they will connect with others like themselves and assimilate information faster than we did, faster than we could dream of."

All appreciated the old man's hopeful spirit and the beauty he saw.

"My mind keeps returning to the gentle people of Tibet." Abhay went on between a few coughs. "If my mind wanders, I hope it does so in worthy directions. Their children are so bright and inquisitive and good. They will bring good things to the world."

"That is my hope as well," said Zvi.

Ethan and Rina nodded in warm appreciation of such people and such ideas and such hope.

The meeting ended shortly later and the two guests moved into an adjacent cottage where they'd stay a few days before returning to California. They'd much to consider, especially the idea of working with Peter Whitt at PAMD.

That evening, Ethan and Rina went over Abhay's prophecy. They imagined a village in Tibet where a thirteen-year-old receives a gift from his parents which took them long hours of toil to provide. It's an older computer yet one that will give their child many hours of creative experience. When the village's power switches on in the evening, the computer comes to life on a simple wooden table in a modest living area with bedding and small rugs off to the side.

A spark of electricity awakes the computer and its microprocessor begins to direct information. Bits of data flow between the chip's internal blocks, transmitting data to connect the screen, mouse, and keyboard. A blue cursor blinks in the upper-left corner of the screen, a booting sequence begins, and routines run. A working system has come to life.

The child is excited. Teachers say a wireless system is coming to the village and everyone in the village imagines the wonders that will mean. Vast information, unlimited communication. The child can't wait for the day.